I0593716

James H. Graff, Charles J. Lever

A Day's Ride

a life's romance

James H. Graff, Charles J. Lever

A Day's Ride
a life's romance

ISBN/EAN: 9783337351083

Printed in Europe, USA, Canada, Australia, Japan

Cover: Foto ©Andreas Hilbeck / pixelio.de

More available books at **www.hansebooks.com**

A DAY'S RIDE:

A LIFE'S ROMANCE.

BY

CHARLES LEVER,

AUTHOR OF "CHARLES O'MALLEY," "HARRY LORREQUER,"
ETC., ETC.

Fifth Edition.

LONDON:
CHAPMAN AND HALL, 193, PICCADILLY
1866.

A DAY'S RIDE: A LIFE'S ROMANCE.

CHAPTER I.

It has been said, that any man, no matter how small and insignificant the post he may have filled in life, who will faithfully record the events in which he has borne a share, even though incapable of himself deriving profit from the lessons he has learned, may still be of use to others—sometimes a guide, sometimes a warning. I hope this is true. I like to think it so, for I like to think that even I—A. S. P.— if I cannot adorn a tale, may at least point a moral.

Certain families are remarkable for the way in which peculiar gifts have been transmitted for ages. Some have been great in arms, some in letters, some in statecraft, displaying in successive generations the same high qualities which had won their first renown. In an humble fashion, I may lay claim to belong to this category. My ancestors have been apothecaries for one hundred and forty odd years. Joseph Potts, "drug and condiment man," lived in the reign of Queen Anne, at Lower Liffey-street, No. 87; and to be remembered passingly, has the name of Mr. Addison amongst his clients; the illustrious writer having, as it would appear, a peculiar fondness for "Potts's Linature," whatever that may have been; for the secret died out with my distinguished forefather. There was Michael Joseph Potts, "licensed for chemicals," in Mary's Abbey, about thirty years later; and so we come on to Paul Potts and Son, and to then, Launcelot Peter Potts, "Pharmaceutical Chemist to his Excellency and the Irish Court," the father of him who now bespeaks your indulgence.

1

My father's great misfortune in life was the ambition to rise above the class his family had adorned for ages. He had, as he averred, a soul above senna, and a destiny higher than black drop. He had heard of a tailor's apprentice becoming a great general. He had himself seen a wig-maker elevated to the wooksack; and he kept continually repeating, "Mine is the only walk in life that leads to no high rewards. What matters it whether my mixtures be addressed to the refined organisation of rank or the ' dura ilia rasorum '—I shall live and die an apothecary. From every class are men selected for honours save mine, and though it should rain baronetcies, the bloody hand would never fall to the lot of a compounding chemist."

"What do you intend to make of Algernon Sydney, Mr. Potts?" would say one of his neighbours. "Bring him up to your own business? A first-rate connection to start with in life."

"My own business, Sir? I'd rather see him a chimney-sweep."

"But, after all, Mr. Potts, being so to say, at the head of your profession——"

"It is not a profession, Sir. It is not even a trade. High science and skill have long since left our insulted and out-raged ranks; we are mere commission agents for the sale of patent quackeries. What respect has the world any longer for the great phials of ruby, and emerald, and marine blue, which, at nightfall, were once the magical emblems of our mysteries, seen afar through the dim mists of louring atmospheres, or throwing their lurid glare upon the passers-by. What man, now, would have the courage to adorn his surgery—I suppose you would prefer I should call it a ' shop'—with skeleton fishes, snakes, or a stuffed alligator? Who, in this age of chemical infidelity, would surmount his door with the ancient symbols of our art—the golden pestle and mortar? Why, Sir, I'd as soon go forth to apply leeches in a herald's tabard, or a suit of Milan mail. And what have they done, Sir?" he would ask, with a roused indignation—"what have they done by their reforms? In invading the mystery of medicine, they have ruined its prestige. The precious drops you once regarded as the essence of an elixir vitæ, and whose efficacy lay in your faith, are now so much strychnine, or creosote, which you take with fear and think over with foreboding."

I suppose it can only be ascribed to that perversity which seems a great element in human nature, that, exactly in the direct ratio of my father's dislike to his profession was *my* fondness for it. I used to take every opportunity of stealing into the laboratory, watching intently all the curious proceedings that went on there, learning the names and properties of the various ingredients, the gases, the minerals, the salts, the essences; and although, as may be imagined, science took, in these narrow regions, none of her loftiest flights, they were to me the most marvellous and high-soaring efforts of human intelligence. I was just at that period of life—the first opening of adolescence—when fiction and adventure have the strongest hold upon our nature, my mind filled with the marvels of Eastern romance, and imbued with a sentiment, strong as any conviction, that I was destined to a remarkable life. I passed days in dreamland—what I should do in this or that emergency; how rescue myself from such a peril; how profit by such a stroke of fortune; by what arts resist the machinations of this adversary; how conciliate the kind favour of that. In the wonderful tales that I read, frequent mention was made of alchemy and its marvels, now, the search was for some secret of endless wealth ; now, it was for undying youth or undecaying beauty; while in other stories, I read of men who had learned how to read the thoughts, trace the motives, and ultimately sway the hearts of their fellow-men, till life became to them a mere field for the exercise of their every will and caprice, throwing happiness and misery about them as the humour inclined. The strange life of the laboratory fitted itself exactly to this phase of my mind.

The wonders it displayed, the endless combinations and transformations it effected, were as marvellous as any that imaginative fiction could devise; but even these were nothing compared to the mysterious influence of the place itself upon my nervous system, particularly when I found myself there alone. In the tales with which my head was filled, many of them the wild fancies of Grimm, Hoffman, or Musæus, nothing was more common than to read how some eager student of the black art, deep in the mystery of forbidden

1—2

knowledge, had, by some chance combination, by some mere
accidental admixture of this ingredient with that, suddenly
arrived at the great SECRET, that terrible mystery which for
centuries and centuries had evaded human search.   How
often have I watched the fluid as it boiled and bubbled in the
retort, till I thought the air globules, as they came to the
surface, observed a certain rhythm and order.   Were these,
words ?   Were they symbols of some hidden virtue in the
liquid ?   Were there intelligences to whom these coulds peak,
and thus reveal a wondrous history ?   And then, again,
with what an intense eagerness have I gazed on the lurid
smoke that arose from some smelting mass, now fancying
that the vapour was about to assume form and substance,
and now, imagining that it lingered lazily, as though waiting
for some cabalistic word of mine to give it life and being ?
How heartily did I censure the folly that had ranked
alchemy amongst the absurdities of human invention.   Why
rather had not its facts been treasured and its discoveries
recorded, so that, in some future age a great intelligence
arising, might classify and arrange them, showing, at least,
what were practicable and what were only evasive.   Alche-
mists were, certainly, men of pure lives, self-denying, and
humble.   They made their art no stepping-stone to worldly
advancement or success, they sought no favour from princes,
nor any popularity from the people ; but, retired and estranged
from all the pleasures of the world, followed their one pursuit, unnoticed and unfriended.   How cruel, therefore, to
drag them forth from their lonely cells, and expose them to
the gaping crowd as devil worshippers !   How inhuman to
denounce men whose only crimes were lives of solitude and
study !   The last words of Peter von Vordt, burned for a
wizard, at Haarlem, in 1306, were, " Had they left this poor
head a little longer on my shoulders, it would have done
more for human happiness than all this bonfire ! "
     How rash and presumptuous is it, besides, to set down any
fixed limits to man's knowledge !   Is not every age an
advance upon its predecessors, and are not the commonest
acts of our present civilisation perfect miracles as compared
with the usages of our ancestors ?   But why do I linger on
this theme, which I only introduced to illustrate the temper
of my boyish days ?   As I grew older, books of chivalry and

romance took possession of my mind, and my passion grew for lives of adventure. Of all kinds of existence, none seemed to me so enviable as that of those men, who, regarding life as a vast ocean, hoisted sail, and set forth, not knowing nor caring whither, but trusting to their own manly spirit for extrication out of whatever difficulties might beset them. What a narrow thing, after all, was our modern civilisation, with all its forms and conventionalities, with its gradations of rank and its orders! How hopeless for the adventurous spirit to war with the stern discipline of an age that marshalled men in ranks like soldiers, and told that each could only rise by successive steps! How often have I wondered was there any more of adventure left in life? Were there incidents in store for him who, in the true spirit of an adventurer, should go in search of them? As for the newer worlds of Australia and America, they did not possess for me much charm. No great association linked them with the past; no echo came out of them of that heroic time of feudalism, so peopled with heart-stirring characters. The life of the bush or the prairie had its incidents, but they were vulgar and commonplace; and worse, the associates and companions of them were more vulgar still. Hunting down Pawnees or buffaloes was as mean and ignoble a travesty of feudal adventure, as was the gold diggings at Bendigo of the learned labours of the alchemist. The perils were unexciting, the rewards prosaic and commonplace. No. I felt that Europe—in some remote regions—and the East—in certain less visited tracts—must be the scenes best suited to my hopes. With considerable labour I could spell my way through a German romance, and I saw, in the stories of Fouqué, and even of Goethe, that there still survived in the mind of Germany many of the features which gave the colouring to a feudal period. There was, at least, a dreamy indifference to the present, a careless abandonment to what the hour might bring forth, so long as the dreamer was left to follow out his fancies in all their mysticism, that lifted men out of the vulgarities of this work-o'-day world; and I longed to see a society where learning consented to live upon the humblest pittance, and beauty dwelt unflattered in obscurity.

I was now entering upon manhood, and my father—having

with that ambition so natural to an Irish parent who aspires
highly for his only son, destined me for the Bar—made me a
student of Trinity College, Dublin.

What a shock to all the romance of my life were the
scenes into which I now was thrown! With hundreds of
companions to choose from, I found not one congenial to me.
The reading men, too deeply bent upon winning honours,
would not waste a thought upon what could not advance
their chances of success. The idle, only eager to get through
their career undetected in their ignorance, passed lives of
wild excess or stupid extravagance.

What was I to do amongst such associates? What I did
do—avoid them, shun them, live in utter estrangement from
all their haunts, their ways, and themselves. If the proud
man who has achieved success in life encounters immense
difficulties when, separating himself from his fellows, he
acknowledges no companionship, nor admits any to his confidence, it may be imagined what must be the situation of
one who adopts this isolation without any claim to superiority whatever. As can easily be supposed, I was the butt
of my fellow-students, the subject of many sarcasms and
practical jokes. The whole of my Freshman year was a
martyrdom. I had no peace, was rhymed on by poetasters,
caricatured by draughtsmen, till the name of Potts became
proverbial for all that was eccentric, ridiculous, and absurd.

Curran has said "one can't draw an indictment against a
nation;" in the same spirit did I discover "one cannot fight
his whole division." For a while I believe I experienced a
sort of heroism in my solitary state; I felt the spirit of a
Coriolanus in my heart, and muttered, "I banish *you!*" but
this self-supplied esteem did not last long, and I fell into a
settled melancholy. The horrible truth was gradually forc-
ing its way slowly, clearly, through the mists of my mind,
that there might be something in all this sarcasm, and I can
remember to this hour, the day—ay, and the very place—
wherein the questions flashed across me: Is my hair as limp,
my nose as long, my back as arched, my eyes as green as
they have pictured them? Do I drawl so fearfully in my
speech? Do I drag my heavy feet along so ungracefully?
Good Heavens? have they possibly a grain of fact to sustain
all this fiction against me?

And if so—horrible thought—am I the stuff to go forth and seek adventures? Oh, the ineffable bitterness of this reflection! I remember it in all its anguish, and even now, after years of such experience as have befallen few men, I can recal the pain it cost me. While I was yet in the paroxysm of that sorrow, which assured me that I was not made for doughty deeds, nor to captivate some fair princess, I chanced to fall upon a little German volume entitled Wald Wandelungen und Abentheure, von Heinrich Stebbe. Forest rambles and adventures, and of a student, too! for so Herr Stebbe announces himself, in a short introduction to the reader. I am not going into any account of his book. It is in Voss's Leipzig Catalogue, and not unworthy of perusal by those who are sufficiently imbued with Germanism to accept the changeful moods of a mystical mind, with all its visionary glimpses of light and shade, its doubts, fears, hopes and fancies, in lieu of real incidents and actual events. Of adventures, properly speaking, he had none. The people he met, the scenes in which he bore his part, were as commonplace as need be. The whole narrative never soared above that bread-and-butter life—Butterbrod-Leben—which Germany accepts as romance; but meanwhile the reflex of whatever passed around him in the narrator's own mind, was amusing; so ingeniously did he contrive to interweave the imaginary with the actual, throwing over the most ordinary pictures of life a sort of hazy indistinctness—meet atmosphere for mystical creation.

If I did not always sympathise with him in his brain-wronght wanderings, I never ceased to take pleasure in his description of scenery, and the heartfelt delight he experienced in journeying through a world so beautful and so varied. There was also a little woodcut frontispiece which took my fancy much, representing him as he stood leaning on his horse's mane, gazing rapturously on the Elbe, from one of the cliffs off the Saxon Switzerland. How peaceful he looked, with his long hair waving gracefully on his neck, and his large soft eyes turned on the scene beneath him. His clasped hands, as they lay on the horse's mane, imparted a sort of repose, too, that seemed to say, " I could linger here ever so long." Nor was the horse itself without a significance in the picture : he was a long-maned, long-tailed, patient-looking beast, well befitting an enthusiast, who doubtless took but little heed of how he went or where. If his lazy eye denoted lethargy, his broad feet and short legs vouched for his sure-footedness.

Why should not I follow Stebbe's example? Surely there was nothing too exalted or extravagant in his plan of life. It was simply to see the world as it was, with the aid of such combinations as a fertile fancy could contribute; not to distort events, but to arrange them, just as the landscape painter in the licence of his craft moves that massive rock more to the foreground, and throws that stone pine a little further to the left of his canvas. There was, indeed, nothing to prevent my trying the experiment. Ireland was not less rich in picturesque scenery than Germany, and if she boasted no such mighty stream as the Elbe, the banks of the Black-water and the Nore were still full of woodland beauty ; and, then, there was lake scenery unrivalled throughout Europe.

L turned to Stebbe's narrative for details of his outfit. His horse he bought at Nordheim for two hundred and forty gulden—about ten pounds; his saddle and knapsack cost him a little more than forty shillings ; with his map, guide-book, compass, and some little extras, all were comprised within twenty pounds sterling—surely not too costly an equipage for one who was adventuring on a sea wide as the world itself.

As *my* trial was a mere experiment, to be essayed on the most limited scale, I resolved not to buy, but only hire, a horse, taking him by the day, so that if any change of mind or purpose supervened, I should not find myself in any embarrassment.

A fond uncle had just left me a legacy of a hundred pounds, which besides, was the season of the long vacation ; thus did everything combine to favour the easy execution of a plan, which I determined forthwith to put into practice.

"Something quiet and easy to ride, Sir, you said?" repeated Mr. Dycer after me, as I entered his great establish-ment for the sale and hire of horses. "Show the gentleman four hundred and twelve."

Oh, Heaven forbid!" I exclaimed, in my ignorance; "such a number would only confuse me."

"You mistake me, Sir," blandly interposed the dealer ;

" I meant the horse that stands at that number. Lead him out, Tim. He's gentle as a lamb, Sir, and, if you find he suits you, can be had for a song.—I mean a ten pound note."

" Has he a long mane and tail ?" I asked, eagerly.

" The longest tail and the fullest mane I ever saw. But here he comes." And with the word, there advanced towards us, at a sort of easy amble, a small-sized cream-coloured horse, with white mane and tail. Knowing nothing of horseflesh, I was fain to content myself with such observations as other studies might supply me with ; and so I closely examined his head, which was largely developed in the frontal region, with moral qualities fairly displayed. He had memory large, and individuality strong ; nor was wit, if it exist in the race, deficient. Over the orbital region the depressions were deep enough to contain my closed fist, and when I remarked upon them to the groom, he said, " 'Tis his teeth will tell you the rayson of that ;" a remark which I suspect was a sarcasm upon my general ignorance.

I liked the creature's eye. It was soft, mild, and con-templative ; and although not remarkable for brilliancy, possessed a subdued lustre that promised well for temper and disposition.

"Ten shillings a day—make it three half-crowns by the week, Sir. You'll never hit upon the like of him again," said the dealer, hurriedly, as he passed me, on his other avocations.

" Better not lose him, Sir ; he's well known at Batty's, and they'll have him in the circus again, if they see him. Wish you saw him with his fore-legs on a table, ringing the bell for his breakfast."

" I'll take him by the week, though, probably, a day or two will be all I shall need."

" Four hundred and twelve for Mr. Potts," Dycer screamed out. "Shoe's removed, and to be ready in the morning."

CHAPTER II.

I HAD heard and read frequently of the exhilarating sensations of horse exercise. My fellow-students were full of
stories of the hunting-field and the race-course. Wherever,
indeed, a horse figured in a narrative, there was an almost
certainty of meeting some incident to stir the blood and
warm up enthusiasm. Even the passing glimpses one
caught of sporting prints in shop-windows were suggestive
of the pleasure imparted by a noble and chivalrous pastime.

I never closed my eyes all night, revolving such thoughts
in my head. I had so worked up my enthusiasm, that I felt
like one who is about to cross the frontier of some new land
where people, language, ways, and habits are all unknown
to him. "By this hour to-morrow night," thought I, "I
shall be in the land of strangers, who have never seen, nor
so much as heard of me. There, will invade no traditions of
the scoffs and jibes I have so long endured; none will have
received the disparaging estimate of my abilities, which my
class-fellows love to propagate ; I shall simply be the
traveller who arrived at sundown mounted on a cream-
coloured palfrey—a stranger, sad-looking, but gentle withal,
of courteous address, blandly demanding lodging for the
night. "Look to my horse, ostler," shall I say, as I enter
the honeysuckle-covered porch of the inn. "Blondel"—I
will call him Blondel—"is accustomed to kindly usage."
With what quiet dignity, the repose of a conscious position,
do I follow the landlord as he shows me to my room. It is
humble, but neat and orderly. I am contented. I tell him
so. I am sated and wearied of luxury; sick of a gilded and
glittering existence. I am in search of repose and solitude.
I order my tea ; and, if I ask the name of the village, I take
care to show by my inattention that I have not heard the
answer, nor do I care for it.

Now I should like to hear how they are canvassing me in

the bar, and what they think of me in the stable. 1 am, doubtless, a peer, or a peer's eldest son. I am a great writer, the wondrous poet of the day; or the pre-Raphaelite artist; or I am a youth heart-broken by infidelity in love; or, mayhap, a dreadful criminal. I liked this last the best, the interest was so intense; not to say that there is, to men who are not constitutionally courageous, a strong pleasure in being able to excite terror in others.

But I hear a horse's feet on the silent street. I look out. Day is just breaking. Tim is holding Blondel at the door. My hour of adventure has struck, and noiselessly descending the stairs, I issue forth.

"He is a trifle tender on the fore-feet, your honour," said Tim, as I mounted, "but when you get him off the stones on a nice piece of soft road, he'll go like a four-year old.

"But he *is* young, Tim, isn't he?" I asked, as I tendered him my half-crown.

"Well, not to tell your honour a lie, he is not," said Tim, with the energy of a man whose veracity had cost him little than a spasm.

"How old would you call him, then?" I asked, in that affected ease that seemed to say, "Not that it matters to me if he were Methuselah."

"I couldn't come to his age exactly, your honour," he replied. "but I remember seeing him fifteen years ago, dancing a hornpipe, more by token for his own benefit; it was at Cooke's Circus, in Abbey-street, and there wasn't a hair's difference between him now and then, except, perhaps, that he had a star on the forehead, where you just see the mark a little darker now."

"But that is a star, plain enough," said I, half vexed.

"Well, it is, and it is not," muttered Tim, doggedly, for he was not quite satisfied with my right to disagree with him.

"He's gentle, at all events?" I said, more confidently.

"He's a lamb!" replied Tim. "If you were to see the way he lets the Turks run over his back, when he's wounded in Timour the Tartar, you wouldn't believe he was a livin' baste."

"Poor fellow!" said I, caressing him. He turned his mild eye upon me, and we were friends from that hour.

What a glorious morning it was, as I gained the outskirts
of the city, and entered one of those shady alleys that lead to
the foot of the Dublin mountains!   The birds were opening
their morning hymn, and the earth, still fresh from the night
dew, sent up a thousand delicious perfumes.   The road on
either side was one succession of handsome villas or orna-
mental cottages, whose grounds were laid out in the perfection of landscape gardening.   There were but few persons
to be seen at that early hour, and in the smokeless chimneys
and closed shutters I could read that all slept—slept in that
luxurious hour when Nature unveils, and seems to revel in
the sense of unregarded loveliness.   "Ah, Potts," said I,
"thou hast chosen the wiser part; thou wilt see the world
after thine own guise, and not as others see it."   Has my
reader not often noticed that in a picture-gallery the
slightest change of place, a move to the left or right, a
chance approach or retreat, suffices to make what seemed a
hazy confusion of colour and gloss a rich and beautiful
picture?   So is it in the actual world, and just as much
depends on the point from which objects are viewed.   Do
not be discouraged, then, by the dark aspects of events.   It
may be that by the slightest move to this side or to that,
some unlooked-for sunlight shall slant down and light up all
the scene.   Thus musing, I gained a little grassy strip that
ran along the roadside, and, gently touching Blondel with
my heel, he broke out into a delightful canter.   The motion,
so easy and swimming, made it a perfect ecstasy to sit there
floating at will through the thin air, with a moving panorama of wood, water, and mountain around me.

Emerging at length from the thickly wooded plain, I
began the ascent of the Three Rock Mountain, and, in my
slackened speed, had full time to gaze upon the bay beneath
me, broken with many a promontory, backed by the broad
bluff of Howth, and the more distant Lambay.   No, it is *not*
finer than Naples.   I did not say it was; but, seeing it as I
then saw it, I thought it could not be surpassed.   Indeed, I
went further, and defied Naples in this fashion:

Though no volcano's lurid light
Over thy blue sea steals along,
Nor Pescator beguiles the night
With cadence of his simple song;

Though none of dark Calabria's daughters
With tinkling lute thy echoes wake,
Mingling their voices with the waters,
As 'neath the prow the ripples break ;

Although no cliffs with myrtle crown'd,
Reflected in thy tide, are seen,
Nor olives, bending to the ground,
Relieve the laurel's darker green ;

Yet—yet——

Ah, there was the difficulty—I had begun with the plaintiff, and I really hadn't a word to say for the defendant; and so, voting comparisons odious, I set forward on my journey.

As I rode into Enniskerry to breakfast, I had the satisfaction of overhearing some very flattering comments upon Blondel, which rather consoled me for some less laudatory remarks upon my own horsemanship. By the way, can there possibly be a more ignorant sarcasm than to say a man rides like a tailor? Why, of all trades, who so constantly sits straddle-legged as a tailor? and yet he is the especial mark of this impertinence.

I pushed briskly on after breakfast, and soon found myself in the deep shady woods that lead to the Dargle. I hurried through the picturesque demesne, associated as it was with a thousand little vulgar incidents of city junkettings, and rode on for the Glen of the Downs. Blondel and I had now established a most admirable understanding with each other. It was a sort of reciprocity by which *I* bound myself never to control *him*, he in turn consenting not to unseat *me*. He gave the initiative to the system, by setting off at his pleasant little rocking canter whenever he chanced upon a bit of favourable ground, and invariably pulled up when the road was stony or uneven; thus showing me that he was a beast with what Lord Brougham would call " a wise discretion." In like manner he would halt to pluck any stray ears of wild oats that grew along the hedge sides, and occasionally slake his thirst at convenient streamlets. If I dismounted to walk at his side, he moved along unheld, his head almost touching my elbow, and his plaintive blue eye mildly beaming on me with an expression that almost spoke —nay, it did speak. I'm sure I felt it, as though I could swear to it, whispering, " Yes, Potts, two more friendless

creatures than ourselves are not easy to find. The world
wants not either of us; not that we abuse it, despise it, or
treat it ungenerously—rather the reverse, we incline favourably towards it, and would, occasion serving, befriend it—but
we are not, so to say, 'of it.' There may be, here and there,
a man or a horse that would understand or appreciate us,
but they stand alone—they are not belonging to classes.
They are, like ourselves, exceptional." If his expression
said this much, there was much unspoken melancholy in his
sad glance, also, which seemed to say, "What a deal of
sorrow could I reveal if I might—what injuries—what
wrong—what cruel misconceptions of my nature and disposition—what mistaken notions of my character and
intentions! What pretentious stupidity, too, have I seen
preferred before me—creatures with, mayhap, a glossier
coat or a more silky forelock——" "Ah, Blondel, take
courage—men are just as ungenerous, just as erring !"
"Not that I have not had my triumphs, too," he seemed to
say, as, cocking his ears, and ambling with a more elevated
toss of the head, his tail would describe an arch like a waterfall ; "no salmon-coloured silk stockings danced sarabands
on *my* back; I was always ridden in the Haute Ecole by
Monsieur L'Etrier himself, the stately gentleman in jack-
boots and long-waisted dress-coat, whose five minutes no
persuasive bravos could ever prolong." I thought—nay, I
was certain at times—that I could read in his thoughtful
face the painful sorrows of one who had outlived popular
favour, and who had survived to see himself supplanted and
dethroned.

There are no two destinies which chime in so well together
as that of him who is beaten down by sheer distrust of himself, and that of the man who has seen better days. Although
the one be just entering on life, while the other is going out
of it, if they meet on the threshold, they stop to form a friendship. Now, though Blondel was not a man, he supplied to my
friendlessness the place of one.

The sun was near its setting, as I rode down the little hill
into the village of Ashford, a picturesque little spot in the
midst of mountains, and with a bright clear stream bounding
through it, as fearlessly as though in all the liberty of open
country. I tried to make my entrance what stage people

call effective. I threw myself, albeit a little jaded, into an attitude of easy indifference, slouched my hat to one side, and suffered the sprig of laburnum, with which I had adorned it, to droop in graceful guise over one shoulder. The villagers stared; some saluted me; and taken, perhaps, by the cool acquiescence of my manner, as I returned the courtesy, seemed well disposed to believe me of some note.

I rode into the little stable-yard of the "Lamb" and dismounted. I gave up my horse, and walked into the inn. I don't know how others feel it—I greatly doubt if they will have the honesty to. tell—but for myself, I confess that I never entered an inn or an hotel without a most uncomfortable conflict within : a struggle made up of two very antagonistic impulses—the wish to seem something important, and a lively terror lest the pretence should turn out to be costly. Thus swayed by opposing motives, I sought a compromise by assuming that I was incog. ; for the present a nobody, to be treated without any marked attention, and to whom the acme of respect would be a seeming indifference.

"What is your village called?" I said, carelessly, to the waiter, as he laid the cloth.

"Ashford, your honour. 'Tis down in all the books," answered the waiter.

"Is it noted for anything, or is there anything remarkable in the neighbourhood?"

"Indeed, there is, Sir, and plenty. There's Glenmalure and the Devil's Glen ; and there's Mr. Snow Malone's place, that everybody goes to see ; and there's the fishing of Doyle's river—trout, eight, nine, maybe twelve, pounds' weight; and there's Mr. Reeve's cottage—a Swiss cottage belike—at Kinmacreedy; but, to be sure, there must be an order for that."

"I never take much trouble," I said, indolently. "Who have you got in the house at present?"

"There's young Lord Keldrum, Sir, and two more with him, for the fishing; and the next room to you here, there's Father Dyke, from Inistioge, and he's going, by the same token, to dine with the lord to-day."

"Don't mention to his lordship that I am here," said I, hastily. "I desire to be quite unknown down here." The waiter promised obedience, without vouchsafing any misgivings as to the possibility of his disclosing what he did not know.

To his question as to my dinner, I carelessly said, as if I were in a West-end club, "Never mind soup—a little fish—a cutlet and partridge. Or order it yourself—I am indifferent." The waiter had scarcely left the room when I was startled by the sound of voices so close to me as to seem at my side. They came from a little wooden balcony to the adjoining room, which, by its pretentious bow-window, I recognised to be the state apartment of the inn, and now in the possession of Lord Keldrum and his party. They were talking away in that gay, rattling, discursive fashion very young men do amongst each other, and discussed fishing-flies, the neighbouring gentlemen's seats, and the landlady's niece.

"By the way, Kel," cried one, " it was in your visit to the bar that you met your priest, wasn't it ?"

"Yes; I offered him a cigar, and we began to chat together, and so I asked him to dine with us to-day."

"And he refused ? "

"Yes; but he has since changed his mind, and sent a message to say he'll be with us at eight."

"I should like to see your father's face, Kel, when he heard of your entertaining the Reverend Father Dyke at dinner."

"Well, I suppose he would say it was carrying conciliation a little too far; but as the adage says, ' A la guerre——' "

At this juncture, another burst in amongst them, calling out, "You'd never guess who's just arrived here, in strict incog., and having bribed Mike, the waiter, to silence. Burgoyne ! "

"Not Jack Burgoyne ? "

"Jack himself. I had the portrait so correctly drawn by the waiter, that there's no mistaking him; the long hair, green complexion, sheepish look, all perfect. He came on a hack, a little cream-coloured pad he go at Dycer's, and fancies he's quite unknown."

"What *can* he be up to, now ? "

"I think I have it," said his lordship. "Courtenay has got two three-year olds down here at his uncle's, one of them under heavy engagements for the spring meetings. Master Jack has taken a run down to have a look at them."

"By Jove, Kel, you're right! he's always wide awake, and that stupid leaden-eyed look he has, has done him good service in the world."

"I say, old Oxley, shall we dash in and unearth him. Or shall we let him fancy that we know nothing of his being here at all?"

"What does Hammond say?"

"I'd say, leave him to himself," replied a deep voice; "you can't go and see him without asking him to dinner; and he'll walk into us after, do what we will."

"Not, surely, if we don't play," said Oxley.

"Wouldn't he though? Why he'd screw a bet out of a bishop."

"I'd do with him as Tomkinson did," said his lordship; "he had him down at his lodge in Scotland, and bet him fifty pounds that he couldn't pass a week without a wager. Jack booked the bet and won it, and Tomkinson franked the company."

"What an artful villain my counterpart must be!" I said. I stared in the glass to see if I could discover the sheepishness they laid such stress on. I was pale, to be sure, and my hair a light brown, but so was Shelley's; indeed, there was a wild, but soft expression, in my eyes that resembled his, and I could recognise many things in our natures that seemed to correspond. It was the poetic dreaminess, the lofty abstractedness from all the petty cares of every-day life, which vulgar people set down as simplicity; and thus,

> The soaring thoughts that reached the stars,
> Seemed ignorance to *them*.

As I uttered the consolatory lines, I felt two hands firmly pressed over my eyes, while a friendly voice called out, "Found out, old fellow! run fairly to earth!" "Ask him if he knows you," whispered another, but in a voice I could catch.

"Who am I, Jack?" cried the first speaker.

"Situated as I now am," I replied, "I am unable to pro-

2

nounce; but of one thing I am assured—I am certain I am not called Jack."

The slow and measured intonation of my voice seemed to electrify them, for my captor relinquished his hold and fell back, while the two others, after a few seconds of blank surprise, burst into a roar of laughter; a sentiment which the other could not refrain from, while he struggled to mutter some words of apology.

"Perhaps I can explain your mistake," I said, blandly; "I am supposed to be extremely like the Prince of Salms Hökinshauven——"

"No, no!" burst in Lord Keldrum, whose voice I recognised, "we never saw the prince. The blunder of the waiter led us into this embarrassment; we fancied you were——"

"Mr. Burgoyne," I chimed in.

"Exactly; Jack Burgoyne; but you're not a bit like him."

"Strange, then; but I'm constantly mistaken for him; and when in London, I'm actually persecuted by people calling out, 'When did you come up, Jack?' 'Where do you hang out?' 'How long do you stay?' 'Dine with me to-day—to-morrow—Saturday?' and so on; and although, as I have remarked, these are only so many embarrassments for me, they all show how popular must be my prototype." I had purposely made this speech of mine a little long, for I saw by the disconcerted looks of the party that they did not see how to wind up "the situation," and, like all awkward men, I grew garrulous where I ought to have been silent. While I rambled on, Lord Keldrum exchanged a word or two with one of his friends; and, as I finished, he turned towards me, and, with an air of much courtesy, said,—

"We owe you every apology for this intrusion, and hope you will pardon it; there is, however, but one way in which we can certainly feel assured that we have your forgiveness—that is, by your joining us. I see that your dinner is in preparation, so pray let me countermand it, and say that you are our guest."

"Lord Keldrum," said one of the party, presenting the speaker; "my name is Hammond, and this is Captain Oxley, Coldsteams Guards."

I saw that this move required an exchange of ratifications, and so I bowed, and said, "Algernon Sydney Potts."

"There are Staffordshire Pottses?"

"No relation," I said, stiffly. It was Hammond who made the remark, and with a sneering manner that I could not abide.

"Well, Mr. Potts, it is agreed," said Lord Keldrum, with his peculiar urbanity, "we shall see you at eight. No dressing. You'll find us in this fishing costume you see now."

I trust my reader, who has dined out any day he pleased and in any society he has liked these years past, will forgive me if I do not enter into any detailed account of my reasons for accepting this invitation. Enough if I freely own that to me, A. S. Potts, such an unexpected honour was about the same surprise as if I had been announced governor of a colony, or bishop in a new settlement.

"At eight, sharp, Mr. Potts."

"The next door down the passage."

"Just as you are, remember!" were the three parting admonitions with which they left me.

CHAPTER III.

WHO has not experienced the charm of the first time in his life, when totally removed from all the accidents of his station, the circumstance of his fortune, and his other belongings, he has taken his place amongst perfect strangers, and been estimated by the claims of his own individuality? Is it not this which gives the almost ecstasy of our first tour—our first journey? There are none to say, "Who is this Potts that gives himself these airs?" "What pretension has he to say this, or order that?" "What would old Peter say if he saw his son to-day?" with all the other "What has the world come tos?" and "What are we to see nexts?" I say, it is with a glorious sense of independence that one sees him-

2—2

self emancipated from all these restraints, and recognises his freedom to be that which nature has made him.

As I sat on Lord Keldrum's left—Father Dyke was on his right—was I in any real quality other than I ever am? Was my nature different, my voice, my manner, my social tone, as I received all the bland attentions of my courteous host? And yet, in my heart of hearts, I felt that if it were known to that polite company I was the son of Peter Potts, 'pothecary, all my conversational courage would have failed me. I would not have dared to assert fifty things I now declared, nor vouched for a hundred that I as assuredly guaranteed. If I had had to carry about me traditions of the shop in Mary's Abbey, the laboratory, and the rest of it, how. could I have had the nerve to discuss any of the topics on which I now pronounced so authoritatively? And yet, these were all accidents of my existence—no more ME than was the colour of *his* whiskers mine who vaccinated me for cow-pock. The man Potts was himself through all; he was neither compounded of senna and salts, nor amalgamated with sarsaparilla and the acids ; but by the cruel laws of a harsh conventionality it was decreed otherwise, and the trade of the father descends to the son in every estimate of all he does, and says, and thinks. The converse of the proposition I was now to feel in the success I obtained in this company. I was, as the Germans would say, " Der Herr Potts SELBST, nicht nach seinen Begebenheiten"—the man Potts, not the creature of his belongings.

The man thus freed from his " antecedents," and owning no " relatives," feels like one to whom a great, a most unlimited credit has been opened, in matter of opinion. Not reduced to fashion his sentiments by some supposed standard becoming his station, he roams at will over the broad prairie of life, enough if he can show cause why he says this or thinks that, without having to defend himself for his parentage, and the place he was born in. Little wonder if, with such a sam to my credit, I drew largely on it; little wonder if I were dogmatical and demonstrative ; little wonder if, when my reason grew wearied with facts, I reposed on my imagination in fiction.

Be it remembered, however, that I only became what I have set down here after an excellent dinner, a considerable quantity of champagne, and no small share of claret, strong-bodied enough to please the priest. From the moment we sat down to table, I conceived for him a sort of distrust. He was painfully polite and civil; he had a soft, slippery, Clare accent; but there was a malicious twinkle in his eye that showed he was by nature satirical. Perhaps because we were more reading men than the others that it was we soon found ourselves pitted against each other in argument, and this not upon one, but upon every possible topic that turned up. Hammond, I found, also, stood by the priest; Oxley was *my* backer; and his lordship played umpire. Dyke was a shrewd, sarcastic dog in his way, but he had no chance with me. How mercilessly I treated his church!—he pushed me to it—what an expose did I make of the Pope and his government, with all their extortions and cruelties! how ruthlessly I showed them up as the sworn enemies of all freedom and enlightenment! The priest never got angry. He was too cunning for that, and he even laughed at some of my anecdotes, of which I related a great many.

" Don't be so hard on him, Potts," whispered my lord, as the day wore on; " he's not one of us, you know !"

This speech put me into a flutter of delight. It was not alone that he called me Potts, but there was also an accept-ance of me as one of his own set. We were, in fact, hence-forth " nous autres." Enchanting recognition, never to be forgotten !

"But what would you do with us?" said Dyke, mildly remonstrating against some severe measures we of the landed interest might be yet driven to resort to.

" I don't know—that is to say—I have not made up my mind whether it were better to make a clearance of you altogether, or to bribe you."

" Bribe us by all means, then !" said he, with a most serious earnestness.

" Ah ! but could we rely upon you ? " I asked.

"That would greatly depend upon the price."

" I'll not haggle about terms, nor I'm sure would Kel-drum," said I, nodding over to his lordship.

" You are only just to me, in that," said he, smiling.

" That's all fine talking for you fellows who had the luck

to be first on the list, but what are poor devils like Oxley and myself to do?" said Hammond. "Taxation comes down to second sons."

"And the 'Times' says that's all right," added Oxley.

"And I say it's all wrong; and I say more," I broke in: "I say that of all the tyrannies of Europe, I know of none like that newspaper. Why, Sir, whose station, I would ask, now-a-days, can exempt him from its impertinent criticisms? Can Keldrum say—can I say—that to-morrow or next day we shall not be arraigned for this, that, or t'other? I choose, for instance, to manage my estate—the property that has been in my family for centuries—the acres that have descended to us by grants as old as Magna Charta. I desire, for reasons that seem sufficient to myself, to convert arable into grass land. I say to one of my tenant farmers—it's Hedgeworth—no matter, I shall not mention names, but I say to him——"

"I know the man," broke in the priest; "you mean Hedgeworth Davis, of Mount Davis."

"No, Sir, I do not," said I, angrily, for I resented this attempt to run me to earth.

"Hedgeworth! Hedgeworth! It ain't that fellow that was in the Rifles; the 2nd battalion, is it?" said Oxley.

"I repeat," said I, "that I will mention no names."

"My mother had some relatives Hedgeworths, they were from Herefordshire. How odd, Potts, if we should turn out to be connections! you said that these people were related to you."

"I hope," I said, angrily, "that I am not bound to give the birth, parentage, and education of every man whose name I may mention in conversation. At least, I would protest that I have not prepared myself for such a demand upon my memory."

"Of course not, Potts. It would be a test no man could submit to," said his lordship.

"That Hedgeworth, who was in the Rifles, exceeded all the fellows I ever met in drawing the long bow. There was no country he had not been in, no army he had not served with; he was related to every celebrated man in Europe; and, after all, it turned out that his father was an attorney at

Market Harborough, and sub-agent to one of our fellows who had some property there." This was said by Hammond, who directed the speech entirely to me.

"Confound the Hedgeworths, all together," Oxley broke in. "They have carried us miles away from what we were talking of."

This was a sentiment that met my heartiest concurrence, and I nodded in friendly recognition to the speaker, and drank off my glass to his health.

"Who can give us a song? I'll back his reverence here to be a vocalist," cried Hammond. And, sure enough, Dyke sang one of the national melodies with great feeling and taste. Oxley followed with something in less perfect taste, and we all grew very jolly. Then there came a broiled bone and some devilled kidneys, and a warm brew which Hammond himself concocted—a most insidious liquor, which had a strong odour of lemons, and was compounded, at the same time, of little else than rum and sugar.

There is an adage that says "in vino veritas," which I shrewdly suspect to be a great fallacy; at least, as regards my own case, I know it to be totally inapplicable. I am, in my sober hours—and I am proud to say that the exceptions from such are of the rarest—one of the most veracious of mortals; indeed, in my frank sincerity, I have often given offence to those who like a courteous hypocrisy better than an ungraceful truth. Whenever, by any chance, it has been my ill-fortune to transgress these limits, there is no bound to my imagination. There is nothing too extravagant or too vain-glorious for me to say of myself. All the strange incidents of romance that I have read, all the travellers' stories, newspaper accidents, adventures by sea and land, wonderful coincidences, unexpected turns of fortune, I adapt to myself, and coolly relate them as personal experiences. Listeners have afterwards told me that I possess an amount of consistence, a verisimilitude in these narratives perfectly marvellous, and only to be accounted for by supposing that I myself must, for the time being, be the dupe of my own imagination. Indeed, I am sure such must be the true explanation of this curious fact. How, in any other mode, explain the rash wagers, absurd and impossible engagements I have contracted in such moments, backing myself to leap

twenty-three feet on the level sward; to dive in six fathoms
water and fetch up Heaven knows what of shells and marine
curiosities from the bottom; to ride the most unmanageable
of horses; and, single-handed and unarmed, to fight the
fiercest bulldog in England? Then, as to intellectual feats,
what have I not engaged to perform? Sums of mental
arithmetic; whole newspapers committed to memory after
one reading ; verse compositions, on any theme, in ten
languages; and once, a written contract to compose a whole
opera, with all the scores, within twenty-four hours. To a
nature thus strangely constituted, wine was a perfect magic
wand, transforming a poor, weak, distrustful, modest man,
into a hero; and yet, even with such temptatious, my excesses were extremely rare and unfrequent. Are there many,
I would ask, that could resist the passport to such a dreamland, with only the penalty of a headache the next morning ?
Some one would, perhaps, suggest that these were enjoyments to pay forfeit on. Well, so they were; but I must
not anticipate. And now to my tale.

To Hammond's brew there succeeded one by Oxley, made
after an American receipt, and certainly both fragrant and
insinuating, and then came a concoction made by the priest,
which he called "Father Hosey's pride." It was made in a
bowl, and drunk out of lemon-rinds, ingeniously fitted into
the wine-glasses. I remember no other particulars about it,
though I can call to mind much of the conversation that preceded it. How I gave a long historical account of my family,
that we came originally from Corsica, the name Potts being
a corruption of Pozzo, and that we were of the same stock as
the celebrated diplomatist Pozzo di Borgo. Our unclaimed
estates in the island were of fabulous value, but in asserting
my right to them I should accept thirteen mortal duels, the
arrears of a hundred and odd years unscored off, in anticipation of which I had at one time taken lessons from Angelo in
fencing, which led to the celebrated challenge they might
have read in "Galignani," where I offered to meet any swordsman in Europe for ten thousand Napoleons, giving choice of
the weapon to my adversary. With a tear to the memory of
the poor French colonel that I killed at Sedan, I turned the
conversation. Being in France, I incidentally mentioned
some anecdotes of military life, and how I had invented the

rifle called after Minié's name, and, in a moment of good nature, given that excellent fellow my secret.

"I will say," said I, "that Minié has shown more gratitude than some others nearer home, but we'll talk of rifled cannon another time."

In an episode about bear-shooting, I mentioned the Emperor of Russia, poor dear Nicholas, and told how we had once exchanged horses, mine being more strong-boned, and a weight-carrier, his a light Caucasian mare, of purest breed, "the dam of that creature you may see below in the stable now," said I, carelessly. "'Come and see me one of these days, Potts,' said he, in parting; 'come and pass a week with me at Constantinople.' This was the first intimation he had ever given of his project against Turkey, and when I told it to the Duke of Wellington, his remark was a muttered 'Strange fellow, Potts—knows everything!' though he made no reply to me at the time."

It was somewhere about this period that the priest began with what struck me as an attempt to outdo me as a storyteller, an effort I should have treated with the most contemptuous indifference but for the amount of attention bestowed on him by the others. Nor was this all, but actually I perceived that a kind of rivalry was attempted to be established, so that we were pitted directly against each other. Amongst the other self-delusions of such moments was the profound conviction I entertained that I was master of all games of skill and address, superior to Major A. at whist, and able to give Staunton a pawn and the move at chess. The priest was just as vainglorious. "He'd like to see the man who'd play him a game of 'spoiled five'"—whatever that was—"or drafts; ay, or, though it was not his pride, a bit of backgammon."

"Done, for fifty pounds; double on the gammon!" cried I.

"Fifty fiddlesticks!" cried he; "where would you or I find as many shillings?"

"What do you mean, Sir?" said I, angrily. "Am I to suppose that you doubt my competence to risk such a contemptible sum, or is it to your own inability alone you would testify?"

A very acrimonious dispute followed, of which I have no

clear recollection. I only remember how Hammond was
out-and-out for the priest, and Oxley too tipsy to take *my*
part with any efficiency. At last—how arranged I can't
say—peace was restored, and the next thing I can recal was
listening to Father Dyke giving a long, and of course a most
fabulous, history of a ring that he wore on his second finger.
It was given by the Pretender, he said, to his uncle, the
celebrated Carmelite monk, Lawrence O'Kelly, who for years
had followed the young prince's fortunes. It was an onyx,
with the letters C. E. S. engraved on it. Keldrum took an
immense fancy to it; he protested that everything that
attached to that unhappy family possessed in his eyes an
uncommon interest. "If you have a fancy to take up
Potts's wager," said he, laughingly, "I'll give you fifty
pounds for your signet ring."

The priest demurred—Hammond interposed—then there
was more discussion, now warm, now jocose. Oxley tried to
suggest something, which we all laughed at. Keldrum
placed the backgammon board meanwhile, but I can give no
clear account of what ensued, though I remember that the
terms of our wager were committed to writing by Hammond,
and signed by Father D. and myself, and in the conditions
there figured a certain ring, guaranteed to have belonged to,
and been worn by, his Royal Highness Charles Edward, and
a cream-coloured horse, equally guaranteed as the produce
of a Caucasian mare presented by the late Emperor Nicholas
to the present owner. The document was witnessed by all
three, Oxley's name written in two letters, and a flourish.

After that, I played, and lost!

CHAPTER IV

I CAN recal to this very hour the sensations of headache
and misery with which I awoke the morning after this
debauch. Racking pain it was, with a sort of tremulous
beating all through the brain, as though a small engine had

been set to work there, and that piston, and boiler, and con-
necting rod were all banging, fizzing, and vibrating amid my
fevered senses. I was, besides, much puzzled to know where
I was, and how I had come there. Controversial divinity,
genealogy, horse-racing, the peerage, and " double sixes"
were dancing a wild cotillon through my brain; and
although a waiter more than once cautiously obtruded his
head into the room, to see if I were asleep, and as guardedly
withdrew it again, I never had energy to speak to him, but
lay passive and still, waiting till my mind might clear, and
the cloud-fog that obscured my faculties might be wafted
away.

At last—it was towards evening—the man, possibly
becoming alarmed at my protracted lethargy, moved somewhat briskly through the room, and with that amount of
noise that showed he meant to arouse me, disturbed chairs
and fire-irons indiscriminately.

" Is it late or early ? " asked I, faintly.

" 'Tis near five, Sir, and a beautiful evening," said he,
drawing nigh, with the air of one disposed for colloquy.

I didn't exactly like to ask where I was, and tried to
ascertain the fact by a little circumlocution. " I suppose,"
said I, yawning, " for all that is to be done in a place like
this, when up, one might just as well stay abed, eh ? "

" 'Tis the snuggest place anyhow," said he, with that
peculiar disposition to agree with you so characteristic in an
Irish waiter.

" No society ? " sighed I.

" No, indeed, Sir."

" No theatre ? "

" Devil a one, Sir."

" No sport ? "

" Yesterday was the last of the season, Sir; and signs on
it, his lordship and the other gentleman was off immediately
after breakfast."

" You mean Lord—Lord—" A mist was clearing slowly
away, but I could not yet see clearly.

" Lord Keldrum, Sir; a real gentleman every inch of
him."

" Oh yes ! to be sure—a very old friend of mine," muttered
I. " And so he's gone, is he ? "

"Yes, Sir; and the last word he said was about your honour."

"About me—what was it?"

"Well, indeed, Sir," replied the waiter, with a hesitating and confused manner, "I didn't rightly understand it; but as well as I could catch the words, it was something about hoping your honour had more of that wonderful breed of horses the Emperor of Roossia gave you."

"Oh yes! I understand," said I, stopping him abruptly. "By the way, how is Blondel—that is, my horse—this morning?"

"Well, he looked fresh and hearty, when he went off this morning at daybreak——"

"What do you mean?" cried I, jumping up in my bed. "Went off? where to?"

"—With Father Dyke on his back; and a neater hand he couldn't wish over him. 'Tim,' says he, to the ostler, as he mounted, 'there's a five-shilling piece for you, for hansel, for I won this baste last night, and you must drink my health and wish me luck with him.'"

I heard no more, but sinking back into the bed, I covered my face with my hands, overcome with shame and misery. All the mists that had blurred my faculties had now been swept clean away, and the whole history of the previous evening was revealed before me. My stupid folly, my absurd boastfulness, my egregious story-telling—not to call it worse—were all there; but, shall I acknowledge it? what pained me not less poignantly was the fact that I ventured to stake the horse I had merely hired, and actually lost him at the play-table.

As soon as I rallied from this state of self-accusation, I set to work to think how I should manage to repossess myself of my beast, my loss of which might be converted into a felony. To follow the priest and ransom Blondel was my first care. Father Dyke would most probably not exact an unreasonable price; he, of course, never believed one word of my nonsensical narrative about Schamyl and the Caucasus, and he'd not revenge upon Potts sober the follies of Potts tipsy. It is true my purse was a very slender one, but Blondel to anyone unacquainted with his pedigree, could not be a costly animal; fifteen pounds—twenty, certainly—

ought to buy what the priest would call "every hair on his tail."

It was now too late in the evening to proceed to execute the measures I had resolved on, and so I determined to lie still and ponder over them. Dismissing the waiter, with an order to bring me a cup of tea about eight o'clock, I resumed my cogitations. They were not pleasant ones: Potts a byword for the most outrageous and incoherent balderdash and untruth—Potts in the "Hue and Cry"—Potts in the dock—Potts in the pillory—Potts paragraphed in "Punch" —portrait of Potts, price one penny!—these were only a few of the forms in which the descendant of the famous Corsican family of Pozzo di Borgo now presented himself to my imagination.

The courts and quadrangles of Old Trinity ringing with laughter, the coarse exaggerations of tasteless scoffers, the jokes and sneers of stupidity, malice, and all uncharitableness, rang in my ears as if I heard them. All possible and impossible versions of the incident passed in review before me: my father, driven distracted by impertinent inquiries, cutting me off with a shilling, and then dying of mortification and chagrin—rewards offered for my apprehension— descriptions, not in any way flatteries, of my personal appearance—paragraphs of local papers hinting that the notorious Potts was supposed to have been seen in our neighbourhood yesterday, with sly suggestions about looking after stabledoors, &c. I could bear it no longer. I jumped up, and rang the bell violently.

"You know this Father Dyke, waiter? In what part of the country does he live?"

"He's parish priest of Inistioge," said he; "the snuggest place in the whole county."

"How far from this may it be?"

"It's a matter of five-and-forty miles; and by the same token, he said he'd not draw bridle till he got home to-night, for there was a fair at Grague to-morrow, and if he wasn't pleased with the baste he'd sell him there."

I groaned deeply, for here was a new complication, entirely unlooked for, "You can't possibly mean," gasped I out, "that a respectable clergyman would expose for sale a horse lent to him casually by a friend?" for the thought

struck me that this protest of mine should be thus early on
record.

The waiter scratched his head and looked confused.
Whether another version of the event possessed him, or
that my question staggered his convictions, I am unable to
say, but he made no reply.   "It is true," continued I, in the
same strain, " that I met his reverence last night for the first
time.   My friend Lord Keldrum made us acquainted; but
seeing him received at my noble friend's board, I naturally
felt, and said to myself, 'The man Keldrum admits to his
table is the equal of anyone.'   Could anything be more
reasonable than that ? "

" No, indeed, Sir; nothing," said the waiter, obsequiously.

" Well, then," resumed I, "some day or other it may
chance that you will be called on to remember and recal this
conversation between us; if so, it will be important that you
should have a clear and distinct memory of the fact, that
when I awoke in the morning, and asked for my horse, the
answer you made me was——What was the answer you
made me ? "

" The answer I med was this," said the fellow, sturdily,
and with an effrontery I can never forget—"the answer I
med was, that the man that won him took him away."

" You're an insolent scoundrel," cried I, boiling over with
passion, " and if you don't ask pardon for this outrage on
your knees, I'll include you in the indictment for conspiracy."

So far from proceeding to the penitential act I proposed,
the fellow grinned from ear to ear, and left the room.   It
was a long time before I could recover my wonted calm and
composure.   That this rascal's evidence would be fatal to me
if the question ever came to trial, was as clear as noonday;
not less clear was it that he knew this himself.

" I must go back at once to town," thought I.   " I will
surrender myself to the law.   If a compromise be impossible,
I will perish at the stake."

I forgot there was no stake, but there was wool-carding,
and oakum-picking, and wheel-treading, and oyster-shell
pounding, and other small plays of this nature, infinitely
more degrading to humanity than all the cruelties of our
barbarous ancestors.

Now, in no record of lives of adventure had I met any

account of such trials as these. The Silvio Pellicos of Pentonville are yet unwritten martyrs. Prison discipline would vulgarise the grandest epic that ever was conceived. "Anything rather than this," said I, aloud. "Proscribed, outlawed, hunted down, but never, grey-coated and hair-clipped, shall a Potts be sentenced to the 'crank,' or black-holed as refractory!—Bring me my bill," cried I, in a voice of indignant anger. "I will go forth into the world of darkness and tempest—I will meet the storm and the hurricane; better all the conflict of the elements than man's—than man's——" I wasn't exactly sure what, but there was no need of the word, for a gust of wind had just flattened my umbrella in my face as I issued forth, and left me breathless, as the door closed behind me.

CHAPTER V.

As I walked onward against the swooping wind and the plashing rain, I felt a sort of heroic ardour in the notion of breasting the adverse waves of life so boldly. It is not every fellow could do this: throw his knapsack on his shoulder, seize his stick, and set out in storm and blackness. No, Potts, my man; for downright inflexibility of purpose, for bold and resolute action, you need yield to none! It was, indeed, an awful night; the thunder rolled and crashed with scarce an interval of cessation; forked lightning tore across the sky in every direction; while the wind swept through the deep glen, smashing branches and uplifting large trees like mere shrubs. I was soon completely drenched, and my soaked clothes hung around with the weight of lead; my spirits, however, sustained me, and I toiled along, occasionally in a sort of wild bravado, giving a cheer as the thunder rolled close above my head, and trying to sing, as though my heart were as gay and my spirits as light as in an hour of happiest abandonment.

Jean Paul has somewhere the theory that our Good

Genius is attached to us from our birth by a film fine as gossamer, and which few of us escape rupturing in the first years of youth, thus throwing ourselves at once without chart or pilot upon the broad ocean of life. He, however, more happily constituted, who feels the guidance of his guardian spirit, recognises the benefits of its care, and the admonitions of its wisdom, *he* is destined to great things. Such men discover new worlds beyond the seas, carry conquest over millions, found dynasties, and build up empires; they whom the world regard as demigods having simply the wisdom of being led by fortune, and not severing the slender thread that unites them to their destiny. Was I, Potts, in this glorious category? Had the lesson of the great moralist been such a warning to me that I had preserved the filmy link unbroken; I really began to think so; a certain impulse, a whispering voice within, that said, "Go on!" On, ever onward! seemed to be the accents of that Fate, which had great things in store for me, and would eventually make me illustrious.

No illusions of your own, Potts, no phantasmagoria of your own poor heated fancy, must wile you away from the great and noble part destined for you. No weakness, no faintheartedness, no shrinking from toil, nor even peril. Work hard to know thoroughly for what Fate intends you; read your credentials well, and then go to your post unflinchingly. Revolving this theory of mine, I walked ever on. It opened a wide field, and my imagination disported in it, as might a wild mustang over some vast prairie. The more I thought over it, the more did it seem to me the real embodiment of that superstition which extends to every land and every family of men. We are Lucky when, submitting to our Good Genius, we suffer ourselves to be led along unhesitatingly; we are Unlucky when, breaking our frail bonds, we encounter life unguided and unaided.

What a docile, obedient, and believing pupil did I pledge myself to be. Fate should see that she had no refractory nor rebellious spirit in me, no self-indulgent voluptuary, seeking only the sunny side of existence, but a nature ready to confront the rugged conflict of life, and to meet its hardships, if such were my allotted path.

I applied the circumstances in which I then found myself

to my theory, and met no difficulty in the adaptation. Blondel was to perform a great part in my future. Blondel was a symbol selected by fate to indicate a certain direction. Blondel was a lamp by which I could find my way in the dark paths of the world. With Blondel, my Good Genius would walk beside me, or occasionally get up on the crupper, but never leave me or desert me. In the high excitement of my mind, I felt no sense of bodily fatigue, but walked on, drenched to the skin, alternately shivering with cold or burning with all the intensity of fever. In this state was it that I entered the little inn of Ovoco soon after daybreak, and stood dripping in the bar, a sad spectacle of exhaustion and excitement. My first question was, "Has Blondel been here?" and before they could reply, I went on with all the rapidity of delirium to assure them that deception of me would be fruitless; that Fate and I understood each other thoroughly, travelled together on the best of terms, never disagreed about anything, but by a mutual system of give and take, hit it off like brothers. I talked for an hour in this strain, and then my poor faculties, long struggling and sore pushed, gave way completely, and I fell into brain fever.

I chanced upon kind and good-hearted folk, who nursed me with care and watched me with interest; but my illness was a severe one, and it was only in the sixth week that I could be about again, a poor, weak, emaciated creature, with failing limbs and shattered nerves. There is an indescribable sense of weariness in the mind after fever, just as if the brain had been enormously over-taxed and exerted, and that in the pursuit of all the wild and fleeting fancies of delirium it had travelled over miles and miles of space. To the depressing influence of this sensation is added the difficulty of disentangling the capricious illusions of the sick-bed from the actual facts of life; and in this maze of confusion my first days of convalescence were passed. Blondel was my great puzzle. Was he a reality, or a mere creature of imagination? Had I really ridden him as a horse, or only as an idea? Was he a quadruped with mane and tail, or an allegory invented to typify destiny? I cannot say what hours of painful brain labour this inquiry cost me, and what intense research into myself. Strange enough, too, though I came out of the investigation convinced of his existence,

3

I arrived at the conclusion that he was a "horse and something more." Not that I am able to explain myself more fully on that head, though, if I were writing this portion of my memoirs in German, I suspect I could convey enough of my meaning to give a bad headache to anyone indulgent enough to follow me.

I set out once more upon my pilgrimage on a fine day of June, my steps directed to the village of Inistioge, where Father Dyke resided. I was too weak for much exertion, and it was only after five days of the road I reached at nightfall the little glen in which the village stood. The moon was up, streaking the wide market-places with long lines of yellow light between the rows of tall elm-trees, and tipping with silvery sheen the bright eddies of the beautiful river that rolled beside it. Over the granite cliffs that margined the stream, laurel, and arbutus, and wild holly clustered in wild luxuriance, backed higher up again by tall pine-trees, whose leafy summits stood out against the sky; and lastly, deep within a waving meadow, stood an old ruined abbey, whose traceried window was now softly touched by the moonlight. All was still and silent, except the rush of the rapid river, as I sat down upon a stone bench to enjoy the scene and luxuriate in its tranquil serenity. I had not believed Ireland contained such a spot, for there was all the trim neatness and careful propriety of an English village, with that luxuriance of verdure and wild beauty so eminently Irish. How was it that I had never heard of it before? Were others aware of it, or was the discovery strictly my own? Or can it possibly be that all this picturesque loveliness is but the effect of a mellow moon? While I thus questioned myself, I heard the sound of a quick footstep rapidly approaching, and soon afterwards the pleasant tone of a rich voice humming an opera air, I arose, and saw a tall, athletic-looking figure, with rod and fishing-basket, approaching me.

"May I ask you, Sir," said I, addressing him, "if this village contains an inn?"

"There is, or rather there was, a sort of inn here," said he, removing his cigar as he spoke; "but the place is so little visited, that I fancy the landlord found it would not answer, and so it is closed at this moment."

"But do visitors—tourists—never pass this way?"

"Yes; and a few salmon-fishers, like myself, come occasionally in the season; but then we dispose ourselves in little lodgings, here and there, some of us with the farmers, one or two of us with the priest."

"Father Dyke?" broke I in.

"Yes; you know him, perhaps?"

"I have heard of him, and met him, indeed," added I, after a pause. "Where may his house be?"

"The prettiest spot in the whole glen. If you'd like to see it in this picturesque moonlight, come along with me."

I accepted the invitation at once, and we walked on together. The easy, half-careless tone of the stranger, the loose, lounging stride of his walk, and a certain something in his mellow voice, seemed to indicate one of those natures which, so to say, take the world well—temperaments that reveal themselves almost immediately. He talked away about fishing, as he went, and appeared to take a deep interest in the sport, not heeding much the ignorance I betrayed on the subject, nor my ignoble confession that I had never adventured upon anything higher than a worm and a quill.

"I'm sure," said he, laughingly, "Tom Dyke never encouraged you in such sporting tackle, glorious fly-fisher as he is."

"You forget, perhaps," replied I, "that I scarcely have any acquaintance with him. We met once only at a dinner party."

"He's a pleasant fellow," resumed he; "devilish wide-awake, one must say; up to most things in this same world of ours."

"That much, my own brief experience of him can confirm," said I, dryly, for the remark rather jarred upon my feelings."

"Yes," said he, as though following out his own train of thought. "Old Tom is not a bird to be snared with coarse lines. The man must be an early riser that catches him napping."

I cannot describe how this irritated me. It sounded like so much direct sarcasm upon my weakness and want of acuteness.

3—2

"There's the 'Rosary;' that's his cottage," said he, taking
my arm, while he pointed upward to a little jutting promontory of rock over the river, surmounted by a little
thatched cottage almost embowered in roses and honey-
suckles.   So completely did it occupy the narrow limits
of ground, that the windows projected actually over the
stream, and the creeping plants that twined through the
little balconies hung in tangled masses over the water.
"Search where you will through the Scottish and Cumberland scenery, I defy you to match that," said my companion;
"not to say that you can hook a four-pound fish from that
little balcony on any summer evening while you smoke your
cigar."

"It is a lovely spot, indeed," said I, inhaling with ecstasy
the delicious perfume which, in the calm night air, seemed
to linger in the atmosphere.

"He tells me," continued my companion—"and I take
his word for it, for I am no florist—that there are seventy
varieties of the rose on and around that cottage. I can
answer for it, that you can't open a window without a great
mass of flowers coming, in showers, over you. I told him,
frankly, that if I were his tenant for longer than the fishing
season, I'd clear half of them away."

"You live there, then?" asked I, timidly.

"Yes, I rent the cottage, all but two rooms, which he
wished to keep for himself, but which he now writes me
word may be let, for this month and the next, if a tenant
offer. Would you like them?" asked he, abruptly.

"Of all things—that is—I think so—I should like to see
them first!" muttered I, half startled by the suddenness of
the question.

"Nothing easier," said he, opening a little wicket as he
spoke, and beginning to ascend a flight of narrow steps cut
in the solid rock. "This is a path of my designing," continued he, "the regular approach is on the other side; but
this saves fully half a mile of road, though it be a little
steep."

As I followed him up the ascent, I proposed to myself a
variety of questions, such as, where and how I was to procure accommodation for the night, and in what manner to
obtain something to eat, of which I stood much in need?

and I had gained a little flower-garden at the rear of the cottage before I could resolve any of these difficult points.

"Here we are," said he, drawing a long breath. "You can't see much of the view at this hour; but to-morrow, when you stand on this spot, and look down that reach of the river, with Mont Alto in the background, you'll tell me if you know anything finer!"

"Is that Edward?" cried a soft voice; and at the same instant a young girl came hastily out of the cottage, and throwing her arms around my companion, exclaimed, "How you have alarmed me! What could possibly have kept you out so late?"

"A broad-shouldered fish, a fellow weighing twelve pounds at the very least, and who, after nigh three hours' playing, got among the rocks, and smashed my tackle."

"And you lost him?"

"That did I, and some twenty yards of gut, and the top splice of my best rod, and my temper besides. But I'm forgetting: Mary, here is a gentleman who will, I hope, not refuse to join us at supper.—My sister."

By the manner of presentation, it was clear that he expected to hear my name, and so I interposed, "Mr. Potts—Algernon Sydney Potts."

The young lady curtseyed slightly, muttered something like a repetition of the invitation, and led the way into the cottage.

My astonishment was great at the "interior" now before me, for though all the arrangements bespoke habits of comfort and even luxury, there was a studious observance of cottage style in everything, the bookshelves, the tables, the very pianoforte, being all made of white unvarnished wood! and I now perceived that the young lady herself, with a charming coquetry, had assumed something of the costume of the Oberland, and wore her bodice laced in front, and covered with silver embroidery both tasteful and becoming.

"My name is Crofton," said my host, as he disengaged himself of his basket and tackle; "we are almost as much strangers here as yourself. I came here for the fishing, and mean to take myself off when it's over."

"I hope not, Edward," broke in the girl, who was now,

with the assistance of a servant woman, preparing the table for supper; "I hope you'll stay till we see the autumn tints on those trees."

"My sister is just as great an enthusiast about sketching as I am for salmon-fishing," said he, laughingly; "and for my own part, I like scenery and landscape very well, but think them marvellously heightened by something like sport. Are you an angler?"

"No," said I; "I know nothing of the gentle craft."

"Fond of shooting, perhaps? Some men think the two sports incompatible."

"I am as inexpert with the gun as the rod," said I, diffidently.

I perceived that the sister gave a sly look under her long eyelashes towards me, but what its meaning, I could not well discover. Was it depreciation of a man who avowed himself unacquainted with the sports of the field, or was it a quiet recognition of claims more worthy of regard? At all events, I perceived that she had very soft, gentle-looking grey eyes, a very fair skin, and a profusion of beautiful brown hair. I had not thought her pretty at first. I now saw that she was extremely pretty, and her figure, though slightly given to fulness, the perfection of grace.

Hungry, almost famished as I was, with a fast of twelve hours, I felt no impatience so long as she moved about in preparation for the meal. How she disposed the little table equipage, the careful solicitude with which she arranged the fruit and the flowers—not always satisfied with her first dispositions, but changing them for something different— all interested me vastly, and when at last we were summoned to table, I actually felt sorry and disappointed.

Was it really so delicious, was the cookery so exquisite? I own frankly that I am not a trustworthy witness, but if my oath could be taken, I am willing to swear that I believe there never were such salmon-steaks, such a pigeon-pie, and such a damson-tart served to mortals as these. My enthusiasm, I suspect, must have betrayed itself in some outward manifestation, for I remember Crofton laughingly having remarked,—

"You will turn my sister's head, Mr. Potts, by such flatteries; all the more, since her cookery is self-taught."

"Don't believe him, Mr. Potts; I have studied all the great masters of the art, and you shall have an omelette to-morrow for breakfast, Brillat Savarin himself would not despise."

I blushed at the offer of an hospitality so neatly and delicately insinuated, and had really no words to acknowledge it, nor was my confusion unfavourably judged by my hosts. Crofton marked it quickly and said,—

"Yes, Mr. Potts, and I'll teach you to hook a trout afterwards. Meanwhile, let us have a glass of Sauterne together; we drink it out of green glasses, to cheat ourselves into the fancy that it's Rhenish."

"'Am Rhein, am Rhein, da wachsen unsere Reben,'" said I, quoting the students' song.

"Oh, have you been in Germany?" cried she, eagerly.

"Alas! no," said I. "I have never travelled." I thought she looked disappointed as I said this. Indeed, I already wished it unsaid, but her brother broke in with,—

"We are regular vagabonds, Mr. Potts. My sister and myself have had a restless paroxysm for the last three years of life, and what with seeking cool spots for the summer and hot climates for winter, we are scarcely ever off the road."

"Like the gentleman, I suppose, who ate oysters for appetite, but carried his system so far as to induce indigestion." My joke failed; nobody laughed, and I was overwhelmed with confusion, which I was fain to bury in my strawberries and cream.

"Let us have a little music, Mary," said Crofton. "Do you play, or sing, Mr. Potts?"

"Neither. I do nothing," cried I, in despair. "As Sydney Smith says, 'I know something about the Romans,' but, for any gift or grace which could adorn society, or make time pass more pleasantly, I am an utter bankrupt."

The young girl had, while I was speaking, taken her place at the pianoforte, and was half listlessly suffering her hands to fall in chords over the instrument.

"Come out upon this terrace, here," cried Crofton to me. "and we'll have our cigar. What I call a regular luxury after a hard day is to lounge out here in the cool night air, and enjoy one's weed while listening to Spohr or Beethoven."

It was really delightful. The bright stars were all reflected in the calm river down below, and a thousand odours floated softly on the air as we sat there.

Are there not in every man's experience short periods in which he seemed to have lived longer than during whole years of life? They tell us there are certain conditions of the atmosphere, inappreciable as to the qualities, which seem to ripen wines, imparting to young fresh vintages all the mellow richness of age, all the depth of flavour, all the velvety softness of time. May there not possibly be influences which similarly affect our natures? May there not be seasons in which changes as great as these are wrought within us? I firmly believe it, and as firmly that such a period was that in which I sat on the balcony over the Nore, listening to Mary Crofton as she sang, but just as often lost to every sound, and deep in a heaven of blended enjoyments, of which no one ingredient was in the ascendant. Starry sky, rippling river, murmuring night winds, perfumed air, floating music, all mingling as do the odours of an incense, and, like an incense, filling the brain with a delicious intoxication.

Hour after hour must have passed with me in this half-conscious ecstasy, for Crofton at last said,—

"There, where you see that pinkish tint through the grey, that's the sign of breaking day, and the signal for bedtime. Shall I show you your room?"

"How I wish this could last for ever!" cried I, rapturously; and then, half ashamed of my warmth, I stammered out a good night, and retired.

CHAPTER VI.

Our life at the Rosary for it was *our* life now of which I have to speak—was one of unbroken enjoyment. On fine days we fished, that is, Crofton did, and I loitered along some river's bank till I found a quiet spot to plant my rod, and stretch myself on the grass, now reading, oftener dreaming, such glorious dreams as only come in the leafy shading of summer time, to a mind enraptured with all around it. The lovely scenery and the perfect solitude of the spot ministered well to my fanciful mood, and left me free to weave the most glittering web of incident for my future. So utterly was all the past blotted from my memory, that I recalled nothing of existence more remote than my first evening at the cottage. If for a parting instant a thought of bygones would obtrude, I hastened to escape from it as from a gloomy reminiscence. 1 turned away as would a dreamer who dreaded to awaken out of some delicious vision, and who would not face the dull aspect of reality. Three weeks thus glided by of such happiness as I can scarcely yet recal without emotion! The Croftons had come to treat me like a brother; they spoke of family events in all freedom before me; talked of the most confidential things in my presence, and discussed their future plans and their means as freely in my hearing as though I had been kith and kin with them. I learned that they were orphans, educated and brought up by a rich, eccentric uncle, who lived in a sort of costly reclusion in one of the Cumberland dales; Edward, who had served in the army, and been wounded in an Indian campaign, had given up the service in a fit of impatience of being passed over in promotion. His uncle resented the rash step by withdrawing the liberal allowance he had usually made him, and they quarrelled. Mary Crofton, espousing her brother's side, quitted her guardian's roof to join his, and thus had they rambled about the world for two or three years, on means scanty enough, but still sufficient to provide for those who neither sought to enter society nor partake of its pleasures.

As I advanced in the intimacy, I became depository of the secrets of each. Edward's was the sorrow he felt for having involved his sister in his own ruin, and been the means of separating her from one so well able and so willing to befriend her. Hers was the more bitter thought that their narrow means should prejudice her brother's chances of recovery, for his chest had shown symptoms of dangerous disease requiring all that climate and consummate care might do to overcome. Preyed on incessantly by this reflection,

unable to banish it, equally unable to resist its force, she took
the first and only step she had ever adventured without his
knowledge, and written to her uncle a long letter of explanations and entreaty.

I saw the letter; and read it carefully. It was all that
sisterly love and affection could dictate, accompanied by a
sense of dignity, that if her appeal should be unsuccessful, no
slight should be passed upon her brother, who was unaware
of the step thus taken. To express this sufficiently, she was
driven to the acknowledgment that Edward would never
have himself stooped to the appeal ; and so careful was she
of his honour in this respect, that she repeated—with what
appeared to me unnecessary insistence—that the request
should be regarded as hers, and hers only. In fact, this was
the uppermost sentiment in the whole epistle. I ventured to
say as much, and endeavoured to induce her to moderate in
some degree the amount of this pretension; but she resisted
firmly and decidedly. Now, I have recorded this circumstance
here—less for itself than to mention how by its means this
little controversy led to a great intimacy between us—inducing us, while defending our separate views to discuss
each other's motives, and even characters, with the widest
freedom. I called her enthusiast, and in return she styled
me worldly and calculating; and, indeed, I tried to seem so,
and fortified my opinions by prudential maxims and severe
reflections I should have been sorely indisposed to adopt in
my own case. I believe she saw all this. I am sure she
read me aright, and perceived that I was arguing against
my own convictions. At all events, day after day went
over, and no answer came to the letter. I used to go each
morning to the post in the village to inquire, but always
returned with the same disheartening tidings, "Nothing to-
day!"

One of these mornings it was, that I was returning dis-
consolately from the village, Crofton, whom I believed at
the time miles away on the mountains, overtook me. He
came up from behind, and passing his arm within mine,
walked on some minutes without speaking. I saw plainly
there was something on his mind, and I half dreaded lest he
might have discovered his sister's secret, and have disap-
proved of my share in it.

"Algy," said he, calling me by my Christian name, which he very rarely did, "I have something to say to you. Can I be quite certain that you'll take my frankness in good part?"

"You can," I said, with a great effort to seem calm and assured.

"You give me your word upon it?"

"I do," said I, trying to appear bold; "and my hand be witness of it."

"Well," he resumed, drawing a long breath, "here it is: I have remarked that for above a week back you have never waited for the postboy's return to the cottage, but always have come down to the village yourself."

I nodded assent, but said nothing.

"I have remarked, besides," said he, "that, when told at the office there was no letter for you, you came away sad-looking and fretted, scarcely spoke for some time, and seemed altogether downcast and depressed."

"I don't deny it," I said, calmly.

"Well," continued he, "some old experiences of mine have taught me that this sort of anxiety has generally but one source, with fellows of *our* age, and which simply means that the remittance we have counted upon as certain, has been, from some cause or other, delayed. Isn't that the truth?"

"No," said I, joyfully, for I was greatly relieved by his words; "no, on my honour, nothing of the kind."

"I may not have hit the thing exactly," said he, hurriedly, "but I'll be sworn it is a money matter, and if a couple of hundred pounds be of the least service——"

"My dear, kind-hearted fellow," I broke in, "I can't endure this longer; it is no question of money; it is nothing that affects my means, though I half wish it were, to show you how cheerfully I could owe you my escape from a difficulty—not, indeed, that I need another tie to bind me to you——" But I could say no more, for my eyes were swimming over, and my lips trembling.

"Then," cried he, "I have only to ask pardon for thus obtruding upon your confidence."

I was too full of emotion to do more than squeeze his hand affectionately, and thus we walked along, side by side, neither

uttering a word.   At last, and as it were with an effort, by a
bold transition to carry our thoughts into another and very
different channel, he said, "Here's a letter from old Dyke,
our landlord.   The worthy father has been enjoying himself
in a tour of English watering-places, and has now started
for a few weeks up the Rhine.   His account of his holiday,
as he calls it, is amusing; nor less so is the financial accident
to which he owes the excursion.   Take it, and read it," he
added, giving me the epistle.   "If the style be the man, his
reverence is not difficult to decipher."

I bestowed little attention on this speech, uttered, as I perceived, rather from the impulse of starting a new topic, than
anything else, and taking the letter half mechanically, I
thrust it in my pocket.   One or two efforts we made at conversation were equally failures, and it was a relief to me
when Crofton, suddenly remembering some night-lines he had
laid in a mountain lake a few miles off, hastily shook my
hand, and said, "Good-bye till dinner-time."

When I reached the cottage, instead of entering, I strolled
into the garden, and sought out a little summer-house of
sweet briar and honeysuckle, on the edge of the river.
Some strange, vague impression was on me, that I needed
time and place to commune with myself and be alone; that
a large unsettled account lay between me and my conscience, which could not be longer deferred; but, of what
nature, how originating, and how tending, I know nothing
whatever.

I resolved to submit myself to a searching examination,
to ascertain what I might about myself.   In my favourite
German authors I had frequently read that men's failures in
life were chiefly owing to neglect of this habit of self investigation; that though we calculate well the dangers and difficulties of an enterprise, we omit the more important estimate
of what may be our capacity to effect an object, what are our
resources, wherein our deficiencies.

"Now for it," I thought, as I entered the little arbour,
—"now for it, Potts; kiss the book, and tell the whole truth
and nothing but the truth."

As I said this, I took off my hat and bowed respectfully
around to the members of an imaginary court.   "My name,"
said I, in a clear and respectful voice, "is Algernon Sydney

Potts. If I be pushed to the avowal, I am sorry it *is* Potts! Algernon Sydney do a deal, but they can't do everything—not to say that—captious folk see a certain bathos in the collocation with my surname. Can a man hope to make such a name illustrious? Can he aspire to the notion of a time when people will allude to the great Potts, the celebrated Potts, the immortal Potts?" I grew very red, I felt my cheek on fire as I uttered this, and I suddenly bethought me of Mr. Pitt, and I said aloud, "and, if Pitt, why not Potts?" That was a most healing recollection. I revelled in it for a long time. "How true is it," I continued, "that the halo of greatness illumines all within its circle, and the man is merged in the grandeur of his achievements. The men who start in life with high sounding designations have but to fill a foregone pledge—to pay the bill that Fortune has endorsed. Not so was our case, Pitt. To us is it to lay every foundation stone of our future greatness. There was nothing in *your* surname to foretel you would be a Minister of State at one-and-thirty—there is no letter of *mine* to indicate what I shall be. But what is it that I am to be? Is it Poet, Philosopher, Politician, Soldier, or Discoverer? Am I to be great in Art, or illustrious in Letters? Is there to be an ice tract of Behring's Straits called Potts's Point, or a planet styled Pottsium Sidus? And when centuries have rolled over, will historians have their difficulty about the first Potts, and what his opinions were on this subject or that?"

Then came a low soft sound of half suppressed laughter, and then the rustle of a muslin dres hastily brushing through the trees. I rushed out from my retreat, and hurried down the walk. No one to be seen—not a soul; not a sound, either, to be heard.

"No use hiding, Mary," I called out, "I saw you all the time; my mock confession was got up merely to amuse you. Come out boldly and laugh as long as you will." No answer. This refusal amazed me. It was like a disbelief in my assertion. "Come, come!" I cried, "you can't pretend to think I was serious in all this vain-glorious nonsense. Come, Mary, and let us enjoy the laugh at it together. If you don't, I shall be angry. I'll take it ill—very ill."

Still no reply. Could I, then, have been deceived? Was

it a mere delusion? But no; I heard the low laugh, and
the rustle of the dress, and the quick tread upon the gravel,
too plainly for any mistake, and so I returned to the cottage
in chagrin and ill-temper. As I passed the open windows of
the little drawing-room I saw Mary seated at her work, with,
as was her custom, an open book on a little table beside her.
Absorbed as she was, she did not lift her head, nor notice
my approach till I entered the room.

" You have no letter for me? " she cried, in a voice of sor-
rowful meaning.

" None," said I scrutinising her closely, and sorely puzzled
what to make of her calm deportment. " Have you been out
in the garden this morning? " I asked, abruptly.

" No," said she, frankly.

" Not quitted the house at all ? "

" No. Why do you ask? " cried she, in some surprise.

" I'll tell you," I said, sitting down at her side, and speaking in a low and confidential tone; " a strange thing has
just happened to me." And with that I narrated the incident, glossing over, as best I might, the absurdity of my
soliloquising, and the nature of the self-examination I was
engaged in. Without waiting for me to finish, she broke in
suddenly with a low laugh, and said,

" It must have been Rose."

" And who is Rose? " I asked, half sternly.

" A cousin of ours, a mere school-girl, who has just arrived.
She came by the mail this morning, when you were out.
But here she is, coming up the walk. Just step behind that
screen, and you shall have your revenge. I'll make her tell
everything."

I had barely time to conceal myself, when, with a merry
laugh, a fresh, girlish voice called out, " I've seen him ! I
have seen him, Mary ! I was sitting on the rock beside the
river, when he came into the summer-house, and, fancying
himself alone and unseen, proceeded to make his confession
to himself."

" His confession ! What do you mean ? "

" I don't exactly know whether that be the proper name
for it, but it was a sort of self-examination, not very painful,
certainly, inasmuch as it was rather flattering than otherwise."

"I really cannot understand you, Rose."

"I'm not surprised," said she, laughing again. "It was some time before I could satisfy myself that he was not talking to somebody else, or reading out of a book, and when, peeping through the leaves, I perceived he was quite alone, I almost screamed out with laughing."

"But why, child? What was the absurdity that amused you?"

"Fancy the creature. I need not describe him, Molly. You know him well, with his great staring light-green eyes, and his wild yellow hair. Imagine his walking madly to and fro, tossing his long arms about in uncouth gestures, while he asked himself seriously whether he wouldn't be Shakespeare, or Milton, or Michael Angelo, or Nelson. Fancy his gravely inquiring of himself what remarkable qualities predominated in his nature: was he more of a sculptor, or a politician, or had fate destined him to discover new worlds, or to conquer the old ones? If I hadn't been actually listening to the creature, and occasionally looking at him, too, I'd have doubted my senses. Oh, dear! shall I ever forget the earnest absurdity of his manner as he said something about the 'immortal Potts.'"

The reminiscence was too much for her, for she threw herself on a sofa, and laughed immoderately. As for me, unable to endure more, and fearful that Mary might finish by discovering me, I stole from the room, and rushed out into the wood.

What is it that renders ridicule more insupportable than vituperation? Why is the violence of passion itself more easy to endure than the sting of sarcastic satire? What weak spot in our nature does this peculiar passion assail? And again, why are all the noble aspirations of high-hearted enthusiasm, the grand self-reliance of daring minds, ever to be made the theme of such scoffings? Have the scorners never read of Wolfe, of Murat, or of Nelson? Has not a more familiar instance reached them of one who foretold to an unwilling senate the time when they would hang in expectancy on his words, and treasure them as wisdom? Cruel, narrow-minded, and unjust world, with whom nothing succeeds except success!

The man who contracts a debt is never called cheat till

his inability to discharge it has been proven clearly and
beyond a doubt; but he who enters into an engagement with
his own heart to gain a certain prize, or reach a certain goal,
is made a mockery and a sneer by all whose own humble
faculties represent such striving as impossible. From thoughts
like these I went on to speculate whether I should ever be
able, in the zenith of my great success, to forgive those captious and disparaging critics who had once endeavoured to
damp my ardour and bar my career. I own I found it ex-
ceedingly difficult to be generous, and in particular to that
young minx of sixteen who had dared to make a jest of my
pretensious.

I wandered along thus for hours. Many a grassy path of
even sward led through the forest, and taking one of those
which skirted the stream, I strolled along, unconscious alike
of time and place. Out of the purely personal interests which
occupied my mind sprang others, and I bethought me with
a grim satisfaction of the severe lesson Mary must have, ere
this, read Rose upon her presumption and her flippancy,
telling her, in stern accents, how behind that screen the man
was standing she had dared to make the subject of her
laughter. Oh, how she blushes! what flush of crimson
shame spreads over her face, her temples, and her neck;
what large tears overflow her lids, and fall along her
cheeks. I actually pity her suffering, and am pained at her
grief.

"Spare her, dear Mary!" I cry out; "after all, she is
but a child. Why blame her that she cannot measure
greatness, as philosophers measure mountains, by the
shadow?"

Egotism, in every one of its moods and tenses, must have
a strong fascination. I walked on for many a mile while
thus thinking, without the slightest sense of weariness, or
any want of food. The morning glided over, and the hot
noon was passed, and the day was sobering down into the
more solemn tints of coming evening, and I still loitered, or
lay in the tall grass deep in my musings.

In taking my handkerchief from my pocket, I accidently
drew forth the priest's letter, and in a sort of half-indolent
curiosity, proceeded to read it, The hand was cramped and
rugged, the writing that of a man to whom the manual part

of correspondence is a heavy burden, and who consequently incurs such labour as rarely as is possible. The composition had all the charm of ease, and was as unstudied as need be; the writer being evidently one who cared little for the graces of style, satisfied to discuss his subject in the familiar terms of his ordinary conversation.

Although I did not mean to impose more than an extract from it on my reader, I must reserve even that much for my next chapter.

CHAPTER VII.

FATHER DYKE was one of those characters which Ireland alone produces—a sporting priest. In France, Spain, or Italy, the type is unknown. Time was, when the abbé, elegant, witty, and well-bred, was a great element of polished life; when his brilliant conversation and his insidious address threw all the charm of culture over a society which was only rescued from coarseness by the marvellous dexterity of such intellectual gladiators. They have passed away, like many other things brilliant and striking : the gilded coach, the red-heeled slipper, and the supper of the regency; the powdered marquise, for a smile of whose dimpled mouth the deadly rapier has flashed in the moonlight; the perfumed beauty, for one of whose glances a poet would have racked his brain to render worthily in verse ; the gilded *salon* where, in a sort of incense, all the homage of genius was offered up before the altar of loveliness—gone are they all !

Au fond, the world is pretty much the same, although we drive to a club dinner in a one-horse brougham ; and if we meet the curé of St. Roch, we find him to be rather a morose middle-aged man with a taste for truffles, and a talent for silence. It is not as the successor of the witty abbé that I adduce the sporting priest, but simply as a variety of the ecclesiastical character which, doubtless, a very few more

A.

years will have consigned to the realm of history. He, too, will be a bygone! Father Tom, as he was popularly called, never needing any more definite designation, was tam Marte quam Mercurio, as much poacher as priest, and made his sporting acquirements subservient to the demands of an admirable table. The thickest salmon, the curdiest trout, the fattest partridge, and the most tender woodcock, smoked on his board, and, rumour said, cooked with a delicacy that more pretentious houses could not rival. In the great world, nothing is more common than to see some favoured individual permitted to do things which, by common voice, are proclaimed impracticable or improper. With a sort of prescriptive right to outrage the ordinances of society, such people accept no law but their own inclination, and seem to declare, that they are altogether exempt from the restraints that bind other men. In a small way and an humble sphere, Father Tom enjoyed this privilege, and there was not in his whole county to be found one man churlish or ungenerous enough to dispute it; and thus was he suffered to throw his line, snap his gun, or unleash his dog in precincts where many with higher claims had been refused permission.

It was not alone that he enjoyed the invigorating pleasure of field sports in practice, but he delighted in everything which bore any relationship to them. There was not a column of "Bell's Life" in which he had not his sympathy— the pigeon match, the pedestrian, the Yankee trotter, the champion for the silver sculls at Chelsea, the dog "Billy," were all subjects of interest to him. Never did the most inveterate blue stocking more delight in the occasion of meeting a great celebrity of letters, than did he when chance threw him in the way of the jock who rode the winner at the Oaks, or the "Game Chicken" who punished the "Croydon Pet" in the prize ring. But now for the letter, which will as fully reveal the man as any mere description. It was a narrative of races he had attended, and rowing matches he had witnessed, with little episodes of hawking, badger drawing, and cock fighting intermixed :

"I came down here—Brighton—to swim for a wager of five-and-twenty sovereigns against a Major Blayse, of the Third Light Dragoon Guards; we made the match after

mess at Aldershott, when neither of us was anything to
speak of too sober; but as we were backed strongly—he
rather the favourite—there was no way of drawing the bet.
I beat him after a hard struggle; we were two hours and
forty minutes in the water, and netted about sixty pounds
besides. We dined with the depôt in the evening, and I won
a ten-pound note on a question of whether there ought to be
saffron in the American drink called 'greased lightning;'
but this was not the only piece of luck that attended me, as
you shall hear. As I was taking my morning canter on the
Downs, I perceived that a stranger—a jockey-like fellow, not
quite a gentleman, but near it—seemed to keep me in view;
now riding past, now behind me, and always bestowing his
whole attention on my nag. Of course, I showed the beast
off to the best, and handled him skilfully. I thought to
myself, he likes the pony; he'll be for making me an offer
for him. I was right. I had just seated myself at breakfast, when the stranger sent his card, with a request to speak
to me. He was a foreigner, but spoke very correct English,
and his object was to learn if I would sell my horse. It is
needless to say that I refused at once. The animal suited
me, and I was one of those people who find it excessively
difficult to be mounted to their satisfaction. I needed temper,
training, action, gentleness, beauty, high-courage, and perfect
steadiness, and a number of such-like seeming incongruities.
He looked a little impatient at all this; he seemed to say,
'I know all this kind of nonsense; I have heard ship-loads
of such gammon before. Be frank, and say what's the
figure; how much do you want for him?' He looked this, I
say; but he never uttered a word, and at last I asked him,
"'Are you a dealer?'
"'Well,' said he, with an arch smile, 'something in that
line.'
"'I thought so,' said I. 'The pony is a rare good one.'
"He nodded assent.
"'He can jump a bar of his own height?'
"Another nod.
"'And he's as fresh on his legs——'
"'As if he were not twenty-six years old,' he broke in.
"'Twenty-six fiddle-sticks! Look at his mouth; he has
an eight-year old mouth.'

4—2

"'I know it,' said he, dryly; 'and so he had fourteen years ago. Will you take fifty sovereigns for him?' he added, drawing out a handful of gold from his pocket.

"'No,' said I, firmly; 'nor sixty, nor seventy, nor eighty!'

"'I am sorry to have intruded upon you,' said he, rising, 'and I beg you to excuse me. The simple fact is, that I am one who gains his living by horses, and it is only possible for me to exist by the generosity of those who deal with me.'

"This appeal was a home-thrust, and I said, 'What can you afford to give?'

"'All I have here,' said he, producing a handful of gold, and spreading it on the table.

"We set to counting, and there were sixty-seven sovereigns in the mass. I swept off the money into the palm of my hand, and said, 'The beast is yours.'

"He drew a long breath, as if to relieve his heart of a load of care, and said, 'Men of *my* stamp, and who lead such lives as I do, are rarely superstitious.'

"'Very true,' said I, with a nod of encouragement for him to go on.

"'Well,' said he, resuming, 'I never thought for a moment that any possibility could have made me so. If ever there was a man that laughed at lucky and unlucky days, despised omens, sneered at warnings, and scorned at predictions, I was he; and yet I have lived to be the most credulous and the most superstitious of men. It is now fourteen years and twenty-seven days—I remember the time to an hour—since I sold that pony to the Prince Ernest von Saxenhausen, and since that day I never had luck. So long as I owned him all went well with me. I ought to tell you that I am the chief of a company of equestrians, and one corps, know as Klam's Kunst-Reiters, was the most celebrated on the Continent. In three years I made three hundred thousand guilders, and if the devil had not induced me to sell " Schatzchen "—that was his name—I should be this day as rich as Heman Rothschild! From the hour he walked out of the circus our calamities began. I lost my wife by fever at Wiesbaden, the most perfect high-school horsewoman in Europe; my son, of twenty years of age, fell and dislocated his neck; the year after, at Vienna, my daughter Gretchen was blinded riding through a fiery hoop at Homburg; and four years later, all the company died of yellow fever at the Havannah, leaving me utterly beggared and ruined. Now these, you would say, though great misfortunes, are all in the course of common events. But what will you say when, on the eve of each of them, "Schatzchen" appeared to me in a dream, performing some well-known feat or other, and bringing down, as he ever did, thunders of applause; and never did he so appear without a disaster coming after. I struggled hard before I suffered this notion to influence me. It was years before I even mentioned it to anyone; and I used for a while to make a jest of it in the circus, saying, "Take care of yourselves to-night, for I saw 'Schatzchen.'" Of course they were not the stuff to be deterred by such warnings, but they became so at last. That they did, and were so terrified, so thoroughly terrified, that the day after one of my visions not a single member of the troupe would venture on a hazardous feat of any kind; and if we performed at all, it was only some common-place exercises, with few risks, and no daring exploits whatever. Worn out with evil fortune, crushed and almost broken-hearted, I struggled on for years, secretly determining, if ever I should chance upon him, to buy back Schatzchen with my last penny in the world. Indeed, there were moments in which such was the intense excitement of my mind, I could have committed a dreadful crime to regain possession of him. We were on the eve of embarking for Ostend the other night, when I saw you riding on the Downs, and I came ashore at once to track you out, for I knew him, though fully half a mile away. None of my comrades could guess what detained me, nor understand why I asked each of them in turn to lend me whatever money he could spare. It was in this way I made up the little purse you see. It was thus provided that I dared to present myself to-day before you.'

"As he gave me this narrative his manner grew more eager and excited, and I could not help feeling that his mind, from the long-continued pressure of one thought, had received a serious shock. It was exactly one of those cases which physicians describe as leaving the intellect unimpaired, while some one faculty is under the thraldom of a dominant and all-pervading impression. I saw this more palpably, when, having declined to accept more than his original offer of fifty pounds, I replaced the remainder in his hand, he evinced scarcely any gratitude for my liberality, so totally was he engrossed by the idea that the horse was now his own, and that Fortune would no longer have any pretext for using him so severely as before.

"'I don't know—I cannot know,' said he, 'if fortune means to deal more kindly by me than heretofore, but I feel a sort of confidence in the future now; I have a kind of trustful courage as to what may come, that tells me no disaster will deter me, no mishap cast me down.'

"These were his words as he arose to take his leave. Of his meeting with the pony I am afraid to trust myself to speak. It was such an overflow of affection as one might witness from a long absent brother on being once again restored to his own. I cannot say that the beast knew him, nor would I go so far as to assert that he did not, for certainly some of his old instincts seemed gradually to revive within him on hearing certain words; and when ordered to take a respectful farewell of me, the pony planted a foreleg on each of his master's shoulders, and, taking off his hat with his teeth, bowed twice or thrice in the most deferential fashion. I wished them both every success in life, and we parted. As I took my evening's stroll on the pier, I saw them embark for Ostend, the pony sheeted most carefully, and every imaginable precaution taken to ensure him against cold. The man himself was poorly clad and indifferently provided against the accidents of the voyage. He appeared to feel that the disparity required a word of apology, for he said, in a whisper: '*It*'ll soon furnish me with a warm cloak; it'll not leave me long in difficulties!' I assure you, my dear Crofton, there was something contagious in the poor fellow's superstition, for, as he sailed away, the thought lay heavily on my heart, 'What if I, too, should have parted with my good luck in life? How if I have bartered my fortune for a few pieces of money?' The longer I dwelt on this theme, the more forcibly did it strike me. My original possession of the animal was accomplished in a way that aided the illusion. It was thus I won him on a hit of back-gammon!"

As I read thus far, the paper dropped from my hands, my head reeled, and in a faint dreamy state, as if drugged by

some strong narcotic, I sank, I know not how long, unconscious. The first thing which met my eyes on awakening,
was the line, "I won him on a hit of backgammon!" The
whole story was at once before me. It was of Blondel I was
reading! Blondel was the beast whose influence had swayed
one man's destiny. So long as he owned him, the world
went well and happily with him; all prospered and succeeded. It was a charm like the old lamp of Aladdin.
And this was the treasure I had lost. So far from imputing an ignorant superstition to the German, I concurred in
every speculation, every theory of his invention. The man
had evidently discovered one of those curious problems in
what we rashly call the doctrine of chances. It was not the
animal himself that secured good fortune, it was that, in
his "circumstances," what Strauff calls "die umringende
Begebenheiten" of his lot, this creature was sure to call
forth efforts and develop resources in his possessor, of which,
without his aid, he would have gone all through life
unconscious.

The vulgar notion that our lives are the sport of accident
—the minute too early or too late—the calm that detained
us—the snow-storm that blocked the road—the chance
meeting with this or that man, which we lay such stress on
—what are they in reality but trivial incidents without force
or effect, save that they impel to action? They call out
certain qualities in our nature by which our whole characters
become modified. Your horse balks at a fence and throws
you over his head; the fall is not a very grave one, and you
are scarcely hurt; you have fallen into a turnip-field, and the
honest fellow, who is hoeing away near, comes kindly to your
aid, and, in good Samaritan fashion, bathes your temples and
restores you. When you leave him at last, you go forth with
a kindlier notion of human nature; you recognise the tie
"that makes the whole world kin," and you seem to think
that hard toil hardens not the heart, nor a life of labour
shuts out generous sympathies—the lesson is a life one. But
suppose that in your fall you alight on a bed of choice tulips,
you descend in the midst of a rich parterre of starry
anemones, and that your first conscious struggles are met
with words of anger and reproach; instead of sorrow for
your suffering, you hear sarcasms on your horsemanship, and

insults on your riding—no sympathy, no kindness, no generous anxiety for your safety, but all that irritate and offend—more thought, in fact, for the petals of a flower than for the ligaments of your knee,—then, too, is the lesson a life one, and its fruit will be bitter memories for many a year. The events of our existence are in reality nothing, save in our treatment of them. By Blondel, I recognised one of those suggestive influences which mould fate by moulding temperament. The deep-reflecting German saw this: it was clear *he* knew that in that animal was typified all that his life might become. Why should not I contest the prize with him ? Blondel was charged with another destiny as well as his.

I turned once more to the letter, but I could not bear to read it; so many were the impertinent allusions to myself, my manner, my appearance, and my conversation. Still more insulting were the speculations as to what class or condition I belonged to. "He puzzled us completely," wrote the priest, "for while unmistakably vulgar in many things, there were certain indications of reading and education about him that refuted the notion of his being what Keldrum thought—an escaped counter-jumper! The Guardsman insisted he was a valet; my own impression was, the fellow had kept a small circulating library, and gone mad with the three-volume novels. At all events, I have given him a lesson which, whether profitable or not to *him*, has turned out tolerably well for *me*. If ever you chance to hear of him—his name was Podder or Pedder, I think—pray let me know, for my curiosity is still unslaked about him." He thence went off to a sort of descriptive catalogue of my signs and token, so positively insulting, that I cannot recal it; the whole winding up: "Add to all these, an immense pomposity of tone, with a lisp, and a Dublin accent, and you can scarcely mistake him." Need I say, benevolent reader, that fouler calumnies were never uttered, nor more unfounded slanders ever pronounced ?

It is not in this age of photography that a man need defend his appearance. By the aid of sun and collodion, I may, perhaps, one day convince you that I am not so devoid of personal graces as this foul-mouthed priest would persuade you. I am, possibly, in this pledge, exceeding the exact

limits which this publication may enable me to sustain. I
may be contracting an engagement which cannot be, con-
sistent with its principles, fulfilled. If so, I must be your
artist; but I swear to you, that I shall not flatter. Potts,
painted by himself, shall be a true portrait. Meanwhile, I
have time to look out for my canvas, and you will be patient
enough to wait till it be filled.

Again to this confounded letter:

"There is another reason" (wrote Dyke) "why I should
like to chance upon this fellow." ("This fellow" meant
me.) "I used to fancy myself unequalled in the imaginative
department of conversation, by the vulgar called lying. Here,
I own, with some shame, he was my match. A more fear-
less, determined, go-ahead liar, I never met. Now, as one
who deems himself no small proficient in the art, I would
really like to meet him once more. We could approach each
other like the augurs of old, and agree to be candid and
free-spoken together, exchanging our ideas on this great
topic, and frankly communicating any secret knowledge each
might deem that he possessed. I'd go a hundred miles to
pass an evening with him alone, to hear from his own lips
the sort of early training and discipline his mind went
through: who were his first instructors, what his original
inducements. Of one thing I feel certain: a man thus constituted has only to put the curb upon his faculty to be
most successful in life, his perils will all lie in the exuberance
of his resources: let him simply bend himself to believe in
some of the impositions he would force upon others. Let
him give his delusions the force acquired by convictions, and
there is no limit to what he may become. Be on the look
out, therefore, for him, as a great psychological phenomenon,
the man who outlied

"Your sincerely attached friend,
"THOMAS DARCY DYKE.

"P.S.—I have just remembered his name. It was Potts:
the villain said from the Pozzo di Borgo family. I'm sure
with this hint you can't fail to run him to earth; and I
entreat of you spare no pains to do it."

There followed here some more impertinent personalities
as clues to my discovery, which my indulgent reader will

graciously excuse me if I do not stop to record; enough to
say they were as unfounded as they were scurrilous.

Another and very different train of thought, however, soon
banished these considerations. This letter had been given
me by Crofton, who had already read it; he had perused all
this insolent narrative about me before handing it to me, and,
doubtless. in so doing, had no other intention than to convey,
in the briefest and most emphatic way to me, that I was
found out. It was simply saying. in the shortest possible
space. "Thou art the man !" Oh. the ineffable shame and
misery of that thought ' Oh, the bitterness of feeling ! How
my character should now be viewed and my future discussed!
"Only think, Mary," I fancied I heard him say—" only think
who our friend should turn out to be—this same Potts: the
fellow that vanquished Father Dyke in story-telling, and
outlied the priest ! And here we have been lavishing kindness and attentions upon one who, after all, is little better
than a swindler. sailing under false colours and fictitious
credentials; for who can now credit one syllable about his
having written those verses he read for us, or composed that
tale of which he told us the opening ? What a lesson in
future about extending confidence to utter strangers ! What
caution and reserve should it not teach us! How guarded
should we be not to suffer ourselves to be fascinated by the
captivations of manner and the insinuating charms of
address ! If Potts had been less prepossessing in appearance, less gifted and agreeable—if, instead of being a consummate man of the world, with the breeding of a courtier
and the knowledge of a scholar, he had been a pedantic
puppy with a lisp and a Dublin accent——" Oh, ignominy
and disgrace ! these were the very words of the priest in
describing me, which came so aptly to my memory, and I
grew actually sick with shame as I recalled them. I next
became angry. Was this conduct of Crofton's delicate or
considerate ? Was it becoming in one who had treated me
as his friend thus abruptly to conclude our intimacy by an
insult ? Handing me such a letter was saying, "There's a
portrait, can you say anyone it resembles ?" How much
more generous had he said, " Tell me all about this wager of
yours with Father Dyke—I want to hear *your* account of it,
for old Tom is not the most veracious of mortals, nor the

most mealy-mouthed of commentators. Just give me *your* version of the incident, Potts, and I am satisfied it will be the true one." That's what he might, that's what he ought to have said. I can swear it is what I, Potts, would have done by *him*, or by any other stranger whose graceful manners and pleasing qualities had won my esteem and conciliated my regard. I'd have said, " Potts, I have seen enough of life to know how unjust it is to measure men by one and the same standard. The ardent, impassioned nature cannot be ranked with the cold and calculating spirit. The imaginative man has the same necessity for the development of his creative faculty as the strongly muscular man of bodily exercise. He must blow off the steam of his invention, or the boiler will not contain it. You and Le Sage and Alexandre Dumas are a category. You are not the Clerks of a Census Commission, or Masters in Equity. You are the chartered libertines of fiction. Shake out your reefs, and go free—free as the winds that waft you!"

To all these reflections came the last one. "I must be up and doing, and that speedily! I will recover Blondel, if I devote my life to the task. I will regain him, let the cost be what it may. Mounted upon that creature, I will ride up to the Rosary; the time shall be evening; a sun just sunk behind the horizon shall have left in the upper atmosphere a golden and rosy light, which shall tip his mane with a softened lustre, and shed over my own features a rich Titian-like tint. 'I come,' will I say, 'to vindicate the fair fame of one who once owned your affection. It is Potts, the man of impulse, the child of enthusiasm, who now presents himself before you. Poor, if you like to call him so, in worldly craft or skill, poor in its possessions, but rich, boundlessly rich, in the stores of an ideal wealth. Blondel and I are the embodiment of this idea. These fancies you have stigmatised as lies are but the pilot balloons by which great minds calculate the currents in that upper air they are about to soar in.'"

And, last of all, there was a sophistry that possessed a great charm for my mind, in this wise : to enable a man, humble as myself, to reach that station in which a career of adventure should open before him, some ground must be won, some position gained. That I assume to be something that

I am not, is simply to say that I trade upon credit. If my
future transactions be all honourable and trustworthy—if by
a fiction, only known to my own heart, I acquire that
eminence from which I can distribute benefits to hundreds—
who is to stigmatise me as a fraudulent trader ?

Is it not a well-known fact, that many of those now
acknowledged as the wealthiest of men, might, at some time or
other of their lives, have been declared insolvent had the real
state of their affairs been known ? The world, however, had
given them its confidence, and time did the rest. Let the
same world be but as generous towards *me !* The day will
come, I say it confidently and boldly, the day will come when
I can "show my books," and "point to my balance-sheet."
When Archimedes asked for a base on which to rest his
lever, he merely uttered the great truth, that some one fixed
point is essential to the success of a motive power.

It is by our use or abuse of opportunity we are either good
or bad men. The physician is not less conversant with
noxious drugs than the poisoner ; the difference lies in the
fact that the one employs his skill to alleviate suffering, the
other, to work out evil and destruction. If I, therefore, but
make some feigned station in life the groundwork from
which I can become the benefactor of my fellow-men, I shall
be good and blameless. My heart tells me how well and how
fairly I mean by the world : I would succour the weak, console the afflicted, and lift up the oppressed ; and if to carry
out grand and glorious conceptions of this kind all that be
needed is a certain self-delusion which may extend its
influence to others, "Go in," I say, " Potts ; be all that
your fancy suggests—

> Dives, honoratis, pulcher, rex denique regum—
> Be rich, honoured and fair, a prince or a begum—

but, above all, never distrust your destiny, or doubt your
star."

CHAPTER VIII.

So absorbed was I in the reflections of which my last chapter is the record, that I utterly forgot how time was speeding, and perceived at last, to my great surprise, that I had strayed miles away from the Rosary, and that evening was already near. The spires and roofs of a town were distant about a mile at a bend of the river, and for this I now made, determined on no account to turn back, for how could I ever again face those who had read the terrible narrative of the priest's letter, and before whom I could only present myself as a cheat and impostor?

"No," thought I, "my destiny points onward—and to Blondel; nothing shall turn me from my path." Less than an hour's walking brought me to the town, of which I had but time to learn the name—New Ross. I left it in a small steamer for Waterford, a little vessel in correspondence with the mail packet for Milford, and which I learned would sail that evening at nine.

The same night saw me seated on the deck, bound for England. On the deck, I say, for I had need to husband my resources, and travel with every imaginable economy, not only because my resources were small in themselves, but that having left all that I possessed of clothes and baggage at the Rosary, I should be obliged to acquire a complete outfit on reaching England.

It was a calm night, with a starry sky and a tranquil sea, and, when the cabin passengers had gone down to their berths, the captain did not oppose my stealing "aft" to the quarter-deck, where I could separate myself from the some-what riotous company of the harvest labourers that thronged the forepart of the vessel. He saw, with that instinct a sailor is eminently gifted with, that I was not of that class by which I was surrounded, and with a ready courtesy he admitted me to the privilege of isolation.

"You are going to enlist, I'll be bound," said he, as he passed me in his short deck walk. "Ain't I right?"

"No," said I; "I'm going to seek my fortune."

"Seek your fortune!" he repeated, with a slighting sort of laugh. "One used to read about fellows doing that in story books when a child, but it's rather strange to hear of it now-a-days."

"And may I presume to ask why should it be more strange now than formerly? Is not the world pretty much what it used to be? Is not the drama of life the same stock piece our forefathers played ages ago? Are not the actors and the actresses made up of the precise materials their ancestors were? Can you tell me of a new sentiment, a new emotion, or even a new crime? Why, therefore, should there be a seeming incongruity in reviving any feature of the past?"

"Just because it won't do, my good friend," said he, bluntly. "If the law catches a fellow lounging about the world in these times, it takes him up for a vagabond."

"And what can be finer, grander, or freer than a vagabond?" I cried, with enthusiasm. "Who, I would ask you, sees life with such philosophy? Who views the wiles, the snares, the petty conflicts of the world with such a reflective calm as his? Caring little for personal indulgence, not solicitous for self-gratification, he has both the spirit and the leisure for observation. Diogenes was the type of the vagabond, and see how successive ages have acknowledged his wisdom."

"If I had lived in *his* day, I'd have set him picking oakum for all that!" he replied.

"And probably, too, would have sent the 'blind old bard to the crank,'" said I.

"I'm not quite sure of whom you are talking," said he; "but if he was a good ballad-singer, I'd not be hard on him."

"O! Menin aeide Thea Peleiadeo Achilleos!" spouted I out, in rapture.

"That ain't high Dutch," asked he, "is it?"

"No," said I, proudly. "It is ancient Greek—the godlike tongue of an immortal race."

"Immortal rascals!" he broke in. "I was in the fruit

trade up in the Levant there, and such scoundrels as these Greek fellows I never met in my life."

"By what and whom made so?" I exclaimed, eagerly. "Can you point to a people in the world who have so long resisted the barbarising influence of a base oppression? Was there ever a nation so imbued with high civilisation, as to be enabled for centuries of slavery to preserve the traditions of its greatness? Have we the record of any race but this, who could rise from the slough of degradation to the dignity of a people?"

"You've been a play-actor, I take it?" asked he, dryly.

"No, Sir, never!" replied I, with some indignation.

"Well, then, in the Methody line? You've done a stroke of preaching, I'll be sworn."

"You would be perjured in that case, Sir," I rejoined, as haughtily.

"At all events, an auctioneer," said he, fairly puzzled in his speculations.

"Equally mistaken there," said I, calmly; "bred in the midst of abundance, nurtured in affluence, and educated with all the solicitous care that a fond parent could bestow——"

"Gammon!" said he, bluntly. "You are one of the swell mob in distress!"

"Is this like distress?" said I, drawing forth my purse in which were seventy-five sovereigns, and handing it to him. "Count over that, and say how just and how generous are your suspicions."

He gravely took the purse from me, and, stooping down to the binnacle light, counted over the money, scrutinising carefully the pieces as he went.

"And who is to say this isn't 'swag?'" said he, as he closed the purse.

"The easiest answer to that," said I, "is, would it be likely for a thief to show his booty, not merely to a stranger, but to a stranger who suspected him?"

"Well, that is something, I confess," said he, slowly.

"It ought to be more—it ought to be everything. If distrust were not a debasing sentiment, obstructing the impulses of generosity and even invading the precincts of justice, you would see far more reason to confide in, than to disbelieve me."

" I've been done pretty often afore now," he muttered, half to himself.

" What a fallacy that is !" cried I, contemptuously. " Was not the pittance that some crafty impostor wrung from your compassion well repaid to you in the noble self-consciousness of your generosity ? Did not your venison on that day taste better when you thought of his pork chop ? Had not your Burgundy gained flavour by the memory of the glass of beer that was warming the half chilled heart in *his* breast ? Oh, the narrow mockery of fancying that we are not better by being deceived ! "

" How long is it since you had your head shaved ?" he asked, dryly.

" I have never been the inmate of an asylum for lunatics," said, I divining and answering the impertinent insinuation.

" Well, I own you are a rum 'un," said he, half musingly.

" I accept even this humble tribute to my originality," said I, with a sort of proud defiance. " I am well aware how *he* must be regarded who dares to assert his own individuality."

" I'd be very curious to know," said he, after a pause of several minutes, " how a fellow of your stamp sets to work about gaining his livelihood? What's his first step? how does he go about it ? "

I gave no other answer than a smile of scornful meaning.

" I meant nothing offensive," resumed he, " but I really have a strong desire to be enlightened on this point."

" You are doubtless impressed with the notion," said I, boldly, " that men possessed of some distinct craft, or especial profession, are alone needed by the world of their fellows. That one must be doctor, or lawyer, or baker, or shoemaker, to gain his living, as if life had no other wants than to be clothed, and fed, and physicked, and litigated. As if humanity had not its thousand emotional moods, its way-ward impulses, its trials and temptations, all of them more needing guidance, support, direction, and counsel, than the sickest patient needs a physician. It is on this world that I throw myself; I devote myself to guide infancy, to console age, to succour the orphan, and support the widow—morally, I mean."

"I begin to suspect you are a most artful vagabond," said he, half angrily.

"I have long since reconciled myself to the thought of an unjust appreciation," said I. "It is the consolation dull men accept when confronted with those of original genius. You can't help confessing that all your distrust of me has grown out of the superiority of my powers, and the humble figure you have presented in comparison with me."

"Do you rank modesty amongst these same powers?" he asked, slyly.

"Modesty I reject," said I, "as being a conventional form of hypocrisy."

"Come down below," said he, "and take a glass of brandy-and-water. It's growing chilly here, and we shall be the better of something to cheer us."

Seated in his comfortable little cabin, and with a goodly array of liquors before me to choose from, I really felt a self-confidence in the fact, that, if I were not something out of the common, I could not then be there. "There must be in my nature," thought I, "that element which begets success, or I could not always find myself in situations so palpably beyond the accidents of my condition."

My host was courtesy itself; no sooner was I his guest than he adopted towards me a manner of perfect politeness. No more allusions to my precarious mode of life, never once a reference to my adventurous future. Indeed, with an almost artful exercise of good breeding, he turned the conversation towards himself, and gave me a sketch of his own life.

It was not in any respects a remarkable one; though it had its share of those mishaps and misfortunes which every sailor must have confronted. He was wrecked in the Pacific, and robbed in the Havannah; had his crew desert him at San Francisco, and was boarded by Riff pirates, and sold in Barbary just as every other blue jacket used to be, and I listened to the story, only marvelling what a dreary sameness pervades all these narratives. Why, for one trait of the truthful to prove his tale, I could have invented fifty. There were no little touches of sentiment or feeling; no relieving lights of human emotion in his story. I never felt, as I

5

listened, any wish that he should be saved from shipwreck, baffle his persecutors, or escape his captors; and I thought to myself, "This fellow has certainly got no narrative gusto." Now for *my* turn : we had each of us partaken freely of the good liquor before us. The captain in his quality of talker, I, in my capacity of listener, had filled and refilled several times. There was not anything like inebriety, but there was that amount of exultation, a stage higher than mere excitement, which prompts men, at least men of temperaments like mine, not to suffer themselves to occupy rear rank positions, but at any cost to become foreground and prominent figures.

"You have heard of the M'Gillicuddys, I suppose?" asked I. He nodded, and I went on. "You see, then, at this moment before you the last of the race. I mean, of course, of the elder branch, for there are swarms of the others, well to do and prosperous also, and with fine estated properties. I'll not weary you with family history. I'll not refer to that remote time when my ancestors wore the crown, and ruled the fair kingdom of Kerry. In the Annals of the Four Masters, and also in the Chronicles of Thealbogh O'Faudlemh, you'll find a detailed account of our house. I'll simply narrate for you the immediate incident which has made me what you see me—an outcast and a beggar :

"My father was the tried and trusted friend of that noble-hearted, but mistaken man, Lord Edward Fitzgerald. The famous attempt of the year 'eight was concerted between them, and all the causes of its failure, secret as they are and for ever must be, are known to him who now addresses you. I dare not trust myself to talk of these times or things, lest I should by accident let drop what might prove strictly confidential. I will but recount one incident, and that a personal one, of the period. On the night of Lord Edward's capture, my father, who had invited a friend—deep himself in the conspiracy—to dine with him, met his guest on the steps of his hall door. Mr. Hammond—this was his name—was pale and horror-struck, and could scarcely speak, as my father shook his hand. 'Do you know what has happened, Mac?' said he to my father. 'Lord Edward is taken, Major Sirr and his party have tracked him to his hiding-place; they have got hold of all our papers, and we are lost.

By this time to-morrow every man of us will be within the walls of Newgate.'

"'Don't look so gloomily, Tom,' said my father, 'Lord Edward will escape them yet; he's not a bird to be snared so easily; and after all we shall find means to slip our cables, too. Come in, and enjoy your sirloin and a good glass of port, and you'll view the world more pleasantly.' With a little encouragement of this sort he cheered him up, and the dinner passed off agreeably enough; but still my father could see that his friend was by no means at his ease, and at every time the door opened he would start with a degree of surprise that augured anxiety of some coming event. From these and other signs of uneasiness in his manner, my father drew his own conclusions, and with a quick intelligence of look communicated his suspicions to my mother, who was herself a keen and shrewd observer.

"'Do you think, Matty,' said he, as they sat over their wine, 'that I could find a bottle of the old green seal if I was to look for it in the cellar? It has been upwards of forty years there, and I never touch it save on especial occasions; but an old friend like Hammond deserves such a treat.'

"My father fancied that Hammond grew paler as he thus alluded to their old friendship, and he gave my mother a rapid glance of his sharp eye, and, taking the cellar key, he left the room. Immediately outside the door, he hastened to the stable, and saddled and bridled a horse, and slipping quietly out, he rode for the sea-coast, near the Skerries. It was sixteen miles from Dublin, but he did the distance within the hour. And well was it for him that he employed such speed! With a liberal offer of money, and the gold watch he wore, he secured a small fishing-smack to convey him over to France, for which he sailed immediately. I have said it was well that he employed such speed; for, after waiting with suppressed impatience for my father's return from the cellar, Hammond expressed to my mother his fears lest my father might have been taken ill. She tried to quiet his apprehensions, but the very calmness of her manner served only to increase them. 'I can bear this no longer,' cried he, at last, rising, in much excitement, from his chair; 'I must see what has become of him!' At the same moment the door was suddenly flung open, and an officer of police,

5—2

in full uniform, presented himself. 'He has got away,
Sir,' said he, addressing Hammond; 'the stable-door is
open, and one of the horses missing.'

"My mother, from whom I heard the story, had only time
to utter a 'Thank God!' before she fainted. On recovering
her senses, she found herself alone in the room. The traitor
Hammond and the police had left her without even calling
the servants to her aid."

"And your father—what became of him?" asked the
skipper, eagerly.

"He arrived in Paris in sorry plight enough; but,
fortunately, Clarke, whose influence with the Emperor was
unbounded, was a distant connection of our family. By his
intervention my father obtained an interview with his
Majesty, who was greatly struck by the adventurous spirit
and daring character of the man; not the less so because he
had the courage to disabuse the Emperor of many notions
and impressions he had conceived about the readiness of
Ireland to accept French assistance.

"Though my father would much have preferred taking
service in the army, the Emperor, who had strong prejudices
against men becoming soldiers who had not served in every
grade from the ranks upwards, opposed this intention, and
employed him in a civil capacity. In fact, to his management were entrusted some of the most delicate and difficult
secret negotiations; and he gained a high name for acuteness
and honourable dealing. In recognition of his services, his
name was inscribed in the Grand Livre for a considerable
pension; but at the fall of the dynasty, this, with hundreds
of others equally meritorious, was annulled; and my father,
worn out with age and disappointment together, sank at last,
and died at Dinant, where my mother was buried but a few
years previously. Meanwhile, he was tried and found guilty
of high treason in Ireland, and all his lands and other
property forfeited to the Crown. My present journey was
simply a pilgrimage to see the old possessions that once
belonged to our race. It was my father's last wish that I
should visit the ancient home of our family, and stand upon
the hills that once acknowledged us as their ruler. He
never desired that I should remain a French subject; a
lingering love for his own country mingled in his heart with

a certain resentment towards France, who had certainly treated him with ingratitude; and almost his last words to me were, 'Distrust the Gaul.' When I told you a while back that I was nurtured in affluence, it was so to all appearance; for my father had spent every shilling of his capital on my education, and I was under the firm conviction that I was born to a very great fortune. You may judge the terrible revulsion of my feelings when I learned that I had to face the world almost, if not actually, a beggar.

"I could easily have attached myself as a hanger-on of some of my well-to-do relations. Indeed, I will say for them, that they showed the kindest disposition to befriend me; but the position of a dependent would have destroyed every chance of happiness for me, and so I resolved that I would fearlessly throw myself upon the broad ocean of life, and trust that some sea current or favouring wind would bear me at last into a harbour of safety."

"What can you do?" asked the skipper, curtly.

"Everything, and nothing! I have, so to say, the 'sentiment' of all things in my heart, but am not capable of executing one of them. With the most correct ear, I know not a note of music; and though I could not cook you a chop, I have the most excellent appreciation of a well-dressed dinner."

"Well," said he, laughing, "I must confess I don't suspect these to be exactly the sort of gifts to benefit your fellow-man."

"And yet," said I, "it is exactly to individuals of this stamp that the world accords its prizes. The impresario that provides the opera could not sing nor dance. The general who directs the campaign might be sorely puzzled how to clean his musket or pipeclay his belt. The great minister who imposes a tax might be totally unequal to the duty of applying its provisions. Ask him to gauge a hogshead of spirits, for instance. *My* position is like *theirs*. I tell you, once more, the world wants men of wide conceptions and far-ranging ideas—men who look to great results and grand combinations."

"But, to be practical, how do you mean to breakfast to-morrow morning?"

" At a moderate cost, but comfortably : tea, rolls, two
eggs, and a rumpsteak with fried potatoes."

" What's your name?" said he, taking ont his note-book.
" I mustn't forget you when I hear of you next."

" For the present, I call myself Potts—Mr. Potts, if you
please."

" Write it here, yourself," said he, handing me the pencil.
And I wrote in a bold, vigorons hand, "Algernon Sydney
Potts," with the date.

" Preserve that autograph, captain," said I; "it is in no
spirit of vanity I say it, but the day will come yon'll refuse
a ten-pound note for it."

" Well, I'd take a trifle less just now," said he, smiling.

He sat for some time gravely contemplating the writing,
and, at length, in a sort of half soliloquy, said, " Bob would
like him—be would suit Bob." Then, lifting his head, be
addressed me: " I have a brother in command of one of the
P. and O. steamers—just the fellow for *you*. He has got
ideas pretty much like your own about success in life, and
won't be persuaded that he isn't the first seaman in the
English navy ; or that he hasn't a plan to send Cherbourg
and its breakwater sky high, at twenty-four hours' warning."

" An enthusiast—a visionary, I have no doubt," said I,
contemptuously.

" Well, I think you might be more merciful in your judgment of a man of your own stamp," retorted be, laughing.
" At all events, it would be as good as a play to see yon
together. If you should chance to be at Malta, or
Marseilles, when the *Clarence* touches there, just ask for
Captain Rogers; tell him you know me, that will be
enough."

" Why not give me a line of introduction to him ?" said I,
with an easy indifference. " These things serve to clear
away the awkwardness of a self-presentation."

" I don't care if I do," said he, taking a sheet of paper,
and beginning " Dear Bob,"—after which be paused and
deliberated, muttering the words " Dear Bob " three or four
times over below his breath.

" ' Dear Bob,' " said I, aloud, in the tone of one dictating to
an amanuensis,—" ' This brief note will be handed to you by

a very valued friend of mine, Algernon Sydney Potts, a man so completely after your own heart that I feel a downright satisfaction in bringing you together.'"

"Well, that ain't so bad," said he, as he uttered the last words which fell from his pen—"'in bringing you together.'"

"Go on," said I, dictatorially, and continued: "'Thrown by a mere accident myself into his society, I was so struck by his attainments, the originality of his views, and the wide extent of his knowledge of life——' Have you *that* down?"

"No," said he, in some confusion; "I am only at 'entertainments.'"

"I said '*at*-tainments,' Sir," said I, rebukingly, and then repeating the passage word for word, till he had written it,—"'that I conceived for him a regard and an esteem rarely accorded to others than our oldest friends.' One word more: 'Potts, from certain circumstances, which I cannot here enter upon, may appear to you in some temporary inconvenience as regards money——'"

Here the captain stopped, and gave me a most significant look: it was at once an appreciation and an expression of drollery.

"Go on," said I, dryly. "'If so,'" resumed I, "'be guardedly cautious neither to notice his embarrassment nor allude to it; above all, take especial care that you make no offer to remove the inconvenience, for he is one of those whose sensibilities are so fine, and whose sentiments so fastidious, that he could never recover, in his own esteem, the dignity compromised by such an incident.'"

"Very neatly turned," said he, as he re-read the passage. "I think that's quite enough."

"Ample. You have nothing more to do than sign your name to it."

He did this, with a verificatory flourish at foot, folded and sealed the letter, and handed it to me, saying,—

"If it weren't for the handwriting Bob would never believe all that fine stuff came from *me*; but you'll tell him it was after three glasses of brandy-and-water that I dashed it off—that will explain everything."

I promised faithfully to make the required explanation,

and then proceeded to make some inquiries about this brother Bob, whose nature was in such a close affinity with my own. I could learn, however, but little beyond the muttered acknowledgment that Bob was a " queer 'un," and that there was never his equal for " falling upon good luck, and spending it after," a description which, when applied to my own conscience, told an amount of truth that was actually painful.

"There's no saying," said I, as I pocketed the letter, " if this epistle should ever reach your brother's hand, my course in life is too wayward and uncertain for me to say in what corner of the earth fate may find me; but if we *are* to meet, you shall hear of it. Rogers "—I said this in all the easy familiarity which brandy inspired—" I'll tell your brother of the warm and generous hospitality you extended to me, at a time that, to all seeming, I needed such attentions—at a time, I say, when none but myself could know how independently I stood as regarded means; and of one thing be assured, Rogers, he whose caprice it now is to call himself Potts, is your friend, your fast friend, for life."

He wrung my hand cordially—perhaps it was the easiest way for an honest sailor, as he was, to acknowledge the patronising tone of my speech—but I could plainly see that he was sorely puzzled by the situation, and possibly very well pleased that there was no third party to be a spectator of it.

" Throw yourself there on that sofa," said he, " and take a sleep." And with that piece of counsel he left me, and went up on deck.

CHAPTER IX.

NEXT mornings are terrible things, whether one awakes to the thought of some awful run of ill luck at play, or with the racking headache of new port, or a very "fruity" Burgundy. They are dreadful, too, when they bring memories—vague and indistinct, perhaps—of some serious altercations, passionate words exchanged, and expressions of defiance reciprocated; but, as a measure of self-reproach and humiliation, I know not any distress can compare with the sensation of awaking to the consciousness that our cups have so ministered to imagination, that we have given a mythical narrative of ourself and our belongings, and have built up a card edifice of greatness that must tumble with the first touch of truth.

It was a sincere satisfaction to me that I saw nothing of the skipper on that " next morning." He was so occupied with all the details of getting into port, that I escaped his notice, and contrived to land unremarked. Little scraps of my last night's biography would obtrude themselves upon me, mixed up strangely with incidents of that same skipper's life, so that I was actually puzzled at moments to remember whether *he* was not the descendant of the famous rebel friend of Lord Edward Fitzgerald and *I* it was who was sold in the public square at Tunis.

These dissolving views of an evening before are very difficult problems—not to *you*, most valued reader, whose conscience is not burglariously assaulted by a riotous imagination, but to the poor weak Potts-like organisations, the men who never enjoy a real sensation, or taste a real pleasure, save on the hypothesis of a mock situation.

I sat at my breakfast in the "Goat" meditating these things. The grand problem to resolve was this : Is it better to live a life of dull incidents and common-place events in one's own actual sphere, or, creating, by force of imagination, an ideal status, to soar into a region of higher conceptions, and more pictorial situations ? What could existence in the first case offer me ? A wearisome beaten path, with nothing to interest, nothing to stimulate me. On the other side, lay glorious regions of lovely scenery, peopled with figures the most graceful and attractive. I was at once the associate of the wise, the witty, and the agreeable, with wealth at my command, and great prizes within my reach. Illusions all! to be sure ; but what are not illusions—if by that word you take mere account of permanence ? What is it in this world that we love to believe real is not illusionary—the question of duration being the only difference ? Is not beauty perish-

able? Is not wit soon exhausted? What becomes of the
proudest physical strength after middle life is reached?
What of eloquence when the voice fails or loses its facility of
inflexion?

All these considerations, however convincing to myself,
were not equally satisfactory as regarded others, and so I
sat down to write a letter to Crofton, explaining the reasons
of my sudden departure, and enclosing him Father Dyke's
epistle, which I had carried away with me. I began this
letter with the most firm resolve to be truthful and accurate.
I wrote down, not only the date, but the day, "'Goat,'
Milford," followed, and then, "My dear Crofton,—It would
ill become one who has partaken of your generous hospitality,
and who, from an unknown stranger, was admitted to the
privilege of your intimacy, to quit the roof beneath which the
happiest hours of his life were passed without expressing the
deep shame and sorrow such a step has cost him, while he
bespeaks your indulgence to hear the reason." This was my
first sentence, and it gave me uncommon trouble. I desired
to be dignified, yet grateful, proud in my humility, grieved
over an abrupt departure, but sustained by a manly confidence
in the strength of my own motives. If I read it over once, I
read it twenty times ; now deeming it too diffuse, now fear-
ing lest I had compressed my meaning too narrowly. Might
it not be better to open thus : " Strike, but hear me, dear
Crofton, or, before condemning the unhappy creature whose
abject cry for mercy may seem but to increase the presumption of his guilt, and in whose faltering accents may
appear the signs of a stricken conscience, read over, dear
friend, the entire of this letter, weigh well the difficulties and
dangers of him who wrote it, and say, is he not rather a
subject for pity than rebuke? Is not this more a case for a
tearful forgiveness than for chastisement and reproach?"

Like most men who have little habit of composition, my
difficulties increased with every new attempt, and I became
bewildered and puzzled what to choose. It was vitally
important that the first lines of my letter should secure the
favourable opinion of the reader ; by one unhappy word, one
ill-selected expression, a whole case might be prejudiced. I
imagined Crofton angrily throwing the epistle from him with
an impatient " Stuff and nonsense ! a practised humbugger !"

or, worse, again, calling out, "Listen to this, Mary. Is not Master Potts a cool hand? Is not this brazening it out with a vengeance?" Such a thought was agony to me; the very essence of my theory about life was to secure the esteem and regard of others. I yearned after the good opinion of my fellowmen, and there was no amount of false-hood I would not incur to obtain it. No, come what would of it, the Croftons must not think ill of me. They must not only believe me guiltless of ingratitude, but some one whose gratitude was worth having. It will elevate them in their own esteem if they suppose that the pebble they picked up in the highway turned out to be a ruby. It will open their hearts to fresh impulses of generosity; they will not say to each other, "Let us be more careful another time; let us be guarded against showing attention to mere strangers; remember how we were taken in by that fellow Potts; what a specious rascal he was—how plausible, how insinuating!" but rather, "We can afford to be confiding, our experiences have taught us trustfulness. Poor Potts is a lesson that may inspire a hopeful belief in others." How little benefit can any one in his own individual capacity confer upon the world, but what a large measure of good may be distributed by the way he influences others. Thus, for instance, by one well sustained delusion of mine, I inspire a fund of virtues which, in my merely truthful character, I could never pre-tend to originate. "Yes," thought I, "the Croftons shall continue to esteem me; Potts shall be a beacon to guide, not a sunken rock to wreck them."

Thus resolving, I sat down to inform them that on my return from a stroll, I was met by a man bearing a telegram, informing me of the dying condition of my father's only brother, my sole relative on earth; that, yielding only to the impulse of my affection, and not thinking of preparation, I started on board of a steamer for Waterford, and thence for Milford on my way to Brighton. I vaguely hinted at great expectations and so on, and then approaching the difficult problem of Father Dyke's letter, I said, "I enclose you the priest's letter, which amused me much. With all his shrewdness, the worthy churchman never suspected how completely my friend Keldrum and myself had humbugged him, nor did he discover that our little dinner and the episode

that followed it were the subjects of a wager between ourselves. His marvellous cunning was thus for once at fault,
as I shall explain to you more fully when we meet, and prove
to you that, upon this occasion at least, he was not deceiver
but dupe!" I begged to have a line from him to the
"Crown Hotel, Brighton," and concluded.

With this act, I felt I had done with the past, and now
addressed myself to the future. I purchased a few cheap
necessaries for the road, as few and as cheap as was well
possible; I said to myself, fortune shall lift you from the
very dust of the high road, Potts, not one advantageous
adjunct shall aid your elevation!

The train by which I was to leave, did not start till noon,
and to while away time I took up a number of the *Times*,
which the "Goat" appeared to receive at third or fourth
hand. My eye fell upon that memorable second column, in
which I read the following :—

"Left his home in Dublin on the 8th ult., and not since
been heard of, a young gentleman, aged about twenty-two
years, five feet nine and a quarter in height, slightly
formed, and rather stooped in the shoulders, features pale
and melancholy, eyes greyish, inclining to hazel, hair
light brown, and worn long behind. He had on at his
departure——"

I turned impatiently to the foot of the advertisement, and
found that to any one giving such information as might lead
to his discovery, was promised a liberal reward, on application to Messrs. Potts and Co., Compounding Chemists and
Apothecaries, Mary's Abbey. I actually grew sick with
anger as I read this. To what end was it that I built up a
glorious edifice of imaginative architecture, if by one miserable touch of coarse fact it would crumble into clay? To
what purpose did I intrigue with Fortune to grant me a
special destiny, if I were thus to be classed with runaway
traders or strayed terriers? I believe in my heart I could
better have borne all the terrors of a charge of felony, than
the lowering, debasing, humiliating condition, of being
advertised for on a reward.

I had long since determined to be free as regarded the
ties of country. I now resolved to be equally so with
respect to those of family. I will be Potts no longer. I

will call myself for the future—let me see—what shall it
be that will not involve a continued exercise of memory, and
the troublesome task of unmarking my linen ?   I was forgetting in this that I had none, all my wearables being left
behind at the Rosary.   Something with an initial P, was
requisite, and after much canvassing, I fixed on Pottinger.
If by an unhappy chance I should meet one who remembered
me as Potts, I reserved the right of mildly correcting him by
saying, "Pottinger, Pottinger! the name Potts was given
me when at Eton for shortness."   They tell us that amongst
the days of our exultation in life, few can compare with that
in which we exchange a jacket for a tailed coat : the spring
from the tadpole to the full-grown frog : the emancipation
from boyhood into adolescence is certainly very fascinating.
Let me assure my reader that the bound from a monosyllabic
name to a high-sounding epithet of three syllables, is almost
as enchanting as this assumption of the *toga virilis*.   I had
often felt the terrible brevity of Potts; I had shrunk from
answering the question " What name, Sir ? " from the
indescribable shame of saying, Potts ; but Pottinger could be
uttered slowly and with dignity.   One could repose on the
initial syllable, as if to say, " Mark well what I am saying :
this is a name to be remembered."   With that, there must
have been great and distinguished Pottingers, rich men, men
of influence and acres ; from these I could at leisure select a
parentage.

" Do you go by the twelve-fifteen train, Sir ? " asked the
waiter, breaking in upon these meditations.   " You have no
time to lose, Sir."

With a start, I saw it was already past twelve, so I paid
my bill with all speed, and taking my knapsack in my hand,
hurried away to the train.   There was considerable confusion as I arrived, a crush of cabs, watermen, and porters,
blocked the way, and the two currents of an arriving and
departing train struggled against and confronted each other.
Amongst those, who like myself were bent on entering the
station-house, was a young lady in deep mourning, whose
frail proportions and delicate figure gave no prospect of
resisting the shock and conflict before her.   Seeing her so
destitute of all protection, I espoused her cause, and after a
valorous effort and much buffeting, I fought her way for her

to the ticket-window, but only in time to hear the odious crash of a great bell, the bang of a glass door, and the cry of a policeman on duty, " No more tickets, gentlemen! the train is starting!"

" Oh, what shall I do!" cried she, in an accent of intense agony, inadvertently addressing the words to myself. " What shall I do!"

" There's another train to start at three-forty," said I, consolingly. "I hope that waiting will be no inconvenience to you. It is a slow one, to be sure, stops everywhere, and only arrives in town at two o'clock in the morning."

I heard her sob ; I distinctly heard her sob behind her thick black veil, as I said this ; and to offer what amount of comfort I could, I added, " I, too, am disappointed, and obliged to await the next departure, and if I can be of the least service in any way——"

" Oh, no, Sir ! I am very grateful to you, but there is nothing—I mean—there is no help for it!" And here her voice dropped to a mere whisper.

" I sincerely trust," said I, in an accent of great deference and sympathy, " that the delay may not be the cause of grave inconvenience to you ; and although a perfect stranger, if any assistance I can offer——"

" No, Sir; there is really nothing I could ask from your kindness. It was in turning back to bid good-bye a second time to my mother——" Here her agitation seemed to choke her, for she turned away, and said no more.

" Shall I fetch a cab for you?" I asked. " Would you like to go back till the next train starts?"

" Oh, by no means, Sir ! We live three miles from Milford; and besides, I could not bear——" Here again she broke down, but added, after a pause, " It is the first time I have been away from home!"

With a little gentle force, I succeeded in inducing her to enter the refreshment-room of the station, but she would take nothing; and after some attempts to engage her in conversation to while away the dreary time, I perceived that it would be a more true politeness not to obtrude upon her sorrow: and so I lighted my cigar, and proceeded to walk up and down the long terrace of the station. Three trunks, or rather two and a hat-box, kept my knapsack company on the side of the tramway, and on these I read, inscribed in a large hand, "Miss K. Herbert, per steamer *Ardent*, Ostend." I started. Was it not in that direction my own steps were turned! Was not Blondel in Belgium, and was it not in search of him that I was bent? "Oh, Fate!" I cried; "what subtle device of thine is this? What wily artifice art thou now engaged in? Is this a snare, or is it an aid? Hast thou any secret purpose in this rencontre, for with thee, there are no chances, no accidents in thy vicissitudes, all is prepared and fitted, like a piece of door carpentry?" and then I fell into weaving a story for the young lady: She was an orphan. Her father, the curate of the little parish she lived in, had just died, leaving herself and her mother in direst distress. She was leaving home—the happy home of her childhood (I saw it all before me—cottage, and garden, and little lawn, with its one cow and two sheep, and the small green wicket beside the road), and she was leaving all these to become a governess to an upstart, mill-owning, vulgar family at Brussels. Poor thing, how my heart bled for her! What a life of misery lay before her! What trials of temper and of pride! The odious children—I know they are odious—will torture her to the quick; and Mrs. Treddles, or whatever her detestable name is, will lead her a terrible life from jealousy, and she'll have to bear everthing, and cry over it in secret, remembering the once happy time in that honeysuckled porch, where poor papa used to read Words-worth for them.

What a world of sorrow on every side! and how easily might it be made otherwise. What gigantic efforts are we for ever making for something which we never live to enjoy. Striving to be freer, greater, better governed, and more lightly taxed, and all the while forgetting that the real secret is to be on better terms with each other; more generous, more forgiving, less apt to take offence, or bear malice. Of mere material goods, there is far more than we need. The table would accommodate more than double the guests, could we only agree to sit down in orderly fashion; but here we have one occupying three chairs, while another crouches on the floor, and some even prefer smashing the furniture to letting some more humbly born take a place near them. I wish they would listen to me on this theme. I

wish, instead of all this social science humbug and art-union
balderdash, they would hearken to the voice of a plain man,
saying, Are you not members of one family—the individuals
of one household ? Is it not clear to you, if you extend the
kindly affections you now reserve for the narrow circ'e
wherein you live to the wider area of mankind, that, while
diffusing countless blessings to others, you will yourself
become better, more charitable, more kind-hearted, wider in
reach of thought, more catholic in philanthropy? I can
imagine such a world, and feel it to be a Paradise—a world
with no social distinctions, no inequalities of condition, and,
consequently, no insolent pride of station, nor any degrading
subserviency of demeanour, no rivalries, no jealousies—love
and benevolence everywhere. In such a sphere, the calm
equanimity of mind by which great things are accomplished,
would in itself constitute a perfect heaven. No impatience
of temper, no passing irritation——

"Where the——are you driving to, Sir?" cried I, as a
fellow with a brass-bound trunk in a hand-barrow came
smash against my shin.

"Don't you see, Sir, the train is just starting?" said he,
hastening on; and I now perceived that such was the case,
and that I had barely time to rush down to the pay-office
and secure my ticket.

"What class, Sir?" cried the clerk.

"Which has she taken?" said I forgetting all save the
current of my own thoughts.

"First or second, Sir?" repeated he impatiently.

"Either, or both," replied I in confusion and he flung
me back some change and a blue card, closing the little
shutter with a bang that announced the end of all colloquy.

"Get in, Sir, !"

"Which carriage?"

"Get in, Sir!"

"Second-class? Here you are!" called out an official,
as he thrust me almost rudely into a vile mob of travellers.

The bell rang out and two snorts and a scream followed,
then a heave and a jerk, and away we went. As soon as I
had time to look around me, I saw that my companions were
all persons of an humble order of the middle class—the small
shopkeepers and traders probably of the locality we were

leaving. Their easy recognition of each other, and the
natural way their conversation took up local matters, soon
satisfied me of this fact, and reconciled me to fall back upon
my own thoughts for occupation and amusement. This was
with me the usual prelude to a sleep, to which I was quietly
composing myself soon after. The droppings of the conversation around me, however, prevented this; for the talk
had taken a discussional tone, and the differences of opini n
were numerous. The question debated was, whether a certain Sir Samuel Somebody was a great rogue, or only unfortunate. The reasons for either opinion were well put and
defended, showing that the company, like most others of
that class in life in England, had cultivated their faculties of
judgment and investigation by the habit of attending trials
or reading reports of them in newspapers.

After the discussion on his morality, came the question,
Was he alive or dead?

"Sir Samuel never shot himself, Sir," said a short pluffy
man with an asthma. "I've known him for years, and I
can say he was not a man to do such an act."

"Well, Sir, the Ostrich and the United Brethren offices
are both of your opinion," said another; "they'll not pay the
policy on his life."

"The law only recognises death on production of the
body," sagely observed a man in shabby black, with a satin
neckcloth, and whom I afterwards perceived was regarded
as a legal authority.

"What's to be done then, if a man be drowned at sea, or
burned to a cinder in a lime-kiln?"

"Ay, or by what they call spontaneous combustion, that
doesn't leave a shred of you?" cried three objectors in turn.

"The law provides for these emergencies with its usual
wisdom, gentlemen. Where death may not be actually proven
it can be often inferred."

"But who says that Sir Samuel is dead?" broke in the
asthmatic man, evidently impatient at the didactic tone of
the attorney. "All we know of the matter is a letter of his
own signing, that when these lines are read I shall be no
more. Now, is that sufficient evidence of death to induce an
insurance company to hand over some eight or ten thousand
pounds to his family?"

6

" I believe you might say thirty thousand, Sir," suggested a mild voice from the corner.

"Nothing of the kind," interposed another; " the really heavy polices on his life was held by an old Cumberland baronet, Sir Elkanah Crofton, who first established Whalley in the iron trade. I've heard it from my father fifty times, when a child, that Sam Whalley entered Milford in a fustain jacket, with all his traps in a handkerchief."

At the mention of Sir Elkanah Crofton, my attention was quickly excited; this was the uncle of my friends at the Rosary, and I was at once curious to hear more of him.

"Fustain jacket or not, he had a good head on his shoulders," remarked one.

"And luck, Sir; luck, which is better than any head," sighed the meek man, sorrowfully.

"I deny that, deny it totally," broke in he of the asthma. "If Sam Whalley hadn't been a man of first-rate order, he never could have made that concern what it was—the first foundry in Wales."

"And what is it now, and where is he?" asked the attorney, triumphantly.

"At rest, I hope." murmured the sad man.

"Not a bit of it, Sir," said the wheezing voice, in a tone of confidence; " take *my* word for it, he's alive and hearty, somewhere or other, ay, and we'll hear of him one of these days: he'll be smelting metals in Africa, or cutting a canal through the Isthmus of Heaven knows what, or prime minister of one of those rajahs in India. He's a clever dog, and he knows it too. I saw what he thought of himself the day old Sir Elkanah came down to Fairbridge."

"To be sure you were there that morning," said the attorney; "tell us about that meeting."

"It's soon told," resumed the other. "When Sir Elkanah Crofton arrived at the house we were all in the garden. Sir Samuel had taken me there to see some tulips, which he said were the finest in Europe, except some at the Hague. Maybe it was that the old baronet was vexed at seeing nobody come to meet him, or that something else had crossed him, but as he entered the garden I saw he was sorely out of temper.

"'How d'ye do, Sir Elkanah?'" said Whalley to him, coming up pleasantly. 'We scarcely expected you before dinner-time. My wife and my daughters,' said he, introducing them; but the other only removed his hat ceremoniously, without ever noticing them in the least.

"'I hope you had a pleasant journey, Sir Elkanah?'" said Whalley, after a pause, while, with a short jerk of his head, he made signs to the ladies to leave them.

"'I trust I am not the means of breaking up a family party?' said the other, half sarcastically. 'Is Mrs. Whalley——'

"'Lady Whalley, with your good permission, Sir,' said Samuel, stiffly.

"'Of course—how stupid of me! I should remember you had been knighted. And, indeed, the thought was full upon me as I came along, for I scarcely suppose that if higher ambitions had not possessed you, I should find the farm buildings and the outhouse in the state of ruin I see them.'

"'They are better by ten thousand pounds than the day on which I first saw them; and I say it in the presence of this honest townsman here, my neighbour'—meaning *me*—'that both *you* and they were very creaky concerns when I took you in hand.'

"I thought the old baronet was going to have a fit at these words, and he caught hold of my arm and swayed backwards and forwards all the time, his face purple with passion.

"'Who made you, Sir? who made you?' cried he, at last, with a voice trembling with rage.

"'The same hand that made us all,' said the other, calmly. 'The same wise Providence that, for his own ends, creates drones as well as bees, and makes rickety old baronets as well as men of brains and industry.'

"'You shall rue this insolence—it shall cost you dearly, by Heaven!' cried out the old man, as he gripped me tighter. 'You are a witness, Sir, to the way I have been insulted. I'll foreclose your mortgage—I'll call in every shilling I have advanced—I'll sell the house over your head——'

"'Ay! but the head without a roof over it will hold itself higher than your own, old man. The good faculties and good

6—2

health God has given me are worth all your title-deeds twice told. If I walk out of this town as poor as the day I came into it, I'll go with the calm certainty that I can earn my bread—a process that would be very difficult for *you* when you could not lend out money on interest.'

" ' Give me your arm, Sir, back to the town,' said the old baronet to me ; ' I feel myself too ill to go all alone.'

" ' Get him to step into the house and take something,' whispered Whalley in my ear, as he turned away and left us. But I was afraid to propose it, indeed, if I had, I believe the old man would have had a fit on the spt, for he trembled from head to foot, and drew long sighs, as if recovering out of a faint.

" ' Is there an inn near this,' asked he, ' where I can stop? and have you a doctor here ? "

" ' You can have both, Sir Elkanah," said I.

" ' You know me, then?—you know who I am ?' said he, hastily, as I called him by his name.

" ' That I do, Sir, and I hold my place under you ; my name is Shore.'

" ' Yes, I remember,' said he, vaguely, as he moved away. When we came to the gate on the road he turned around full and looked at the house, overgrown with that rich red creeper that was so much admired. ' Mark my words, my good man,' said he—' mark them well, and as sure as I live, I'll not leave one stone on another of that dwelling there.' "

" He was promising more than he could perform," said the attorney.

" I don't know that," sighed the meek man ; " there's very little that money can't do in this life."

" And what has become of Whalley's widow—if she be a widow ?" asked one.

" She's in a poor way. She's up at the village yonder, and, with the help of one of her girls, she's trying to keep a children's school."

" Lady Whalley's school ?" exclaimed one, in half sarcasm.

" Yes; but she has taken her maiden name again since this disaster, and calls herself Mrs. Herbert."

" Has she more than one daughter, Sir ? " I asked of the last speaker.

"Yes, there are two girls ; the younger one, they tell me, is going, or gone, abroad, to take some situation or other—a teacher, or a governess."

"No, Sir," said the pluffy man, "Miss Kate has gone as companion to an old widow lady at Brussels—Mrs. Keats. I saw the letter that arranged the terms—a trifle less per annum than her mother gave to her maid."

"Poor girl!" sighed the sad man. "It's a dreary way to begin life!"

I nodded assentingly to him, and with a smile of gratitude for his sympathy. Indeed, the sentiment had linked me to him, and made me wish to be beside him. The conversation now grew discursive, on the score of all the difficulties that beset women when reduced to make efforts for their own support; and though the speakers were men well able to understand and pronounce upon the knotty problem, the subject did not possess interest enough to turn my mind from the details I had just been hearing. The name of Miss Herbert on the trunks showed me now who was the young lady I had met, and I reproached myself bitterly with having separated from her, and thus forfeited the occasion of befriending her on her journey. We were to sup somewhere about eleven, and I resolved that I would do my utmost to discover her, if in the train; and I occupied myself now with imagining numerous pretexts for presuming to offer my services on her behalf. She will readily comprehend the disinterested character of my attentions. She will see that I come in no spirit of levity, but moved by a true sympathy and the respectful sentiment of one touched by her sorrows. I can fancy her coy diffidence giving way before the deferential homage of my manner ; and in this I really believe I have some tact. I was not sorry to pursue this theme undisturbed by the presence of my fellow-travellers, who had now got out at a station, leaving me all alone to meditate and devise imaginary conversations with Miss Herbert. I rehearsed to myself the words by which to address her, my bow, my gesture, my faint smile, a blending of melancholy with kindliness, my whole air a union of the deference of the stranger with something almost fraternal. These pleasant musings were now rudely routed by the return of my fellow-travellers, who came hurrying back to their places at the banging summons of a great bell.

"Everything cold, as usual. It is a perfect disgrace how the public are treated on this line!" cried one.

"I never think of anything but a biscuit and a glass of ale, and they charged me elevenpence halfpenny for that."

"The directors ought to look to this. I saw those ham sandwiches when I came down here last Tuesday week."

"And though the time-table gives us fifteen minutes, I can swear, for I laid my watch on the table, that we only got nine and a half."

"Well, I supped heartily off that spiced round."

"Supped, supped! Did you say you had supped here, Sir?" asked I, in anxiety.

"Yes, Sir; that last station was Trentham. They give us nothing more now till we reach town."

I lay back with a faint sigh, and, from that moment, took no note of time till the guard cried "London!"

CHAPTER X.

"YOUNG lady in deep mourning, Sir—crape shawl and bonnet, Sir," said the official, in answer to my question, aided by a shilling fee; "the same as asked where was the station for the Dover line."

"Yes, yes; that must be she."

"Got into a cab, Sir, and drove off straight for the Sou'-Eastern."

"She was quite alone?"

"Quite, Sir; but she seems used to travelling— got her traps together in no time, and was off in a jiffy."

"Stupid dog!" thought I; "with every advantage position and accident can confer, how little this fellow reads of character. In this poor forlorn, heart-weary orphan, he only sees something like a commercial traveller!"

"Any luggage, Sir? Is this yours?" said he, pointing to a woolsack.

"No," said I, haughtily: "my servants have gone forward with my luggage. I have nothing but a knapsack." And with an air of dignity I flung it into a Hansom, and ordered the driver to set me down at the South-Eastern. Although using every exertion, the train had just started when I arrived, and a second time was I obliged to wait some hours at a station. Resolving to free myself from all the captivations of that tendency to day-dreaming—that fatal habit of suffering my fancy to direct my steps, as though in pursuit of some settled purpose—I calmly asked myself whither I was going—and for what? Before I had begun the examination, I deemed myself a most candid, truth-observing, frank witness, and now I discovered that I was casuistical and "dodgy" as an Old Bailey lawyer. I was haughty and indignant at being so catechised. My conscience, on the shallow pretext of being greatly interested about me, was simply prying and inquisitive. Conscience is all very well when one desires to appeal to it, and refer some distinct motive or action to its appreciation; but it is scarcely fair, and certainly not dignified, for conscience to go about seeking for little accusations of this kind or that. What liberty of action is there, besides, to a man who carries a "detective" with him wherever he goes? And lastly, conscience has the intolerable habit of obtruding its opinion upon details, and will not wait to judge by results. Now, when I have won the race, come in first, amid the enthusiastic cheers of thousands, I don't care to be asked, however privately, whether I did not practise some little bit of rather unfair jockeyship. I never could rightly get over my dislike to the friend who would take this liberty with me; and this is exactly the part conscience plays, and with an insufferable air of superiority, too, as though to say, "None of your shuffling with *me*, Potts! That will do all mighty well with the outer world, but *I* am not to be humbugged. You never devised a scheme in your life that I was not by at the cookery, and saw how you mixed the ingredients and stirred

the pot! No, no, old fellow, all your little secret rogueries
will avail you nothing here !"

Had these words been actually addressed to me by a living
individual, I could not have heard them more plainly than
now they fell upon my ear, uttered, besides, in a tone of
cutting, sarcastic derision. " I will stand this no longer !"
cried I, springing up from my seat and flinging my cigar
angrily away. " I'm certain no man ever accomplished any
high and great destiny in life who suffered himself to be
bullied in this wise; such irritating, pestering impertinence
would destroy the temper of a saint, and break down the
courage and damp the ardour of the boldest. Could great
measures of statecraft be carried out—could battles be won—
could new continents be discovered, if at every strait and
every emergency, one was to be interrupted by a low
voice, whispering, ' Is this *all* right? Are there no flaws
here? You live in a world of frailties, Potts. You are
playing at a round game, where every one cheats a little,
and where the rogueries are never remembered against him
who wins. Bear that in your mind, and keep your cards
" up.""'

When I was about to take my ticket, a dictum of the
great moralist struck my mind : " Desultory reading has
slain its thousands and tens of thousands;" and if desultory
reading, why not infinitely more so desultory acquaintance.
Surely, our readings do not impress us as powerfully as the
actual intercourse of life. It must be so. It is in this daily
conflict with our fellow-men that we are moulded and
fashioned, and the danger is, to commingle and confuse the
impressions made upon our hearts—to cross the writing on
our natures so often that nothing remains legible ! " I will
guard against this peril," thought I. " I will concentrate
my intentions and travel alone." I slipped a crown into a
guard's hand and whispered, " Put no one in here if you can
help it." As I jogged along, all by myself, I could not help
feeling that one of the highest privileges of wealth must be,
to be able always to buy solitude—to be in a position to say,
" None shall invade me. The world must contrive to go
round without a kick from *me*. I am a self-contained and
self-suffering creature." If I were Rothschild I'd revel in
this sentiment; it places one so immeasurably above that

busy ant-hill where one sces the creatures hurrying, hastening, and fagging "till their hearts are broken." One feels
himself a superior intelligence—a being above the wants and
cares of the work-a-day world around him.

"Any room here?" cried a merry voice, breaking in
upon my musing, and at the same instant a young fellow,
in a grey travelling suit and a wideawake, flung a dressing-
bag and a wrapper carelessly into the carriage, and so reck-
lessly as to come tumbling over me. He never thought of
apology, however, but continued his remarks to the guard,
who was evidently endeavouring to induce him to take a
place elsewhere. "No, no!" cried the young man; "I'm
all right here, and the cove with the yellow hair won't object
to my smoking."

I heard these words as I sat in the corner, and I need
scarcely say how grossly the impertinence offended me.
That the privacy I had paid for should be invaded was bad
enough, but that my companion should begin acquaintance
with an insult was worse again, and so I determined on no
account, nor upon any pretext, would I hold intercourse with
him, but maintain a perfect silence and reserve so long as
our journey lasted.

There was an insufferable jauntiness and self-satisfaction
in every movement of the new arrival, even to the reckless
way he pitched into the carriage three small white canvas
bags, carefully sealed and docketed; the address—which I
read—being, "To H.M.'s Minister and Envoy at ——, by
the Hon. Grey Buller, Attaché, &c." So, then, this was one
of the Young Guard of Diplomacy, one of those sucking
Talleyrands, which form the hope of the Foreign-Office and
the terror of middle-class English abroad.

"Do you mind smoking?" asked he, abruptly, as he
scraped his lucifer match against the roof of the carriage,
showing, by the promptitude of his action, how little he
cared for my reply.

"I never smoke, Sir, except in the carriages reserved for
smokers," was my rebukeful answer.

"And I always do," said he, in a very easy tone.

Not condescending to notice this rude rejoinder, I drew
forth my newspaper, and tried to occupy myself with its
contents.

"Anything new ?" asked he, abruptly.

"Not that I am aware, Sir. I was about to consult the paper."

"What paper is it ?"

"It is the *Banner*, Sir, at your service," said I, with a sort of sarcasm.

"Rascally print—a vile, low, radical, mill-owning organ. Pitch it away!"

"Certainly not, Sir. Being for *me* and *my* edification, I will beg to exercise my own judgment as to how I deal with it."

"It's deuced low, that's what it is, and that's exactly the fault of all our daily papers. Their tone is vulgar; they reflect nothing of the opinions one hears in society. Don't you agree with me?"

I gave a sort of muttering dissent, and he broke in quickly,—

"Perhaps not; it's just as likely *you* would not think them low, but take *my* word for it, *I*'m right."

I shook my head negatively, without speaking.

"Well, now," cried he, "let us put the thing to the test. Read out one of those leaders. I don't care which, or on what subject. Read it out, and I pledge myself to show you at least one vulgarism, one flagrant outrage on good breeding, in every third sentence."

"I protest, Sir," said I, haughtily, "I shall do no such think. I have come here neither to read aloud nor take up the defence of the public press."

"I say, look out !" cried he; "you'll smash something in that bag you're kicking there. If I don't mistake, it's Bohemian glass. "No, no; all right," said he, examining the number, "it's only Yarmouth bloaters."

"I imagined these contained dispatches, Sir," said I, with a look of what he ought to have understood as withering scorn.

"You did, did you ?" cried he, with a quick laugh. "Well, I'll bet you a sovereign I make a better guess about *your* pack than you've done about *mine*."

"Done, Sir; I take you," said I, quickly.

"Well; you're in cutlery, or hardware, or lace goods. or ribbons, or alpaca cloth, or drugs, ain't you ?"

"I am not, Sir," was my stern reply.

"Not a bagman?"

"Not a bagman, Sir."

"Well, you're an usher in a commercial academy, or 'our own correspondent,' or a telegraph clerk?"

"I'm none of these, Sir. And I now beg to remind you, that instead of one guess, you have made about a dozen."

"Well, you've won, there's no denying it," said he, taking a sovereign from his waistcoat pocket and handing it to me. "It's deuced odd how I should be mistaken. I'd have sworn you were a bagman!" But for the impertinence of these last words I should have declined to accept his lost bet, but I took it now as a sort of vindication of my wounded feelings. "Now it's all over and ended," said he, calmly, "what are you? I don't ask out of any impertinent curiosity, but that I hate being foiled in a thing of this kind. What are you?"

"I'll tell you what I am, Sir," said I, indignantly, for now I was outraged beyond endurance—"I'll tell you, Sir, what I am, and what I feel myself—one singularly unlucky in a travelling companion."

"Bet you a five-pound note you're not," broke he in. "Give you six to five on it, in anything you like."

"It would be a wager almost impossible to decide, Sir."

"Nothing of the kind. Let us leave it to the first pretty woman we see at the station, the guard of the train, the fellow in the pay-office, the stoker if you like."

"I must own, Sir, that you express a very confident opinion of your case."

"Will you bet?"

"No, Sir, certainly not."

"Well, then, shut up, and say no more about it. If a man won't back his opinion, the less he says the better."

I lay back in my place at this, determined that no provocation should induce me to exchange another word with him. Apparently, he had not made a like resolve, for he went on: "It's all bosh about appearances being deceptive, and so forth. They say 'not all gold that glitters;' my notion is, that with a fellow who really knows life, no disguise that was ever invented will be successful: the way a man wears his hair"—here he looked at mine—"the sort

of gloves he has, if there be anything peculiar in his waistcoat, and, above all, his boots. I don't believe the devil was
ever more revealed in his hoof than a snob by his shoes." A
most condemnatory glance at my extremities accompanied
this speech.

"Must I endure this sort of persecution all the way to
Dover?" was the question I asked of my misery.

"Look out, you're on fire!" said he, with a dry laugh.
And, sure enough, a spark from his cigarette had fallen on
my trousers, and burned a round hole in them.

"Really, Sir," cried I, in passionate warmth, "your
conduct becomes intolerable."

"Well, if I knew you preferred being singed, I'd have
said nothing about it. What's this station here? Where's
your 'Bradshaw?'"

"I have got no 'Bradshaw,' Sir," said I, with dignity.

"No 'Bradshaw!' A bagman without 'Bradshaw!' Oh,
I forgot, you ain't a bagman. Why are we stopping here?
something smashed, I suspect. Eh! what! isn't that she?
Yes, it is! Open the door!—let me out, I say! Confound
the lock!—let me out!" While he uttered these words, in
an accent of the wildest impatience, I had but time to see a
lady, in deep mourning, pass on to a carriage in front, just
as, with a preliminary snort, the train shook, then backed,
and at last set out on its thundering course again. "Such a
stunning fine girl!" said he, as he lighted a fresh cigar;
"saw her just as we started, and thought I'd run her to
earth in this carriage. Precious mistake I made, eh, wasn't
it? All in black—deep black—and quite alone!"

I had to turn towards the window, not to let him perceive
how his words agitated me, for I felt certain it was Miss
Herbert he was describing, and I felt a sort of revulsion to
think of the poor girl being subjected to the impertinence of
this intolerable puppy.

"Too much style about her for a governess; and yet,
somehow, she wasn't, so to say—you know what I mean—
she wasn't altogether *that*; looked frightened, and people of
real class never look frightened."

"The daughter of a clergyman, probably," said I, with a
tone of such reproof as I hoped must check all levity.

"Or a flash maid! some of them, now-a-days, are wonderful swells; they've got an art of dressing, and making-up that is really surprising."

"I have no experience of the order, Sir," said I, gravely.

"Well, so I should say. *Your* beat is in the haberdashery or hosiery line, eh?"

"Has it not yet occurred to you, Sir," asked I, sternly, "that an acquaintanceship brief as ours should exclude personalities, not to say——" I wanted to add "impertinences," but his grey eyes were turned full on me, with an expression so peculiar, that I faltered, and could not get the word out.

"Well, go on—out with it: not to say what?" said he, calmly.

I turned my shoulder towards him, and nestled down into my place.

"There's a thing, now," said he, in a tone of the coolest reflection—"there's a thing, now, that I never could understand, and I have never met the man to explain it. Our nation, as a nation, is just as plucky as the French—no one disputes it; and yet take a Frenchman of *your* class—the *commis-voyageur*, or anything that way—and you'll just find him as prompt on the point of honour as the best noble in the land. He never utters an insolent speech without being ready to back it."

I felt as if I were choking, but I never uttered a word.

"I remember meeting one of those fellows—traveller for some house in the wine trade—at Avignon. It was at table d'hote, and I said something slighting about Communism, and he replied, 'Monsieur, je suis Fouriériste, and you insult me.' Thereupon, he sent me his card by the waiter—'Paul Deloge, for the house of Gougon, père et fils.' I tore it, and threw it away, saying, 'I never drink Bordeaux wines.' 'What do you say to a glass of Hermitage, then?' said he, and flung the contents of his own in my face. Wasn't that very ready? *I* call it as neat a thing as could be."

"And you bore that outrage," said I, in triumphant delight; "you submitted to a flagrant insult like that at a public table?"

"I don't know what you call 'bearing it,'" said he; "the

thing was done, and I had only to wipe my face with my napkin."

"Nothing more?" said I, sneeringly.

"We went out, afterwards, if you mean *that*," said he, quietly, "and he ran me through here." As he spoke, he proceeded, in leisurely fashion, to unbutton the wrist of his shirt, and baring his arm midway, showed me a pinkish cicatrice of considerable extent. "It went, the doctor said, within a hair's breath of the artery."

I made no comment upon this story. From the moment I heard it, I felt as though I was travelling with the late Mr. Palmer, of Rugeley. I was, as it were, in the company of one who never would have scrupled to dispose of me, at any moment and in any way that his fancy suggested. My code respecting the Duel was to regard it as the last, the very last, appeal in the direst emergency of dishonour. The men who regarded it as the settlement of slight differences, I deemed assassins. They were no more safe associates for peaceful citizens than a wolf was a meet companion for a flock of South Downs. The more I ruminated on this theme, the more indignant grew my resentment, and the question assumed the shape of asking, "Is the great mass of man-kind to be hectored and bullied by some half-dozen scoundrels with skill at the small sword?" Little knew I that in the ardour of my indignation I had uttered these words aloud— spoken them with an earnest vehemence, looking my fellow-traveller full in the face, and frowning.

"Scoundrel is strong, eh?" said he, slowly; "*very* strong!"

"Who spoke of a scoundrel?" asked I, in terror, for his confounded calm, cold manner, made my very blood run chilled.

"Scoundrel is exactly the sort of word," added he, deliberately, "that once uttered can only be expiated in one way. You do not give me the impression of a very bright individual, but certainly you can understand so much."

I bowed a dignified assent; my heart was in my mouth as I did it, and I could not, to save my life, have uttered a word. My predicament was highly perilous; and all incurred by what?—that passion for adventure that had

led me forth out of a position of easy obscurity into a world
of strife, conflict, and difficulty. Why had I not stayed at
home? What foolish infatuation had ever suggested to me
the Quixotism of these wanderings? Blondel had done it
all. Were it not for Blondel, I had never met Father Dyke,
talked myself into a stupid wager, lost what was not my
own; in fact, every disaster sprang out of the one before it,
just as twig adheres to branch and branch to trunk. Shall
I make a clean breast of it, and tell my companion my whole
story? Shall I explain to him that at heart I am a creature
of the kindliest impulses and most generous sympathies, that
I overflow with good intentions towards my fellows, and that
the problem I am engaged to solve is how shall I dispense
most happiness? Will he comprehend me? Has he a
nature to appreciate an organisation so fine and subtle as
mine? Will he understand that the fairy who endows us
with our gifts at birth is reckoned to be munificent when she
withholds only one high quality, and with me that one was
courage? I mean the coarse, vulgar, combative sort of
courage that makes men prize-fighters and bargees, for as to
the grander species of courage, I imagine it to be my distinguishing feature.

The question is, will he give me a patient hearing, for my
theory requires nice handling, and some delicacy in the
developing. He may cut me short in his bluff, abrupt way,
and say, "Out with it, old fellow, you want to sneak out of
this quarrel." What am I to reply? I shall rejoin: "Sir,
let us first inquire if it be a quarrel. From the time of
Atrides down to the Crimean war, there has not been one
instance of a conflict that did not originate in misconceptions, and has not been prolonged by delusions! Let us take
the Peloponnesian war." A short grunt beside me here cut
short my argumentation. He was fast, sound asleep, and
snoring loudly. My thoughts at once suggested escape.
Could I but get away I fancied I could find space in the
world, never again to see myself his neighbour.

The train was whirling along between deep chalk
cuttings, and at a furious pace; to leap out was certain
death. But was not the same fate reserved for me if I
remained? At last I heard the crank-crank of the break!
We were nearing a station; the earth walls at either side

receded; the view opened; a spire of a church, trees, houses
appeared; and our speed diminishing, we came bumping,
throbbing, and snorting into a little trim garden-like spot,
that at the moment seemed to me a paradise.

I beckoned to the guard to let me out—to do it noiselessly
I slipped a shilling into his hand. I grasped my knapsack
and my wrapper, and stole furtively away. Oh, the
happiness of that moment as the door closed without
awakening him!

"Anywhere—any carriage—what class you please,"
muttered I. "There, yonder," broke I in, hastily—"where
that lady in mourning has just got in."

"All full there, Sir," replied the man; "step in here."
And away we went.

My compartment contained but one passenger; he wore
a gold band round his oil-skin cap, and seemed the captain
of a mail steamer, or Admiralty agent; he merely glanced
at me as I came in, and went on reading his newspaper.

"Going north, I suppose?" said he, bluntly, after a pause
of some time. "Going to Germany?"

"No," said I, rather astonished at his giving me this
destination. "I'm for Brussels."

"We shall have a rough night of it, outside; glass is
falling suddenly, and the wind has chopped round to the
south'ard and east'ard!"

"I'm sorry for it," said I. "I'm but an indifferent
sailor."

"Well, I'll tell you what to do: just turn into my cabin,
you'll have it all to yourself; lie down flat on your back the
moment you get aboard; tell the steward to give you a
strong glass of brandy-and-water—the captain's brandy say,
for it is rare old stuff, and a perfect cordial, and my name
ain't Slidders if you don't sleep all the way across."

I really had no words for such unexpected generosity;
how was I to believe my ears at such a kind proposal of a
perfect stranger. Was it anything in my appearance that
could have marked me out as an object for these attentions?
"I don't know how to thank you enough," said I, in confusion; "and when I think that we meet now for the first
time——"

"What does that signify," said he, in the same short way.

"I've met pretty nigh all of you by this time. I've been a matter of eleven years on this station!"

"Met pretty nigh all of us!" What does that mean? Who and what are we? He can't mean the Pottses, for I'm the first who ever travelled even thus far! But I was not given leisure to follow up the inquiry, for he went on to say how in all that time of eleven years he had never seen threatenings of a worse night than that before us.

"Then why venture out?" asked I, timidly.

"They must have the bags over there, that's the reason," said he, curtly; "besides, who's to say when he won't meet dirty weather at sea—one takes rough and smooth in this life, eh?"

The observation was not remarkable for originality, but I liked it. I like the reflective turn, no matter how beaten the path it may select for its exercise.

"It's a short trip—some five or six hours at most," said he; "but it's wonderful what ugly weather one sees in it. It's always so in these narrow seas."

"Yes," said I, concurringly, "these petty channels, like the small events of our life, are often the sources of our greatest perils."

He gave a little short grunt: it might have been assent, and it might possibly have been a rough protest against further moralising; at all events, he resumed his paper, and read away without speaking. I had time to examine him well, now, at my leisure, and there was nothing in his face that could give me any clue to the generous nature of his offer to me. No, he was a hard-featured, weather-beaten, rather stern sort of man, verging on fifty-seven or eight. He looked neither impulsive nor confiding, and there was in the shape of his mouth, and the curve of the lines around it, that peremptory and almost cruel decision that marks the sea captain. "Well," thought I, "I must seek the explanation of the riddle elsewhere. The secret sympathy that moved him must have its root in *me*; and, after all, history has never told that the dolphins who were charmed by Orpheus were peculiar dolphins, with any special fondness for music, or an ear for melody; they were ordinary creatures of the deep—fish, so to say, taken "ex-medio acervo" of delphinity. The marvel of their captivation lay

7

in the spell of the enchanter. It was the thrilling touch of
his fingers, the tasteful elegance of *his* style, the voluptuous
enthralment of the sounds he awakened, that worked the
miracle. This man of the sea has, therefore, been struck by
something in my air, bearing, or address; one of those
mysterious sympathies which are the hidden motives that
guide half our lives, had drawn him to me, and he said to
himself, 'I like that man. I have met more pretentious
people, I have seen persons who desire to dominate and
impose more than he, but there is that about him that,
somehow, appeals to the instincts of my nature, and I can
say I feel myself his friend already.'"

As I worked at my little theory, with all the ingenuity I
knew how to employ on such occasions, I perceived that he
had put up his newspaper, and was gathering together, in
old traveller fashion, the odds and euds of his baggage.

"Here we are," said he, as we glided into the station,
"and in capital time, too. Don't trouble yourself about your
traps. My steward will be here presently, and take all your
things down to the packet along with my own. Our steam
is up, so lose no time in getting aboard."

I had never less inclination to play the loiterer. The
odious *attaché* was still in my neighbourhood, and until I
had got clear out of his reach I felt anything but security.
He, I remembered, was for Calais, so that, by taking the
Ostend boat, I was at once separating myself from his
detestable companionship. I not only, therefore, accepted
the captain's offer to leave all my effects to the charge of
the steward, but no sooner had the train stopped, than I
sprang out, hastened through the thronged station, and
made at all my speed for the harbour.

Is it to increase the impediments to quitting one's country,
and, by interposing difficulties, to give the exile additional
occasion to think twice about expatriating himself, that the
way from the railroad to the dock at Dover is made so
circuitous and almost impossible to discover? Are these
obstacles invented in the spirit of those official details which
make banns on the church-door, and a delay of three weeks
precede a marriage? as though to say, Halt, impetuous
youth, and bethink you whither you are going! Are these
amongst the wise precautions of a truly paternal rule? If

so, they must occasionally even transcend the original intention, for when I reached the pier, the packet had already begun to move, and it was only by a vigorous leap that I gained the paddle-box, and thus scrambled on board.

"Like every one of you," growled out my weather-beaten friend; "always within an ace of being left behind."

"Every one of us!" muttered I. "What can he have known of the Potts family, that he dares to describe us thus characteristically? And who ever presumed to call us loiterers or sluggards?"

"Step down below, as I told you," whispered he. "It's a dirty night, and we shall have bucketing weather outside." And with this friendly hint I at once complied, and stole down the ladder. "Show that gentleman into my state-room, steward," called he out from above. "Mix him something warm, and look after him."

"Ay, ay, Sir," was the brisk reply, as the bustling man of brandy and basins threw open a small door, and ushered me into a little den, with a mingled odour of tar, Stilton, and wet mackintoshes. "All to yourself here, Sir," said he, and vanished.

CHAPTER XI.

I TAKE it for granted that all special "charities" have had their origin in some specific suffering. At least, I can aver that my first thought on landing at Ostend was, "Why has no great philanthropist thought of establishing such an institution as a Refuge for the Sea-sick?" I declare this publicly, that if I ever become rich, a consummation which, looking to the general gentleness of my instincts, the wide benevolence of my nature, and the kindliness of my temperament, mankind might well rejoice at—if, I repeat, I ever become rich, one of the first uses of my affluence will be to endow such an establishment. I will place it in some one of our popular ports, say Southampton. Surrounded with all the charms of inland scenery, rich in every rustic association, the patient shall never be reminded of the scene of his late sufferings. A velvety turf to stroll on, with a leafy shade above his head, the mellow lowing of cattle in his ears, and the fragrant odours of meadow-sweet and hawthorn around, I would recal the sufferer from the dread memories of the slippery deck, the sea-washed stairs, or the sleepy state-room. For the rattle of cordage, and the hoarse trumpet of the skipper, I would substitute the song of the thrush or the blackbird; and, instead of the thrice odious steward and his basin, I would have trim maidens of pleasing aspect to serve him with syllabubs. I will not go on to say the hundred devices I would employ to cheat memory out of a gloomy record, for I treasure the hope that I may yet live to carry out my theory, and have a copyright in my invention.

It was with sentiments deeply tinctured by the above that I tottered, rather than walked, towards the "Hôtel Royal." It was a bright moonlight night, and, as if in mockery of the weather outside, as still and calm as might be. Many a picturesque effect of light and shade met me as I went: quaint old gables flaring in a strong flood of moonlight, showed outlines the strangest and oddest; twinkling lamps shone out of tall, dark-sided, old houses, from which strains of music came plaintively enough in the night air; the sounds of a prolonged revel rose loudly out of that deep-pillared château-like building in the Place, and in the quiet alley adjoining, I could catch the low song of a mother as she tried to sing her baby to sleep. It was all human in every touch and strain of it. And did I not drink it in with rapture? Was it not in a transport of gratitude that I thanked Fortune for once again restoring me to land? "O Earth, Earth!" says the Greek poet, "how art thou inter-woven with that nature that first came from thee!" Thus musing, I reached the inn, where, though the hour was a late one, the household was all active and astir.

"Many passengers arrived, waiter?" said I, in the easy, careless voice of one who would not own to sea-sickness.

"Very few, Sir; the severe weather has deterred several from venturing across."

"Any ladies?"

"Only one, Sir; and, poor thing, she seems to have suffered fearfully. She had to be carried from the boat, and when she tried to walk upstairs, she almost fainted. There might have been some agitation, however, in that, for she expected some one to have met her here; and when she heard that he had not arrived, she was completely overcome."

"Very sad, indeed," said I, examining the *carte* for supper.

"Oh yes, Sir; and being in deep mourning, too, and a stranger away for the first time from her country."

I started, and felt my heart bounding against my side.

"What was it you said about deep mourning, and being young and beautiful?" asked I, eagerly.

"Only the mourning, Sir—it was only the mourning I mentioned; for she kept her veil close down, and would not suffer her face to be seen."

"Bashful as beautiful! modest as she is fair!" muttered I. "Do you happen to know whither she is going?"

"Yes, Sir; her luggage is marked 'Brussels.'"

"It is she! It is herself!" cried I, in rapture, as I turned away, lest the fellow should notice my emotion. "When does she leave this?"

"She seems doubtful, Sir; she told the landlady that she is going to reside at Brussels; but never having been abroad before, she is naturally timid about travelling even so far alone."

"Gentle creature, why should she be exposed to such hazards? Bring me some of this fricandeau with chicory, waiter, and a pint of Beaune; fried potatoes, too.—Would that I could tell her to fear nothing," thought I. "Would that I could just whisper, 'Potts is here; Potts watches over you; Potts will be that friend, that brother, that should have come to meet you! Sleep soundly, and with a head at ease. You are neither friendless nor forsaken!'"

I feel I must be naturally a creature of benevolent instincts; for I am never so truly happy as when engaged in a work of kindness. Let me but suggest to myself a labour of charity,

some occasion to sorrow with the afflicted, to rally the weak-
hearted, and to succour the wretched, and I am infinitely
more delighted than by all the blandishment of what is
called "society." Men have their allotted parts in life, just
as certain fruits are meet for certain climates. Mine was the
grand comforting line. Nature meant me for a consoler. I
have none of those impulsive temperaments which make
what are called jolly fellows. I have no taste for those
excesses which go by the name of conviviality. I can, it is
true, be witty, anecdotic, and agreeable; I can spice conversation with epigram, and illustrate argument by apt
example; but my forte is tenderness.

"Is not this veal a little tough, waiter?" said I, in gentle
remonstrance.

"Monsieur is right," said he, bowing; "but if a morsel of
cold pheasant would be acceptable—mademoiselle, the lady
in mourning, has just taken a wing of it——"

"Bring it directly.—Oh, ecstasy of ecstasies! We are
then, as it were, supping together—served from the same
dish!—May I have the honour?" said I, filling out a glass
of wine and bowing respectfully and with an air of deep
devotion across the table. The pheasant was exquisite, and
I ate with an epicurean enjoyment. I called for another
pint of Beaune, too. It was an occasion for some indulgence,
and I could not deny myself. No sooner had the waiter left
me alone, than I burst into an expansive acknowledgment
of my happiness. "Yes, Potts," said I, "you are richer in
that temperament of yours than if you owned half California.
That boundless wealth of good intentions is a well no pumping can exhaust. Go on doing imaginary good for ever.
You are never the poorer for all the orphans you support,
all the distresses you relieve. You rescue the mariner from
shipwreck without wetting your feet. You charge at the
head of a squadron without the peril of a scratch. All
blessed be the gift which can do these things!"

You call these delusions; but is it a delusion to be a king,
to deliver a people from slavery, to carry succour to a drowning crew? I have done all of these; that is, I have gone
through every changeful mood of hope and fear that accom-
panies these actions, sipping my glass of Beaune between
whiles.

When I found myself in my bedroom I had no inclination for sleep; I was in a mood of enjoyment too elevated for mere repose. It was so delightful to be no longer at sea, to feel rescued from the miseries of the rocking ship and the reeking cabin, that I would not lose the rapture of forgetfulness. I was in the mood for great things, too, if I only knew what they were to be. "Ah!" thought I, suddenly, "I will write to *her*. She shall know that she is not the friendless and forsaken creature that she deems herself; she shall hear that, though separated from home, friends, and country, there is one near to watch over and protect her, and that Potts devotes himself to her service." I opened my desk, and in all the impatience of my ardour began :—

"'DEAR MADAM'——Quære : Ought I to say 'dear'? We are not acquainted, and can I presume upon the formula that implies acquaintanceship? No. I must omit 'dear;' and then 'Madam' looks fearfully stern and rigid, particularly when addressed to a young unmarried lady; she is certainly not 'Madam' yet, surely. I can't begin 'Miss.' What a language is ours! How cruelly fatal to all the tenderer emotions is a dialect so matter-of-fact and formal. If I could only start with 'Gentilissima Signora,' how I could get on! What an impulse would the words lend me! What 'way on me' would they impart for what was to follow! In our cast-metal tongue there is nothing for it but the third person: 'The undersigned has the honour,' &c., &c. This is chilling—it is positively repulsive. Let me see, will this do?—

"'The gentleman who was fortunate enough to render you some trivial service at the Milford station two day ago, having accidentally learned that you are here and unprovided with a protector, in all humility offers himself to afford you every aid and counsel in his power. No stranger to the touching interest of your life, deeply sensible of the delicacy that should surround your steps, if you deign to accept his devoted services, he will endeavour to prove himself, by every sentiment of respect, your most faithful, most humble, and most grateful servant.

"'P.S.—His name is Potts.'

"Yes, all will do but the confounded postscript. What a terrible bathos—'His name is Potts.' What if I say : 'One

word of reply is requested, addressed to Algernon Sydney
Pottinger, at this hotel?'"

I made a great many copies of this document, always
changing something as I went. I felt the importance of
every word, and fastidiously pondered over each expression
I employed. The bright sun of morning broke in at last
upon my labours and found me still at my desk, still composing. All done, I lay down and slept soundly.

"Is she gone, waiter?" said I, as he entered my room
with hot water. "Is she gone?"   •

"Who, Sir?" asked he, in some astonishment.

"The lady in black, who came over in the last mail
packet from Dover; the young lady in deep mourning, who
arrived all alone."

"No, Sir. She has sent all round the hotels this morning
to inquire after some one who was to have met her here,
but apparently without success."

"Give her this; place it in her own hand, and, as you are
leaving the room, say, in a gentle voice: 'Is there an
answer, mademoiselle?' You understand?"

"Well, I believe I do," said he, significantly, as he slyly
pocketed the half-Napoleon fee I had tendered for his
acceptance.

Now the fellow had thrown into his countenance—a
painfully astute and cunning face it was—one of those expressive looks which actually made me shudder. It seemed
to say, "This is a conspiracy, and we are both in it."

"You are not for a moment to suppose," said I, hurriedly,
"that there is one syllable in that letter which could compromise me, or wound the delicacy of the most susceptible."

"I am convinced that monsieur has written it with most
consummate skill," said he, with a supercilious grin, and left
the room.

How I detest the familiarity of a foreign waiter! The
fellows cannot respond to the most ordinary question without
an affectation of showing off their immense acuteness and
knowledge of life. It is their eternal boast how they read
people, and with what an instinctive subtlety they can
decipher all the various characters that pass before them.
Now this impertinent lacquey, who is to say what has he not
imputed to me? Utterly incapable as such a creature must

necessarily be of the higher and nobler motives that sway men of my order, he will doubtless have ascribed to me the most base and degenerate motives.

I was wrong in speaking one word to the fellow. I might have said, "Take that note to Number Fourteen, and ask if there be an answer;" or better still if I had never written at all, but merely sent in my card to ask if the lady would vouchsafe to accord me an audience of a few minutes. Yes, such would have been the discreet course; and then I might have trusted to my manner, my tact, and a certain something in my general bearing, to have brought the matter to a successful issue. While I thus meditated, the waiter re-entered the room, and, cautiously closing the door, approached me with an ostentatious pretence of secrecy and mystery.

"I have given her the letter," said he, in a whisper.

"Speak up!" said I, severely; "what answer has the lady given?"

"I think you'll get the answer presently," said he, with a sort of grin that actually thrilled through me.

"You may leave the room," said I, with dignity, for I saw how the fellow was actually revelling in the enjoyment of my confusion.

"They were reading it over together for the third time when I came away," said he, with a most peculiar look.

"Whom do you mean? who are they that you speak of?"

"The gentleman that she was expecting. He came by the 9.40 train from Brussels. Just in time for your note." As the wretch uttered these words, a violent ringing of bells resounded along the corridor, and he rushed out without waiting for more.

I turned in haste to my note-book; various copies of my letter were there, and I was eager to recal the expressions I had employed in addressing her. Good Heavens! what had I really written? Here were scraps of all sorts of absurdity; poetry, too! verses to the "Fair Victim of a recent War," with a number of rhymes for the last word, such as "low," "snow," "mow," &c.—all evidences of composition under difficulty.

While I turned over these rough copies, the door opened, and a large, red-faced, stern-looking man, in a suit of red-brown tweed, and with a heavy stick in his hand, entered;

he closed the door leisurely after him, and I half thought
that I saw him also turn the key in the lock. He advanced
towards me with a deliberate step, and, in a voice measured
as his gait, said,—

"I am Mr. Jopplyn, Sir—I am Mr. Christopher
Jopplyn."

"I am charmed to hear it, Sir," said I, in some confusion,
for, without the vaguest conception of wherefore, I suspected
lowering weather ahead.

"May I offer you a chair, Mr. Jopplyn? Won't you be
seated? We are going to have a lovely day, I fancy—a
great change after yesterday."

"Your name, Sir," said he, in the same solemnity as
before—"your name I apprehend to be Porringer?"

"Pottinger, if you permit me; Pottinger, not Porringer."

"It shall be as you say, Sir: I am indifferent what you
call yourself." He heaved something that sounded like a
hoarse sigh, and proceeded: "I have come to settle a small
account that stands between us. Is that document your
writing?" As he said this, he drew, rather theatrically,
from his breast-pocket the letter I had just written, and extended it towards me. "I ask, Sir—and I mean you to
understand that I will suffer no prevarication—is that
document in your writing?"

I trembled all over as I took it, and for an instant I
determined to disavow it; but in the same brief space I
bethought me that my denial would be in vain. I then tried
to look boldly, and brazen it out; I fancied to laugh it off as
a mere pleasantry, and, failing in courage for each of these,
I essayed, as a last resource, the argumentative and discussional line, and said,—

"If you will favour me with an indulgent hearing for a
few minutes, Mr. Jopplyn, I trust to explain to your complete
satisfaction, the circumstances of that epistle."

"Take five, Sir—five," said he, laying a ponderous
silver watch on the table as he spoke, and pointing to the
minute hand.

"Really, Sir," said I, stung by the peremptory and
dictatorial tone he assumed, "I have yet to learn that
intercourse between gentlemen is to be regulated by clock-

work, not to say that I have to inquire by what right you ask me for this explanation."

"One minute gone," said he, solemnly.

"I don't care if there were fifty," said I, passionately. "I disclaim all pretension of a perfect stranger to obtrude himself upon me, and by the mere assumption of a pompous manner and an imposing air, to inquire into my private affairs."

"There are two!" said he, with the same solemnity.

"Who is Mr. Jopplyn—what is he to me?" cried I, in increased excitement, "that he presents himself in my apartment like a commissary of police? Do you imagine, Sir, because I am a young man, that this—this—impertinence"—Lord what a gulp it cost me—"is to pass unpunished? Do you fancy that a red beard and a heavy walking-cane are to strike terror into me? You may think, perhaps, that I am unarmed——"

"Three!" said he, with a bang of his stick on the floor, that made me actually jump with the stick.

"Leave the room, Sir," said I. "It is my pleasure to be alone—the apartment is mine—I am the proprietor here. A very little sense of delicacy, a very small amount of good breeding, might show you, that when a gentleman declines to receive company, when he shows himself indisposed to the society of strangers——"

"One minute more, now," said he, in a low growl, while he proceeded to button up his coat to the neck, and make preparation for some coming event.

My heart was in my mouth; I gave a glance at the window; it was the third story, and a leap out would have been fatal. What would I not have given for one of those weapons I had so proudly proclaimed myself possessed. There was not even a poker in the room. I made a spring at the bell-rope, and before he could interpose, gave one pull that, though it brought down the cord, resounded through the whole house.

"Time is up, Porringer," said he, slowly, as he replaced the watch in his pocket, and grasped his murderous-looking cane.

There was a large table in the room, and I entrenched myself at once behind this, armed with a light cane chair, while I screamed murder in every language I could command. Failing to reach me across the table, my assailant tried to dodge me by false starts, now at this side, now at that. Though a large fleshy man, he was not inactive, and it required all my quickness to escape him. These manœuvres being unsuccessful, he very quickly placed a chair beside the table and mounted upon it. I now hurled my chair at him; he warded off the blow and rushed on; with one spring I bounded under the table, reappearing at the opposite side just as he had reached mine. These tactics we now pursued for several minutes, when my enemy suddenly changed his attack, and descending from the table, he turned it on edge: the effort required strength. I seized the moment and reached the door; I tore it open in some fashion, gained the stairs—the court—the streets—and ran ever onward with the wildness of one possessed with no time for thought, nor any knowledge to guide; I turned left and right, choosing only the narrowest lanes that presented themselves, and at last came to a dead halt at an open drawbridge, where a crowd stood waiting to pass.

"How is this? What's all the hurry for? Where are you running this fashion?" cried a well-known voice. I turned, and saw the skipper of the packet.

"Are you armed? Can you defend me?" cried I, in terror; "or shall I leap in and swim for it?"

"I'll stand by you. Don't be afraid, man," said he, drawing my arm within his; "no one shall harm you. Were they robbers?"

"No, worse—assassins!" said I, gulping, for I was heartily ashamed of my terror, and determined to show "cause why" in the plural.

"Come in here, and have a glass of something," said he, turning into a little cabaret, with whose penetralia he seemed not unfamiliar. "You're all safe here," said he, as he closed the door of a little room. "Let's hear all about it, though I half guess the story already."

I had no difficulty in perceiving, from my companion's manner, that he believed some sudden shock had shaken my faculties, and that my intellects were for the time deranged; nor was it very easy for me to assume sufficient calm to disabuse him of his error, and assert my own perfect coherency.

"You have been out for a lark," said he, laughingly. "I see it all. You have been at one of those tea-gardens and got into a row with some stout Fleming. All the young English go through that sort of thing. Ain't I right?"

"Never more mistaken in your life, captain. My conduct since I landed would not discredit a canon of St. Paul's. In fact, all my habits, my tastes, my instincts, are averse to every sort of junketing. I am essentially retiring, sensitive, and, if you will, over fastidious in my choice of associates. My story is simply this." My reader will readily excuse my repeating what is already known to him. It is enough if I say, that the captain, although anything rather than mirthful, held his hand several times over his face, and once laughed out loudly and boisterously.

"You don't say it was Christy Jopplyn, do you?" said he, at last. "You don't tell me it was Jopplyn?"

"The fellow called himself Jopplyn; but I know nothing of him beyond that."

"Why, he's mad jealous about that wife of his; that little woman with the corkscrew curls and the scorbutic face, that came over with us. Oh! you did not see her aboard, you went below at once, I remember; but there was she, in her black ugly, and her old crape shawl——"

"In mourning?"

"Yes. Always in mourning. She never wears anything else, though Christy goes about in colours, and not particular as to the tint, either."

There came a cold perspiration over me as I heard these words, and perceived that my proffer of devotion had been addressed to a married woman, and the wife of the "most jealous man in Europe."

"And who is this Jopplyn?" asked I, haughtily, and in all the proud confidence of my present security.

"He's a railway contractor—a shrewd sort of fellow, with plenty of money, and a good head on his shoulders; sensible on every point except his jealousy."

"The man must be an idiot," said I, indignantly, "to rush indiscriminately about the world with accusations of this kind. Who wants to supplant him? Who seeks to rob him of the affections of his wife?"

"That's all very well, and very specious," said he, gravely, "but if men will deliberately set themselves down at a writing-table, hammering their brains for fine sentiments, and toiling to find grand expressions for their passion, it does not require that a husband should be as jealous as Christy Jopplyn to take it badly. I don't think I'm a rash or a hasty man, but I know what I'd do in such a circumstance."

"And pray, what would *you* do?" said I, half impertinently.

"I'd just say, 'Look here, young gent, is this balderdash here your hand? Well, now, eat your words. Yes, eat them. I mean what I say. Eat up that letter, seal and all, or, by my oath, I'll break every bone in your skin!'"

"It is exactly what I intend," cried a voice, hoarse with passion; and Jopplyn himself sprang into the room, and dashed at me.

The skipper was a most powerful man, but it required all his strength, and not very gingerly exercised either, to hold off my enraged adversary. "Will you be quiet, Christy?" cried he, holding him by the throat. "Will you just be quiet for one instant, or must I knock you down?"

"Do! do! by all means," muttered I, for I thought if he were once on the ground, I could finish him off with a large pewter measure that stood on the table.

With a rough shake the skipper had at last convinced the other that resistance was useless, and induced him to consent to a parley.

"Let him only tell *you*," said he, "what he has told *me*, Christy."

"Don't strike, but hear me," cried I; and safe in my stockade behind the skipper, I recounted my mistake.

"And *you* believe all this?" asked Jopplyn of the skipper, when I had finished.

"Believe it—I should think I do! I have known him since he was a child that high, and I'll answer for his good conduct and behaviour."

Heaven bless you for that bail bond, though endorsed in a lie, honest ship-captain! and I only hope I may live to requite you for it.

Jopplyn was appeased; but it was the suppressed wrath of a brown bear rather than the vanquished anger of a man. He had booked himself for something cruel, and he was miserable to be balked. Nor was I myself—I shame to own it—an emblem of perfect forgiveness. I know nothing harder than for a constitutionally timid man of weak proportions, to forgive the bullying superiority of brute force. It is about the greatest trial human forgiveness can be subjected to; so that when Jopplyn, in a vulgar spirit of reconciliation, proposed that we should go and dine with him that day, I declined the invitation with a frigid politeness.

"I wish I could persuade you to change your plans," said he, "and let Mrs, J. and myself see you at six."

"I believe I can answer for him that it is impossible," broke in the skipper; while he added in a whisper, "They never can afford any delay—they have to put on the steam at high pressure from one end of Europe to t'other."

What could he possibly mean by imputing such haste to my movements, and who were "they" with whom he thus associated me? I would have given worlds to ask, but the presence of Jopplyn prevented me, and so I could simply assent with a sort of foolish laugh, and a muttered "Very true—quite correct."

"Indeed, how you manage to be here now, I can scarcely imagine," continued the skipper. "The last of yours that went through this took a roll of bread and a cold chicken with him into the train, rather than halt to eat his supper—but I conclude you know best."

What confounded mystification was passing through his marine intellects I could not fathom. To what guild or brotherhood of impetuous travellers had he ascribed me? Why should I not "take mine ease in mine inn?" All this was very tantalising and irritating, and pleading a pressing engagement, I took leave of them both, and returned to the hotel.

I was in need of rest and a little composure. The incident of the morning had jarred my nerves and disconcerted me much. But a few hours ago, and life had seemed to me like a flowery meadow, through which, without path or track, one might ramble at will; now it rather presented the aspect of a vulgar kitchen garden, fenced in, and divided, and partitioned off, with only a few very stony alleys to walk in. "This boasted civilisation of ours," exclaimed I, "what is it but snobbery? Our class distinctions—our artificial inter-courses—our hypocritical professions—our deference for externals, are they not the flimsiest pretences that ever were fashioned? Why has no man the courage to make short work of these, and see the world as it really is? Why has not some one gone forth, the apostle of frankness and plain speaking, the same to prince as to peasant? What I would like, would be a ramble through the less visited parts of Europe—countries in which civilisation slants in just as the rays of a setting sun steal into a forest at evening. I would buy me a horse. Oh, Blondel," thought I, suddenly, "am I not in search of you? Is it not in the·hope to recover you that I am here, and, with you for my companion, am I not content to roam the world, taking each incident of the way with the calm of one who asks little of his fellow-man save a kind word as he passes, and a God speed as he goes?" I knew perfectly that, with any other beast for my "mount," I could not view the scene of life with the same bland com-posure. A horse that started, that tripped, that shied, reared, kicked, cromed his neck, or even shook himself, as certain of these beasts do, would have kept me in a paroxysm of anxiety and uneasiness, the least adapted of all modes for thoughtfulness and reflection. Like an ill-assorted union, it would have given no time save for squabble and recrimina-tion. But Blondel almost seemed to understand my mission, and lent himself to its accomplishment. There was none of the obtrusive selfishness of an ordinary horse in his ways. He neither asked you to remark the glossiness of his skin, nor the graceful curve of his neck; he did not passage nor curvet. Superior to the petty arts by which vulgar natures present themselves to notice, he felt that destiny had given him a duty, and he did it.

Thus thinking, I returned once more to the spirit which had first sent me forth to ramble, to wander through the world, spectator, not actor; to be with my fellow-men in sympathy, but not in action; to sorrow and rejoice as they did, but, if possible, to understand life as a drama, in which, so long as I was the mere audience, I could never be painfully afflicted or seriously injured by the catastrophe: a wonderful philosophy, but of which up to the present, I could not boast any pre-eminent success.

CHAPTER XII.

I GREW impatient to leave Ostend : every association con-
nected with the place was unpleasant. I hope I am not
unjust in my estimate of it. I sincerely desire to be neither
unjust to men nor cities, but I thought it vulgar and
commonplace. I know it is hard for a watering-place to be
otherwise; there is something essentially low in the green-
baize and bathing-house existence—in that semi-nude
sociality, begun on the sands and carried out into deep water,
which I cannot abide. I abhor, besides, a lounging population in fancy toilets, a procession of donkeys in scarlet
trappings, elderly gentlemen with pocket-telescopes, and
fierce old ladies with camp-stools. The worn-out debauchees
come to recruit for another season of turtle and whitebait;
the half-faded victims of twenty polkas per night, the tire-
some politician, pale from a long session, all fiercely bent on
fresh diet and sea-breezes, are perfect antipathies to me, and
I would rather seek companionship in a Tyrol village than
amidst these wounded and missing of a London season.

With all this I wanted to get away from the vicinity of
the Jopplyns—they were positively odious to me. Is not
the man who holds in his keeping one scrap of your handwriting which displays you in a light of absurdity, far more
your enemy than the holder of your protested bill? I own
I think so. Debt is a very human weakness; like disease, it
attacks the best and the noblest amongst us. You may pity
the fellow that cannot meet that acceptance, you may be
sorry for the anxiety it occasions him, the fruitless running
here and there, the protestations, promises, and even lies,
he goes through, but no sense of ludicrous scorn mingles
with your compassion, none of that contemptuous laughter
with which you read a copy of absurd verses or a maudlin
love-letter. Imagine the difference of tone in him who says:
"That's an old bill of poor Potts's; he'll never pay it now,
and I'm sure I'll never ask him." Or, "Just read those
lines; would you believe that any creature out of Hanwell

8

could descend to such miserable drivel as that? It was one Potts who wrote it."

I wonder, could I obtain my manuscript from Jopplyn before I started? What pretext could I adduce for the request? While I thus pondered, I packed up my few wearables in my knapsack and prepared for the road. They were, indeed, a very scanty supply, and painfully suggested to my mind the estimate that waiters and hotel-porters must form of their owner. "Cruel world," muttered I, "whose maxim is, 'By their outsides shall ye judge them.' Had I arrived here with a travelling-carriage and a 'fourgon,' what respect and deference had awaited me! how courteous the landlord, how obliging the head waiter! Twenty attentions which could not be charged for in the bill had been shown me, and even had I, in superb dignity, declined to descend from my carriage while the post-horses were being harnessed, a levee of respectful flunkeys would have awaited my orders. I have no doubt but there must be something very intoxicating in all this homage. The smoke of the hecatombs must have affected Jove as a sort of chloroform, or else he would never have sat there sniffing them for centuries. Are you ever destined to experience these sensations, Potts? Is there a time coming when anxious ears will strain to catch your words, and eyes watch eagerly for your slightest gestures? If such an era should ever come, it will be a great one for the masses of mankind, and an evil one for snobbery. Such a lesson as I will read the world on humility in high places, such an example will I give of one elevated, but uncorrupted, by fortune."

"Let the carriage come to the door," said I, closing my eyes, as I sunk into my chair in reverie. "Tell my people to prepare the entire of the Hôtel de Belle Vue for my arrival, and my own cook to preside in the kitchen."

"Is this to go by the omnibus?" said the waiter, suddenly, on entering my room in haste. He pointed to my humble knapsack.

"Yes," said I, in deep confusion—"yes, that's my leggage—at least, all that I have here at this moment. Where is the bill? Very moderate, indeed," muttered I, in a tone of approval. "I will take care to recommend your house; atttendance prompt, and the wines excellent."

"Monsieur is complimentary," said the fellow with a grin; "he only experimented upon a 'small Beaune' at one-twenty the bottle."

I scowled at him, and he shrank again.

"And this *objet* is also monsieur's," said he, taking up a small white canvas bag which was enclosed in my railroad wrapper.

"What is it?" cried I, taking it up. I almost fell back as I saw that it was one of the dispatch-bags of the Foreign-office, which in my hasty departure from the Dover train I had accidentally carried off with me. There it was, addressed to "Sir Shalley Doubleton, H.M's Envoy and Minister at Hesse-Kalbbratonstadt, by the Hon. Grey Buller, Attaché," &c.

Here was not alone what might be construed into a theft, but what it was well possible might comprise one of the gravest offences against the law: it might be high treason itself! Who would ever credit my story, coupled as it was with the fact of my secret escape from the carriage—my precipitate entrance into the first place I could find, not to speak of the privacy I observed by not mixing with the passengers in the mail packet, by keeping myself estranged from all observation in the captain's cabin? Here, too, was the secret of the skipper's politeness to me : he saw the bag, and believed me to be a Foreign-office messenger, and this was his meaning, as he said, "I can answer for him, he can't delay much here." Yes; this was the entire mystification by which I obtained his favour, his politeness, and his protection. What was to be done in this exigency? Had the waiter not seen the bag, and with the intincts of his craft calmly perused the address on it, I believe, nay, I am quite convinced, I should have burned it and its contents on the spot. The thought of his evidence against me in the event of a discovery, however, entirely routed this notion, and, after a brief consideration, I resolved to convey the bag to its destination, and trump up the most plausible explanation I could of the way it came into my possession. His excellency, I reasoned, will doubtless be too delighted to receive his dispatches to inquire very minutely as to the means by which they were recovered, nor is it quite impossible that he may feel bound to mark my zeal for the public service by some token of recognition. This

was a pleasant turn to give to my thoughts, and I took it with
all the avidity of my peculiar temperament. "Yes," thought
I, "it is just out of trivial incidents like this a man's fortune
is made in life. For one man who mounts to greatness by
the great entrance and the state staircase, ten thousand slip
in by *la petite Porte*. It is, in fact, only by these chances
that obscure genius obtains acknowledgment. How, for
example, should this great diplomatist know Potts if some
accident should not throw them together? Raleigh flung
his laced jacket in a puddle, and for his reward he got a
proud Queen's favour. A village apothecary had the good
fortune to be visiting the state apartments at the Pavilion
when George the Fourth was seized with a fit; he bled him,
brought him back to consciousness, and made him laugh by
his genial and quaint humour. The king took a fancy to
him, named him his physician, and made his fortune. I
have often heard it remarked by men who have seen much of
life, that nobody, not one, goes through the world without
two or three such opportunities presenting themselves. The
careless, the indolent, the unobservant, and the idle, either
fail to remark, or are too slow to profit by them. The sharp
fellows, on the contrary, see in such incidents all that they
need to led them to success. Into which of these categories
you are to enter, Potts, let this incident decide."

Having by a reference to my John Murray ascertained the
whereabouts of the capital of Hesse-Kalbbratonstadt, I took
my place at once on the rail for Cologne, reading myself up
on its beauty and its belongings as I went. There is, however, such a dreary sameness in these small ducal states,
that I am ashamed to say how little I gleaned of anything
distinctive in the case before me. The reigning sovereign
was of course married to a grand-duchess of Russia, and he
lived at a country seat called Ludwig's Lust, or Carl's Lust,
as it might be, "took little interest in politics"—how should
he?—and "passed much of his time in mechanical pursuits,
in which he had attained considerable proficiency;" in other
words, he was a middle-aged gentleman, fond of his pipe,
and with a taste for carpentry. Some sort of connection
with our own royal family had been the pretext for having a
resident minister at his court, though what he was to do
when he was there seemed not so easy to say. Even John,

glorious John, was puzzled how to make a respectable half-page out of his capital, though there was a dome in the Byzantine style, with an altar-piece by Peter von Grys, the angels in the corner being added afterwards by Hans Lüders; and there was a Hof Theatre, and an excellent inn, the " Schwein," by Kramm, where the sausages of home manu-facture were highly recommendable, no less than a table wine of the host's vineyard, called "Magenschmerzer," and which, Murray adds, would doubtess, if known, find many admirers in England; and lastly, but far from leastly, there was a Music Garten, where popular pieces were performed very finely by an excellent German band, and to which promenade, all the fashion of the capital nightly resorted.

I give you all these details respected reader, just as I got them in my "Northern Germany," and not intending to obtrude any further description of my own upon you; for who, I would ask, could amplify upon his Handbook? What remains to be noted after John has taken the inventory? has he forgotten a nail or a saint's shin-bone? With him for a guide, a man may feel that he has done his Europe con-scientiously ; and though it be hard to treasure up all the hard names of poets, painters, priests, and warriors, it is not worse than botany, and about as profitable.

For the same reason that I have given above, I spare my reader all the circumstances of my journey, my difficulties about carriage, my embarrassments about steamboats and cab fares, which were all of the order that Brown and Jones have experienced, are experiencing, and will continue to ex-perience, till the arrival of that millenniary period when we shall all converse in any tongue we please.

It was at nightfall that I drove into Kalbbratonstadt, my postillion announcing my advent at the gates, and all the way to the Platz where the inn stood, by a volley of whip-crack-ings which might have announced a grand-duke or a prima donna. Some casements were hastily opened as we rumbled along, and the guests of a *café* issued hurriedly into the street to watch us, but these demonstrations over, I gained the "Schwein" without further notice, and descended.

Herr Kramm looked suspiciously at the small amount of luggage of the traveller who arrived by "extra post," but, like an honest German, he was not one to form rash

judgments, and so he showed me to a comfortable apartment,
and took my orders for supper in all respectfulness. He
waited upon me also at my meal, and gave me opportunity for conversation. While I ate my Carbonade mit
Kartoffel-Salad, therefore, I learned that, being already nine
o'clock, it was far too late au hour to present myself at
the English Embassy—for so he designated our minister's
residence ; that at this advanced period of the night there
were but few citizens out of their beds : the ducal candle was
always extinguished at half-past eight, and only roisterers
and revellers kept it up much later. My first surprise over,
I owned I liked all this. It smacked of that simple patriarchal existence I had so long yearned after. Let the
learned explain it, but there is, I assert, something in the
early hours of a people that guarantee habits of simplicity,
thrift, and order. It is all very well to say that people can
be as wicked at eight in the evening as at two or three in
the morning; that crime cares little for the clock, nor does
vice respect the chronometer ; but does experience confirm
this, and are not the small hours notorious for the smallest
moralities ?   The grand-duke, who is fast asleep at nine, is
scarcely disturbed by dreams of cruelties to his people. The
police minister, who takes his bed-room candle at the same
hour, is seldom harassed by devising new schemes of torture
for his victims. I suffered my host to talk largely of his
town and its people, and probably such a listener rarely
presented himself, for he certainly improved the occasion.
He assured me, with a gravity that vouched for the conviction, that the capital, though by no means so dear as London
or Paris, contained much if not all these more pretentious
cities could boast. There was a court, a theatre, a promenade, a public fountain, and a new gaol, one of the largest
in all Germany. Jenny Lind had once sung at the opera on
her way to Vienna ; and to prove how they sympathised in
every respect with greater centres of population, when the
cholera raged at Berlin, they, too, lost about four hundred of
their townsfolk. Lastly, he mentioned, and this boastfully,
that though neither wanting organs of public opinion, nor
men of adequate ability to guide them, the Kalbbratoners
had never mixed themselves up in politics, but proudly maintained that calm and dignified attitude which Europe would

one day appreciate; that is, if she ever arrived at the crowning knowlege of the benefit of letting her differences be
decided by some impartial umpire.

More than once, as I heard him, I muttered to myself,
"Potts, this is the very spot you have sought for; here is all
the tranquil simplicity of the village, with the elevated
culture of a great city. Here are sages and philosophers
clad in homespun, Beauty herself in linsey-wolsey. Here
there are no vulgar rivalries of riches, no contests in fine
clothes, no opposing armies of yellow plush. Men are great
by their faculties, not in their flunkeys. How elevated must
be the tone of their thoughts, the style of their conversation,
and what a lucky accident it was that led you to that goal to
which all your wishes and hopes have been converging!—
For how much can a man live—a single gentleman like
myself—here in your city?" asked I of my host.

He sat down at this, and filling himself a large goblet of
my wine—the last in the bottle—he prepared for a lengthy
séance. "First of all," said he, "how would he wish to live?
Would he desire to mingle in our best circles, equal to any
in Europe, to know Herr von Krugwitz, and the Gnädige
Frau von Steinhaltz?"

"Well," thought I, "these be fair ambitions." And I
said, "Yes, both of them."

"And to be on the list of the court dinners? There are
two yearly, one at Easter, the other on his highness's birth-
day, whom may providence long protect!"

"To this also might he aspire."

"And to have a stall at the Grand Opera, and a carriage
to return visits—twice in carnival time—and to live in a
handsome quarter, and dine every day at our *table d'hôte*
here with General von Beulwitz and the Hofrath von
Schlaffrichter? A life like this is costly, and would scarcely
be comprised under two thousand florins a year."

How my heart bounded at the notion of refinement, culture, elevated minds, and polished habits : "science," indeed,
and the "musical glasses," all for one hundred and sixty
pounds per annum.

"It is not improbable that you will see me your guest for
many a day to come," said I, as I ordered another bottle,
and of a more generous vintage, to honour the occasion.

My host offered no opposition to my convivial projects—nay, he aided them by saying,

" If you have really an appreciation for something super-excellent in wine, and wish to taste what Freiligrath calls ' der Deutschen Nectar,' I'll go and fetch you a bottle."

"Bring it by all means," said I. And away he went on his mission.

" Providence blessed me with two hands," said he, as he re-entered the room, "and I have brought two flasks of Lieb Herzenthaler."

There is something very artistic in the way your picture-dealer, having brushed away the dust from a Mieris or a Gerard Dow, places the work in a favourite light before you, and then stands to watch the effect on your countenance. So, too, will your man of rare manuscripts and illuminated missals offer to your notice some illegible treasure of the fourth century; but these are nothing to the mysterious solemnity of him who, uncorking a bottle of rare wine, waits to note the varying sensations of your first enjoyment down to your perfect ecstasy.

I tried to perform my part of the piece with credit: I looked long at the amber-coloured liquor in the glass, I sniffed it and smiled approvingly; the host smiled too, and said "Ja." Not another syllable did he utter, but how expressive was that "Ja !" "Ja" meant, "You are right, Potts, it is the veritable wine of 1764, bottled for the Herzog Ludwig's marriage; every drop of it is priceless. Mark the odour how it perfumes the air around us ; regard the colour —the golden hair of Venus can alone rival it; see how the oily globules cling to the glass !" "Ja" meant all this, and more.

As I drank off my glass, I was sorely puzzled by the precise expression in which to couch my approval; but he supplied it and said, "Is it not Göttlich?" and I said it *was* Göttlich ; and while we finished the two bottles, this solitary phrase sufficed for converse between us, "Göttlich" being uttered by each as he drained his glass, and Göttlich being re-echoed by his companion.

There is great wisdom in reducing our admiration to a word ; giving, as it were, a cognate number to our estimate of anything. Wherever we amplify we usually blunder : we employ epithets that disagree, or, in even less questionable taste, soar into extravagances that are absurd. Besides, our moods of highest enjoyment are not such as dispose to talkativeness: the ecstasy that is most enthralling is self-contained. Who on looking at a glorious landscape does not feel the insufferable bathos of the descriptive enthusiast beside him? How grateful would he own himself if he would be satisfied with one word for his admiration. And if one needs this calm repose, this unbroken peace, for the enjoyment of scenery, equally is it applicable to our appreciation of a curious wine. I have no recollection that any further conversation passed between us, but I have never ceased, and most probably never shall cease, to have a perfect memory of the pleasant ramble of my thoughts as I sat there sipping, sipping. I pondered long over a plan of settling down in this place for life, by what means I could realise sufficient to live in that elevated sphere the host spoke of. If Potts *père* —I mean my father—were to learn that I were received in the highest circles, admitted to all that was most socially exclusive, would he be induced to make an adequate provision for me? He was an ambitious and a worldly man; would he see in these beginnings of mine the seeds of future greatness? Fathers, I well knew, are splendidly generous to their successful children, and " the poor they send empty away." It is so pleasant to aid him who does not need assistance, and such a hopeless task to be always saving him who *will* be drowned.

My first care, therefore, should be to impress upon my parent the appropriateness of his contributing his share to what already was an accomplished success. " Wishing, as the French say, to make you a part in my triumph, dear father, I write these lines." How I picture him to my mind's eye as he reads this, running frantically about to his neighbours, and saying, " I have got a letter from Algy— strange boy—but as I always foresaw, with great stuff in him, very remarkable abilities. See what he has done! struck out a perfect line of his own in life; just the sort of thing genius alone can do. He went off from this one morning by way of a day's excursion, never returned—never wrote. All my efforts to trace him were in vain. I advertised, and offered rewards, did everything, without success;

and now, after all this long interval, comes a letter by this
morning's post to tell me that he is well, happy, and prosperous.   He is settled, it appears, in a German capital with
a hard name, a charming spot, with every accessory of enjoyment in it : men of the highest culture, and women of
most graceful and attractive manner; as he himself writes,
'the elegance of a Parisian *salon* added to the wisdom of the
professor's cabinet.'   Here is Algy living with all that is
highest in rank and most distinguished in station; the
favoured guest of the prince, the bosom friend of the English·
minister ; his advice sought for, his counsel asked in every
difficulty; trusted in the most ·important state offices, and
taken into the most secret councils of the duchy.   Though
the requirements of his station make heavy demands upon
his means, very little help from me will enable him to
maintain a position which· a few years more will have con-
solidated into a rank recognised throughout Europe."   Would
the flintiest of fathers, would the most primitive rock-hearted
of parents resist an appeal like this?   It is no hand to
rescue from the waves is sought, but a little finger to help
to affluence.   "Of course you'll do it, Potts, and do it
liberally; the boy is a credit to you.   He will place your
name where you never dreamed to see it.   What do you
mean to settle on him?   Above all things, no stinginess;
don't disgust him."
    I hear these and such-like on every hand; even the most
close-fisted and miserly of our acquaintances will be generous
of their friend's money; and I think I hear the sage remarks
with which they season advice with touching allusions to
that well-known ship that was lost for want of a small out-
lay in tar.   "Come down handsomely, Potts," says a resolute man, who has sworn never to pay a sixpence of his
son's debts.   "What better use can we make of our hoard-
ings than to render our young people happy?"   I don't
like the man who says this, but I like his sentiments; and I
am much pleased when he goes on to remark that "there is
no such good investment as what establishes a successful son.
Be proud of the boy, Potts, and thank your stars that he had
a soul above senna, and a spirit above sal volatile!"
    As I invent all this play of dialogue for myself, and pic-
ture the speakers before me, I come at last to a small peevish

little fellow named Lynch, a merchant tailor, who lived next door to us, and enjoyed much of my father's confidence. "So, they tell me you have heard from that runaway of yours, Potts. Is it true? What face does he put upon his disgraceful conduct? What became of the livery-stable-keeper's horse? Did he sell him, or ride him to death? A bad business if he should ever come back again, which, of course, he's too wise for. And where is he now, and what is he at?"

"You may read this letter, Mr. Lynch," replies my father; "he is one who can speak for himself." And Lynch reads and sniggers, and reads again. I see him as plainly as if he were but a yard from me. "I never heard of this ducal capital before," he begins, "but I suppose it's like the rest of them—little obscure dens of pretentious poverty, plenty of ceremony, and very little to eat. How did he find it out? What brought him there?"

"You have his letter before you, Sir," says my parent, proudly. "Algernon Sydney is, I imagine, quite competent to explain what relates to his own affairs."

"Oh, perfectly, perfectly; only that I can't really make out how he first came to this place, nor what it is that he does there now that he's in it."

My father hastily snatches the letter from his hands, and runs his eye rapidly along to catch the passage which shall confute the objector and cover him with shame and confusion. He cannot find it at once. "It is this. No, it is on this side. Very strange, very singular indeed; but as Algernon must have told me—" Alas! no, father, he has not told you, and for the simple reason that he does not know it himself. For though I mentioned with becoming pride the prominent stations Irishmen now hold in most of the great states of Europe, and pointed to O'Donnel in Spain, MacMahon in France, and the Field-Marshal Nugent in Austria, I utterly forgot to designate the high post occupied by Potts in the Duchy of Hesse Kalbbratonstadt. To determine what this should be was now of imminent importance, and I gave myself up to the solution with a degree of intentness and an amount of concentration that set me off sound asleep.

Yes, benevolent reader, I will confess it, questions of a

complicated character have always affected me, as the inside
of a letter seems to have struck Tony Lumkin—" all buzz."
I start with the most loyal desire to be acute and penetrat-
ing; I set myself to my task with as honest a disposition to
do my best as ever man did; I say, " Now, Potts, no self-
indulgence, no skulking; here is a knotty problem, here is
a case for your best faculties in their sharpest exercise; "
and if any one come in upon me about ten minutes after this
resolve, he will see a man who could beat Sancho Panza in
sleeping !

Of course this tendency has often cost me dearly; I have
missed appointments, forgotten assignations, lost friends
through it. My character, too, has suffered, many deeming
me insupportably indolent, a sluggard quite unfit for any
active employment. Others, more mercifully hinting at
some " cerebral cause," have done me equal damage; but
there happily is an obverse on the medal, and to this som-
nolency do I ascribe much of the gentleness and all the
romance of my nature. It is your sleepy man is ever benevolent, he loves ease and quiet for others as for himself.
What he cultivates is the tranquil mood that leads to
slumber, and the calm that sustains it. The very operations
of the mind in sleep are broken, incoherent, undelineated—
just like the waking occupations of an idle man; they are
thoughts that cost so little to manufacture, that he can afford
to be lavish of them. And now—Good-night !

CHAPTER XIII.

BREAKFAST over, I took a walk through the town. Though
in a measure prepared for a scene of unbustling quietude and
tranquillity, I must own that the air of repose around, far
surpassed all I had imagined. The streets through which I
sauntered were grass-grown and untrodden; the shops were

but half open; not an equipage, nor even a horseman was to be seen. In the Platz, where a sort of fruit-market was held, a few vendors of grapes, peaches, and melons sat under large crimson umbrellas, but there seemed few purchasers, except a passing schoolboy, carefully scanning the temptations in which he was about to invest his kreutzer.

The most remarkable feature of the place, however, and it is one which, through a certain significance, has always held its place in my memory, was that, go where one would, the palace of the grand-duke was sure to finish the view at one extremity of the street. In fact, every alley converged to this one centre, and the royal residence stood like the governor's chamber in a panopticon gaol. There did my mind for many a day picture him sitting like a huge spider watching the incautious insects that permeated his web. I imagined him fat, indolent, and apathetic, but yet, with a gaoler's instincts, ever mindful of every stir and movement of the prisoners below. With a very ordinary telescope he must be master of everything that went on, and the humblest incident could not escape his notice. Was it the consciousness of this surveillance that made every one keep the house? Was it the feeling that the "Gross Herzogliche" eye never left them, that prevented men being abroad in the streets and about their affairs as in other places? I half suspected this, and set to work imagining a state of society thus scanned and scrutinised. But that the general aspect of the town so palpably proclaimed the absence of all trade and industry, I might have compared the whole to a glass hive; but they were all drones that dwelt there, there was not one "busy bee" in the whole of them.

While I rambled thus carelessly along, I came in front of a sort of garden fenced from the street by an iron railing. The laurel, and arbutus, and even the oleander, were there, gracefully blending a varied foliage, and contrasting in their luxuriant liberty so pleasantly with the dull uniformity outside. Finding a gate wide open, I strolled in, and gave myself up to the delicious enjoyment of the spot. As I was deliberating whether this was a public garden or not, I found myself before a long, low, villa-like building, with a colonnade in front. Over the entrance was a large shield, which on nearer approach I recognised to contain the arms

of England.　This, therefore, was the legation, the residence
of our minister, Sir Shalley Doubleton.　I felt a very British
pride and satisfaction to see our representative lodged so
splendidly.　With all the taxpayer's sentiment in my heart,
I rejoiced to think that he who personated the nation should,
in all his belongings, typify the wealth, the style, and the
grandeur of England, and in the ardour of this enthusiasm,
I hastened back to the inn for the dispatch-bag.

Armed with this, and a card, I soon presented myself at
the door.　On the card I had written, " Mr. Pottinger presents his respectful compliments, and requests his excellency
will favour him with an audience of a few minutes for an explanation."

I had made up my mind to state that my servant, in removing my smaller luggage from the train, had accidentally
carried off this Foreign Office bag, which, though at considerable inconvenience, I had travelled much out of my way
to restore in person.　I had practised this explanation as I
dressed in the morning, I had twice rehearsed it to an orange-
tree in the garden, before which I had bowed till my back
ached, and I fancied myself perfect in my part.　It would, I
confess, have been a great relief to me to have had only the
slightest knowledge of the great personage before whom I
was about to present myself, to have known was he short or
tall, young or old, solemn or easy-mannered, had he a loud
voice and an imperious tone, or was he of the soft and silky
order of his craft.　I'd have willingly entertained his
" gentleman " at a moderate repast for some information on
these points, but there was no time for the inquiry, and so I
rang boldly at the bell.　The door opened of itself at the
summons, and I found myself in a large hall with a plaster
cast of the Laocoon, and nothing else.　I tried several of the
doors on either side, but they were all locked.　A very
handsome and spacious stair of white marble led up from the
middle of the hall, but I hesitated about venturing to ascen t
this, and once more repaired to the bell outside, and repeate l
my summons.　The loud clang re-echoed through the arched
hall, the open door gave a responsive shake, and that was
all.　No one came; everything was still as before.　I was
rather chagrined at this.　The personal inconvenience was
less offensive than the feeling how foreigners would comment

on such want of propriety, what censures they would pass on such an ill-arranged household. I rang again, this time with an energy that made the door strike some of the plaster from the wall, and, with a noise like cannon, "What the hangman "—I am translating—" is all this ? " cried a voice thick with passion; and, on looking up, I saw a rather elderly man, with a quantity of curly yellow hair, frowning savagely on me from the balcony over the stair. He made no sign of coming down, but gazed sternly at me from his eminence.

"Can I see his excellency the minister ? " said I, with dignity.

" Not if you stop down there, not if you continue to ring the bell like an alarm for fire, not if you won't take the trouble to come up-stairs."

I slowly began the ascent at these words, pondering what sort of a master such a man must needs have. As I gained the top, I found myself in front of a very short, very fat man, dressed in a suit of striped gingham, like an over ple-thoric zebra, and wheezing painfully, in part from asthma, in part from agitation. He began again:

" What the hangman do you mean by such a row? Have you no manners, no education ? Where were you brought up that you enter a dwelling-house like a city in storm ? "

" Who is this insolent creature that dares to address me in this wise ? What ignorant menial can have so far for-gotten my rank and his insignificance ? "

" I'll tell you all that presently," said he; " there's his ex-cellency's bell." And he bustled away, as fast as his un-wieldly size would permit, to his master's room.

I was outraged and indignant. There was I, Potts—no, Pottinger—Algernon Sydney Pottinger—on my way to Italy and Greece, turning from my direct road to consign with safety a dispatch-bag which many a less conscientious man would have chucked out of his carriage window and for-gotten—there I stood to be insulted by a miserable stone-polishing, floor-scrubbing, carpet-twigging Hausknecht? Was this to be borne? was it to be endured? Was a man of station, family, and attainments, to be the object of such indignity ? "

Just as I had uttered this speech aloud, a very gentle voice addressed me, saying:

"Perhaps I can assist you?   Will you be good enough to say what you want?"

I started suddenly, looked up, and whom should I see before me but that Miss Herbert, the beautiful girl in deep mourning that I had met at Milford, and who now, in the same pale loveliness, turned on me a look of kind and gentle meaning.

"Do you remember me?" said I, eagerly.   "Do you remember the traveller—a pale young man, with a Glengary cap and a plaid overcoat—who met you at Milford?"

"Perfectly," said she, with slight twitch about the mouth like a struggle against a smile.   "Will you allow me to repay you now for your politeness then?   Do you wish to see his excellency?"

I'm not very sure what it was I replied, but I know well what was passing through my head.   If my thoughts could have spoken, it would have been in this wise:

"Angel of loveliness, I don't care a brass farthing for his excellency.   It is not a matter of the slightest moment to me if I never set eyes on him.   Let me but speak to you, tell you the deep impression you have made upon my heart; how, in my ardour to serve you, I have already been involved in an altercation that might have cost me my life; how I still treasure up the few minutes I passed beside you as the Elysian dream of all my life ——"

"I am certain, Sir," broke she in while I spoke—I repeat, I know not what—"I am certain, Sir, that you never came here to mention all this to his excellency."

There was a severe gravity in the way that she said these words that recalled me to myself, but not to any consciousness of what I had been saying; and so, in my utter discomfiture, I blundered out something about the lost dispatches and the cause of my coming.

"If you'll wait a moment here," said she, opening a door into a neatly furnished room, "his excellency shall hear of your wish to see him."   And before I could answer, she was gone.

I was now alone, but in what wild perplexity and anxiety! How came she here?   What could be the meaning of her presence in this place? The minister was an unmarried man, so much my host had told me. How then reconcile this fact with the presence of one who had left England but a few days ago, as some said, to be a governess or a companion? Oh, the agony of my doubts, the terrible agony of my dire misgivings! What a world of iniquity do we live in, what vice and corruption are ever around us! It was but a year or two ago, I remember, that the *Times* newspaper had exposed the nefarious schemes of a wretch who had deliberately invented a plan to entrap those most unprotected of all females. The adventures of this villain had become part of the police literature of Europe. Young and attractive creatures, induced to come abroad by promises of the most seductive kind, had been robbed by this man of all they possessed, and deserted here and there throughout the Continent. I was so horror-stricken by the terrors my mind had so suddenly conjured up, that I could not acquire the calm and coolness requisite for a process of reasoning. My over-active imagination, as usual, went off with me, clearing obstacles with a sweeping stride, and steeple-chasing through fact as though it were only a gallop over grass land.

"Poor girl, well might you look confused and overwhelmed at meeting me! well might the flush of shame have spread over your neck and shoulders, and well might you have hurried away from the presence of one who had known you in the days of your happy innocence!" I am not sure that I didn't imagine I had been her playfellow in childhood, and that we had been brought up from infancy together. My mind then addressed itself to the practical question, What was to be done? Was I to turn my head away while this iniquity was being enacted? was I to go on my way, forgetting the seeds of that misery whose terrible fruits must one day be a shame and an open ignominy? or was I to arraign this man, great and exalted as he was, and say to him, "Is it thus you represent before the eyes of the foreigner the virtues of that England we boast to be the model of all morality? Is it thus you illustrate the habits of your order? Do you dare to profane what, by the fiction of diplomacy, is called the soil of your country, by a life that you dare not pursue at home? The Parliament shall hear of it; the *Times* shall ring with it; that magnificent institution,

9

the common sense of England, long sick of what is called
secret diplomacy, shall learn at last to what uses are applied
the wiles and snares of this deceitful craft, its extraordinary
and its private missions, its hurried messengers with their
bags of corruption ——"

I was well "into my work," and was going along
slappingly, when a very trim footman, in a nankeen
jacket, said :—

"If you will come this way, Sir, his excellency will see
you."

He led me through three or four *salons* handsomely
furnished and ornamented with pictures, the most conspicuous of which, in each room, was a life-sized portrait
of the same gentleman, though in a different costume—now
in the Windsor uniform, now as a Guardsman, and, lastly, in
the full dress of the diplomatic order. I had but time to
guess that this must be his excellency, when the servant
announced me and retired.

It is in deep shame that I own that the aspect of the
princely apartments, the silence, the implied awe of the
footman's subdued words as he spoke, had so routed all my
intentions about calling his excellency to account, that I
stood in his presence timid and abashed. It is an ignoble
confession wrung out of the very heart of my snobbery, that
no sooner did I find myself before that thin, pale, grey-
headed man, who, in a light silk dressing-gown and slippers,
sat writing away, than I gave up my brief, and inwardly
resigned my place as a counsel for injured innocence.

He never raised his head as I entered, but continued his
occupation without noticing me, muttering below his breath
the words as they fell from his pen. "Take a seat," said he,
curtly, at last. Perceiving, now, that he was fully aware of
my presence, I sat down without reply. "This bag is late,
Mr. Paynter," said he, blandly, as he laid down his pen and
looked me in the face.

"Your excellency will permit me, in limine, to observe
that my name is not Paynter."

"Possibly, Sir," said he, haughtily ; "but you are evidently
before me for the first time, or you would know that, like
my great colleague and friend, Prince Metternich, I have made
it a rule through life never to burden my memory with what-

ever can be spared it, and of these are the patronymics of all
subordinate people; for this reason, Sir, and to this end,
every cook in my establishment answers to the name of
Honoré, my valet is always Pierre, my coachman Jacob, my
groom is Charles, and all foreign messengers I call Paynter.
The original of that appellation is, I fancy, superannuated or
dead, but he lives in some twenty successors who carry canvas
reticules as well as he."

"The method may be convenient, Sir, but it is scarcely
complimentary," said I, stiffly.

"Very convenient," said he, complacently. "All consuls
I address as Mr. Sloper. You can't fail to perceive how it
saves time, and I rather think that in the end they like it
themselves. When did you leave town?"

"I left on Saturday last. I arrived at Dover by the
express train, and it was there that the incident befel me
by which I have now the honour to stand before your
excellency."

Instead of bestowing the slightest attention on this
exordium of mine, he had resumed his pen and was writing
away glibly as before. "Nothing new stirring, when you
left?" said he, carelessly.

"Nothing, Sir. But to resume my narrative of explanation——"

"Come to dinner, Paynter; we dine at six," said he, rising
hastily; and, opening a glass door into a conservatory,
walked away, leaving me in a mingled state of shame,
anger, humiliation, and, I will state, of ludicrous embarrassment, which I have no words to express.

"Dinner! No," exclaimed I, "if the alternative were a
hard crust and a glass of spring water! not if I were to fast
till this time to-morrow! Dine with a man who will no.
condescend to acknowledge even my identity, who will not
deign to call me by my name, but only consents to regard
me as a pebble on the seashore, a blade of grass in a wide
meadow! Dine with him, to be addressed as Mr. Paynter,
and to see Pierre, and Jacob, and the rest of them looking
on me as one of themselves! By what prescriptive right
does this man dare to insult those who, for aught he can tell,
are more than his equals in ability. Does the accident—and
what other can it be than accident—of his station confer this

privilege ?   How would he look if one were to retort with
his own impertinence ?   What, for instance, if I were to say,
' I always call small diplomatists, Bluebottles ; you'll not be
offended if, just for memory's sake, I address you as Bluebottle—Mr. Bluebottle, of course ? ' "

I was in ecstasies at this thought.   It seemed to vindicate
all my insulted personality, all my outraged and injured
identity.   " Yes," said I, " I will dine with him ; six o'clock
shall see me punctual to the minute, and determined to
avenge the whole insulted family of the Paynters.   I defy
him to assert that the provocation came not from *his* side.   I
dare him to show cause why I should be the butt of *his*
humour, any more than he of *mine*.   I will be prepared to
make use of his own exact words in repelling my impertinence, and say, ' Sir, you have exactly embodied *my*
meaning ; you have to the letter expressed what this morning I felt on being called Mr. Paynter, you have, besides this,
had the opportunity of experiencing the sort of pain such an
impertinence inflicts, and you are now in a position to guide
you as to how far you will persist in it for the future.' "

I actually revelled in the thought of this reprisal, and
longed for the moment to come in which, indolently thrown
back in my chair, I should say, " Bluebottle, pass the
Madeira," with some comment on the advantage all the
Bluebottles have in getting their wine duty free.   Then,
with what sarcastic irony I should condole with him over
his wearisome, dull career, eternally writing home platitudes
for blue-books, making Grotius into bad grammar, and
vamping up old Puffendorf for popular reading.   " Ain't
you sick of it all, B.-B. ? " I should say, familiarly ; " is not
the unreality of the whole thing offensive ?   Don't you feel
that a dispatch is a sort of formula in which Madrid might be
inserted for Moscow, and what was said of Naples might be
predicated of Norway ? "   I disputed a long time with
myself at what precise period of the entertainment I should
unmask my battery and open fire.   Should it be in the
drawing-room, before dinner ?   Should it be immediately
after the soup, with the first glass of sherry ?   Ought I to
wait till the dessert, and that time when a sort of easy
intimacy had been established which might be supposed to
prompt candour and frankness ?   Would it not be in better

taste to defer it till the servants had left the room ? To expose him to his household seemed scarcely fair.

These were all knotty points, and I revolved them long and carefully, as I came back to my hotel, through the same silent street.

~~~~~~~~~~~~~~~~~~

CHAPTER XIV.

" Don't keep a place for me at the *table d'hôte* to-day, Kramm," said I, in an easy carelessness; "I dine with his excellency. I couldn't well get off the first day, but to-morrow I promise you to pronounce upon your good cheer."

I suppose I am not the first man who has derived consequence from the invitation it had cost him misery to accept. How many in this world of snobbery have felt that the one sole recompense for long nights of *ennui* was the fact that their names figured amongst the distinguished guests in the next day's *Post*?

" It is not a grand dinner to-day, is it?" asked Kramm.

" No, no, merely a family party ; we are very old chums, and have much to talk over."

" You will then go in plain black, and with nothing but your ' decorations.' "

" I will wear none," said I, " none; not even a ribbon." And I turned away to hide the shame and mortification his suggestion had provoked.

Punctually at six o'clock I arrived at the legation ; four powdered footmen were in the hall, and a decent-looking personage in black preceded me up the stairs, and opened the double doors into the drawing-room, without, however, announcing me, or paying the slightest attention to my mention of " Mr. Pottinger."

Laying down his newspaper as I entered, his excellency came forward with his hand out, and though it was the least imaginable touch, and his bow was grandly ceremonious, his smile was courteous and his manner bland.

"Charmed to find you know the merit of punctuality," said he. "To the untravelled English, six means seven, or even later. You may serve dinner, Robins. Strange weather we are having," continued he, turning to me; "cold, raw, and uncongenial."

We talked "barometer" till, the door opening, the *maître d'hôtel* announced, "His excellency is served;" a rather unpolite mode, I thought, of ignoring his company, and which was even more strongly impressed by the fact that he walked in first, leaving me to follow.

At the table a third "cover" was just being speedily removed as we entered, a fact that smote at my heart like a blow. The dinner began, and went on with little said; a faint question from the minister as to what the dish contained and a whispered reply constituted most of the talk, and an occasional cold recommendation to me to try this or that *entrée*. It was admirable in all its details, the cookery exquisite, the wines delicious, but there was an oppression in the solemnity of it all that made me sigh repeatedly. Had the butler been serving a high mass, his motions at the sideboard could scarcely have been more reverential.

"If you don't object to the open air, we'll take our coffee on the terrace," said his excellency; and we soon found ourselves on a most charming elevation, surrounded on three sides with orange-trees, the fourth opening a magnificent view over a fine landscape with the Taunus mountains in the distance.

"I can offer you at least a good cigar," said the minister, as he selected with great care two from a number on a silver plateau before him. "These, I think, you will find recommendable; they are grown for myself at Cuba, and prepared after a receipt only known to one family."

In all this there was a dignified civility, not at all like the impertinent freedom of his manner in the morning. He never, besides, addressed me as Mr. Paynter; in fact, he did not advert to a name at all, not giving me the slightest pretext for that reprisal I had come so charged with; and, as to opening the campaign myself, I'd as soon have commenced acquaintance with a tiger by a pull at his tail. We were now alone; the servants had retired, and there we sat, silently smoking our cigars in apparent ease, but, one of us at least, in a frame of mind the very opposite to tranquillity. What a rush and conflict of thought was in my head! Why had not *she* dined with us? Was her position such as that the presence of a stranger became an embarrassment? Good heaven! was I to suppose this, that, and the other? What was there in this man that so imposed on me, that when I wanted to speak I only could sigh, and that I felt his presence like some overpowering spell? It was that calm, self-contained, quiet manner—cold rather than austere, courteous without cordiality—that chilled me to the very marrow of my bones. Lecture *him* on the private moralities of his life! ask *him* to render me an account of his actions! address *him* as Bluebottle!——

"With such tobacco as that, one can drink Bordeaux," said he. "Help yourself."

And I did help myself—freely, repeatedly. I drank for courage, as a man might drink from thirst or fever, or for strength in a moment of fainting debility. The wine was exquisite, and my heart beat more forcibly, and I felt it.

I cannot follow very connectedly the course of events; I neither know how the conversation glided into politics, nor what I said on that subject. As to the steps by which I succeeded in obtaining his excellency's confidence, I know as little as a man does of the precise moment in which he is wet through in a Scotch mist. I have a dim memory of talking in a very dictatorial voice, and continually referring to my "entrance into public life," with reference to what Peel "said," and what the Duke "told me."

"What's the use of writing home?" said his excellency, in a desponding voice. "For the last five years I have called attention to what is going on here: nobody minds, nobody heeds it. Open any blue-book you like, and will you find one solitary dispatch from Hesse-Kalbbratonstadt?"

"I cannot call one to mind."

"Of course you can't. Would you believe it, when the Zeringer party went out, and the Schlaffdorfers came in, I was rebuked—actually rebuked—for sending off a special messenger with the news? And then came out a dispatch in cipher, which being interpreted contained this stupid doggrel :—

> 'Strange that such difference should be
> 'Twixt Tweedle-dum and Tweedle-dee.'

"I ask, Sir, is it thus the affairs of a great country can be carried on? The efforts of Russia here are incessant: a certain personage—I will mention no names—loves caviar, he likes it fresh, there is a special *estaffette* established to bring it! I learned, by the most insidious researches, his fondness for English cheese; I lost no time in putting the fact before the cabinet I represented, that while timid men looked tremblingly towards France, the thoughtful politician saw the peril of Hesse-Kalbbratonstadt. I urged them to lose no time : 'The grand-duchess has immense influence—countermine her,' said I, 'countermine her with a Stilton ;' and, would you believe it, Sir, they have not so much as sent out a Chedder! What will the people of England say one of these days when they learn, as learn they shall, that at this mission here I am alone—that I have neither secretary nor *attaché*, paid or unpaid—that since the Crimean war the whole weight of the legation has been thrown upon me—nor is this all, but that a systematic course of treachery—I can't call it lies—has been adopted to entrap me, if such were possible? My dispatches are unreplied to, my questions all unanswered. I stand here with the peace of Europe in my hands, and none to counsel nor advise me. What will you say, Sir, to the very last dispatch I have received from Downing Street? It runs thus :—

"'I am instructed by his lordship to inform you, that he views with indifference your statement of the internal condition of the grand-duchy, but is much struck by your charge for sealing-wax.

"'I have, Sir, &c.'

"This is no longer to be endured. A public servant who has filled some of the most responsible of official stations—I was eleven years at Tragotà, in the Argentine Republic ; I was a *chargé* at Oohululoo for eight months—the only European who ever survived an autumn there; they then sent the special to Cabanhos to negotiate the Salt-sprat treaty; after that——"

Here my senses grew muddy: the grey dim light, the soft influences of a good dinner and a sufficiency of wine, the drowsy tenor of the minister's voice, all conspired, and I slept as soundly as if in my bed. My next conscious moment was as his excellency moved his chair back, and said,—

"I think a cup of tea would be pleasant; let us come into the drawing-room."

CHAPTER XV.

On entering the drawing-room, his excellency presented me to an elderly lady, very thin, and very wrinkled, who received me with a cold dignity, and then went on with her crochet-work. I could not catch her name, nor, indeed, was I thinking of it; my whole mind was bent upon the question, Who could she be? For what object was she there? All my terrible doubts of the morning now rushed forcibly back to my memory, and I felt that never had I detested a human being with the hate I experienced for her. The pretentious stiffness of her manner, the haughty self-possession she wore, were positive outrages; and, as I looked at her, I felt myself muttering, "Don't imagine that your heavy black moiré, or your rich falls of lace, impose upon *me*. Never fancy that this mock austerity deceives one who reads human nature as he reads large print. I know, and I abhor you, old woman! That a man should be to the other sex as a wolf to the fold, the sad experience of daily life too often teaches; but that a woman should be false to woman, that all the gentle instincts we love to think feminine, should be debased to treachery and degraded into snares for betrayal, this is an offence that cries aloud to Heaven!

"No more tea—none!" cried I, with an energy, that

nearly made the footman let the tray fall, and so far startled the old lady, that she dropped her knitting, with a faint cry. As for his excellency, he had covered his face with the *Globe*, and, I believe, was fast asleep.

I looked about for my hat to take my leave, when a sudden thought struck me. "I will stay. I will sit down beside this old creature, and, for once, at least, in her miserable life, she shall hear from the lips of a man a language that is not that of the debauchee. Who knows what effect one honest word of a true-hearted man may not work? I will try, at all events," said I, and approached her. She did not, as I expected, make room for me on the sofa beside her, and I was, therefore, obliged to take a chair in front. This was so far awkward that it looked formal; it gave somewhat the character of accusation to my position, and I decided to obviate the difficulty by assuming a light, easy, cheerful manner at first, as though I suspected nothing.

"It's a pleasant little capital, this Kalbbratonstadt," said I, as I lay back in my chair.

"Is it?" said she, dryly, without looking up from her work.

"Well, I mean," said I, "it seems to have its reasonable share of resources. They have their theatre, and their music garden, and their promenades, and their drives to—to——"

"You'll find all the names set down there," said she, handing me a copy of Murray's 'Handbook' that lay beside her.

"I care less for names than facts, madam," said I, angrily, for her retort had stung me, and routed all my previous intention of a smooth approach to the fortress. "I am one of those unfashionable people who never think the better of vice because it wears French gloves, and goes perfumed with Ess bouquet."

She took off her spectacles, wiped them, looked at me, and went on with her work without speaking.

"If I appear abrupt, madam," said I, "in this opening, it is because the opportunity I now enjoy may never occur again, and may be of the briefest even now. We meet by what many would call an accident—one of those incidents which the thoughtless call chance directed my steps to this place; let me hope that that which seemed a hazard may bear all the fruits of maturest combination, and that the weak words of one frail, even as yourself, may not be heard by you in vain. Let me, therefore, ask you one question— only one—and give me an honest answer to it."

"You are a very singular person," said she, "and seem to have strangely forgotten the very simple circumstance that we meet for the first time now."

"I know it, I feel it; and that it may also be for the last and only time is my reason for this appeal to you. There are persons who, seeing you here, would treat you with a mock deference, address you with a counterfeit respect, and go their ways; who would say to their selfish hearts, 'It is no concern of mine, why should it trouble me?' But I am not one of these. I carry a conscience in my breast; a conscience that holds its daily court, and will even to-morrow ask me, 'Have you been truthful, have you been faithful? When the occasion served to warn a fellow-creature of the shoal before him, did you cry out, "Take soundings! you are in shallow water?" or, "Did you with slippery phrases gloss over the peril, because it involved no danger to yourself?"'"

"Would that same conscience be kind enough to suggest that your present conduct is an impertinence, Sir?"

"So it might, madam; just as the pilot is impertinent when he cries out 'Hard, port! breakers ahead!'"

"I am therefore to infer, Sir," said she, with a calm dignity, "that my approach to a secret danger—of which I can have no knowledge—is a sufficient excuse for the employment of language on your part, that, under a less urgent plea, had been offensive?"

"You are," said I, boldly.

"Speak out, then, Sir, and declare what it is."

"Nay, madam, if the warning find no echo within, my words are useless. I have said I would ask you a question."

"Well, Sir, do so."

"Will you answer it frankly? Will you give it all the weight and influence it should bear, and reply to it with that truthful spirit that conceals nothing?"

"What is your question, Sir? You had better be

speedy with it, for I don't much trust to my continues
patience."

I arose at this, and, passing behind the back of my chair
leaned my arms on the upper rail, so as to confront he
directly; and then, in the voice of an accusing angel, I said
"Old woman, do you know where you are going?"

"I protest, Sir," said she, rising, with an indignation
shall not forget—"I protest, Sir, you make me actually doub
if I know where I am!"

"Then let me tell you, madam," said I, with the voice o
one determined to strike terror into her heart—"let me tel
you; and may my words have the power to awaken you
even now, to the dreadful consequences of what you are
about!"

"Shalley! Shalley!" cried she in amazement, "is thi:
gentleman deranged, or is it but the passing effect of you:
conviviality?" And with this she swept out of the room
leaving me there alone, for I now perceived—what seemec
also to have escaped her—that the minister had slippec
quietly away some time before, and was doubtless at tha
same moment in the profoundest of slumbers.

I took my departure at once. There was no leavetaking:
to delay me, and I left the house in a mood little according
with the spirit of one who had partaken of its hospitalities
I am constrained to admit I was the very reverse of satisfiec
with myself. It was cowardly and mean of me to wreal
my anger on that old woman, and not upon him whc
was the really great offender. He it was I should have
arraigned; and with the employment of a little artifice anc
some tact, how terrible I might have made even my jest
ing levity! how sarcastic my sneers at fashionable vice
Affecting utter ignorance about his life and habits, I coulc
have incidently thrown out little episodes of all the men
who have wrecked their fortunes by abandoned habits. I
would have pointed to this man who made a brilliant opening
in the House, and that who had acquired such celebrity al
the Bar; I would have shown the rising statesman tarnished
the future chief justice disqualified; I would have said
"Let no man, however modest his character or unfrequented
his locality, imagine that the world takes no note of his
conduct; in every class he is judged by his peers, and you

and I, Doubleton, will as assuredly be arraigned before the
bar of society as the pickpocket will be charged before the
beak!"

I continued to revolve these and such like thoughts
throughout the entire night. The wine I had drunk fevered
and excited me, and added to that disturbed state which my
own self-accusings provoked. Doubts, too, flitted across my
mind whether I ought not to have maintained a perfect
silence towards the others, and reserved all my eloquence for
the poor girl herself. I imagined myself taking her hand
between both mine, while, with averted head, she sobbed as
if her heart would break, and, saying, "Be comforted, poor
stricken deer! be comforted; I know all. One who is far
from perfect himself, sorrows with and compassionates you;
he will be your friend, your adviser, your protector. I will
restore you to that home you quitted in innocence. I will
bring you back to that honeysuckled porch where your pure
heart expanded in home affections." Nothing shall equal
the refined delicacy of my manner; that mingled reserve
and kindness—a sort of cross between a half-brother and a
canon of St. Paul's—shall win her over to repentance, and
then to peace. How I fancied myself at intervals of time
visiting that cottage, going, as the gardener watches some
cherished plant, to gaze on the growing strength I had nurtured, and enjoy the luxury of seeing the once drooping flower
expanding into fresh loveliness and perfume. "Yes, Potts,
this would form one of those episodes you have so often
longed to realise." And then I went on to fancy a long
heroic struggle between my love and that sentiment of
respect for worldly opinion which is dear to every man, the
years of conflict wearing me down in health, but exalting me
immensely in every moral consideration. Let the hour of
crowning victory at last come, I should take her to my bosom
and say, "There is rest for thee here!"

"His excellency begs that you will call at the legation,
as early as you can this morning," said a waiter, entering with the breakfast tray; and I now perceived that
I had never gone to bed, or closed my eyes during the
night.

"How did this message come?" I asked.

"By the chasseur of his excellency."

"And how addressed ? "

" 'To the gentleman who dined yesterday at the legation.' "

I asked these questions to ascertain how far he persisted
in the impertinence of giving me a name that was not mine,
and I was glad to find, that on this occasion no transgresion
had occurred.

I hesitated considerably about going to him. Was I to
accept that slippery morality that says, "I see no more than
I please in the man I dine with," or was I to go boldly on
and denounce this offender to himself? What if he were to
say, "Potts, let us play fair ! put your own cards on the table,
and let us see are you always on the square? Who is your
father? how does he live ? Why have you left home, and
how ? What of that horse you have——"

"No, no, not stolen— on my honour, not stolen !"

"Well, ain't it ugly? Isn't the story one that any relating
might, without even a spice of malevolence, make marvellously disagreeable? Is the tale such as you'd wish to
herald you into any society you desired to mix with ?" It
was in this high, easy, and truly companionable style that
conscience kept me company, while I ate two eggs and a
plate of buttered toast. "After all," thought I, "might it
not prove a great mistake not to wait on him? How if, in
our talk over politics last night, I may have dropped some
remarkable expression, a keen appreciation of some statesman, an extraordinary prediction of some coming crisis?
Maybe it is to question me more fully about my 'views' of
the state of Europe." Now I am rather given to "views of
the state of Europe." I like that game of patience, formed
by shuffling up all the govenments of the Continent, and
then seeing who is to have the most "tricks," who's to win
all the kings, and who the knaves. "Yes," thought I,
"this is what he is at. These diplomatic people are con-
summately clever at pumping; their great skill consists in
extracting information from others and adapting it to their
own uses. Their social condition confers the great advantage
of intercourse with whatever is remarkable for station, influence, and ability; and I think I hear his excellency muttering to himself, "remarkable man that—large views—great
reach of thought—wish I could see more of him; must try

what polite attentions may accomplish.' Well," said I, with
a half sigh, "it is the old story, *Sic vos non vobis;* and
I suppose it is one of the curses on Irishmen that, from
Edmund Burke to Potts, they should be doomed to cram
others. I will go. What signifies it to *me?* I am none
the poorer in dispensing my knowledge than is the night-
ingale in discoursing her sweet music to the night air, and
flooding the groves with waves of melody: like *her*, I give of
an affluence that never fails me." And so I set out for the
legation.

As I walked along through the garden, a trimly-dressed
French maid passed me, turned, and repassed, with a look
that had a certain significance. "It was monsieur dined
here yesterday?" said she, interrogatively; and as I smiled
assent, she handed me a very small-sealed note, and disappeared.

It bore no address, but the word Mr. ——; a strange, not
very ceremonious direction. "But, poor girl," thought I,
"she knows me not as Potts, but as Protector. I am not
the individual, but the representative of that wide-spread
benevolence that succours the weak and consoles the afflicted.
I wonder has she been touched by my devotion? has she
imagined—oh, that she would!—that I have followed her
hither, that I have sworn a vow to rescue and to save her?
or is this note the cry of a sorrow-struck spirit, saying,
'Come to my aid ere I perish?'"

My fingers trembled as I broke the seal; I had to wipe
a tear from my eye ere I could begin to read. My agitation
was great, it was soon to be greater. The note contained
very few words; they were these:—

"SIR,—I have not communicated to my brother, Sir
Shalley Doubleton, any circumstance of your unaccountable
conduct yesterday evening. I hope that my reserve will be
appreciated by you, and

"I am, your faithful servant,

"MARTHA KEATS."

I did not faint, but I sat down on the grass, sick and faint,
and I felt the great drops of cold perspiration burst out

over my forehead and temples. " So," muttered I, " the venerable person I have been lecturing is his excellency's own sister! My exhortations to a changed life have been addressed to a lady doubtless as rigid in morals as austere in manners." Though I could recal none of the words I employed, I remembered but too well the lesson I intended to convey, and I shuddered with disgust at my own conduct. Many a time have I heard severest censure on the preacher who has from the pulpit scattered words of doubtful application to the sinners beneath; but here was I making a direct and most odious attack upon the life and habits of a lady of immaculate behaviour! Oh, it was too—too bad! A whole year of sackcloth and ashes would not be penance for such iniquity. How could she have forgiven it? what consummate charity enabled her to pardon an offence so gross and so gratuitous? Or is it that she foresaw consequences so grave, in the event of disclosure, that she dreaded to provoke them? What might not an angry brother, in such a case, be warranted in doing? Would the world call any vengeance exorbitant? I studied her last phrase over and over, "I hope my reserve will be appreciated by you." This may mean, "I reserve the charge—I hold it over you as a bail bond for the future; diverge ever so little from the straight road, and I will say, 'Potts, stand forward and listen to your indictment.'" She may have some terrible task in view for me, some perilous achievement which I cannot now refuse. This old woman may be to me as was the Old Man of the Sea to Sindbad. I may be fated to carry her for ever on my back, and the dread of her be a living nightmare to me. "At such a price, existence has no value," said I, in despair. "Worse even than the bondage is the feeling that I am no longer, to my own heart, the great creature I love to think myself. Instead of Potts the generous, the high-spirited, the confiding, the self-denying, I am Potts the timorous, the terror-stricken, and the slave."

Out of my long and painful musings on the subject, I bethought me of a course to take. I would go to her and say :—

" Listen to this parable : I remember once, when a member of the phrenological club, a stupid jest was played off upon the society by some one presenting us with the cast of a

well-known murderer's skull, and asking for our interpreta-
tions of its development. We gave them with every care
and deliberation; we pointed out the fatal protuberances of
crime, and indicated the depressions, which showed the
absence of all prudential restraints; we demonstrated all the
evidences of badness that were there, and proved that, with
such a head, a man must have thought killing no murder.
The rejoinder to our politeness was a small box that arrived
by the mail, labelled, 'The original of the cast forwarded on
the 14th.' We opened it, and found a pumpkin! The foolish
jester fancied that he had cast an indelible stain upon
phrenology, quite forgetting the fact that his pumpkin had
personated a skull which, had it ever existed, would have
presented the characteristics we gave it." I would say,
"Now, madam, make the application, and say, do you not
rather commend than condemn? are you not more ready
to applaud than upbraid me?"

Second thoughts rather deterred me from this plan; the
figurative line is often dangerous with elderly people. It is
just as likely she would mistake the whole force of my
illustration, and bluntly say, "I'd beg to remark, Sir, I am
not a pumpkin!"

"No. I will not adventure on this path; there is no need
that I should ever meet her again, or, if I should, we may
meet as utter strangers. This resolve made, I arose boldly,
and walked on towards the house.

His excellency, I learned, was at home, and had been for
some time expecting me. I found him in his morning-room,
in the same costume and same occupation as on the day
before.

"There's the *Times*," said he, as I entered; "I shall be
ready for you presently;" and worked away without lifting
his head.

Affecting to read, I set myself to regard him with attention. Vast piles of papers lay around him on every side;
the whole table, and even the floor at his feet, was littered
with them. "Would," thought I—"would that these writers
for the Radical press, these scurrilous penny-a-liners who
inveigh against a bloated and pampered aristocracy, could
just witness the daily life of labour of one of these spoiled
children of fortune. Here is this man, doubtless reared in

10

ease and affluence, and see him how he toils away, from
sundown to dawn, unravelling the schemes, tracing the
wiles, and exposing the snares of these crafty foreigners.
Hark! he is muttering over the subtle sentence he has just
written: 'I am much grieved about Maria's little girl, but I
hope she will escape being marked by the malady.' " A
groan that broke from me here startled him, and he looked
up:
      " Ah! yes, by the way, I want you, Paynter."
      " I am not Paynter, your excellency, my name is ——"
      " Of course, you have your own name, for your own
peculiar set; but don't interrupt.   I have a special service
for you, and will put it in the 'extraordinaries.'   I have
taken a little villa on the lake of Como for my sister, but
from the pressure of political events I am not able to accompany her there.   She is a very timid traveller and cannot
posibly go alone.   You'll take charge of her, therefore,
Paynter—there don't be fussy—you'll take charge of her,
and a young lady who is with her, and you'll see them
housed and established there.   I suppose she will prefer to
travel slowly, some thirty miles or so a day, post-horses
always, and strictly avoiding railroads; but you can talk it
over together yourselves.   There was a Bobus to have come
out ——"
      " A Bobus!"
      " I mean a doctor—I call every doctor, Bobus—but some-
thing has detained him, or, indeed, I believe he was drowned;
at all events, he's not come, and you'll have to learn how to
measure out ether, and drop morphine;—the "companion"
will help you.   And keep an account of your expenses,
Paynter—your own expenses for F.O.—and don't let her fall
sick at any out-of-the-way place, which she has rather a
knack of doing; and, above all, don't telegraph on any
account.   Come and dine—six."
      " If you will excuse me at dinner, I shall be obliged.   I
have a sort of half engagement."
      " Come in about nine, then," said he, "for she'd like to talk
over some matters.   Look out for a carriage, too; I don't
fancy giving mine if you can get another.   One of those great
roomy German things with a cabriolet front, for Miss—I
forget her name—would prefer a place outside.   Kramm, the

landlord, can help you to search for one; and let it be dusted, and aired, and fumigated, and the drag examined, and the axles greased—in a word, have your brains about you, Paynter. Good-by." Exit as before.

~~~~~~~~~~~~~~~~~~

CHAPTER XVI.

THERE is no denying it, I have led a life of far more than ordinary happiness. The white squares in the chequer of my existence have certainly equalled the black ones, and it is not every man can say as much. I suspect I owe a great share of this enjoyment to temperament, to a disposition not so much remarkable for opposing difficulties, as for deriving all the possible pleasure from any fortunate conjuncture. This gift I know I possess. I am not one of those strong natures which, by their intrinsic force, are ever impressing their own image on the society they live in. I am a weak, frail, yielding creature, but my very pliancy has given me many a partnership in emotions which, with a more rugged temperament, I had not partaken of. When one has wept over a friend's misfortunes and awakes to the consciousness that no ill has befallen himself, he feels as some great millionnaire might feel who has bestowed a thousand pounds in charity and yet knows he is never the poorer. With the proud consciousness of this fresh title to men's admiration, he has the secret satisfaction of knowing that he will go clothed in purple as before. and fare to-day as sumptuously as yesterday. Do you, most generous of readers, call this selfishness? It is the very reverse. It is the grand culminating point of human sympathy.

I have a great deal more to say about myself. It is a theme I am really fond of, but I am not exactly sure that you

10—2

are like-minded, or that this is the fittest place for it. I
return to events.

It was on a bright, breezy morning of the early autumn
that a heavy old German travelling carriage—a waggon !—
rattled over the uneven pavement of Kalbbratonstadt, and
soon gaining one of the long forest alleys, rolled noiselessly
over the smooth sward. Within sat an elderly lady with a
due allowance of air cushions, toy terriers, and guide-books;
in the rumble were a man and a maid; and in the cabriolet
in front were a pale but placid girl, with large grey eyes and
long lashes, and he who now writes these lines beside her.
They who had only known me a few months back as a freshman of Trinity would not have recognised me now, as I sat
with a long peaked travelling-cap, a courier's belt and bag at
my side, and the opening promise of a small furry moustache
on my upper lip; not to say that I had got up a sort of supercilious air of contemptuous pity for the foreigner, which I
had observed to be much in favour with the English abroad.
It cost me dear to do this, and nothing but the consciousness
that it was one of the requirements of my station could have
made me assume it, for in my heart of hearts, I revelled in
enjoyment of all around me. I liked the soft, breezy, balmy
air, the mellow beech wood, the grassy turf overgrown with
violets, the wild notes of the frightened wood-pigeon, the very
tramp-tramp of the massive horses, with their scarlet tassels
and their jingling bells, all pleased and interested me. Not to
speak of her who, at my side, felt a very child's delight at
every novelty of the way.

"What would I have said to anyone who, only a fortnight ago, had promised me such happiness as this ? " said I
to my companion, as we drove along, while the light
branches rustles pleasantly over the roof of the carriage,
darkening the shade around us, or occasionally deluging us
with the leaves as we passed.

"And are you then so very happy ? " asked she, with a
pleasant smile.

"Can you doubt it ? or rather, is it that, as the emotion
does not extend to yourself, you *do* doubt it ? "

"Oh, as for me," cried she, joyfully, " it is very different.
I have never travelled till now—seen nothing, actually
nothing. The veriest common-places of the road, the

peasants' costumes, their wayside cottages, the little shrines they kneel at, are all objects of picturesque interest to me, and I am ready to exclaim at each moment, 'Oh! why cannot we stop here? shall we ever see anything so beautiful again as this?'"

"And hearing you talk thus, you can ask me am I so very happy!" said I, reproachfully.

"What I meant was, is it not stupid to have no companion of your own turn of mind, none with whom you could talk, without condescending to a tone beneath you, just as certain stories are reduced to words of one syllable for little children?"

"Mademoiselle is given to sarcasm, I see," said I, half peevishly.

"Nothing of the kind," said she, blushing slightly. "It was in perfect good faith. I wished you a more suitable companion. Indeed, after what I had heard from his excellency about you, I was terrified at the thought of my own insufficiency."

"And pray what *did* he say of me?" asked I, in a flutter of delight.

"Are you very fond of flattery?"

"Immensely!"

"Is it not possible that praise of you could be so exaggerated as to make you feel ashamed?"

"I should say, perfectly impossible; that is, to a mind regulated as mine, over-elation could never happen. Tell me, therefore, what he said?"

"I can't remember one-half of it; he remarked how few men in the career—I conclude he meant diplomacy—could compare with you; that you had such just views about the state of Europe, such an accurate appreciation of public men. I can't say how many opportunities you mustn't have had, and what valuable uses you have not put them to. In a word, I felt that I was about to travel with a great statesman and a consummate man of the world, and was terrified accordingly."

"And now that the delusion is dispelled, how do you feel?"

"But is it dispelled? Am I not shocked with my own temerity in daring to talk thus lightly with one so learned?"

" If so," said I, " you conceal your embarrassment wonder-
fully."

And then we both laughed, but I am not quite sure it was
at the same joke.

" Do you know where you are going? " said I, taking out
a travelling map as a means of diverting our conversation
into some higher channel.

" Not in the least."

" Nor care ? "

" Nor care."

" Well, I must say, it is a most independent frame of
mind. Perhaps you could extend this fine philosophy, and
add, ' Nor with whom ! ' "

I was not at all conscious of what an impertinence I had
uttered till it was out; nor, indeed, even then, till I remarked
that her cheek had become scarlet, and her eyes double as
dark as their wont.

" Yes," said she, " there is one condition for which I
should certainly stipulate—not to travel with anyone who
could needlessly offend me."

I could have cried with shame : I could have held my
hand in the flame of a fire to expiate my rude speech. And
so I told her ; while I assured her at the same time, with
marvellous consistency, that it was not rude at all; that it
was entirely misconception on her part; that *nous autres
diplomates*—Heaven forgive me the lying assumption !—had
a way of saying little smartnesses that don't mean much ;
that we often made our coin ring on the table, though it
turned out bad money when it came to be looked at; that
Talleyrand did it, and Walewsky did it, and I did it—we all
did it !

Now, there was one most unlucky feature in all this. It
was only a few minutes before this passage occurred, that I
said to myself, " Potts, here is one whose frank, fresh,
generous nature claims all your respect and devotion. No
nonsense of your being this, that, and t'other here. Be
truthful and be honest; neither pretend to be man of fortune
nor man of fashion ; own fairly to her by what chance you
adventured upon this strange life; tell her, in a word, you
are the son of Potts—Potts the 'pothecary—and neither a
hero nor a plenipotentiary ! "

I have no doubt, most amiable of readers, that nothing can seem possibly more easy than to have done all this. You deem it the natural and ordinary course; just as, for instance, a merchant in good credit and repute would feel no repugnance to calling all his creditors together to inspect his books, and see that, though apparently solvent, he was, in truth, utterly bankrupt. And yet there is some difficulty in doing this. Does not the law of England expressly declare that no man need criminate himself? Who accuses you, then, Potts? And then I bethought me of the worthy old alderman, who, on learning that "Robinson Crusoe" was a fiction, exclaimed, "It may be so; but I have lost the greatest pleasure of my life in hearing it. What a profound philosophy was there in that simple avowal! With what illusions are we not cheered on through life; how unreal the joys that delight and the triumphs that elate us! for we are all hypochondriacs, and are as often cured with bread pills as with bold remedies. "Yes," thought I, "this young girl is happy in the thought that her companion is a person of rank, station, and influence; she feels a sort of self-elation in being associated with one endowed with all worldly advantages. Shall I rob her of this illusion? Shall I rudely deprive her of what imparts a charm to her existence, and gives a sort of romantic interest to her daily life? Harsh and needless would be the cruelty!"

While I thus argued with myself, she had opened her guide-book, and was eagerly reading away about the road we were travelling. "We are to halt at Bömerstein, are we not?" asked she.

"Yes," said I, "we rest there for the night. It is one of those little villages of which a German writer has given us a striking picture."

"Auerstadt," broke she in.

"So you have read him? You read German?"

"Yes, tolerably; that is, well enough for Schiller and Uhland, but not well enough for Jean Paul and Goethe."

"Never mind; trust me for a guide, you shall now venture upon both."

"But how will you be able to give up time valuable as yours to such teachings? Would it be fair of me, besides, to steal hours that ought to be devoted to your country?"

Though I had not the slightest imaginable ground to suspect any secret sarcasm in this speech, my guilty conscience made me feel it as a perfect torture. "She knows me," thought I, "and this sneer at my pretended importance is intended to overwhelm me."

"As to my country's claims," said I, haughtily, "I make light of them. All that I have seen of life only shows the shallowness of what is called the public service. I am resolved to leave it, and for ever."

"And for what?"

"A life of retirement—obscurity if you will."

"It is what I should do if I were a man."

"Indeed!"

"Yes. I have often reflected over the delight I have felt in walking through some man's demesne, revelling in the enjoyment of its leafy solitude, its dreary shade, its sunlit vistas, and I have thought, 'If all these things, not one of which are mine, can bring such pleasure to my heart, why should I not adopt the same philosophy in life, and be satisfied with enjoying without possessing? A very humble lot would suffice for one, nothing but great success could achieve the other.'"

"What becomes, then, of that great stimulus to good they call labour?"

"Oh, I should labour, too. I'd work at whatever I was equal to. I'd sew, and knit, and till my garden, and be as useful as possible."

"And I would write," said I, "enthusiastically, as though I were plotting out my share in this garden of Eden. "I would write all sorts of things : reviews, and histories, and stories, and short poems, and, last of all, the 'Confessions of Algernon Sydney Potts.'"

"Oh, what a shocking title! How could such names have met together? That shocking epithet Potts would vulgarise it all!"

"I really cannot agree with you," said I, angrily.

"Without," said she, "you meant it for a sort of quiz; and that Potts was to be a creature of absurdity and folly, a pretender and a snob."

I felt as if I was choking with passion; but I tried to laugh, and say, "Yes, of course."

"That would be good fun enough," went she on. "I'd like, if I could, to contribute to that. You should invent the situations, and leave me occasionally to supply the reflective part."

"It would be charming, quite delightful."

"Shall we do it, then? Let us try it, by all means. We might begin by imagining Potts in search of this, that, or t'other—love, happiness, solitude, climate, scenery, anything, in short. Let us fancy him on a journey, try and personate him, that would be the real way. Do you, for instance, be Potts, and I'll be his sister Susan. It will be the best fun in the world, as we go along, to see everything, note every-thing, and discuss everything Pottswise.

"It would be too ridiculous, too absurd," said I, sick with anger.

"Not a bit; we are travelling with our old grandmother, we are making the tour of Europe, and keeping our journal. Every evening we compare notes of what we have seen. Pray do so; I'm quite wild to try it."

"Really," said I, gravely, "it is a sort of trifling I should find it very difficult to descend to. I see no reason, besides, to associate the name of Potts with what you are pleased to call snobbery!"

"Could you help it? Could you, with all the best will in the world, make Potts a man of distinction? Wouldn't he, in spite of you, be low, vulgar, inquisitive, and obtrusive? Wouldn't you find him thrusting himself forward, twenty times a day, into positions he had no right to? Wouldn't the creature be a butt and a dupe ——"

"Shall I own," burst I in, "that it gives me no exalted idea of your taste, if I find that you select for ridicule a person on the mere showing that his name is a monosyllable? And, once for all, I repudiate all share in the scheme, and beg that I may not hear more of it."

I turned away as I said this. She resumed her book, and we spoke no more to each other till we reached our halting-place for the night.

CHAPTER XVII.

I AM forced to the confession, Mrs. Keats was not what is popularly called an agreeable old lady. She spoke seldom, she smiled never, and she had a way of looking at you, a sort of cold astonishment, seeming to say, "How is this? explain yourself," that kept me in a perpetual terror.

My morning's tiff with Miss Herbert had neither been condoned nor expiated when we sat down to dinner, as stiff a party of three as can well be imagined: scarcely a word was interchanged as we ate.

"If you drink wine, Sir, pray order it," said Mrs. Keats to me, in a voice that might have suited an invitation to prussic acid.

"This little wine of the country is very pleasant, madam," said I, courteously, "and I can even venture to recommend it."

"Not to me, Sir. I drink water."

"Perhaps Miss Herbert will allow me?"

"Excuse me, I also drink water."

After a very dreary and painful pause, I dared to express a faint hope that Mrs. Keats had not been fatigued by the day's journey.

She looked at me for a second or two before replying, and then said: "I am really not aware, Sir, that I have manifested any such signs of weariness as would warrant your inquiry. If I should have, however——"

"Oh, I beg you will pardon me, madam," broke I in, apologetically; "my question was not meant for more than a mere ordinary politeness, a matter-of-course expression of my solicitude."

"It will save us both some trouble in future, Sir, if I remark that I am no friend to matter-of-course civilities, and never reply to them."

I felt as though my head and face had been passed across the open door of a blast furnace. I was in a perfect flame, and dared not raise my eye from my plate.

"The waiter is asking if you will take coffee, Sir," said the inexorable old lady to me, as I sat almost stunned and stupid.

"Yes—with brandy—a full glass of brandy in it," cried I, in the half-despair of one who knew not how to rally himself.

"I think we may retire, Miss H.," said Mrs. Keats, rising with a severe dignity that seemed to say, "We are not bound to assist at an orgie." And with a stern stare and a defiant little bow she moved towards the door. I was so awestruck, that I never moved from my place, but stood resting my hand on my chair, till she said, "Do you mean to open the door, Sir, or am I to do it for myself?"

I sprang forward at once, and flung it wide, my face all scarlet with shame.

She passed out, and Miss Herbert followed her. Her dress, however, catching in the doorway, she turned back to extricate it; I seized the moment to stoop down and say, "Do let me see you for one moment this evening—only one moment."

She shook her head in silent negative, and went away.

I sat down at the table, and filled myself a large goblet of wine: I drank it off, and replenished it. It was only this morning, a few brief hours ago, and I would not have changed fortunes with the Emperor of France. Life seemed to open before me like some beautiful alley in a garden, with a glorious vista in the distance. I would not have bartered the place in that cabriolet for the proudest throne in Europe. *She* was there beside me, listening in rapt attention, as I discoursed voyages, travels, memoirs, poetry, and personal adventures. With every changeful expression of lovely sympathy did she follow me through all. I was a hero to us both, myself as much captivated as she was; and now the brief drama was over, the lights were put out, and the theatre closed! How had I destroyed this golden delusion— why had I quarrelled with her, and for what? For a certain Potts, a creature who, in reality, had no existence! "For who is Potts?" said I. "Potts is no more a substance than Caleb Williams or Peregrine Pickle; Potts is the lay figure, that the artist dresses in any costume he requires—a Rachero to-day, a Railway Director to-morrow. What an absurdity in the importance we lend to mere names! Here,

for instance, I take the label off the port, and I hang it round
the neck of the claret decanter: have I changed the quality
of the vintage? have I brought Bordeaux to the meridian of
Oporto? Not a bit of it. And yet a man is to be more the
victim of an accident than a bottle of wine, and his intrinsic
qualities—strength, flavour, and richness—are not to be
tested, but simply implied from the label round his neck!
How narrow-minded, after all, of her, who ought to have
known better! It is thus, however, we educate our women;
this is part and parcel of the false system by which we fancy
we make them companionable. The North American
Indians are far in advance of us in all this: they assign them
their proper places and fitting duties; they feel that, in this
life of ours, order and happiness depend on the due distribu-
tion of burdens, and the Snapping Alligator never feels his
squaw more truly his helpmate than when she is skinning
eels for his dinner."

How I hated that old woman! I don't think I ever
detested a human creature so much as that. I have often
speculated as to whether venomous reptiles have any gratification imparted to them when they inflict a poisonous wound.
Is the mosquito the happier of having stung one's nose?
And, in the same spirit, I should like to know, do the
disagreeable people of this world sleep the better from the
consciousness of having offended us? Is there that great
ennobling sense of a mission fulfilled for every cheek they
set on fire and every heart they depress? and do they
quench hope and extinguish ambition with the same zeal
that the Sun or the Phœnix put out a fire?

"'If you drink wine, Sir, pray order it,'" said I, mimick-
ing her imperious tone. "Yes, madam, I do drink wine, and
I mean to order it, and liberally. I travel at the expense of
that noble old paymaster who only wags his tale the more
the more he has to pay—the British Lion. I go down in
the extraordinaries. I'm on what is called a special service.
'Keep an account of your expenses, Paynter!' Confound
his insolence, he would say 'Puynter.' By the way, I have
never looked how he calls me in my passport. I'm curious
to see if I be Paynter there." I had left the bag containing
this and my money in my room, and I rang the bell, and
told the waiter to fetch it.

The passport set forth in due terms all the dignities, honours, and decorations of the great man who granted it, and who bespoke for the little man who travelled by it all aid and assistance possible, and to let him pass freely, &c. "Mr. Ponto—British subject." "'Ponto!'" What an outrage! This comes of a man making his *maître d'hôtel* his secretary. That stupid French flunkey has converted me into a water-dog. This may explain a good deal of the old lady's rudeness; how could she be expected to be even ordinarily civil to a man called Ponto? She'd say at once, 'His father was an Italian, and of course a courier, or a valet; or he was a foundling, and called after a favourite spaniel.' I'll rectify this without loss of time. If she has not the tact to discover the man of education and breeding by the qualities he displays in intercourse, she shall be brought to admit them by the demands of his self-respect."

I opened my writing-desk and wrote just two lines—a polite request for a few moments of interview, signed "A. S. Pottinger." I wrote the name in a fine text hand, as though to say, "No more blunders, madam, this is large as print."

"Take this to your mistress, François," said I to the courier.

"Gone to bed, Sir."

"Gone to bed! why, it's only eight o'clock."

A shrug and a smile were all he replied.

"And Miss Herbert—can I speak to *her?*"

"Fear not, Sir; she went to her room, and told Clementina not to disturb her."

"It is of consequence, however, that I should see her. I want to make arrangements for to-morrow—the hour we are to start ——"

"Oh! but we are to stop here over to-morrow—I thought monsieur knew that," said the fellow, with the insolent grin of a menial at knowing more than his betters.

"Oh, to be sure we are," said I, laughingly, and affecting to have suddenly remembered it. "I forgot all about it, François; you are quite right. Take a glass of wine, François—or take the bottle with you, that's better." And I handed him a flask of Hocheimer of eight florins, right glad to get rid of his presence and escape further scrutiny from his prying glances.

How relieved I felt when the fellow closed the door after him and left me to " blow off the steam " of my indignation all alone! And was I not indignant? Only to fancy this insolent old woman giving her orders without so much as condescending to communicate with me! I am left to learn her whim by a mere accident, or not learn it at all, and exhibit myself ready to depart at the inn door, and then hear, for the first time, that I may unpack again.

This was unquestionably a studied rudeness, and demanded an equally studied reprisal. She means to discredit my station, and disparage my influence : how shall I reply to her? A vast variety of expedients offered themselves to my mind : I could go off, leaving a fearful letter behind me—a document that would cut her to the very soul with the sarcastic bitterness of its tone; but could I leave without a reconciliation with Miss Herbert—without the fond hope of our meeting as friends. I meant a great deal more, though I wouldn't trust myself to say so. Besides, were I to go away, there were financial considerations to be entertained. I could not, of course, carry off that crimson bag with its gold and silver contents, and yet it was very hard to tear myself from such a treasure.

I say it under correction, for I have never been rich, and, consequently, never in the position to assert it positively, but I declare my firm conviction to be, that no man has ever tasted the unbounded pleasures of a careless liberality on a journey, who has not travelled at some other person's expense. Be as wealthy as you like, let your portmanteau be stuffed full of circular notes, and there will be present at moments of payment the thought, " If I do not allow myself to be cheated here, I shall have all the more to squander, there." But, drawing from the bag of another, no such mean reflection obtrudes. You might as well defraud your lungs of a long inspiration out of the fear of taking more than your share of the atmosphere. There is enough, and will be enough there when you are dust and ashes.

In fact, if I had on one side the " three courses" of the great statesman, I had on the other full thirty reasons against each, and, therefore, I resolved to suspend action and do nothing. And let me here passingly remark that, much as we hear every day about the merits of promptitude and quick-wittedness, in nine cases out of ten in life, I'd rather "give the move than take it." The waiting policy is a rare one; it is the secret of success in love, and of victory in an equity court. And so I determined I'd wait and see what should come of it. I appealed to myself thus: "Potts, you are eminently a man of the world, one who accepts life as it is, with all its crosses and untoward incidents; who knows well that he must play bad cards even oftener than good ones. No impatience, therefore, no rashness; give at least twenty-four hours' thought to any important decision, and let a night's sleep intervene between your first conception of a plan and its adoption." Oh, if the people who are fretting themselves about what is to happen this day ten years, would only remember what a long time it is—that is, counting by the number of events that will occur between this and to-morrow—not to say what incidents are happening at the antipodes that will yet bring joy or sorrow to their hearts—they would keep more of their sympathies for present use, and perhaps be the happier for doing so.

CHAPTER XVIII.

I am about to make a very original observation. I hope its truth may equal its originality. It is, that the man who has never had a sister, is, at his first entrance into life, far more the slave of feminine captivations, than he who has been brought up in a "house full of girls." "Oh, for shame, Mr. Potts! Is this the gallantry we have heard so much of? Is this the spirit of that chivalrous devotion you have been incessantly impressing upon us?" Wait a moment, fair creature; give me one half-minute for an explanation. He

who has not had sisters, has had no experiences of the
behind-scene life of the female world; he has never heard
one syllable about the plans, and schemes, and devices by
which hearts are snared.   He fancies Mary stuck that moss-
rose in her hair in a moment of childish caprice; that Kate
ran after her little sister and showed the prettiest of ankles
in doing it, out of the irrepressible gaiety of her buoyant
spirits.   In a word, he is one who only sees the play when
the house is fully lighted, and all the actors in their grand
costume; he has never witnessed a rehearsal, and has not
the very vaguest suspicion of a prompter.

To him, therefore, who has only experienced the rough
companionship of brothers—or worse still, has lived entirely
alone—the first acquaintanceship with the young-lady world
is such a fascination as no words can describe.   The gentle
look, the graceful gestures, the silvery voices, all the play
and action of natures so infinitely more refined than any he
has ever witnessed, are inexpressibly captivating.   It is not
alone the occupations of their hours, light, graceful, and
picturesque as they are, but all their topics, their thoughts,
seem to soar out of the common-place world he has lived in,
and rise to ideal realms of poetry and beauty.   I say it
advisedly: I do not know of anything so truly Elysian
in life as our first—our very first—experiences of this
kind.

Werther's passion for Charlotte received a powerful
impulse from watching her as she cut bread-and-butter for
the children.   There are vulgar natures who will smile at
this; who cannot enter into the intense far-sightedness of
that poetic conception; that could in one trait of simplicity
embody a whole lifetime with its ennobling duties, its
cheerful sacrifices, its gracefully-borne cares.   Let him,
therefore, who could sneer at Werther, scoff at Potts, as he
owns that he never felt his heart so powerfully drawn to
Kate Herbert as when he watched her making tea for breakfast.   Dressed in a muslin that represented mourning, her
rich hair plainly enclosed in a net, with a noiseless motion,
she glided about, an ideal of gentle sadness, more fascinating
than I can tell.   If she bore any unpleasant memory of our
little difference, she did not show it; her manner was calm
and even kind.   She felt, perhaps, that some compensation

was due to me for the rudeness of that old woman, and was not unwilling to make it.

"You know we are to rest here to-day?" said she, as she busied herself at the table.

"I heard it by a mere chance, and from the courier," said I, peevishly. "I am not quite certain in what capacity Mrs. Keats condescends to regard me, that I am treated with such scant courtesy. Probably you would be kind enough to ascertain this point for me?"

"I shall assuredly not ask," said she, with a smile.

"I certainly promised her brother—I could not do less for a colleague, not to say something more—that I'd see this old lady safe over the Alps. They are looking out for me anxiously enough at Constantinople all this while; in fact, I suspect there will be a nice confusion there through my delay, and I'd not be a bit surprised if they begin to believe that stupid story in the *Nord*. I suppose you saw it?"

"No. What is it about?"

"It is about your humble servant, Miss Herbert, and hints that he has received one hundred purses from the sheiks of the Lebanon not to reach the Golden Horn before they have made their peace with the Grand Vizier."

"And is of course untrue?"

"Of course, every word of it is a falsehood; but there are 'gobemouches' will believe anything. Mark my words, and see if this allegation be not heard in the House of Commons, and some Tower Hamlets member start up to ask if the Foreign Secretary will lay on the table copies of the instructions given to a certain person, and supposed to be credentials of a nature to supersede the functions of our ambassador at the Porte. In confidence, between ourselves, Miss Herbert, so they are! I am entrusted with full powers about the Hatti Homayoun, as the world shall see in good time."

"Do you take your tea strong?" asked she; and there was something so odd and so inopportune in the question, that I felt it as a sort of covert sneer; but when I looked up and beheld that pale and gentle face turned towards me, I banished the base suspicion, and forgetting all my enthusiasm, said,

" Yes, dearest ; strong as brandy ! "

She tried to look grave, perhaps angry ; but in spite of herself, she burst out a laughing.

"I perceive, Sir," said she, "that Mrs. Keats was quite correct when she said that you appear to have moments in which you are unaware of what you say."

Before I could rally to reply, she had poured out a cup of tea for Mrs. Keats, and left the room to carry it to her.

" ' Moments in which I am unaware of what I say '— ' incoherent intervals ' Forbes Winslow would call them : in plain English, I am mad. Old woman, have you dared to cast such an aspersion on me, and to disparage me, too, in the quarter where I am striving to achieve success? For her opinion of me I am less than indifferent; for her judgment of my capacity, my morals, my manners, I am as careless as I well can be of anything ; but these become serious disparagements when they reach the ears of one whose heart I would make my own. I will insist on an explanation—no, but an apology—for this. She shall declare that she used these words in some non-natural sense—that I am the sanest of mortals : she shall give it under her hand and seal : ' I, the undersigned, having in a moment of rash and impatient judgment, imputed to the bearer of this document, Algernon Sydney Potts'—No, Pottinger—' ha, there is a difficulty ! If I be Pottinger, I can never re-become Potts ; if Potts, I am lost—or rather, Miss Herbert is lost to me for ever. What a dire embarrassment ! Not to mention that in the passport I was Ponto ! "

" ' Mrs. Keats desired me to beg you will step up to her room after breakfast, and bring your account-books with you." This was said by Miss Herbert as she entered and took her place at the table.

"What has the old woman got in her head ? " said I, angrily. "I have no account-books—I never had such in my life. When I travel alone, I say to my courier, ' Diomede ' —he is a Greek—' Diomede, pay ; ' and he pays. When Diomede is not with me, I ask, ' How much ? ' and I give it."

" It certainly simplifies travel," said she, gravely.

"It does more, Miss Herbert : it accomplishes the end of travel. Your doctor says, ' Go abroad—take a holiday—turn your back on Downing Street, and bid farewell to cabinet councils.' Where is the benefit of such a course, I ask, if you are to pass the vacation cursing custom-house officers, bullying landlords, and browbeating waiters? I say always, 'Give me a bad dinner if you must, but do not derange my digestion; rather a damp bed than thorns in the pillow.'"

"I am to say that you will see her, however," said she, with that matter-of-fact adhesiveness to the question that never would permit her to join in my digressions.

"Then I go under protest, Miss Herbert—under protest, and, as the lawyers say, without prejudice—that is, I go as a private gentleman, irresponsible and independent. Tell her this, and say, I know nothing of figures: arithmetic may suit the Board of Trade; in the Foreign Department we ignore it. You may add, too, if you like, that from what you have seen of me, I am of a haughty disposition, easily offended, and very vindictive—very!"

"But I really don't think this," said she, with a bewitching smile.

"Not to you, de——" I was nearly in it again : "not to you," said I, stammering and blushing till I felt on fire. I suspect that she saw all the peril of the moment, for she left the room hurriedly, on the pretext of asking Mrs. Keats to take more tea.

"She is sensible of your devotion, Potts; but is she touched by it? Has she said to herself, 'That man is my fate, my destiny—it is no use resisting him; dark and mysterious as he is, I am drawn towards him by an inscrutable sympathy'—or is she still struggling in the toils, muttering to her heart to be still, and to wait? Flutter away, gentle creature," said I, compassionately, "but ruffle not your lovely plumage too roughly; the bars of your cage are not the less impassable that they are invisible. You *shall* love me, and you *shall* be mine!"

To these rapturous fancies there now succeeded the far less captivating thought of Mrs. Keats, and an approaching interview. Can any reader explain why it is, that one sits in quiet admiration of some old woman by Teniers or Holbein, and never experiences any chagrin or impatience at trials which, if only represented in life, would be positively odious?

Why is it that art transcends nature, and that ugliness in
canvas is more endurable than ugliness in the flesh ? Now,
for my own part, I'd rather have faced a whole gallery of
the Dutch school, from Van Eyck to Verhagen, than have
confronted that one old lady who sat awaiting me in
No. 12.

Twice as I sat at my breakfast did François put in his
head, look at me, and retire without a word. "What is the
matter? What do you mean?" cried I, impatiently, at the
third intrusion.

"It is madam that wishes to know when monsieur will be
at leisure to go up-stairs to her."

I almost bounded on my chair with passion. How was I,
I would ask, to maintain any portion of that dignity with
which I ought to surround myself if exposed to such demands as this? This absurd old woman would tear off every
illusion in which I draped myself. What availed all the
romance a rich fancy could conjure up, when that wicked old
enchantress called me to her presence, and in a voice of
thunder said, " Strip off these masqueradings, Potts, I know
the whole story."   " Ay, but," thought I, " she cannot do so:
of me and my antecedents she knows positively nothing."
" Halt there ! " interposes Conscience ; " it is quite enough to
pronounce the coin base without being able to say at what
mint it was fabricated. She knows you, Potts, she knows
you."

There is one great evil in castle-building, and I have
thought very long and anxiously, and I must own fruitlessly
over, how to meet it : it is that one never can get a lease of
the ground to build on. One is always like an Irish cottier,
a tenant at will, likely to be turned out at a moment's
notice, and dispossessed without pity or compassion. The
same language applies to each : "You know well, my good
fellow, you had no right to be there; pack up and be off !"
It's no use saying that it was a bit of waste land unfenced
and untilled; that, until you took it in hand, it was overgrown with nettles and duckweed ; that you dispossessed no
one, and such like. The answer is still the same, " Where's
your title ? Where's your lease ? "

Now, I am curious to hear what injury I was inflicting
on that old woman at No. 12 by any self-deceptions of

mine ? Could the most exaggerated estimate I might form of myself, my present, or my future, in any degree affect *her ?* Who constituted her a sort of ambulatory con-science, to call people's hearts to account at a moment's notice ? It may be seen by the tone of these reflections, that I was fully impressed with the belief through some channel, or by some clue, Mrs. Keats knew all my history, and intended to use her knowledge tyrannically over me.

Oh, that I could only retaliate ! Oh, that I had only the veriest fragment of her past life, out of which to con-struct her whole story. Just as out of a mastodon's molar, Cuvier used to build up the whole monster, never omitting a rib, nor forgetting a vertebra ! How I should like to say to her, and with a most significant sigh, " I knew poor Keats well ! " Could I not make even these simple words convey a world of accusation, blended with sorrow and regret ?

François again, and on the same errand. " Say I am coming ; that I have only finished a hasty breakfast, and that I am coming this instant," cried I. Nor was it very easy for me to repress the more impatient expressions which struggled for utterance, particularly as I saw, or fancied I saw, the fellow pass his hand over his mouth to hide a grin at my expense.

" Is Miss Herbert up stairs ? "

" No, Sir, she is in the garden."

This was so far pleasant. I dreaded the thought of her presence at this interview, and I felt that punishment within the precincts of the gaol was less terrible than on the drop before the populace; and with this consoling reflection I mounted the stairs.

CHAPTER XIX.

I KNOCKED twice before I heard the permission to enter; but scarcely had I closed the door behind me, than the old lady advanced, and curtseying to me with a manner of most reverential politeness, said, "When you learn, Sir, that my conduct has been dictated in the interest of your safety, you will, I am sure, graciously pardon many apparent rudenesses in my manner towards you, and only see in them my zeal to serve you."

I could only bow to a speech, not one syllable of which was in the least intelligible to me. She conducted me courteously to a seat, and only took her own after I was seated.

"I feel, Sir," said she, "that there will be no end to our embarrassments if I do not go straight to my object and say at once that I know you. I tell you frankly, Sir, that my brother did not betray your secret. The instincts of his calling—to *him* second nature—were stronger than fraternal love, and all he said to me was ' Martha, I have found a gentleman who is going south, and who, without inconvenience, can see you safely as far as Como.' I implicitly accepted his words, and agreed to set out immediately. I suspected nothing—I knew nothing. It was only before going down to dinner that the paragraph in the *Courrier du Dimanche* met my eye, and as I read it, I thought I should have fainted. My first determination was not to appear at dinner. I felt that something or other in my manner would betray my knowledge of your secret. My next was to go down and behave with more than usual sharpness. You may have remarked that I was very abrupt, almost, shall I say, rude ? "

I tried to enter a dissent to this, but did not succeed so happily as I meant ; but she resumed :—

"At any cost, however, Sir, I determined that I alone should be the depositary of your confidence. Miss Herbert is to me a comparative stranger ; she is, besides, very young ; she would be in no wise a suitable person to entrust with such a secret, and so I said, I will pretend illness, and remain here for a day ; I will make some pretext of dissatisfaction about the expense of the journey ; I will affect to have had some passing difference, and he can thus leave us ere he be discovered. Not that I desire this, Sir, far from it ; this is the brightest episode in a long life. I never imagined that I should have enjoyed such an honour ; but I have only to think of your safety, and if an old woman,

unobservant, and unremarking as myself, could penetrate
your disguise, why not others more keen-sighted and
inquisitive? Don't you agree with me?"

"There is much force in what you say, madam," said I,
with dignity, "and your words touch me profoundly." I
thought this a happy expression, for it conveyed a sort of
grand condescension that seemed to hit off the occasion.

"You would never guess how I recognised you, Sir,"
said she.

"Never, madam." I could have given my oath to this, if
required.

"Well," said she, with a bland smile, "it was from the
resemblance to your mother!"

"Indeed!"

"Yes; you are far more like *her*, than your father, and
you are scarcely so tall as he was."

"Perhaps not, madam."

"But you have his manner, Sir, the graceful and captivating dignity that distinguished all your house; this
would betray you to the eyes of all who have enjoyed the
high privilege of knowing your family."

The allusion to our house showed that we were royalties,
and I laid my hand on my heart, and bowed as a prince
ought, blandly but haughtily.

"Ah, Sir," said she, with a deep sigh, "your present
enterprise fills me with apprehension. Are you not afraid,
yourself, of the consequences?"

I sighed, too, and if the truth were to be told, I was very
much afraid.

"But, of course, you are acting under advice, and with the
counsel of those well able to guide you."

"I cannot say I am, madam; I am free to tell you that
every step I am now taking is self-suggested."

"Oh, then, let me implore you to pause, Sir," said she,
falling on her knees before me, "let me thus entreat of you
not to go further in a path so full of danger."

"Shall I confess, madam," said I, proudly, "that I do not
see these dangers you speak of."

I thought that on this hint she would talk out, and I
might be able to pierce the veil of the mystery, and discover
who I was; for though very like my mother, and shorter

than my father, I was sorely puzzled about my parentage,
but she only went off into generalities about the state of the
Continent and the condition of Europe generally.   I saw
now that my best chance of ascertaining something about
myself, was to obtain from her the newspaper that first
suggested her discovery of me, and I said half carelessly,
" Let me see the paragraph which struck you in the *Courrier*."

" Ah, Sir, you must excuse me, these ignoble writers have
little delicacy in alluding to the misfortunes of the great;
they seem to revenge the littleness of their own station on
every such occasion."

" You can well imagine, madam, how time has accustomed
me to such petty insults : show me the paper."

" Pray let me refuse you, Sir ; I would not, however
blamelessly, be associated in your mind with what might
offend you."

Again I protested that I was used to such attacks, that I
knew all about the wretched hireling creatures who wrote
them, and that instead of offending, they positively amused
me—actually made me laugh.

Thus urged, she proceeded to search for the newspaper,
and only after some minutes was it that she remembered
Miss Herbert had taken it away to read in the garden.   She
proposed to send the servant to fetch it, but this I would not
permit, pretending at last to concur in her own previously
expressed contempt for the paragraph—but secretly promising myself to go in search of it the moment I should be
at liberty—and once more she resumed the theme of my
rashness, and my dangers, and all the troubles I might
possibly bring upon my family, and the grief I might occasion
my grandmother.

Now as there are few men upon whom the ties of family
and kindred imposed less rigid bonds, I was rather provoked
at being reminded of obligations to my grandmother, and
was almost driven to declare that she weighed for very little
in the balance of my plans and motives.   The old lady, however, rescued me from the indiscretion by a fervent entreaty
that I would at least ask a certain person what he thought
of my present step.

" Will you do this ? " said she, with tears in her eyes.
" Will you do it, now ? "

I promised her faithfully.

"Will you do it here, Sir, at this table, and let me have the proudest memory in my life to recal the incident."

"I should like an hour or two for reflection," said I, pushed very hard by this insistence of hers, for I was sorely puzzled whom I was to write to.

"Oh," said she, still tearfully, "is it not the habit of hesitating, Sir, has cost your house so dearly?"

"No," said I, "we have been always accounted prompt in action and true to our engagements."

Heaven forgive me! but in this vain-glorious speech I was alluding to the motto of the Potts' crest, "*Vigilantibus omnia fausta;*" or, as some one rendered it, "Potts answers to the night-bell."

She smiled faintly at my remark. I wonder how she would have looked had she read the thought that suggested it.

"But you *will* write to him, Sir?" said she, once more.

I laid my hand over what anatomists call the region of the heart, and tried to look like Charles Edward in the prints. Meanwhile, my patience was beginning to fail me, and I felt that if the mystification were to last much longer, I should infallibly lose my presence of mind. Fortunately, the old lady was so full of her theme that she only asked to be let talk away without interruption, with many an allusion to the dear Count and the adored Duchess, and a fervent hope that I might be ultimately reconciled to them both, a wish which I had tact enough to perceive required the most guarded reserve on my part.

"I know I am indiscreet, Sir," said she, at last; "but you must pardon one whose zeal outruns her reason."

And I bowed grandly, as I might have done in extending mercy to some captive taken in battle.

"There is but one favour more, Sir, I have to beg."

"Speak it, madam. As the courtier remarked, if it be possible it *is* done, if impossible it *shall* be done."

"Well, Sir, it is that you will not leave us till you hear from —— " She hesitated as if afraid to say the name, and then added, "the Rue St. Georges. Will you give me this pledge?"

Now, thought this would have been, all things considered,

an arrangement very like to have lasted my life, I could
not help hesitating ere I assented, not to say that our dear
friend of the Rue St. Georges, whoever he was, might
possibly not concur in all the delusions indispensable to my
happiness. I therefore demurred—that is, in legal acceptance, I deferred assent—as though to say, " We'll see."

" At all events, Sir, you'll accompany us to Como ? "

" You have my pledge to that, madam."

" And meanwhile, Sir, you agree with me that it is better
I should continue to behave towards you with a cold and
distant reserve."

" Unquestionably."

" Rarely meeting, seldom or never conversing."

" I should say never, madam; making, in fact, any communication you may desire to reach me through the intervention of that young person—I forget her name."

" Miss Herbert, Sir."

" Exactly; and who appears gentle and unobtrusive."

" She is a gentlewoman by birth, Sir," said the old lady,
tetchily.

" I have no doubt of it, madam, or she would not be found
in association with *you*."

She curtseyed deeply at the compliment, and I bowed as
low, and backing and bowing I gained the door, dying with
eagerness to make my escape.

" Will you pardon me, Sir, if, after all the agitation of
this meeting, I may not feel equal to appear at dinner
to-day ? "

" You will charge that young person to give news of your
health, however," said I, insinuating that I expected to see
Miss Herbert.

" Certainly, Sir; and if it should be your pleasure that she
should dine with you, to preserve appearances —— "

" You are right, madam; your remark is full of wisdom.
I shall expect to meet her." And again I bowed low, and
ere she recovered from another reverential curtsey, I had
closed the door behind me, and was half-way down stairs.

CHAPTER XX.

As between the man who achieves greatness and him who has greatness thrust upon him there lies a whole world of space, so is there an immense interval between one who is the object of his own delusions and him who forms the subject of delusion to others.

My reader may have already noticed that nothing was easier for me than to lend myself to the idle current of my fancy. Most men who build " castles in Spain," as the old adage calls them, do so purely to astonish their friends. *I* indulged in these architectural extravagances in a very different spirit. I built my castle to live in it; from foundation to roof-tree, I planned every detail of it to suit my own taste, and all my study was to make it as habitable and comfortable as I could. Ay, and what's more, live in it I did, though very often the tenure was a brief one; sometimes while breaking my egg at breakfast, sometimes as I drew on my gloves to walk out, and yet no terror of a short lease ever deterred me from finishing the edifice in the most expensive manner. I gilded my architraves and frescoed my ceilings as though all were to endure for centuries; and laid out the gardens and disposed the parterres as though I were to walk in them in my extreme old age. This faculty of lending myself to an illusion by no means adhered to me where the deception was supplied by another; from the moment I entered one of *their* castles, I felt myself in a strange house. I continually forgot where the stairs were, what this gallery opened on, where that corridor led to. No use was it to say, " You are at home here. You are at your own fireside." I knew and I felt that I was not.

By this declaration, I mean my reader to understand that, while ready for any exigency of a story devised by myself, I was perfectly miserable at playing a part written for me by a friend; nor was this feeling diminished by the thought that I really did not know the person I was believed to re-

present; nor had I the very vaguest clue to his antecedents
or belongings.

As I set out in search of Miss Herbert, these were the reflections I revolved, occasionally asking myself, " Is the old
lady at all touched in the upper story ?   Is there not something Private Asylum-ish in these wanderings ? "   But still,
apart from this special instance, she was a marvel of acuteness and good sense.   I found Miss Herbert in a little
arbour at her work; the newspaper on the bench beside
her.

" So," said she, without looking up, " you have been
making a long visit up stairs.   You found Mrs. Keats very
agreeable, or you were so yourself."

" Is there anything wrong hereabouts ? " said I, touching
my forehead with my finger.

" Nothing whatever."

" No fancies, no delusions about certain people ? "

" None whatever."

" None of the family suspected of anything odd, or eccentric ? "

" Not that I have ever heard of.   Why do you ask? "

" Well, it was a mere fancy, perhaps, on my part; but
her manner to-day struck me as occasionally strange—
almost flighty."

" And on what subject ? "

" I am scarcely at liberty to say that; in fact, I am not at
all free to divulge it," said I, mysteriously, and somewhat
gratified to remark that I had excited a most intense curiosity
on her part to learn the subject of our interview.

" Oh, pray do not make any imprudent revelations to me,"
said she, pettishly; " which, apart from the indiscretion,
would have the singular demerit of affording me not the
slightest pleasure.   I am not afflicted with the malady of
curiosity."

" What a blessing to you !   Now, I am the most inquisitive of mankind.   I feel that if I were a clerk in a bank, I'd
spend the day prying into every one's account, and learning
the exact state of his balance-sheet.   If I were employed in
the post-office, no terror of the law could restrain me from
reading the letters.   Tell me that anyone has a secret in his
heart, and I feel I could cut him open to get at it ! "

"I don't think you are giving a flattering picture of yourself in all this," said she, peevishly.

"I am aware of that, Miss Herbert; but I am also one of those who do not trade upon qualities they have no pretension to."

She flushed a deep crimson at this, and after a moment said :

"Has it not occurred to you, Sir, that people who seldom meet except to exchange ungracious remarks, would show more judgment by avoiding each other's society?"

Ob, how my heart thrilled at this pettish speech! In Hans Grüter's "Courtship," he says, "I knew she loved me, for we never met without a quarrel." "I have thought of that too, Miss Herbert," said I, "but there are outward observances to be kept up, conventionalities to be respected."

"None of which, however, require that you should come out and sit here while I am at my work," said she, with suppressed passion.

"I came out here to search for the newspaper," said I, taking it up, and stretching myself on the grassy sward to read at leisure.

She arose at once, and gathering all the articles of her work into a basket, walked away.

"Don't let me hunt you away, Miss Herbert," said I, indolently; "anywhere else will suit me just as well. Pray don't go." But without vouchsafing to utter a word, or even turn her head, she continued her way towards the house.

"The morning she slapped my face," says Hans, " filled the measure of my bliss, for I then saw she could not control her feelings for me." This passage recurred to me as I lay there, and I hugged myself in the thought that such a moment of delight might yet be mine. The profound German explains this sentiment well. "With women," says he, "love is like the idol worship of an Indian tribe; at the moment their hearts are bursting with devotion, they like to cut and wound and maltreat their god. With *them*, this is the ecstasy of their passion."

I now saw that the girl was in love with me, and that she did not know it herself. I take it that the sensations of a man who suddenly discovers that the pretty girl he has been

admiring is captivated by his attentions, are very like what
a head clerk may feel at being sent for by the house, and informed that he is now one of the firm! This may seem a
commercial formula to employ, but it will serve to show my
meaning, and as I lay there on that velvet turf, what a delicious vision spread itself around me. At one moment we
were rich, travelling in splendour through Europe, amassing
art-treasures wherever we went, and despoiling all the great
galleries of their richest gems. I was the associate of all
that was distinguished in literature and science, and my
wife the chosen friend of queens and princesses. How un-
affected we were, how unspoiled by fortune! Approachable
by all, our graceful benevolence seemed to elevate its object
and make of the recipient the benefactor. What a world of
bliss this vile dross men call gold can scatter! "There—
there, good people," said I, blandly, waving my hand, "no
illuminations, no bonfires—your happy faces are the brightest
of all welcomes." Then we were suddenly poor—out of caprice just to see how we should like it—and living in a little
cottage under Snowden, and I was writing, Heaven knows
what, for the periodicals, and my wife rocking a little urchin
in a cradle, whom we constantly awoke by kissing, each pretending that it was all the other's fault, till we ratified a
peace in the same fashion. Then I remembered the night,
never to be forgotten, when I received my appointment as
something in the antipodes, and we went up to town to
thank the great man who bestowed it, and he asked us to
dinner, and he was, I fancied, more than polite to my wife,
and I sulked about it when we got home, and she petted and
caressed me, and we were better friends than ever, and I
swore I would not accept the minister's bounty, and we set
off back again to our cottage in Wales, and there we were
when I came to myself once more.

It is always pleasant—at least I have ever felt it so, on
awaking from a dream, or a reverie—to know that one has
borne himself well in some imaginary crisis of difficulty and
peril. I like to think that I was in no hurry to get into the
long-boat. I am glad I gave poor Dick that last fifty-pound
note—my last in the world—and I rejoice to remember that
I did not run away from that grizzly bear, but sent the four-
pound ball right into the very middle of his forehead. You

feel in all these that the metal of your nature has been tested, and come out pure gold : at all events, *I* did, and was very happy thereat. It was not till after some little time that I could get myself clear out of dreamland, and back to the actual world of small debts and difficulties, and then I bethought me of the newspaper which lay unread beside me.

I began it now, resolved to examine it from end to end, till I discovered the passage that alluded to me. It was so far pleasant reading, that it was novel and original. A very able leader set forth that nothing could equal the blessings of the Pope's rule at Rome—no people were so happy—so prosperous—or so contented—that all the granaries were full, and all the gaols empty, and the only persons of small incomes in the state were the cardinals, and that they were too heavenly-minded to care for it. After this, there came some touching anecdotes of that good man the late King of Naples. And then there was a letter from Frohsdorf, with fifteen francs enclosed to the inhabitants of a village submerged by an inundation. There were pleasant little paragraphs, too, about England, and all the money she was spending to propagate infidelity and spread the slave-trade —the two great and especial objects of her policy—after which came insults to France and injustice to Ireland. The general tone of the print was war with everyone but some twenty or thirty old ladies and gentlemen living in exile somewhere in Bohemia. Now none of these things touched *me*, and I was growing very weary of my search when I lighted upon the following :

" We are informed, on authority that we cannot question, that the young C. de P. is now making the tour of Germany alone and in disguise, his object being to ascertain for himself, how the various relatives of his house, on the maternal side, would feel affected by any movement in France to renew his pretensions. Strange, undignified, and ill advised as such a step must seem, there is nothing in it at all repulsive to the well-known traditions of the younger branch. Our informant himself met the P. at Mayence, and speedily recognised him, from the marked resemblance he bears to the late duchess, his mother ; he addressed him at once by his title, but was met by the cold assurance that he was mis-

taken, and that a casual similarity in features had already
led others into the same error. The general—for our informant is an old and honoured soldier of France—confessed
he was astounded at the *aplomb* and self-possession displayed
by so young a man; and although their conversation lasted
for nearly an hour, and ranged over a wide field, the C. never
'or an instant exposed himself to a detection, nor offered the
slightest clue to his real rank and station. Indeed, he
affected to be English by birth, which his great facility in
the language enabled him to do. When he quitted Mayence
it was for Central Germany."

Here was the whole mystery revealed, and I was no less a
person than a royal prince—very like my mother, but neither
so tall nor robust as my distinguished father! " Oh, Potts!
in all the wildest ravings of your most florid moments you
never arrived at this!"

A very strange thrill went through me as I finished this
paragraph. It came this wise. There is, in one of Hoffman's tales, the story of a man who, in a compact with the
Fiend, acquired the power of personating whomsoever he
pleased, but who, sated at last with the enjoyment of this
privilege, and eager for a new sensation, determined he
would try whether the part of the Devil himself might not
be amusing. Apparently Mephistopheles won't stand joking,
for he resented the liberty by depriving the transgressor of
his identity for ever, and made him become each instant
whatever character occurred to the mind of him he talked
to.

Though the parallel scarcely applied, the very thought of
it sent an anguish thrill through me—a terror so great and
acute that it was very long before I could turn the medal
round and read it on the reverse. There, indeed, was matter
for vain-glory! " It was but t'other day," thought I, " and
Lord Keldrum and his friends fancied I was their intimate
acquaintance, Jack Burgoyne; and though they soon found
out the mistake, the error led to an invitation to dinner, a
delightful evening, and, alas! that I should own, a variety
of consequences, some of which proved less delightful. Now,
however, Fortune is in a more amiable mood : she will have
it that I resemble a prince. It is a project which I neither
aid nor abet; but I am not churlish enough to refuse the

rôle any more than I should spoil the Christmas revelries of a country-house by declining a part in a tableau, or in private theatricals. I say, in the one case as in the other, 'Here is Potts! make of him what you will. Never is he happier than by affording pleasure to his friends.' To what end, I would ask, should I rob that old lady up-stairs at No. 12, evidently a widow, and with not too many enjoyments to solace her old age—why should I rob her of what she herself called the proudest episode in her life? Are not, as the moralists tell us, all our joys fleeting? Why, then, object to this one that it may only last for a few days? Let us suppose it only to endure throughout our journey, and the poor old soul will be so happy, never caring for the fatigues of the road, never fretting about the innkeepers' charges, but delighted to know that his royal highness enjoys himself, and sits over his bottle of Chambertin every evening in the garden, apparently as devoid of care as though he were a bagman."

I cannot say how it may be with others, but, for myself, I have always experienced an immense sense of relief, actual repose, whenever I personated somebody else; I felt as though I had left the man Potts at home to rest and refresh himself, and took an airing as another gentleman; just as I might have spared my own paletot by putting on a friend's coat in a thunderstorm. Now I *did* wish for a little repose, I felt it would be good for me. As to the special part allotted me, I took it just as an obliging actor plays Hamlet or the Cock to convenience the manager. Mrs. Keats likes it, and, I repeat, I do not object to it.

It was evident that the old lady was not going to communicate her secret to her companion, and this was a great source of satisfaction to me. Whatever delusions I threw around Miss Herbert I intended should be lasting. The traits in which I would invest myself to *her* eyes, my personal prowess, coolness in danger, skill in all manly exercises, together with a large range of general gifts and acquirements, I meant to accompany me through all time, and I am a sufficient believer in magnetism to feel assured that by imposing upon *her* I should go no small part of the road to deceiving myself, and that the first step in any gift is to suppose you are eminently suited to it, is a well-known

12

and readily acknowledged maxim.   Women grow pretty from looking in the glass; why should not men grow brave from constantly contemplating their own courage ?

"Yes, Potts, be a Prince, and see how it will agree with you!"

~~~~~~~~~~~~~~

CHAPTER XXI.

MRS. KEATS came down, and our dinner that day was some-what formal.   I don't think any of us felt quite at ease, and, for my own part, it was a relief to me when the old lady asked my leave to retire after her coffee.   "If you should feel lonely, Sir, and if Miss Herbert's company would prove agreeable —— "

"Yes," said I, languidly, "that young person will find me in the garden."   And therewith I gave my orders for a small table under a great weeping-ash, and the usual accom-paniment of my after-dinner hours, a cool flask of Chamber-tin.   I had time to drink more than two-thirds of my Bur-gundy before Miss Herbert appeared.   It was not that the hour hung heavily on me, or that I was not in a mood of considerable enjoyment, but, somehow, I was beginning to feel chafed and impatient at her long delay.   Could she possibly have remonstrated against the impropriety of being left alone with a young man ?   Had she heard, by any mis-chance, that impertinent phrase by which I designated her? Had Mrs. Keats herself resented the cool style of my per-mission by a counter-order ?   "I wish I knew what detains her !" cried I to myself, just as I heard her step on the gravel, and then saw her coming, in very leisurely fashion, up the walk.

Determined to display an indifference the equal of her own, I waited till she was almost close; and then, rising languidly, I offered her a chair with a superb air of Brummelism, while I listlessly said, "Won't you take a seat?"

It was growing duskish, but I fancied I saw a smile on her lip as she sat down.

"May I offer you a glass of wine, or a cigar?" said I, carelessly.

"Neither, thank you," said she, with gravity.

"Almost all women of fashion smoke, now-a-days," I resumed. "The Empress of the French smokes this sort of thing here; and the Queen of Bavaria smokes and chews."

She seemed rebuked at this, and said nothing.

"As for myself," said I, "I am nothing without tobacco —positively nothing. I remember one night—it was the fourth sitting of the Congress at Paris—that Sardinian fellow, you know his name, came to me and said,

"'There's that confounded question of the Danubian Provinces coming on to-morrow, and Gortschakoff is the only one who knows anything about it. Where are we to get at anything like information?'

"'When do you want it, count?' said I.

"'To-morrow, by eleven at latest. There must be at least a couple of hours to study it before the Congress meets.'

"'Tell them to bring in ten candles, fifty cigars, and two quires of foolscap,' said I; 'and let no one pass this door till I ring.' At ten minutes to eleven next morning he had in his hands that memoir which Lord C. said embodied the prophetic wisdom of Edmund Burke with the practical statesmanship of the great Commoner. Perhaps you have read it?"

"No, Sir."

"Your tastes do not probably incline to affairs of state. If so, only suggest what you'd like to talk on. I am indifferently skilled in most subjects. Are you for the poets? I am ready, from Dante to the Bigelow Papers. Shall it be arts? I know the whole thing from Memmling and his long-nosed saints, to Leech and the Punchists. Make it antiquities, agriculture, trade, dress, the drama, conchology, or cock-fighting—I'm your man; so go in, and don't be afraid that you'll disconcert me."

"I assure you, Sir, that my fears would attach far more naturally to my own insufficiency."

12—2

"Well," said I, after a pause, "there's something in that. Macaulay used to be afraid of me. Whenever Mrs. Montagu Stanhope asked him to one of her Wednesday dinners, he always declined if I was to be there. You don't seem surprised at that?"

"No, Sir," said she, in the same quiet, grave fashion.

"What's the reason, young lady," said I, somewhat sternly, "that you persist in saying 'Sir' on every occasion that you address me? The ease of that intercourse that should subsist between us is marred by this Americanism. The pleasant interchange of thought loses the charming feature of equality. How is this?"

"I am not at liberty to say, Sir."

"You are not at liberty to say, young lady?" said I, severely. "You tell me distinctly that your manner towards me is based upon a something which you must not reveal?"

"I am sure, Sir, you have too much generosity to press me on a subject of which I cannot, or ought not, to speak."

That fatal Burgundy had got into my brains, while the princely delusion was uppermost; and if I had been submitted to the thumbscrew now, I would have died one of the Orleans family. "Mademoiselle," said I, grandly, "I have been fortunately, or unfortunately, brought up in a class that never tolerates contradiction. When we ask, we feel that we order."

"Oh, Sir, if you but knew the difficulty I am in —— "

"Take courage, my dear creature," said I, blending condescension with something warmer. "You will at least be reposing your confidence where it will be worthily bestowed."

"But I have promised, not exactly promised, but Mrs. Keats enjoined me imperatively not to betray what she revealed to me."

"Gracious Powers!" cried I, "she has not surely communicated my secret—she has not told you who I am?"

"No, Sir, I assure you most solemnly, that she has not; but being annoyed by what she remarked as the freedom of my manner towards you at dinner, the readiness with which I replied to your remarks, and what she deemed the want of deference I displayed for them, she took me to task this evening, and without intending it, even before she knew, dropped certain expressions which showed me that you were one of the very highest in rank, though it was your pleasure to travel for the moment in this obscurity and disguise. She quickly perceived the indiscretion she had committed, and said, 'Now, Miss Herbert, that an accident has put you in possession of certain circumstances, which I had neither the will nor the right to reveal, will you do me the inestimable favour to employ this knowledge in such a way as may not compromise me.' I told her, of course, that I would; and having remarked how she occasionally—inadvertently, per-haps—used 'Sir,' in addressing you, I deemed the imitation a safe one, while it as constantly acted as a sort of monitor over myself to repress any relapse into familiarity."

"I am very sorry for all this," said I, taking her hand in mine, and employing my most insinuating of manners to-wards her. "As it is more than doubtful that I shall ever resume the station that once pertained to me; as, in fact, it may be my fortune to occupy for the rest of life an humble and lowly condition, my ambition would have been to draw towards me in that modest station such sympathies and affections as might attach to one so circumstanced. My plan was to assume an obscure name, seek out some un-frequented spot, and there, with the love of one—one only—solve the great problem, whether happiness is not as much the denizen of the thatched cottage as of the gilded palace. The first requirement of my scheme was that my secret should be in my own keeping. One can steel his own heart against vain regrets and longings; but one cannot secure himself against the influence of those sympathies which come from without, the unwise promptings of zealous followers, the hopes and wishes of those who read your sub-mission as mere apathy."

I paused and sighed; she sighed too, and there was a silence between us.

"Must she not feel very happy and very proud," thought I, "to be sitting there on the same bench with a prince, her hand in his, and he pouring out all his confidence in her ear? I cannot fancy a situation more full of interest."

"After all, Sir," said she, calmly, "remember that Mrs. Keats alone knows your secret. I have not the vaguest suspicion of it."

"And yet," said I, tenderly, "it is to *you* I would confide it; it is iu *your* keeping I would wish to leave it; it is from *you* I would ask counsel as to my fnture."

"Surely, Sir, it is not to such inexperience as mine you would address yourself in a difficulty?"

"The plan I would carry out demands none of that crafty argnment called 'knowing the world.' All that acquaintance with the by-play of life, its conventionalities and exactions, would be sadly out of place in an Alpine village, or a Tyrolese Dorf, where I mean to pitch my tent. Do you not think that your interest might be persuaded to track me so far?"

"Oh, Sir, I shall never cease to follow your steps with the deepest anxiety."

"Would it not be possible for me to secure a lease of that sympathy?"

"Can you tell me what o'clock it is, Sir?" said she, very gravely.

"Yes," said I, rather put out by so sudden a diversion; "it is a few minutes after nine."

"Pray excuse my leaving you, Sir, but Mrs. Keats takes her tea at nine, and will expect me." And, with a very respectful curtsey, she withdrew, before I could recover my astonishment at this abrupt departnre.

"I trust that my royal highness said nothing indiscreet," muttered I to myself; "though, upon my life, this hasty exit would seem to imply it."

CHAPTER XXII.

WE continued our journey the next morning, but it was not without considerable difficulty that I succeeded in maintainiug my former place in the cabriolet. That stupid old woman faucied that princes were born to be bored, and snggested accordingly that I should travel iuside with her; leaving the macaw and the toy terriers to keep company

with Miss Herbert. It was not only by insisting on an outside place as a measure of health that I at last prevailed,
telling her that Dr. Corvisart was peremptory on two points
regarding me. "Let him," said he, "have abundance of
fresh air, and never be without some young companion."

And so we were again in our little leathern tent, high up
in the fresh breezy atmosphere, above dusty roads, and with
a glorious view over that lovely country that forms the
approach to the Black Forest. The road was hilly, and the
carriage-way a heavy one, but we had six horses who trotted
along briskly, shaking their merry bells, and flourishing their
scarlet tassels, while the postillions cracked their whips or
broke out into occasional bugle performances, principally
intended to announce to the passing peasants that we were
very great folk, and well able to pay for all the noise we required.

I was not ashamed to confess my enjoyment in thus
whirling along at some ten miles the hour, remembering
how that great sage Dr. Johnson had confessed to a like
pleasure, and animated by the inspiriting air and the lovely
landscape, could not help asking Miss Herbert if she did not
feel it "very jolly?"

She assented with a sort of constrained curtsey that by no
means responded to the warmth of my own sensations, and I
felt vexed and chafed accordingly.

"Perhaps you prefer travelling inside?" said I, with some
pique.

"No, Sir."

"Perhaps you dislike travelling altogether?"

"No, Sir."

"Perhaps ——', But I checked myself—and, with a
somewhat stiff air, I said, "Would you like a book?"

"If it would not be rude to read, Sir, while you ——"

"Oh, not at all, never mind me, I have more than enough
to think of. Here are some things by Dumas, and Paul
Féval, and some guide-book trash." And with that I handed
her several volumes, and sank back into my corner in sulky
isolation.

Here was a change! Ten minutes ago all nature smiled
on me; from the lark in the high heavens to the chirping
grasshopper in the tall maize-field, it was one song of joy

and gladness. The very clouds as they swept past threw
new and varied light over the scene, as though to show fresh
effects of beauty on the landscape—the streams went by in
circling eddies, like smiles upon a lovely face—and now all
was sad and crape-covered! "What has wrought this
dreary change?" thought I; "is it possible that the cold
looks of a young woman, good-looking, I grant, but no regular downright beauty after all, can have altered the aspect
of the whole world to you? Are you so poor a creature in
yourself, Potts, so beggared in your own resources, so barren
in all the appliances of thought and reflection, that if your
companion, whoever she or he may be, sulk, you must needs
reflect the humour? Are you nothing but the mirror that
displays what is placed before it?"

I set myself deliberately to scan the profile beside me;
her black veil, drawn down on the side furthest from me,
formed a sort of back-ground, which displayed her pale
features more distinctly. All about the brow and orbit was
beautifully regular, but the mouth was, I fancied, severe;
there was a slight retraction of the upper lip that seemed to
imply over-firmness, and then the chin was deeply indented
—"a sign," Lavater says, "of those who have a will of their
own." "Potts," thought I, "she'd rule you—that's a nature
would speedily master yours. I don't think there's any
softness either, any of that yielding gentleness there, that
makes the poetry of womanhood ; besides, I suspect she's
worldly—those sharply-cut nostrils are very worldly! She
is, in fact,"—and here I unconsciously uttered my thoughts
aloud—"she is, in fact, one to say, 'Potts, how much have
you got a-year? Let us have it in figures.'"

"So you are still ruminating over the life of that interesting creature," said she, laying down her book to laugh ;
"and shall I confess, I lay awake half the night, inventing
incidents and imagining situations for him."

"For whom?" said I, innocently.

"For Potts, of course. I cannot get him out of my head
such as I first fancied he might be, and I see now, by your
unconscious allusion to him, that he has his place in your
imagination also."

"You mistake, Miss Herbert—at least you very much
misapprehend my conception of that character. The Potts

family has a high historic traditior Si.' Constantine Potts
was cup-bearer to Henry II., and I really see no reason why
ridicule should attach to one who may be, most probably,
his descendant."

"I'm very sorry, Sir, if I should have dared to differ with
you ; but when I heard the name first, and in connection
with two such names as Algernon Sydney, and when I
thought by what strange accident did they ever meet in the
one person ———"

"You are very young, Miss Herbert, and therefore not removed from the category of the teachable," said I, with a
grand didactic look. "Let me guard you, therefore, against
the levity of chance inferences. What would you say if a
person named Potts were to make the offer of his hand ? I
mean, if he were a man in all respects acceptable, a gentleman captivating in manner and address, agreeable in person,
graceful and accomplished—what would you reply to his
advances ? "

"Really, Sir, I am shocked to think of the humble opinion
I may be conveying of my sense and judgment, but I'm afraid
I should tell him it is impossible I could ever permit myself
to be called Mrs. Potts."

"But, in Heaven's name, why ?—I ask you why ? "

"Oh, Sir ! don't be angry with me ; it surely does not
deserve such a penalty ; at the worst, it is a mere caprice on
my part."

"I am not angry, young lady, I am simply provoked; I
am annoyed to think that a prejudice so unworthy of you
should exercise such a control over your judgment."

"I am quite ashamed, Sir, to have been the occasion of so
much displeasure to you. I hope and trust you will ascribe
it to my ignorance of life and the world."

"If you are dissatisfied with yourself, Miss Herbert, I have
no more to say," said I, taking up a book, and pretending to
read, while I felt such a disgust with myself, that if I hadn't
been strapped up with a leather apron up to my chin, I
think I should have thrown myself headlong down and let
the wheel pass over me. "What is it, Potts, that is corrupt-
ing and destroying the naturally fine and noble nature you
are certainly endowed with ? Is it this confounded elevation
to princely rank ? If you were not a royal highness would

you have dared to utter such cruelties as these? Would you, in your most savage of moods, have presumed to make that pale cheek paler, and forced a tear-drop into that liquid eye? I always used to think that the greatest effort of a man was to keep him on a level with those born above him. I now find it is far harder to stoop than to stand on tip-toe. Such a pain in the back comes of always bending, and it is so difficult to do it gracefully!"

I was positively dying to be what the French call "*bon prince*," and yet I didn't know how to set about it. I could not take off one of my decorations—a cross, or a ribbon—for I had none; nor give it, because she, being a woman, couldn't wear it. I couldn't make her one of the court ladies, for there was no court; and yet it was clear something should be done, if one only knew what it was. "I suppose now," said I to myself, "a real R.H. would see his way here at once; the right thing to do, the exact expression to use would occur as naturally to his mind as all this embarrassment presents itself to mine. 'Whenever your head cannot guide you,' says a Spanish proverb, 'ask your heart;' and so I did, and my heart spoke thus: 'Tell her, Potts, who you are, and what; say to her, "Listen, young lady, to the words of truth from one who could tell you far more glibly, far more freely, and far more willingly, a whole bushel of lies. It will sit light on his heart that he deceive the old lady inside, but *you* he cannot, will not deceive. Do not deem the sacrifice a light one; it cost St. George far less to go out dragon-hunting than it costs me to slay this small monster who ever prompts me to feats of fancy." ' "

"I am very sorry to be troublesome, Sir, but as we change horses here, I will ask you to assist me to alight; the weather looks very threatening, and some drops of rain have already fallen."

These words roused me from my reverie to action, and I got down, not very dexterously either, for I slipped, and made the postillion laugh, and then I helped her, who accomplished the descent so neatly, so gracefully, showing the least portion of such an ankle, and accidently giving me such a squeeze of the hand! The next moment she was lost to me, the clanking steps were drawn up, the harsh door banged to, and I was alone—all alone in the world.

Like a sulky eagle, sick of the world, I climbed up to my eyrie. I no longer wished for sunshine or scenery ; nay, I was glad to see the postboys put on their overcoats and prepare for a regular down-pour. I liked to think there are some worse off than even Potts. In half-an-hour *they* will be drenched to the skin, and I'll not feel a drop of it!

The little glass slide at my back was now withdrawn, and Miss Herbert's pale, sweet face appeared at it. She was saying that Mrs. Keats urgently entreated I would come inside, that she was so uneasy at my being exposed to such a storm.

I refused, and was about to enter into an account of my ascent of Mont Blanc, when the slide was closed and my listener lost to me.

" Is it possible, Potts," said I, " that she has detected this turn of yours for the imaginative line, and that she will not encourage it, even tacitly ? Has she said, ' There is a young man of genius, gifted marvellously with the richest qualities, and yet such is the exuberance of his fancy that he is positively its slave. Not content to let him walk the earth like other men, she attaches wings to him, and carries him off into the upper air. I will endeavour, however hard the task, to clip his feathers and bring him back to the common haunts of men.' Try it, fair enchantress—try it! "

The rain was now coming down in torrents, and with such swooping gusts ot wind, that I was forced to fasten the leather curtain in front of me, and sit in utter darkness, denied even the passing pleasure of seeing the drenched postboys bobbing up and down on the wet saddles. I grew moody and sad. Every Blue Devil of my acquaintance came to pay his visit to me, and brought a few more of his private friends. I bethought me that I was hourly travelling away further and further from my home; that all this long road must surely be retraced one day or other, though not in a carriage and post, but probably in a one-horse cart, with a mounted gendarme on either side of it, and a string to my two wrists in their bridle hands. I thought of that vulgar herd of mankind so ready to weep over a romance, and yet send the man who acts one to a penal settlement. I thought how I should be described as the artful knave, the accomplished swindler. As if I was the first man who ever took

an exaggerated estimate of his own merits! Go into the
House of Commons, visit the National Gallery, dine at a bar
or a military mess, frequent, in one word, any of the haunts
of men, and with what *piéces pour servir à l'histoire* of self-
deception will you come back loaded!

The sliding window at my back was again drawn aside,
and I heard Miss Herbert's voice:

"If I am not giving you too much trouble, Sir, would you
kindly see if I have not dropped a bracelet—a small jet
bracelet—in the *coupé?*"

"I'm in the dark here, but I'll do my best to find
it."

"We are very nearly so too," said she; "and Mrs. Keats
is fast asleep, quite unmindful of the thunder."

With some struggling I managed to get down on my
knees, and was soon engaged in a very vigorous search.
To aid me, I lighted a lucifer match, and by its flickering
glare I saw right in front of me that beautiful pale face, enclosed as it were in a frame by the little window. She
blushed at the fixedness of my gaze, for I utterly forgot
myself in my admiration, and stared as though at a picture.
My match went out, and I lit another. Alas! there she
was still, and I could not force myself to turn away, but
gazed on in rapture.

"I'm sorry to give you this trouble, Sir," said she, in
some confusion. "Pray never mind it. It will doubtless
be found this evening when we arrive."

Another lucifer, and now I pretended to be in most eager
pursuit; but somehow my eyes would look up and rest upon
her sweet countenance.

"A diamond bracelet, you said?" muttered I, not knowing what I was saying.

"No, Sir, mere jet, and of no value whatever, save to
myself. I am really distressed at all the inconvenience I
have occasioned you. I entreat you to think no more of it."

My match was out and I had not another. "Was ever a
man robbed of such ecstasy for a mere pennyworth of stick
and a little sulphur? O Fortune! is not this downright
cruelty?"

As I mumbled my complaints, I searched away with an
honest zeal, patting the cushions all over, and poking away

into most inscrutable pockets and recesses, while she, in a most beseeching tone, apologised for her request and besought me to forget it.

"Found! found!" cried I, in true delight, as I chanced upon the treasure at my feet.

"Oh, Sir, you have made me *so* happy, and I am so much obliged, and so grateful to you!"

"Not another word, I beseech you," whispered I; "you are actually turning my head with ecstasy. Give me your hand, let me clasp it on your arm, and I am repaid."

"Will you kindly pass it to me, Sir, through the window?" said she, timidly.

"Ah!" cried I, in anguish, "your gratitude has been very fleeting."

She muttered something I could not catch, but I heard the rustle of her sleeve against the window-frame, and dark as it was, pitch dark, I knew her hand was close to me. Opening the bracelet, I passed it round her wrist as reverently as though it were the arm of a Queen of Spain, one touch of whom is high treason. I trembled so, that it was some seconds before I could make the clasp meet. This done, I felt she was withdrawing her hand, when with something like that headlong impulse by which men set their lives on one chance, I seized the fingers in my grasp, and implanted two rapturous kisses on them. She snatched her hand hastily away, closed the window with a sharp bang, and I was alone once more in my darkness, but in such a flutter of blissful delight that even the last reproving gesture could scarcely pain me. It mattered little to me that day that the lightning felled a great pine and threw it across the road, that the torrents were so swollen that we only could pass them with crowds of peasants around the carriage with ropes and poles to secure it, that four oxen were harnessed in front of our leaders to enable us to meet the hurricane, or that the postboys were paid treble their usual fare for all their perils to life and limb. I cared for none of these. Enough for me that, on this day, I can say with Schiller,

> "Ich habe genossen das irdische Glück,
> Ich habe gelebt und geliebt!"

CHAPTER XXIII.

WE arrived at a small inn on the borders of the Titi-see at
nightfall; and though the rain continued to come down un-
ceasingly, and huge masses of cloud hung half way down
the mountain, I could see that the spot was highly picturesque
and romantic.   Before I could descend from my lofty eminence, so strapped and buttoned and buckled up was I, the
ladies had time to get out and reach their rooms.   When I
asked to be shown mine, the landlord, in a very free-and-easy
tone, told me that there was nothing for me but a double-
bedded room, which I must share with another traveller.   I
scouted this proposition at once with a degree of force and,
indeed, of violence, that I fancied must prove irresistible;
but the stupid German, armed with native impassiveness,
simply said, "Take it or leave it, it's nothing to me," and
left me to look after his business.   I stormed and fumed.   I
asked the chambermaid if she knew who I was, and sent for
the Hausknecht to tell him that all Europe should ring with
this indignity.   I more than hinted that the landlord had
sealed his own doom, and that his miserable cabaret had seen
its last days of prosperity.

I asked next, where was the Jew pedlar?   I felt certain
he was a fellow with pencil-cases and pipe-heads, who owned
the other half of the territory.   Could he not be bought up?
He would surely sleep in the cow-house, if it were too wet to
go up a tree!

François came to inform me that he was out fishing; that
he fished all day, and only came home after dark; his man
had told him so much.

" His man?   Why, has he a servant?" asked I.

" He's not exactly like a servant, Sir; but a sort of peasant
with a green jacket and a tall hat and leather gaiters, like a
Tyrolese."

"Strolling actors, I'll be sworn," muttered I; "fellows

taking a week's holiday on their way to a new engagement. How long have they been here?"

"Came on Monday last in the diligence, and are to remain till the twentieth; two florins a-day they give for everything."

"What nation are they?"

"Germans, Sir, regular Germans; never a pipe out of their mouths, master and man. I learned all this from his servant, for they have put up a bed for me in his room."

A sudden thought now struck me: "Why should not François give up his bed to this stranger, and occupy the one in my room?" This arrangement would suit me better, and it ought to be all the same to Hamlet or Goetz, or whatever he was. "Just lounge about the door, François," said I, "till he comes back; and when you see him, open the thing to him, civilly, of course; and if a crown piece, or even two, will help the negotiation, slip it slyly into his hand. You understand?"

François winked like a man who had corrupted customhouse officers in his time, and even bribed bigger functionaries at a pinch.

"If he's in trade, you know, François, just hint that if he sends in his pack in the course of the evening, the ladies might possibly take a fancy to something."

Another wink.

"And throw out—vaguely, of course, very vaguely—that we are swells, but in strict *incog.*"

A great scoundrel was François; he was a Swiss, and could cheat anyone, and, like a regular rogue, never happier than when you gave him a mission of deceit or duplicity. In a word, when I gave him his instructions, I regarded the negotiation as though it were completed, and now addressed myself to the task of looking after our supper, which, with national obstinacy, the landlord declared could not be ready before nine o'clock. As usual, Mrs. Keats had gone to bed immediately on arriving; but when sending me a "Good night" by her maid, she added, "that whenever supper was served, Miss Herbert would come down."

We had no sitting-room save the common room of the inn, a long, low-ceilinged, dreary chamber, with a huge green-tile stove in one corner, and down the centre a great oak table,

which might have served about forty guests. At one end of
this three covers were laid for us, the napkins enclosed in
bone circlets, and the salt in great leaden receptacles—like
big ink bottles—a very ancient brass lamp, giving its dim
radiance over all. It was wearisome to sit down on the
straight-backed wooden chairs, and not less irksome to walk
on the gritty, sanded floor, and so I lounged in one of the
windows, and watched the rain. As I looked, I saw the
figure of a man with a fishing-basket and rod on his shoulder
approaching the house. I guessed at once it was our stranger,
and opening the window a few inches, I listened to hear the
dialogue between him and François. The window was
enclosed in the same porch as the door, so that I could hear
a good deal of what passed. François accosted him familiarly, questioned him as to his sport, and the size of the fish
he had taken. I could not hear the reply, but I remarked
that the stranger emptied his basket, and was dispatching
the contents in different directions; some were for the curé,
and some for the postmaster, some for the brigadier of the
gendarmerie, and one large trout for the miller's daughter.

"A good-looking wench, I'll be sworn," said François, as
he heard the message delivered.

Again the stranger said something, and I thought, from
the tone, angrily, and François responded; and then I saw
them walk apart for a few seconds, during which François
seemed to have all the talk to himself, a good omen, as it
appeared to me, of success, and a sure warranty that the
treaty was signed. François, however, did not come to
report progress, and so I closed the window and sat
down.

"So you have got company to-night, Master Ludwig,"
said the stranger, as he entered, followed by the host, who
speedily seemed to whisper that one of the arrivals was then
before him. The stranger bowed stiffly, but courteously to
me, which I returned not less haughtily; and I now saw that
he was a man about thirty-five, but much freckled, with a
light-brown beard and moustache. On the whole, a good-
looking fellow, with a very upright carriage, and something
of a cavalry soldier in the swing of his gait.

"Would you like it at once, Herr Graf?" said the host,
obsequiously.

"Oh, he's a count, is he?" said I, with a sneer to myself. "These countships go a short way with me."

"You had better consult your other guests; I am ready when they are," said the stranger.

Now, though the speech was polite, and even considerate, I lost sight of the courtesy in thinking that it implied we were about to sup in common, and that the third cover was meant for him.

"I say, landlord," said I, "you don't intend to tell me that you have no private sitting-room, but that ladies of condition must needs come down and sup here with "—I was going to say, "Heaven knows who;" but I halted, and said —"with the general company."

"That, or nothing!" was the sturdy response. "The guests in this house eat here, or don't eat at all; eh, Herr Graf?"

"Well, so far as my experience goes, I can corroborate you," said the stranger, laughing. "Though, you may remember, I have often counselled you to make some change."

"That you have; but I don't want to be better than my father and my grandfather; and the Arch-Duke Charles stopped here in their time, and never quarrelled with his treatment."

I told the landlord to apprise the young lady whenever supper was ready, and I walked to a distant part of the room and sat down.

In about two minutes after, Miss Herbert appeared, and the supper was served at once. I had not met her since the incident of the bracelet, and I was shocked to see how cold she was in her manner, and how resolute in repelling the most harmless familiarity towards her.

I wanted to explain to her that it was through no fault of mine we were to have the company of that odious stranger, that it was one of the disagreeables of these wayside hostels, and to be borne with patience, and that though he was a stage-player, or a sergeant of dragoons, he was reasonably well-bred and quiet. I did contrive to mumble out some of this explanation, but, instead of attending to it, I saw her eyes following the stranger, who had just draped a large riding-cloak over a clothes-horse behind her chair, to serve

13

as a screen. Thanks are all very well, but I'm by no means
certain that gratitude requires such a sweet glance as that,
not to mention that I saw the expression in her eyes for the
first time.

I thought the soup would choke me. I almost hoped it
might. Othello was a mild case of jealousy compared to
me, and I felt that strangling would not half glut my
vengeance. And how they talked!—he complimenting her
on her accent, and she telling him how her first governess
was a Hanoverian from Celle, where they are all such purists.
There was nothing they did not discuss in those detestable
gutturals, and as glibly as if it had been a language meet
for human lips. I could not eat a mouthful, but I drank and
watched them. The fellow was not long in betraying himself: he was soon deep in the drama. He knew every play
of Schiller by heart, and quoted the Wallenstein, the Robbers,
Don Carlos, and Maria Stuart at will; so, too, was he
familiar with Göethe and Lessing. He had all the swinging
intonation of the boards, and declaimed so very professionally
that, as he concluded a passage, I cried out, without knowing
it,

"Take that for your benefit—it's the best you have given
yet."

Oh, Lord, how they laughed! She covered up her face
and smothered it; but he lay back, and holding the table
with both hands, he positively shouted and screamed aloud.
I would have given ten years of life for the courage to have
thrown my glass of wine in his face; but it was no use,
nature had been a niggard to me in that quarter, and I had
to sit and hear it—exactly so, sit and hear it—while they
made twenty attempts to recover their gravity and behave
like ladies and gentlemen, and when, no sooner would they
look towards me, than off they were again as bad as before.

I resolved a dozen cutting sarcasms, all beginning with,
"Whenever I feel assured that you have sufficiently regained
the customary calm of good society," but the dessert was
served ere I could complete the sentence; and now they
were deep in the lyric poets, Uhland, and Korner, and Freiligrath, and the rest of them. As I listened to their enthusiasm, I wondered why people never went into raptures
over a cold in the head. But it was not to end here: there

was an old harpsichord in the room, and this he opened and
set to work on in that fearful two-handed fashion your
German alone understands. The poor old crippled instrument shook on its three legs, while the fourth fell clean off,
and the loose wires jangled and jarred like knives in a tray;
but he only sang the louder, and her ecstasies grew all the
greater too.

Heaven reward you, dear old Mrs. Keats, when you sent
word down that you couldn't sleep a wink, and begging them
to "send that noisy band something and let them go away;"
and then Miss Herbert wished him a sweet good-night, and
he accompanied her to the door, and then there was more
good-night, and I believe I had a short fit, but when I came
to myself he was sitting smoking his cigar opposite me.

"You are no relative, no connection of the young lady who
has just left the room?" said he to me, with a grave manner,
so significant of something under it, that I replied hastily,
"None—none whatever."

"Was that servant who spoke to me in the porch, as I
came in this evening, yours?"

"Yes." This I said more boldly, as I suspected he was
coming to the question François had opened.

"He mentioned to me," said he, slowly, and puffing his
cigar at easy intervals, "that you desire your servant should
sleep in the same room with you. I am always happy to
meet the wishes of courteous fellow-travellers, and so I have
ordered my servant to give you *his* bed; he will sleep up
stairs in what was intended for *you*. Good-night." And
with an insolent nod he lounged out of the room and left me.

CHAPTER XXIV.

My reader is sufficiently acquainted with me by this time
to know that there is one quality in me on which he can
always count with safety—my candour! There may be

13—2

braver men and more ingenious men, there may be, I will
not dispute it, persons more gifted with oratorical powers,
better linguists, better mathematicians, and with higher
acquirements in art; but I take my stand upon candour,
and say, there never lived the man, ancient or modern, who
presented a more open and undisguised section of himself
than I have done, am doing, and hope to do to the end.
And what, I would ask you, is the reason why we have
hitherto made so little progress in that greatest of all
sciences—the knowledge of human nature?   Is it not because we are always engaged in speculating on what goes
on in the hearts of others, guessing, as it were, what people
are doing next door, instead of honestly recording what
takes place in our own house?

You think this same candour is a small quality. Well,
show me one thoroughly honest autobiography. Of all the
men who have written their own memoirs, it is fair to presume that some may have lacked personal courage; some
been deficient in truthfulness; some forgetful of early friendships, and so on. Yet where will you find me one, I only ask
one, who declares, " I was a coward.   I never could speak
truth.   I was by nature ungrateful?"

Now, it would be exactly through such confessions as these
our knowlege of humanity would be advanced. The ship
that makes her voyage without the loss of a spar or a rope,
teaches little; but there is a whole world of information in
the log of the vessel with a great hole in her, all her masts
carried away, the captain invariably drunk, and the crew
mutinous.   Then, we hear of energy and daring and ready-
wittedness, marvellous resource, and indomitable perse-
verance.   Then, we come to estimate a variety of qualities
that are only evoked by danger.   Just as some gallant
skipper might say, " I saw that we couldn't weather the
point, and so I dropped anchor in thirty fathoms, and
determined to trust all to my cables;" or, " I perceived that
we were settling down, so I crowded all sail on, resolved to
beach her."   In the same spirit I would like to read in some
personal memoir, " Knowing that I could not rely on my
courage; feeling that if pressed hard, I should certainly
have told a lie —— "   Oh, if we only could get honesty like
this!   If some great statesman, some grand foreground

figure of his age would sit down to give his trials as they really occurred, we should learn more of life from one such volume than we glean from all the mock memoirs we have been reading for centuries!

It is the special pleading of these records that makes them so valueless; the writer always is bent on making out his case. It is the eternal representation of that spectacle said to be so pleasing to the gods—the good man struggling with adversity. But what we want to see is the weak man, the frail man, the man who has to fight adversity with an old rusty musket and a flint lock, instead of an Enfield rifle, loading at the breech!

I'd not give a rush to see Blondin cross the Falls of Niagara on a tight-rope; but I'd cross the Atlantic to see, say the Lord Mayor, or the Master of the Rolls try it.

Now, much-respected reader, do not for a moment suppose that I have, even in my most vain-glorious of raptures, ever imagined that I was here in these records supplying the void I have pointed out. Remember, that I have expressly told you, such confessions, to be valuable, ought to come from a great man. Painful as the avowal is, I am not a great man! Elements of greatness I have in me, it is true; but there are wants, deficiencies, small little details, many of them—rivets and bolts, as it were—without which the machinery can't work; and I know this, and I feel it.

This digression has all grown out of my unwillingness to mention what mention I must—that I passed my night at the little inn on the table where we supped. I had not courage to assert the right to my bed in the count's room, and so I wrapped myself in my cloak, and with my carpet-bag for a pillow, tried to sleep. It was no use—the most elastic spring-mattress and a down cushion would have failed that night to lull me. I was outraged beyond endurance : *she* had slighted, *he* had insulted me! Such a provocation as he gave me could have but one expiation. He could not, by any pretext, refuse me satisfaction. But was I as ready to ask it? Was it so very certain that I would insist upon this reparation? He was certain to wound, he might kill me! I believe I cried over that thought. To be cut off in the bud of one's youth, in the very spring-time of one's enjoyment—

I could not say of one's utility—to go down unnoticed to the grave, never appreciated, never understood, with vulgar and mistaken judgments upon one's character and motives! I thought my heart would burst with the affliction of such a picture, and I said, "No, Potts, live—live and reply' to such would-be slanderers by the exercise of the qualities of your great nature." Numberless beautiful little episodes came thronging to my memory of good men, men whose personal gallantry had won them a world-wide renown, refusing to fight a duel. "We are to storm the citadel to-morrow, colonel," said one; "let us see which of us will be first up the breach." How I loved that fellow for his speech, and I tortured my mind how, as there was no citadel to be carried by assault, I could apply its wisdom to my own case. What if I were to say, "Count, the world is before us—a world full of trials and troubles. With the common fortune of humanity, we are certain each of us to have our share. What if we meet on this spot, say ten years hence, and see who has best acquitted himself in the conflict?" I wonder what he would say. The Germans are a strange, imaginative, dreamy sort of folk. Is it not likely that he would be struck by a notion so undeniably original? Is it not probable that he would seize my hand with rapture, and say, "Ja! I agree?" Still it is possible that he might not; he might be one of those vulgar matter-of-fact creatures who will regard nothing through the tinted glass of fancy; he might ridicule the project, and tell it at breakfast as a joke. I felt almost smothered as this notion crossed me.

I next bethought me of the privileges of my rank. Could I, as an R.H., accept the vulgar hazards of a personal encounter? Would not such conduct be derogatory in one to whom great destinies might one day be committed? Not that I lent myself, be it remarked, to the delusion of being a prince; but that I felt, if the line of conduct would be objectionable to men in my rank and condition, it inevitably followed that it must be bad. What I could neither do as the descendant of St. Louis, or the son of Peter Potts, must needs be wrong. These were the grievous meditations of that long, long night; and, though I arose from the hard table, weary, and with aching bones, I blessed the pinkishgrey light that ushered in the day. I had scarcely completed a very rapid toilet, when François came with a message from Mrs. Keats, "hoping I had rested well, and begging to know at what hour it was my pleasure to continue the journey." There was an evident astonishment in the fellow's face at the embassy with which he was charged; and though he delivered the message with reasonable propriety, there was a certain something in his look that said, "What delusion is this you have thrown around the old lady?"

"Say that I am ready, François; that I am even impatient to be off, and the sooner we start the better."

This I uttered with all my heart; for I was eager to get away before the odious German should be stirring, and could not subdue my anxiety to avoid meeting him again. There was every reason to expect that we should get off unnoticed, and I hastened out myself to order the horses and stimulate the postillions to greater activity. This was no labour of love, I promise you! The sluggardly inertness of that people passes all belief; entreaties, objurgations, curses, even bribes could not move them. They never admitted such a possibility as haste, and stumped about in their wooden shoes or iron-bound boots, searching for articles of horse-gear under bundles of hay or stacks of firewood, as though it was the very first time in their lives that post-horses had ever been required in that locality. "Make a great people out of such materials as these!" muttered I; "what rubbish to imagine it! How, with such intolerable apathy, are they to be moved? Where everything proceeds at the same regulated slowness, how can justice ever overtake crime? When can truth come up with falsehood? Whichever starts first here, must inevitably win. To urge the creatures on by example, I assisted with my own hands to put on the harness; not, I will own, with much advantage to speed, for I put the collar on upside down, and, in revenge for the indignity, the beast planted one of his feet upon me, and almost drove the cock of his shoe through my instep. Almost mad with pain and passion, I limped away into the garden, and sat down in a damp summer-house. A sleepless night, a lazy ostler, and a bruised foot, are, after all, not stunning calamities; but there are moments when our jarred nerves jangle at the slightest touch, and even the most trivial inconveniences grow to the size of afflictions.

"We began to fear you were lost, Sir," said François, breaking in upon my gloomy reverie, I cannot say how long after. "The horses have been at the door this half-hour, and all the house searching after you."

I did not deign a reply, but followed him, as he led me by a short path to the house. Mrs. Keats and Miss Herbert had taken their places inside the carriage, and, to my ineffable disgust, there was the German chatting with them at the door, and actually presenting a bouquet the landlord had just culled for her. Unable to confront the fellow with that contemptuous indifference which I knew with a little time and preparation I could summon to my aid, I scaled up to my leathern attic and let down the blinds.

"Do you mean," said I, through a small slit in my curtain—"do you mean to sit smoking there all day? Will you never drive on?" And now, with a crash of bolts and a jarring of cordage, like what announced the launch of a small ship, the heavy conveniency lurched, surged, and, after two or three convulsive bounds, lumbered along, and we started on our day's journey. As we bumped along, I remembered that I had never wished the ladies a "good morning," nor addressed them in any way; so completely had my selfish preoccupation immersed me in my own annoyances, that I actually forgot the commonest attentions of every-day life. I was pained by this rudeness on my part, and waited with impatience for our first change of horses to repair my omission. Before, however, we had gone a couple of miles, the little window at my back was opened, and I heard the old lady's voice, asking if I had ever chanced upon a more comfortable country inn, or with better beds?

"Not bad—not bad," said I, peevishly. "I had such a mass of letters to write that I got little sleep. In fact, I scarcely could say I took any rest."

While the old lady expressed her regretful condolences at this, I saw that Miss Herbert pinched her lips together as if to avoid a laugh, and the bitter thought crossed me, "She knows it all!"

"I am easily put out, besides," said I. "That is, at certain times I am easily irritated, and a vulgar German fellow who supped with us last night so ruffled my temper, that I assure you he continued to go through my head till morning."

"Oh, don't call him vulgar!" broke in Miss Herbert; "surely there could be nothing more quiet or unpretending than his manners."

"If I were to hunt for an epithet for a month," retorted I, "a more suitable one would never occur to me. The fellow was evidently an actor of some kind—perhaps a rope-dancer."

She burst in with an exclamation, but at the same time Mrs. Keats interposed, and though her words were perfectly inaudible to me, I had no difficulty in gathering their import, and saw that "the young person" was undergoing a pretty smart lecture for her presumption in daring to differ in opinion with my royal highness. I suppose it was very ignoble of me, but I was delighted at it. I was right glad that the old woman administered that sharp castigation, and I burned even with impatience to throw in a shell myself and increase the discomfiture. Mrs. Keats finished her gallop at last, and I took up the running.

"You were fortunate, madam," said I, "in the indisposition that confined you to your room, and which rescued you from the underbred presumption of this man's manners. I have travelled much, I have mixed largely, I may say with every rank and condition, and in every country of Europe, so that I am not pronouncing the opinion of one totally inadequate to form a judgment——"

"Certainly not, Sir. Listen to that, young lady," muttered she, in a sort of under growl.

"In fact," resumed I, "it is one of my especial amusements to observe and note the forms of civilisation implied by mere conventional habits. If, from circumstances not necessary to particularise, certain advantages have favoured this pursuit ——"

When I had reached thus far in my very pompous preface, the clatter of a horse coming up at full speed arrested my attention, and at the very moment the German himself, the identical subject of our talk, dashed up to the carriage window, and with a few polite words handed in a small volume to Miss Herbert, which it seems he had promised to give her,

but could not accomplish before, in consequence of the
abrupt haste of our departure. The explanation did not
occupy an entire minute, and he was gone and out of sight
at once. And now the little window was closed, and I could
distinctly hear that Mrs. Keats was engaged in one of those
salutary exercises by which age communicates its experiences
to youth. I wished I could have opened a little chink to
listen to it, but I could not do so undetected, so I had to
console myself by imagining all the shrewd and disagreeable
remarks she must have made. Morals has its rhubarb as
well as medicine, wholesome, doubtless, when down, but
marvellously nauseous and very hard to swallow, and I felt
that the young person was getting a full dose; indeed, I
could catch two very significant words, which came and
came again in the allocution, and the very utterance of
which added to their sharpness : " levity," " encouragement."
There they were again!

" Lay it on, old lady," muttered I; " your precepts are
sound; never was there a case more meet for their application. Never mind a little pain either—one must touch the
quick to make the cautery effectual. She will be all the
better for the lesson, and she has well earned it ! "

Oh, Potts! Potts! was this not very hard-hearted and
ungenerous? Why should the sorrow of that young
creature have been a pleasure to you? Is it possible that
the mean sentiment of revenge has had any share in this?
Are you angry with her that she liked that man's conversation and turned to *him* in preference to *you?* You surely
cannot be actuated by a motive so base as this? Is it for
herself, for her own advantage, her preservation, that you
are thinking all this time? Of course it is. And there,
now, I think I hear her sob. Yes, she is crying; the old
lady has really come to the quick, and I believe is not going
to stop there.

" Well," thought I, " old ladies are an excellent invention;
none of these cutting severeties could be done but for them.
And they have a patient persistence in this surgery quite
wonderful, for when they have flayed the patient all over,
they sprinkle on salt as carefully as a pastrycook frosting a
plum-cake."

At last, I did begin to wish it was over. She surely

must have addressed herself to every phase of the question in an hour and a half, and yet I could hear her still grinding, grinding on, as though the efficacy of her precepts, like a homœopathic remedy, were to he increased by trituration. Fortunately, we had to halt for fresh horses, and so I got down to chat with them at the carriage door, and interrupt the lecture. Little was I prepared for the reddened eyes and quivering lips of that poor girl, as she drank off the glass of water she begged me to fetch her, but still less for the few words she contrived to whisper in my ear as I took the glass from her hands.

" I hope you have made me miserable enough *now*."

And with this the window was hanged to, and away we went.

CHAPTER XXV

I WAS so hurt by the last words of Miss Herbert to me, that I maintained throughout the entire day what I meant to he a "dignified reserve," but what I half suspect bore stronger resemblance to a deep sulk. My station had its privileges, and I resolved to take the benefit of them. I dined alone. Yes, on that day I did fall back upon the eminence of my condition, and proudly intimated that I desired solitude. I was delighted to see the dismay this declaration caused. Old Mrs. Keats was speechless with terror. I was looking at her through a chink in the door when Miss Herbert gave my message, and I thought she would have fainted.

" What were his precise words? Give them to me exactly as he uttered them," said she, tremulously, " for there are persons whose intimations are half commands."

" I can scarcely repeat them, madam," said the other, " but

their purport was, that we were not to expect him at dinner,
that he had ordered it to be served in his own room, and at
his own hour."

"And this is very probably all your doing," said the old
lady with indignation. "Unaccustomed to any levity of
behaviour, brought up in a rank where familiarities are never
practised, he has been shocked by your conduct with that
stranger. Yes, Miss Herbert, I say shocked, because, however harmless in intention, such freedoms are utterly unknown in—in certain circles."

"I am sure, madam," replied she, with a certain amount
of spirit, "that you are labouring under a very grave
misapprehension. There was no familiarity, no freedom.
We talked as I imagine people usually talk when they
sit at the same table. Mr. —— I scarcely know his
name ——"

"Nor is it necessary," said the old woman, tartly;
"though, if you had, probably this unfortunate incident
might not have occurred. Sit down there, however, and
write a few lines in my name, hoping that his indisposition
may be very slight, and begging to know if he desire to
remain here to-morrow and take some repose."

I waited till I saw Miss Herbert open her writing-desk,
and then I hastened off to my room to reflect over my answer
to her note. Now that the suggestion was made to me, I
was pleased with the notion of passing an entire day where
we were. The place was Schaffhausen—the famous fall of
the Rhine—not very much as a cataract, but picturesque
withal; pleasant chestnut woods to ramble about and a nice
old inn in a wild old wilderness of a garden that sloped
down to the very river.

Strange perversity is it not! but how naturally one likes
everything to have some feature or other out of keeping
with its intrinsic purport. An inn like an old *château*, a
chief-justice that could ride a steeple-chase, a bishop that
sings Moore's melodies, have an immense attraction for me.
They seem all, as it were, to say, "Don't fancy life is a mere
four-roomed house with a door in the middle. Don't imagine
that all is humdrum, and routine, and regular. Notwithstanding his wig and stern black eyebrows, there is a touch of
romance in that old chancellor's heart that you couldn't beat

out of it with his great mace; and his grace the primate there has not forgotten what made the poetry of his life in days before he ever dreamed of charges or triennial visitations."

By these reflections I mean to convey that I am very fond of an inn that does not look like an inn, but resembles a faded old country-house, or a deserted convent, or a disabled mill. This Schaffhausen Gasthaus looked like all three. It was the sort of place one might come to in a long vacation, to live simply and to go early to bed, take monotony as a tonic, and fancying unbroken quiet to be better than quinine.

"Ah!" thought I, "if it had not been for that confounded German, what a paradise might not this have been to me! Down there in that garden, with the din of the waterfall around us, walking under the old cherry-trees, brushing our way through tangled sweetbriers, and arbutus, and laburnum, what delicious nonsense might I not have poured into her ear. Ay! and not unwillingly had she heard it. That something within that never deceives, that little crimson heart within the rose of conscience tells me that she liked me, that she was attracted by what, if it were not for shame, I would call the irresistible attractions of my nature; and now this creature of braten and beetroot has spoiled all, jarred the instrument and unstrung the chords that might have yielded me such sweet music."

In thinking over the inadequacy of all human institutions, I have often been struck by the fact that while the law gives the weak man a certain measure of protection against the superior physical strength of the powerful ruffian in the street, it affords none against the assaults of the intellectual bully at a dinner party. *He* may maltreat you at his pleasure, batter you with his arguments, kick you with inferences, and knock you down with conclusions, and no help for it all!

"Ah, here comes François with the note." I wrote one line in pencil for answer: "I am sensibly touched by your consideration, and will pass to-morrow here." I signed this with a P., which might mean Prince, Potts, or Pottinger. My reply dispatched, I began to think how I could improve the opportunity. "I will bring her to book,"

thought I ; " I will have an explanation."   I always loved
that sort of thing—there is an almost certainty of emotion ;
now emotion begets tears ; tears, tenderness; tenderness,
consolation ; and when you reach consolation, you are, so to
say, a tenant in possession; your title may be disputable,
your lease invalid, still you are there, on the property, and it
will take time at least to turn you out. " After all," thought
I, "that rude German has but troubled the water for a
moment, the pure well of her affections will by this time
have regained its calm still surface, and I shall see my image
there as before."

My meditations were interrupted, perhaps not unplea-
santly. It was the waiter with my dinner. I am not
unsocial—I am eminently the reverse—I may say, like
most men who feel themselves conversationally gifted, I
like company, I see that my gifts have in such gatherings
their natural ascendancy—and yet, with all this, I have
always felt that to dine splendidly, all alone, was a very
grand thing. Mind, I don't say it is pleasant, or jolly, or
social ; but simply that it is grand to see all that table
equipage of crystal and silver spread out for *you* alone; to
know that the business of that gorgeous candelabrum is to
light *you*; that the two decorous men in black—archdeacons
they might be, from the quiet dignity of their manners—are
there to wait upon *you* ; that the whole sacrifice, from the
caviare to the cheese, was a hecatomb to *your* greatness.   I
repeat, these are all grand and imposing considerations, and
there have been times when I have enjoyed these *Lucullus
cum Lucullo* festivals more than convivial assemblages.   This
day was one of these : I lingered over my dinner in delightful dalliance. I partook of nearly every dish, but, with a
supreme refinement, ate little of any, as though to imply,
" I am accustomed to a very different *cuisine* from this ; it is
not thus that I fare habitually." And yet I was blandly
forgiving, accepting even such humble efforts to please as if
they had been successes. The Cliquot was good, and I drank
no other wine, though various flasks with tempting titles
stood around me.

Dinner over and coffee served, I asked the waiter what
resources the place possessed in the way of amusement.   He
looked blank and even distressed at my question : he had all

his life imagined that the Falls sufficed for everything; he had seen the tide of travel halt there to view them for years. Since he was a boy, he had never ceased to witness the yearly recurring round of tourists who came to see, and sketch, and scribble about them, and so he faintly muttered out a remonstrance,—

"Monsieur has not yet visited the Falls."

"The Falls! why I see them from this, and if I open the window I am stunned with their uproar."

I was really sorry at the pain my hasty speech gave him, for he looked suddenly faint and ill, and after a moment gasped out,—

"But monsieur is surely not going away without a visit to the cataract? the guide-books give two hours as the very shortest time to see it effectually."

"I only gave ten minutes to Niagara, my good friend," said I, "and would not have spared even that, but that I wanted to hold a sprained ankle under the fall."

He staggered, and had to hold a chair to support himself.

"There is, besides, the Laufen Schloss——"

"As to castles," broke I in, "I have no need to leave my own to see all that mediæval architecture can boast. No, no," sighed I out, "if I am to have new sensations, they must come through some other channel than sight. Have you no theatre?"

"No, Sir. None."

"No concert-rooms, no music garden?"

"None, Sir."

"Not even a circus?" said I, peevishly.

"There was, Sir, but it was not attended. The strangers all come to see the Falls."

"Confound the Falls! And what became of the circus?"

"Well, they made a bad business of it; got into debt on all sides, for oil, and forage, and printing placards, and so on, and then they beat a sudden retreat one night, and slipped off, all but two, and, indeed, they were about the best of the company; but somehow they lost their way in the forest, and instead of coming up with their companions, found themselves at daybreak at the outside of the town."

"And these two unlucky ones, what were they?"

"One was the chief clown, Sir, a German, and the other

was a little girl, a Moor they call her; but the cleverest
creature to ride or throw somersaults through hoops of the
whole of them."

"And how do they live now?"

"Very hardly, I believe, Sir; and but for Tintefleck—
that's what they call her—they might starve; but she goes
about with her guitar through the *cafés* of an evening, and
as she has a sweet voice, she picks up a few batzen. But the
maire, I hear, won't permit this any longer, and says that as
they have no passport or papers of any kind, they must be
sent over the frontier as vagabonds."

"Let that maire be brought before *me*," said I, with a
haughty indignation. "Let me tell him in a few brief words
what I think of his heartless cruelty——But no, I was forgetting—I am here incog. Be careful, my good man, that
you do not mention what I have so inadvertently dropped;
remember that I am nobody here; I am Number Five and
nothing more. Send the unfortunate creatures, however,
here, and let me interrogate them. They can be easily
found, I suppose?"

"In a moment, Sir. They were in the Platz just when I
served the pheasant."

"What name does the man bear?"

"I never heard a name for him. Amongst the company
he was called Vaterchen, as he was the oldest of them all;
and, indeed, they seemed all very fond of him."

"Let Vaterchen and Tintefleck, then, come hither. And
bring fresh glasses, waiter."

And I spoke as might an Eastern despot giving his orders
for a "nautch;" and, then, waving my hand, motioned the
messenger away.

CHAPTER XXVI.

HAD Fortune decreed that I should be rich, I believe I would have been the most popular of men. There is such a natural kindness of disposition in me, blended with the most refined sense of discrimination. I love humanity in the aggregate, and, at the same time, with a rare delicacy of sentiment, I can follow through all the tortuous windings of the heart, and actually sympathise in emotions that I never experienced. No rank is too exalted, no lot too humble, for the exercise of my benevolence. I have sat in my arm-chair with a beating, throbbing heart, as I imagined the troubles of a king, and I have drunk my Bordeaux with tears of gratitude as I fancied myself a peasant with only water to slake his thirst. To a man of highly-organised temperament, the privations themselves are not necessary to eliminate the feeling they would suggest. Coarser natures would require starvation to produce the sense of hunger, nakedness to cause that of cold, and so on; the gifted can be in rags, while enclosed in a wadded dressing-gown; they can go supperless to bed after a meal of oysters and toasted cheese; they can, if they will, be fatally wounded as they sit over their wine, or cast away after shipwreck with their feet on the fender. Great privileges all these; happy is he who has them, happy are they amidst whom he tries to spread the blessings of his inheritance !

Amid the many admirable traits which I recognise in myself—and of which I speak not boastfully, but gratefully, being accidents of my nature as far removed from my own agency as the colour of my eyes or the shape of my nose— of these, I say, I know of none more striking than such as fit me to be a patron. I am graceful as a lover, touching as a friend, but I am really great as a protector.

Revelling in such sentiments as these, I stood at my window, looking at the effect of moonlight on the Falls. It seemed to me as though in the grand spectacle before my

eyes I beheld a sort of illustration of my own nature, wherein
generous emotions could come gushing, foaming, and falling,
and yet the source be never exhausted, the flood ever at full.
I ought parenthetically to observe, that the champagne was
excellent, and that I had drunk the third glass of the second
bottle to the health of the Widow Cliquot herself. Thus
standing and musing, I was startled by a noise behind me,
and, turning round, I saw one of the smallest of men in a
little red Greek jacket and short yellow breeches, carefully
engaged in spreading a small piece of carpet on the floor, a
strip like a very diminutive hearth-rug. This done, he gave
a little wild exclamation of "Ho!" and cut a somersault in
the air, alighting on the flat of his back, which he announced
by a like cry of "Ha!" He was up again, however, in an
instant, and repeated the performance three times. He was
about, as I judged by the arrangement of certain chairs, to
proceed to other exercises equally diverting, when I stopped
him by asking who he was.

"Your excellency," said he, drawing himself up to his full
height of, say four feet, "I am Vaterchen!"

Everyone knows what provoking things are certain
chance resemblances, how disturbing to the right current of
thought, how subverting to the free exercise of reason. Now,
this creature before me, in his deeply intended temples, high
narrow forehead, aquiline nose, and resolute chin, was marvellously like a certain great field-marshal with whose
features, notwithstanding the portraits of him, we are all
familiar. It was not of the least use to me that I knew he
was not the illustrious general, but simply a mountebank.
There were the stern traits, haughty and defiant, and do
what I would, the thought of the great man would clash
with the capers of the little one. Owing to this impression,
it was impossible for me to address him without a certain
sense of deference and respect.

"Will you not be seated?" said I, offering him a chair,
and taking one myself. He accepted with all the quiet ease
of good breeding, and smiled courteously as I filled a glass
and passed it towards him.

I pressed my hand across my eyes for a few moments
while I reflected, and I muttered to myself:—

"Oh, Potts, if instead of a tumbler this had really been

the hero, what an evening might this be ! Lives there that man in Europe so capable of feeling in all its intensity the glorious privilege of such a meeting ? Who, like you, would listen to the wisdom distilling from those lips ? Who would treasure up every trait of voice, accent, and manner, remem- bering, not alone every anecdote, but every expression ? Who, like you, could have gracefully led the conversation so as to range over the whole wide ocean of that great life, taking in battles, and sieges, and stormings, and congresses, and scenes of all that is most varied and exciting in exist- ence ? Would not the record of one such night, drawn by you, have been worth all the cold compilations and bleak biographies that ever were written ? You would have pre- sented him as he sat there in front of you." I opened my eyes to paint from the model, and there was the little dog, with his legs straight up on each side of his head and form- ing a sort of gothic arch over his face. The wretch had done the feat to amuse me, and I almost fainted with horror as I saw it.

"Sit down, Sir," said I, in a voice of stern command. "You little know the misery you have caused me."

I refilled his glass and closed my eyes once more. In my old pharmaceutical experiences I had often made bread pills, and remembered well how, almost invariably, they had been deemed successful. What relief from pain to the agonised sufferer had they not given ! What slumber to the sleep- less ! What appetite, what vigour, what excitement ! Why should not the same treatment apply to morals as to medicine ? Why, with faith to aid one, cannot he induce every wished-for mood of mind and thought? The lay figure to support the drapery suffices for the artist, the Venus herself is in his brain. Now, if that little fellow there would neither cut capers nor speak, I ask no more of him. Let him sit firmly as he does now, staring me boldly in the face that way.

"Yes," said I, "lay your hand on the arm of your chair, so, and let the other be clenched thus." And so I placed him. "Never utter a word, but nod to me at rare intervals."

He has since acknowledged that he believed me to be deranged, but as I seemed a harmless case, and he could rely on his activity for escape, he made no objection to my

14—2

directions. The less, too, that he enjoyed his wine immensely, and was at liberty to drink as he pleased.

"Now," thought I, "one glance, only one, to see that he
poses properly."

All right, nothing could be better. His face was turned
slightly to one side, giving what the painters call action to
the head, and he was perfect. I now resigned myself to the
working of the spell, and already I felt its influence over me.
Where and with what was I to begin? Numberless
questions thronged to my mind. I wanted to know a
thousand disputed things, and fully as many that were only
disputed by myself. I felt that as such another opportunity
would assuredly never present itself twice in my life, that the
really great use of the occasion would be to make every
inquiry subsidiary to my own case, to make all my investi-
gations what the Germans would call "Potts-wise." My
intensest anxiety was then to ascertain if, like myself, his
grace started in life with very grand aspirations.

"Did you feel, for instance, when playing practical jokes
on the maids of honour in Dublin, some sixty odd years ago,
that you were only in sportive vein throwing off so much
light ballast to make room for the weightier material that
was to steady you in the storm-tossed sea before you? Have
you experienced the almost necessity of these little expansions
of eccentricity as I have? Was there always in your heart,
as a young man, as there is now in mine, a profound contempt for the opinions of your contemporaries? Did you
continually find yourself repeating, '*Respice finem!* Mark
where I shall be yet?'" There was another investigation
which touched me still more closely, but it was long before
I could approach it. I saw all the difficulty and delicacy of
the inquiry, but with that same recklessness of consequences
which would make me catch at a queen by the back hair if
I was drowning, I clutched at this discovery now, and,
although trembling at my boldness, asked: "Was your
grace ever afraid? I know the impertinence of the
question, but if you only guessed how it concerns me,
you'd forgive it. Nature has made me many things, but
not courageous. Nothing on earth could induce me to risk
life ; the more I reason about it the greater grows my
repugnance. Now, I would like to hear, is this what

anatomists call congenital? Am I likely to grow out of
it? Shall I ever be a dare-devil, intrepid, fire-eating sort of
creature? How will the change come over me? Shall I
feel it coming? Will it come from within, or through
external agencies? and when it has arrived, what shall I
become? Am I destined to drive the Zouaves into the sea
by a bayonet charge of the North Cork Rifles, or shall I
only be great in council, and take weekly trips in the *Fairy*
to Cowes? I'd like to know this, and begin a course of preparation for my position, as I once knew of a militia captain
who hardened himself for a campaign by sleeping every
night with his head on the window-stool."

As I opened my eyes I saw the stern features in front of
me. I thought the words, " I was never afraid, Sir ! " rang
through my brain till they filled every ventricle with their
din.

" Not at Assaye ? "

" No, Sir."

" Not at the Douro ? "

" No, Sir."

" Not at Torres Vedras ? "

" I tell you again, no, Sir ! "

Whether I uttered this last with any uncommon degree of
vehemence or not, I so frightened Vaterchen that he cut a
somersault clean over the chair, and stood grinning at me
through the rails at the back of it. I motioned to him to be
reseated, while, passing my hand across my brow, I waved
away the bright illusions that beset me, and, with a heavy
sigh, re-entered the dull world of reality.

" You are a clown," said I, meditatively. " What is a
clown ? "

He did not answer me in words, but, placing his hands on
his knees, stared at me stedfastly, and then, having fixed
my attention, his face performed a series of the most fearful
contortions I ever beheld. With one horrible spasm he made
his mouth appear to stretch from ear to ear; with another,
his nose wagged from side to side; with a third, his eyebrows went up and down alternately, giving the different
sides of his face two directly antagonistic expressions. I
was shocked and horrified, and called to him to desist.

" And yet," thought I, " there are natures who can

delight in these, and see in them matter for mirth and laughter !"

"Old man," said I, gravely, " has it ever occurred to you, that in this horrible commixture of expression, wherein grief wars with joy and sadness with levity, you are like one who, with a noble instrument before him, should, instead of sweet sounds of harmony, produce wild, unearthly discords, the jangling bursts of fiend-like voices ?"

"The Tintefleck can play indifferently well, your excellency," said he, humbly. "I never had any skill that way myself."

Oh, what a *crassa natura* was here ! What a triple wall of dulness surrounds such dark intelligences!

"And where is the Tintefleck ? Why is she not here?" asked I, anxious to remove the discussion to a ground of more equality.

"She is without, your excellency. She did not dare to present herself till your excellency had desired, and is waiting in the corridor."

"Let her come in," said I, grandly ; and I drew my chair to a distant corner of the room so as to give them a wider area to appear in, while I could, at the same time, assume that attitude of splendid ease and graceful protection I have seen a prince accomplish on the stage at the moment the ballet is about to begin. The door opened, and Vaterchen entered, leading Tintefleck by the hand.

CHAPTER XXVII.

I WAS quite right—Tintefleck's *entrée* was quite dramatic. She tripped into the room with a short step, nor arrested her run till she came close to me, when, with a deep curtsey, she bent down very low, and then, with a single spring backward, retreated almost to the door again. She was very

pretty—dark enough to be a Moor, but with a rich brilliancy
of skin never seen amongst that race, for she was a Calabrian; and as she stood there with her arms crossed before
her, and one leg firmly advanced, and with the foot—a very
pretty foot—well planted, she was like—all the Italian
peasants one has seen in the National Gallery for years
back. There was the same look, half shy; the same elevation of sentiment in the brow, and the same coarseness of
the mouth; plenty of energy, enough and to spare of daring;
but no timidity, no gentleness.

"What is she saying?" asked I of the old man, as I
overheard a whisper pass between them. "Tell me what
she has just said to you."

"It is nothing, your excellency—she is a fool."

"That she may be, but I insist on hearing what it was she
said."

He seemed embarrassed and ashamed, and instead of replying to me, turned to address some words of reproach to
the girl.

"I am waiting for your answer," said I, peremptorily.

"It is the saucy way she has gotten, your excellency, all
from over flattery; and now that she sees there is no
audience here, none but your excellency, she is impatient to
be off again. She'll never do anything for us on the night
of a thin house."

"Is this the truth, Tintefleck?" asked I.

With a wild volubility, of which I could not gather a word,
but every accent of which indicated passion, if not anger, she
poured out something to the other, and then turned as if to
leave the room. He interposed quickly, and spoke to her,
at first angrily, but at last in a soothing and entreating tone,
which seemed gradually to calm her.

"There is more in this than you have told, Vaterchen,"
said I. "Let me know at once why she is impatient to get
away."

"I would leave it to herself to tell your excellency," said
he, with much confusion, "but that you could not understand
her mountain dialect. The fact is," added he, after a great
struggle with himself—"the fact is, she is offended at your
calling her 'Tintefleck.' She is satisfied to be so named
amongst ourselves, where we all have similar nicknames;

but that you, a great personage, high, and rich, and titled, should do so, wounds her deeply. Had you said —— "

Here he whispered me in my ear, and, almost inadvertently, I repeated after him, " Catinka."

" Si, si, Catinka," said she, while her eyes sparkled with an expression of wildest delight, and at the same instant she bounded forward and kissed my hand twice over.

I was glad to have made my peace, and placing a chair for her at the table, I filled out a glass of wine and presented it. She only shook her head in dissent, and pushed it away.

" She has odd ways in everything," said the old man; " she never eats but bread and water. It is her notion, that if she were to taste other food, she'd lose her gift of fortune-telling."

" So, then, she reads destiny, too? " said I, in astonishment.

Before I could inquire further, she swept her hands across the strings of her guitar, and broke out into a little peasant song. It was very monotonous, but pleasing. Of course, I knew nothing of the words nor the meaning, but it seemed as though one thought kept ever and anon recurring in the melody, and would continue to rise to the surface, like the air bubbles in a well. Satisfied, apparently, by the evidences of my approval, she had no sooner finished than she began another. This was somewhat more pretentious, and, from what I could gather, represented a parting scene between a lover and his mistress. There was, at least, a certain action in the song which intimated this. The fervent earnestness of the lover, his entreaties, his prayers, and at last his threatenings, were all given with effect, and there was actually good acting in the stolid defiance she opposed to all; she rejected his vows, refused his pledges, scorned his menaces ; but when he had gone and left her, when she saw herself alone and desolate, then came out a gush of the most passionate sorrow, all the pent-up misery of a heart that seemed to burst with its weight of agony.

If I was in a measure entranced while she was singing, such was the tension of my nerves as I listened, that I was heartily glad when it was over. As for her, she seemed so overcome by the emotion she had parodied, that she bent her head down, covered her face with her hands, and sobbed twice or thrice convulsively.

I turned towards Vaterchen to ask him some question, I forget what, but the little fellow had made such good use of the decanter beside him, while the music went on, that his cheeks were a bright crimson, and his little round eyes shone like coals of fire.

"This young creature should never have fallen amongst such as you!" said I, indignantly; "she has feeling and tenderness—the powers of expression she wields all evidence a great and gifted nature. She has, so to say, noble qualities."

"Noble, indeed!" croaked out the little wretch, with a voice hoarse from the strong Burgundy.

"She might, with proper culture, adorn a very different sphere," said I, angrily. "Many have climbed the ladder of life with humbler pretensions."

"Ay, and stand on one leg on top of it, playing the tambourine all the time," hiccupped he in reply.

I did not fancy the way he carried out my figure, but went on with my reflections :

"Some, but they are few, achieve greatness at a bound —— "

"That's what she does," broke he in. "Twelve hoops and a drum behind them, at one spring—she comes through like a flying-fish."

"I don't know what angry rejoinder was on my lips to this speech, when there came a tap at my door. I arose at once and opened it. It was François, with a polite message from Mrs. Keats, to say how happy it would make her " if I felt well enough to join her and Miss Herbert at tea." For a second or two I knew not what to reply. That I was "well enough," François was sure to report, and in my flushed condition I was, perhaps, the picture of an exaggerated state of convalescence; so, after a moment's hesitation, I muttered out a blundering excuse, on the plea of having a couple of friends with me, "who had chanced to be just passing through the town on their way to Italy."

I did not think François had time to report my answer, when I heard him again at the door. It was, with his mistress's compliments, to say, she "would be charmed if I would induce my friends to accompany me."

I had to hold my hand on my side with laughter as I heard this message, so absurd was the proposition, and so ridiculous seemed the notion of it. This, I say, was the first impression made upon my mind; and then, almost as suddenly, there came another and very different one. "What is the mission you have embraced, Potts?" asked I of myself. "If it have a but or an object, is it not to overthrow the mean and unjust prejudices, the miserable class distinctions, that separate the rich from the poor, the great from the humble, the gifted from the ignorant? Have you ever proposed to yourself a nobler conquest than over that vulgar tyranny by which prosperity lords it over humble fortune? Have you imagined a higher triumph than to make the man of purple and fine linen feel happy in the companionship of him in smock-frock and high-lows? Could you ask for a happier occasion to open the campaign than this? Mrs. Keats is an admirable representative of her class; she has all the rigid prejudices of her condition; her sympathies may rise, but they never fall; she can feel for the sorrows of the well-born, she has no concern for vulgar afflictions. How admirable the opportunity to show her that grace, and genius, and beauty are of all ranks! And Miss Herbert, too, what a test it will be of *her!* If she really have greatness of soul, if there be in her nature a spirit that rises above petty conventionalities and miserable ceremonials, she will take this young creature to her heart like a sister. I think see them with arms entwined—two lovely flowers on one stalk—the dark crimson rose and the pale hyacinth! Oh, Potts! this would be a nobler victory to achieve than to rend battalions with grape, or ride down squadrons with the crash of cavalry.—"I will come, François,'" said I. "Tell Mrs. Keats that she may expect us immediately." I took especial care in my dialogue to keep this prying fellow outside the room, and to interpose in every attempt that he made to obtain a peep within. In this I perfectly succeeded, and dismissed him, without his being able to report any one circumstance about my two travelling friends.

My next task was to inform them of my intentions on

their behalf; nor was this so easy as might be imagined, for Vaterchen had indulged very freely with the wine, and all the mountains of Calabria lay between myself and Tintefleck. With a great exercise of ingenuity, and more of patience, I did at last succeed in making known to the old fellow that a lady of the highest station and her friend were curious to see them. He only caught my meaning after some time, but when he had surmounted the difficulty, as though to show me how thoroughly he understood the request, and how nicely he appreciated its object, he began a series of face contortions of the most dreadful kind, being a sort of programme of what he intended to exhibit to the distinguished company. I repressed this firmly, severely. 1 explained that an artist in all the relations of private life should be ever the gentleman ; that the habits of the stage were no more necessary to carry into the world than the costume. I dilated upon the fact that John Kemble had been deemed fitting company by the First Gentleman of Europe ; and that if his manner could have exposed him to a criticism, it was in, perhaps, a slight tendency to an over-reserve, a cold and almost stern dignity. I'm not sure Vaterchen followed me completely, nor understood the anecdotes I introduced about Edmund Kean and Lord Byron, but I now addressed myself pictorially to Tintefleck—pictorially, I say, for words were hopeless. I signified that a *très grande dame* was about to receive her. I arose, with my skirts expanded in both hands, made a reverent curtsey, throwing my head well back, looking every inch a duchess. But alas for my powers of representation ! she burst into a hearty laugh, and had at last to lay her head on Vaterchen's shoulder out of pure exhaustion.

" Explain to her what I have told you, Sir, and do not sit grinning at me there, like a baboon," said I, in a severe voice.

I cannot say how he acquitted himself, but I could gather that a very lively altercation ensued, and it seemed to me as though she resolutely refused to subject herself to any further ordeals of what academicians call a " private view." No ; she was ready for the ring and the sawdust, and the drolleries of the men with chalk on their faces, but she would not accept high life on any terms. By degrees, and by arguments of his own ingenious devising, however, he did

succeed, and at last she arose with a bound, and cried out
" Eccomi ! "

" Remember," said I to Vaterchen, as we left the room,
" I am doing that which few would have the courage to dare.
It will depend upon the dignity of your conduct, the grace
of your manners, the well-bred ease of your address, to make
me feel proud of my intrepidity, or, sad and painful possibility,
retire covered with ineffable shame and discomfiture. Do
you comprehend me ? "

" Perfectly," said he, standing erect, and giving even in
his attitude a sort of bail bond for future dignity. " Lead
on ! "

This was more familiar than he had been yet; but I
ascribed it to the tension of nerves strung to a high purpose,
and rendering him thus inaccessible to other thoughts than
of the enterprise before him.

As I neared the door of Mrs. Keats' apartment, I hesitated
as to how I should enter. Ought I to precede my friends,
and present them as they followed ? Or would it seem
more easy and more assured if I were to give my arm to
Tintefleck, leaving Vaterchen to bring up the rear ? After
much deliberation, this appeared to be the better course,
seeming to take for granted that, although some peculiarities
of costume might ask for explanation later on, I was about
to present a very eligible and charming addition to the company.

I am scarcely able to say whether I was or was not reassured by the mode in which she accepted the offer of my
arm. At first, the proposition appeared unintelligible, and
she looked at me with one of those wide-eyed stares, as
though to say, " What new gymnastic is this? · What tour
de force, of which I never heard before ? " and then, with a
sort of jerk, she threw my arm up in the air and made a
pirouette under it, of some half-dozen whirls.

Half reprovingly, I shook my head, and offered her my
hand. This she understood at once. She recognised such a
mode of approach as legitimate and proper, and with an
artistic shake of her drapery with the other hand, and a
confident smile, she signified she was ready to go " on."

I was once on a time thrown over a horse's head into a
slate quarry, a very considerable drop it was, and nearly

fatal; on another occasion, I was carried in a small boat over the fall of a salmon weir, and hurried along in the flood for almost three hundred yards; each of these was a situation of excitement and peril, and with considerable confusion as the consequence; and yet I could deliberately recount you every passing phase of my terror, from my first fright down to my complete unconsciousness, with such small traits as would guarantee truthfulness; while, of the scene upon which I now adventured, I preserve nothing beyond the vaguest and most unconnected memory.

I remember my advance into the middle of the room. I have a recollection of a large tea-urn, and beyond it a lady in a turban; another in long ringlets there was. The urn made a noise like a small steamer, and there was a confusion of voices—about what, I cannot tell—that increased the uproar, and we were all standing up and all talking together; and there was what seemed an angry discussion, and then the large turban and the ringlets swept haughtily past me. The turban said, " This is too much, Sir ! " and ringlets added, " Far too much, Sir ! " and as they reached the door, there was Vaterchen on his head, with a branch of candles between his feet to light them out, and Tintefleck, screaming with laughter, threw herself into an arm-chair, and clapped a most riotous applause.

I stood a moment almost transfixed, then dashed out of the room, hurried up stairs to my chamber, bolted the door, drew a great clothes-press against it for further security, and then threw myself upon my bed in one of those paroxysms of mad confusion, in which a man cannot say whether he is on the verge of inevitable ruin, or has just been rescued from a dreadful fate. I would not, if even I could, recount all that I suffered that night. There was not a scene of open shame and disgrace that I did not picture to myself as incurring. I was everywhere in the stocks or the pillory. I wore a wooden placard on my breast, incribed, " Potts, the Impostor." I was running at top speed before hooting and yelling crowds. I was standing with a circle of protecting policemen amidst a mob eager to tear me to pieces. I was sitting on a hard stool while my hair was being cropped a la Pentonville, and a grey suit lay ready for me when it was done. But enough of such a dreary record. I believe I cried myself to sleep at last, and so soundly, too, that it was very late in the afternoon ere I awoke. It was the sight of the barricade I had erected at my door gave me a clue to the past, and again I buried my face in my hands, and wept bitterly.

CHAPTER XXVIII.

I COULD not hear the loud and repeated knockings which were made at my door, as at first waiters, and then the landlord himself, endeavoured to gain admittance. At length, a ladder was placed at the window, and a courageous individual, duly armed, appeared at my casement and summoned me to surrender. With what unspeakable relief did I learn that it was not to apprehend or arrest me that all these measures were taken; they were simply the promptings of a graceful benevolence, a sort of rumoured intimation having got about, that I had taken prussic acid, or was being done to death by charcoal. Imagine a prisoner in a condemned cell suddenly awakened, and hearing that the crowd around him consisted not of the ordinary, the sheriff, Mr. Calcraft and Co., but a deputation of respectable citizens come to offer the representation of their borough or a piece of plate, and then you can have a mild conception of the pleasant revulsion of my feelings. I thanked my public in a short but appropriate address. I assured them, although there was a popular prejudice about doing this sort of thing in November in England, that it was deemed quite unreasonable at other times, and that really in these days of domestic arsenic and conjugal strychnine, nothing but an unreasonable impatience would make a man self-destructive—suicide arguing that as a man was really so utterly valueless, it was worth nobody's while to get rid of him. My explanation over, I ordered breakfast.

"Why not dinner?" said the waiter. "It is close on four o'clock."

"No," said I; "the ladies will expect me at dinner."

"The ladies are near Constance by this, or else the roads are worse than we thought them."

"Near Constance! Do you mean to say they have gone?"

"Yes, Sir, at daybreak; or, indeed, I might say befoie daybreak."

"Gone! actually gone!" was all that I could utter.

"They never went to bed last night, Sir; the old lady was taken very ill after tea, and all the house running here and there for doctors and remedies, and the young lady, though she bore up so well, they tell me she fainted when she was alone in her own room. In fact, it was a piece of confusion and trouble until they started, and we may say, none of us had a moment's peace till we saw them off."

"And how came it that I was never called?"

"I believe, Sir, but I'm not sure, the landlord tried to awake you. At all events, he has a note for you now, for I saw the old lady place it in his hand."

"Fetch it at once," said I; and when he left the room I threw some water over my face, and tried to rally all my faculties to meet the occasion.

When the waiter reappeared with the note, I bade him leave it on the table; I could not venture to read it while he was in the room. At length he went away, and I opened it. These were the contents:

"SIR,—When a person of your rank abuses the privilege of his station, it is supposed that he means to rebuke. Although innocent of any cause for your displeasure, I have preferred to withdraw myself from your notice than incur the chance of so severe a reprimand a second time.

"I am, Sir, with unfeigned sorrow and humility, your most devoted follower and servant,

"MARTHA KEATS.

"To the —— de ——."

This was the whole of it; not a great deal as correspondence, but matter enough for much thought and much

misery. After a long and painful review of my conduct, one
startling fact stood prominently forward, which was, that I
had done something which, had it been the act of a royal
prince, would yet have been unpardonable, but which, if
known to emanate from one such as myself, would have been
a downright outrage.

I went into the whole case, as a man who detests figures
might have gone into a long and complicated account; and
just as he would skip small sums, and pay little heed to
fractions, I aimed at arriving at some grand solid balance
for or against myself.

I felt, that if asked to produce my books, they might run
this wise : Potts, on the credit side, a philanthropist, self-
denying, generous, and trustful ; one eager to do good, thinking no evil of his neighbour, hopeful of everybody, anxious
to establish that brotherhood amongst men which, however
varied the station, could and ought to subsist, and which
needs but the connecting-link of one sympathetic existence to
establish.   On the other side, Potts, I grieve to say, appeared
that which Ferdinand Mendez Pinto was said to be.

When I had rallied a bit from the stunning effect of this
disagreeable " total," I began to wish that I had somebody
to argue the matter out with me.   The way I would put my
case would be thus : "Has not—from the time of Quintus
Curtius down to the late Mr. Sadleir, of banking celebrity—
the sacrifice of one man for the benefit of his fellows, been
recognised as the noblest exposition of heroism ?   Now,
although it is much to give up life for the advantage of
others, it is far more to surrender one's identity, to abandon
that grand capital Ego ! which gives a man his self-esteem
and suggests his self-preservation.   And who, I would ask,
does this so thoroughly as the man who everlastingly palms
himself upon the world for that which he is not ?   According
to the greatest happiness principle, this man may be a real
boon to humanity.   He feeds this one with hope, the other
with flattery; he bestows courage on the weak, confidence
on the wavering.   The rich man can give of his abundance,
but it is out of his very poverty this poor fellow has to
bestow all.   Like the spider, he has to weave his web from
his own vitals, and like the same spider he may be swept
away by some pretentious affectation of propriety."

While I thus argued, the waiter came in to serve dinner. It looked all appetising and nice; but I could not touch a morsel. I was sick at heart; Kate Herbert's last look as she quitted the room was ever before me. Those dark grey eyes—which you stupid folk will go on calling blue—have a sort of reproachful power in them very remarkable. They don't flash out in anger like black eyes, or sparkle in fierceness like hazel; but they emit a sort of steady, fixed, concentrated light, that seems to imply that they have looked thoroughly into you, and come back very sad and very sorry for the inquiry. I thought of the happy days I had passed beside her; I recalled her low and gentle voice, her sweet, half sad smile, and her playful laugh, and I said, " Have I lost all these for ever, and how ? What stupid folly possessed me last evening ? How could I have been so idiotic as not to see that I was committing the rankest of all enormities ? How should I, in my insignificance, dare to assail the barriers and defences which civilisation has established, and guards amongst its best prerogatives ? Was this old buffoon, was this piece of tawdry fringe and spangles a fitting company for that fair and gentle girl ? How artistically false, too, was the position I had taken. Interweaving into my ideal life these coarse realities, was the same sort of outrage as shocks one in some of the Venetian churches, where a lovely Madonna, the work of a great hand, may be seen bedizened and disfigured with precious stones over her drapery. In this was I violating the whole poetry of my existence. These figures were as much out of keeping as would be a couple of Ostade's Boors in a grand Scripture piece by Domenichino.

"And yet, Potts," thought I, " they were *really* living creatures. They had hearts for joy and sorrow and hope and the rest of it. They were pilgrims travelling the self-same road as you were. They were not illusions, but flesh and blood folk, that would shiver when cold, and die of hunger if starved. Were they not then, as such, of more account than all your mere imaginings ? would not the least of their daily miseries outweigh a whole bushel of fancied sorrow ? and is it not a poor selfishness on your part, when you deem some airy conception of your brain of more account than that poor old man and that dark-eyed girl. Last of all, are they not, in all their ragged finery,

15

more 'really true men' than you yourself, Potts, living in
a maze of delusions? They only act when the sawdust
is raked and the lamps are lighted; but you are *en scène*
from dawn to dark, and only lay down one motley to don
another. Is not this wretched? Is it not ignoble? In all
these changes of character, how much of the real man will
be left behind? Will there be one morsel of honest flesh,
when all the lacquer of paint is washed off? And was it—
oh, was it for this you first adventured out on the wide ocean
of life?"

I passed the evening and a great part of the night in such
self-accusings, and then I addressed myself to action. I
bethought me of my future, and with whom and where and
how it might be passed. The bag of money intrusted to me
by the minister to pay the charges of the road was hanging
where I had placed it—on the curtain holder. I opened it,
and found a hundred and forty gold Napoleons, and some ten
or twelve pounds in silver. I next set to count over my own
especial hoard; it was a fraction under a thousand francs.
Forty pounds was truly a very small sum wherewith to
confront a world to which I brought not any art, or trade,
or means of livelihood; I say' forty, because I had not the
shadow of a pretext for touching the other sum, and I
resolved at once to transmit it to the owner. Now what
could be done with so humble a capital? I had heard
of a great general who once pawned a valuable sword—
a sword of honour it was—wherewith to buy a horse, and so
mounted, he went forth over the Alps, and conquered a
kingdom. The story had no moral for me, for somehow I did
not feel as though I were the stuff that conquers kingdoms,
and yet there must surely be a vast number of men in life
with about the same sort of faculties, merits, and demerits as
I have. There must be a numerous Potts family in every
land, well-meaning, right intentioned, worthless creatures,
who, out of a supposed willingness to do anything, always
end in doing nothing. Such people it must be inferred, live
upon what are called their wits, or, in other words, trade
upon the daily accidents of life, and the use to which they
can turn the traits of those they meet with.

I was resolved not to descend to this; no, I had determined to say adieu to all masquerading, and be simply Potts,

the druggist's son, one who had once dreamed of great ambitions, but had taken the wrong road to them. I would
from this hour be an honest, truth-speaking, simple-hearted
creature. What the world might henceforth accord me of its
sympathy should be tendered on honest grounds; nay, more,
in the spirit of those devotees who inspire themselves with
piety by privations, I resolved on a course of self-mortification,
I would not rest till I had made my former self expiate all
the vain-glorious wantonness of the past, and pay in severe
penance for every transgression I had committed. I
began boldly with my reformation. I sat down and wrote
thus:—

"To Mr. Dycer, Stephen's-green, Dublin.
"The gentleman who took away a dun pony from your
livery stables in the month of May last, and who, from
certain circumstances, has not been able to restore the animal,
sends herewith twenty pounds as his probable value. If Mr.
D. conscientiously considers the sum insufficient, the sender
will at some future time, he hopes, make good the difference."

Doubtless my esteemed reader will say at this place, "The
fellow couldn't do less; he need not vaunt himself on a common-place act of honesty, which, after all, might have been
suggested by certain fears of future consequences. His indiscretion amounted to horse-stealing, and horse-stealing is a
felony."

All true, every word of it, most upright of judges: I was
simply doing what I ought, or rather what I ought long since
to have done. But now, let me ask, is this, after all, the
invariable course in life, and is there no merit in doing
what one ought when every temptation points to the other
direction? and lastly, is it nothing to do what a man ought,
when the doing costs exactly the half of all he has in the
world?

Now, if I were, instead of being Potts, a certain great
writer that we all know and delight in, I would improve the
occasion here by asking my reader does he always himself do
the right thing? I would say to him, perhaps with all haste
to anticipate his answer, "Of course you do. You never

15—2

pinch your children, or kick your wife out of bed ; you are a model father and a churchwarden ; but I am only a poor apothecary's son brought up in precepts of thrift and the Dublin Pharmacopœia ; and I own to you, when I placed the half of my twenty-pound crisp clean bank note inside of that letter, I felt I was figuratively cutting myself in two. But I did it "like a man," if that be a proper phrase for an act which I thought god-like. And oh, take my word for it, when a sacrifice hasn't cost you a coach-load of regrets, and a shopful of hesitations about making it, it is of little worth. There's a wide difference between the gift of a sheep from an Australian farmer, or the present of a child's pet lamb, even though the sheep be twice the size of the lamb.

I gave myself no small praise for what I had done, much figurative patting on the back, and a vast deal of that very ambiguous consolation which beggars in Catholic countries bestow in change for alms, by assurance that it will be remembered to you in Purgatory.

"Well," thought I, "the occasion isn't very far off, for my Purgatory begins to-morrow."

CHAPTER XXIX.

I was in a tourist locality, and easily provided myself with a light equipment for the road, resolved at once to take the footpath in life and "seek my fortune." I use these words simply as the expresssion of the utter uncertainty which prevailed as to whither I should go, and what do when I got there.

If there be few more joyous things in life than to start off on foot with three or four choice companions, to ramble through some fine country, rich in scenery, varied in character and interesting in story, there are few more lonely sensations than to set out by oneself, not very decided what way to take, and with very little money to take it.

One of the most grievous features of small means is, certainly, the almost exclusive occupation it gives the mind as to every, even the most trivial, incident that involves cost. Instead of dining on fish and fowl and fruit, you feel eating so many groschen and kreutzers. You are *not* drinking wine, your beverage is a solution of copper batzen in vinegar! When you poke the fire, every spark that flies up the chimney is a baiocco! You come at last to suspect that the sun won't warm you for nothing, and that the very breeze that cooled your brow is only waiting round the corner to ask " for something for himself."

When the rich man lives sparingly, the conscious power of the wealth he might employ if he pleased, sustains him. The poor fellow has no such consolation to fall back on; the closer his coat is examined, the more threadbare will it appear. If it were simply that he dressed humbly and fared coarsely, it might be borne well, but it is the hourly depreciation that poverty is exposed to, makes its true grievance. " An ill-looking "—this means, generally, ill-dressed—"an ill-looking fellow had been seen about the premises at night-fall," says the police report. " A very suspicious character had asked for a bed; his wardrobe was in a 'spotted handkerchief.' The waiter remembers that a fellow, much travel-stained and weary, stopped at the door that evening and asked if there was any cheap house of entertainment in the village." Heaven help the poor wayfarer if anyone has been robbed, any house broken into, any rick set fire to, while he passed through that locality. There is no need of a crowd of witnesses to convict him, since every bend in his hat, every tear in his coat, and every rent in his shoes, are evidence against him.

If I thought over these things in sorrow and humiliation, it was in a very proud spirit that I called to mind how, on that same morning, I deposited the bag with all the money in Messrs. Haber's bank, saw the contents duly counted over, replaced and sealed up, and then addressed to Her Majesty's Minister at Kalbbratonstadt, taking a receipt for the same. " This was only just common honesty," says the reader. Oh, if there is an absurd collocation of words, it is that!

Common honesty! why, there is nothing in this world so
perfectly, so totally uncommon! Never, I beseech you,
undervalue the waiter who restores the ring you dropped in
the coffee-room; nor hold him cheaply who gives back the
umbrella you left in the cab. These seem such easy things
to do, but they are not easy. Men are more or less Cornish
wreckers in life, and very apt to regard the lost article as
treasure-trove. I have said all this to you, amiable reader,
that you may know what it cost me, on that same morning,
not to be a rogue, and not to enrich myself with the goods
of another.

I underwent a very long and searching self-examination
to ascertain why it was I had not appropriated that bag, an
offence which, legally speaking, would only amount to a
breach of trust. I said, "Is it that you had no need of
the money, Potts? Did you feel that your own means
were ample enough? Was it that your philosophy had
made you regard gold as mere dross, and then think that
the load was a burden? Or, taking higher ground, had
you recalled the first teachings of your venerable parent,
that good man and careful apothecary, who had given you
your first perceptions of right and wrong?" I fear that I
was obliged to say No, in turn, to each of these queries. I
would have been very glad to be right, proud to have been a
philosopher, overjoyed to feel myself swayed by moral
motives, but I could not palm the imposition on my conscience, and had honestly to own that the real reason of my
conduct was—I was in love! There was the whole of it!

There was an old sultan once so impressed with an ill
notion of the sex, that whenever a tale of misfortune or
disgrace reached him, his only inquiry as to the source of the
evil was, Who was she? Now my experiences of life have
travelled in another direction, and whenever I read of some
noble piece of heroism, or some daring act of self-devotion, I
don't ask whether he got the Bath or the Victoria Cross, if
he were made a governor here or a vice-governor there, but
who was She that prompted this glorious deed? I'd like to
know all about *her*: the colour of her eyes, her hair; was
she slender or plump; was she fiery or gentle; was it an old
attachment or an acute attack coming after a paroxysm at
first sight?

If I were the great chief of some great public department where all my subordinates were obliged to give heavy security for their honesty, I would neither ask for bail bonds or sureties, but I'd say, " Have you got a wife, or a sweetheart? either will do. Let me look at her. If she be worthy an honest man's love, I am satisfied; mount your high stool and write away."

Oh, how I longed to stand aright in that dear girl's eyes, that she should see me worthy of her! Had she yielded to all my wayward notions and rambling opinions, giving way either in careless indolence or out of inability to dispute them, she had never made the deep impression on my heart. It was because she had bravely asserted her own independence, never conceding where unconvinced, never yielding where unvanquished, that I loved her. What a stupid reverie was that of mine when I fancied her one of those strong-minded, determined women—a thickly-shod, umbrella-carrying female, who can travel alone and pass her trunk through a custom-house. No, she was delicate, timid, and gentle; there was no over-confidence in her, nor the slightest pretension. Rule me? not a bit of it. Guide, direct, support, confirm, sustain me; elevate my sentiments, cheer me on my road in life, making all evil odious in my eyes, and the good to seem better!

I verily believe, with such a woman, an humble condition in life offers more chances of happiness than a state of wealth and splendour. If the best prizes of life are to be picked up around a man's fireside, moderate means, conducing as they do to a home life, would point more certainly to these than all the splendour of grand receptions. If I were, say, a village doctor, a schoolmaster; if I were able to eke out subsistence in some occupation, whose pursuit might place me sufficiently favourably in her eyes. I don't like grocery, for instance, or even "dry goods," but something —it's no fault of mine if the English language be cramped and limited, and that I must employ the odious word "genteel," but it conveys, in a fashion, all that I aim at.

I began to think how this was to be done. I might return to my own country, go back to Dublin, and become Potts and Son—at least son! A very horrid thought, and very hard to adopt.

I might take a German degree in physic, and become an English doctor, say, at Baden, Ems, Geneva, or some other resort of my countrymen on the Continent. I might give lectures, I scarcely well knew on what, still less to whom; or I could start as Professor Potts, and instruct foreigners in Shakespeare. There were at least "three courses" open to me; and to consider them the better, I filled my pipe, and strolled off the high road into a shady copse of fine beech-trees, at the foot of one of which, and close to a clear little rivulet, I threw myself at full length, and thus, like Tityrus, enjoyed the leafy shade, making my meerschaum do duty for the shepherd's reed.

I had not been long thus, when I heard the footsteps of some persons on the road, and shortly after, the sound discontinuing, I judged that they must have crossed into the sward beneath the wood. As I listened I detected voices, and the next moment two figures emerged from the cover and stood before me: they were Vaterchen and Tintefleck.

"Sit down," said I, pointing to each in turn to take a place at either side of me. They had, it is true, been the cause of the great calamity of my life, but in no sense was the fault theirs, and I wished to show that I was generous and open-minded. Vaterchen acceded to my repeated invitation with a courteous humility, and seated himself at a little distance off; but Tintefleck threw herself on the grass, and with such a careless *abandon* that her hair escaped from the net that held it, and fell in great wavy masses across my feet.

"Ay," thought I, as I looked at the graceful outlines of her finely-shaped figure, here is the Amaryllis come to complete the tableau; only I would wish fewer spaugles, and a little more simplicity."

I saw that it was necessary to reassure Vaterchen as to my perfect sanity by some explanation as to my strange mode of travelling, and told him briefly, "that it was a caprice common enough with my countrymen to assume the knapsack, and take the road on foot; that we fancied in this wise we obtained a nearer view of life, and at least gained companionship with many from whom the accident of station might exclude us." I said this with an artful delicacy, meant to imply that I was pointing at a very great and valuable privilege of pedestrianism.

He smiled with a sad, a very sad expression on his features, " But in what wise, highly honoured Sir ? "—he addressed me always as Hoch Ge-ehrter Herr—"could you promise to yourself advantage from such associations as these? I cannot believe you would condescend to know us simply to carry away in memory the little traits that must needs distinguish such lives as our. I would not insult my respect for you by supposing that you come amongst us to note the absurd contrast between our real wretchedness and our mock gaiety; and yet what else is there to gain? What can the poor mountebank teach you beyond this? "

"Much," said I, with fervour, as I grasped his hand, and shook it heartily; " much, if you only gave me this one lesson that I now listen to, and I learn that a man's heart can beat as truthfully under motley as under the embroidered coat of a minister. The man who speaks as you do, can teach me much."

He gave a short but heavy sigh, and turned away his head. He arose after a few minutes, and going gently across the grass, spread his handkerchief over the head and face of the girl, who had at once fallen into a deep sleep.

" Poor thing," muttered he, " it is well she *can* sleep ! She has eaten nothing to-day ! "

" But, surely," said I, " there is some village or some wayside inn near this —— "

" Yes, there is the " Eckstein," a little public about two miles further; but we didn't care to reach it before nightfall. It is so painful to pass many hours in a place and never call for anything; one is ill looked on, and uncomfortable from it; and as we have only what would pay for our supper and lodging, we thought we'd wear away the noon in the forest here; and arrive at the inn by close of day."

"Let me be your travelling companion for to-day," said I, " and let us push forward and have our dinner together. Yes, yes, there is far less of condescension in the offer than you suspect. I am neither great nor milor, I am one of a class like your own, Vaterchen, and what I do for you to-day some one else will as probably do for me to-morrow."

Say what I could, the old man would persist in believing that this was only another of those eccentricities for which Englishmen are famed; and though, with the tact of a native good breeding, he showed no persistence in opposition, I saw plainly enough that he was unconvinced by all my arguments.

While the girl slept, I asked him how he chanced upon the choice of his present mode of life, since there were many things in his tone and manner that struck me as strangely unlike what I should have ascribed to his order.

"It is a very short story," said he; "five minutes will tell it, otherwise I might scruple to impose on your patience. It was thus I became what you see me."

Short as the narrative was, I must keep it for another page.

CHAPTER XXX.

I GIVE the old man's story, as nearly as I can, the way he told it.

"There is a little village on the Lago di Guarda, called Caprini. My family had lived there for some generations. We had a little wine-shop, and though not a very pretentious one, it was the best in the place, and much frequented by the inhabitants. My father was in considerable repute while he lived; he was twice named Syndic of Caprini, and I myself once held that dignity. You may not know, perhaps that the office is one filled at the choice of the townsfolk, and not nominated by the government. Still the crown has its influence in the selection, and likes well to see one of its own partisans in power, and, when a popular candidate does succeed against their will, the government officials take good care to make his berth as uncomfortable as they can. These are small questions of politics to ask you to follow, but they were our great ones; and we were as ardent and excited and eager about the choice of our little local governor as though he wielded real power in a great state.

"When I obtained the syndicate, my great ambition was to tread in the footsteps of my father, old Gustave Gamerra, who had left behind him a great name as the assertor of popular rights, and who had never bated the very least privilege that pertained to his native village, I did my best—not very discreetly, perhaps—for my own sake, but I held my head high against all imperial and royal officials, and I taught them to feel that there was at least one popular institution in the land that no exercise of tyranny could assail. I was over-zealous about all our rights. I raked up out of old archives traces of privileges that we once possessed and had never formally surrendered; I discovered concessions that had been made to us of which we had never reaped the profit; and I was, so to say, ever at war with the authorities, who were frank enough to say, that when my two years of office expired, they meant to give me some wholesome lessons about obedience.

"They were as good as their word. I had no sooner descended to a private station than I was made to feel all the severities of their displeasure. They took away my license to sell salt and tobacco, and thereby fully one half of my little income; they tried to withdraw my privilege to sell wine, but this came from the municipality, and they could not touch it. Upon information that they had suborned, they twice visited my house to search for seditious papers, and, finally, they made me such a mark of their enmity that the timid of the townsfolk were afraid to be seen with me, and gradually dropped my acquaintance. This preyed upon me most of all. I was all my life of a social habit; I delighted to gather my friends around me, or to go and visit them, and to find myself, as I was growing old, growing friendless, too, was a great blow.

"I was a widower, and had none but an only daughter."

When he had reached thus far, his voice failed him, and,

after an effort or two, he could not continue, and turned away
his head and buried it in his hands. Full ten minutes elapsed
before he resumed, which he did with a hard, firm tone, as
though resolved not to be conquered by his emotion.

  "The cholera was dreadfully severe all through the Italian
Tyrol ; it swept from Venice to Milan, and never missed
even the mountain villages, far away up the Alps. In our
little hamlet, we lost one hundred and eighteen souls, and
my Gretchen was one of them.

  "We had all grown to be very hard-hearted to each
other; misfortune was at each man's door, and he had no
heart to spare for a neighbour's grief; and yet such was the
sorrow for her, that they came, in all this suffering and
desolation, to try and comfort and keep me up, and though
it was a time when all such cares were forgotten, the young
people went and laid fresh flowers over her grave every
morning. Well, that was very kind of them, and made me
weep heartily, and, in weeping, my heart softened, and I got
to feel that God knew what was best for all of us, and that
mayhap he had taken her away to spare her greater sorrow
hereafter, and left me to learn that I should pray to go to
her. She had only been in the earth eight days, and I was
sitting alone in my solitary house, for I could not bear to
open the shop, and began to think that I'd never have the
courage to do so again, but would go away and try some
other place and some other means of livelihood—it was while
thinking thus, a sharp, loud knock came to the door, and I
arose, rather angrily, to answer it.

  "It was a sergeant of an infantry regiment, whose
detachment was on march for Peschiera : there were
troubles down there, and the government had to send off
three regiments in all haste from Vienna to suppress them.
The sergeant was a Bohemian, and his regiment the Kinsky.
He was a rough, coarse fellow, very full of his authority,
despising all villagers, and holding Italians in especial contempt. He came to order me to prepare rations and room
for six soldiers, who were to arrive that evening. I answered,
boldly, that I would not. I had served the office of syndic in
the town, and was thus for ever exempt from the 'billet,'
and I led him into my little sitting-room, and showed him
my 'brevet,' framed and glazed, over the chimney. He

laughed heartily at my remonstrance, coolly turned the
'brevet' with its face to the wall, and said,—

"'If you don't want twelve of us instead of six, you'll
keep your tongue quiet, and give us a stoup of your best
wine.'

"I did not wait to answer him, but seized my hat and
hurried away to the Platz Commandant. He was an old
enemy of mine, but I could not help it; his was the only
authority I could appeal to, and he was bound to do me
justice. When I reached the bureau, it was so crowded with
soldiers and townsfolk, some seeking for billets, some insisting on their claim to be free, that I could not get past the
door, and, after an hour's waiting, I was fain to give up the
attempt, and turned back home again, determined to make
my statement in writing, which, after all, might have been
the most fitting.

"I found my doors wide open when I got there, and my
shop crowded with soldiers, who, either seated on the counter
or squatting on their knapsacks, had helped themselves
freely to my wine, even to raising the top of an old cask,
and drinking it in large cups from the barrel, which they
handed liberally to their comrades as they passed.

"My heart was too full to care much for the loss, though
the insult pressed me sorely, and, pushing my way through,
I gained the inner room to find it crowded like the shop.
All was in disorder and confusion. The old musket my
father had carried for many a year, and which had hung
over the chimney as an heirloom, lay smashed in fragments
on the floor; some wanton fellow had run his bayonet
through my 'brevet' as syndic, and hung it up in derision
as a banner; and one, he was a corporal, had taken down
the wreath of white roses that lay on Gretchen's coffin till it
was laid in the earth, and placed it on his head. When I
saw this, my senses left me; I gave a wild shriek, and
dashed both my hands in his face. I tried to strangle him;
I would have torn him with my teeth had they not dragged
me off and dashed me on the ground, where they trampled
on me, and beat me, and then carried me away to prison.

I was four days in prison before I was brought up to be
examined. I did not know whether it had been four or forty,
for my senses had left me and I was mad; perhaps it was

the cold dark cell and the silence restored me, but I came
out calm and collected. I remembered everything to the
smallest incident.

" The soldiers were heard first; they agreed in everything,
and their story had all the air of truth about it. They
owned they had taken my wine, but said that the regiment
was ready and willing to pay for it so soon as I came back,
and that all the rest they had done were only the usual
follies of troops on a march. I began by claiming my
exemption as a syndic, but was stopped at once by being
told that my claim had never been submitted to the
authorities, and that in my outrage on the imperial force I
had forfeited all consideration on that score. My offence
was easily proven. I did not deny it, and I was lectured for
nigh an hour on the enormity of my crime, and then
sentenced to pay a fine of a thousand zwanzigers to the
emperor, and to receive four-and-twenty blows with the
stick. 'It should have been eight-and-forty but for my age,'
he said.

"On the same stool where I sat to hear my sentence was
a circus man, waiting the Platz Commandant's leave to give
some representation in the village. I knew him from his
dress, but had never spoken to him nor he to me; just, however, as the commandant had delivered the words of my
condemnation he turned to look at me; mayhap to see how
I bore up under my misfortune. I saw his glance, and I did
my best to sustain it. I wanted to bear myself manfully
throughout, and not to let anyone know my heart was
broken, which I felt it was. The struggle was, perhaps,
more than I was able for, and, while the tears gushed out
and ran down my cheeks, I burst out laughing, and laughed
away fit after fit, making the most terrible faces all the
while; so outrageously droll were my convulsions, that every
one around laughed too, and there was the whole court
screaming madly with the same impulse, and unable to control it.

"'Take the fool away!' cried the commandant, at last,
'and bring him to reason with a hazel rod.' And they
carried me off, and I was flogged.

"It was about a week after I was down near Commachio
I don't know how I got there, but I was in rags, and had no

money, and the circus people came past and saw me.
'There's the old fellow that nearly killed us with his droll
face,' said the chief. 'I'll give you two zwanzigers a day, my
man, if you'll only give us a few grins like that every evening. Is it a bargain?'

"I laughed. I could not keep now from laughing at
everything, and the bargain was made, and I was a clown
from that hour. They taught me a few easy tricks to help
me in my trade, but it is my face that they care for—none
can see it unmoved."

He turned on me as he spoke with a fearful contortion of
countenance, but, moved by his story, and full only of what I
had been listening to, I turned away and shed tears.

"Yes," said he, meditatively, "many a happy heart is
kindled at the fire that is consuming another. As for myself, both joy and sorrow are dead within me. I am without
hope, and, stranger still, without fear."

"But you are not without benevolence," said I, as I looked
towards the sleeping girl.

"She was so like Gretchen," said he; and he bent down
his head and sobbed bitterly.

I would have asked him some questions about her if I
dared, but I felt so rebuked by the sorrow of the old man,
that my curiosity seemed almost unfeeling.

"She came amongst us a mere child," said he, "and
speedily attached herself to me. I contrived to learn enough
of her dialect to understand and talk to her, and at last she
began to regard me as a father, and even called me such.
It was a long time before I could bear this. Every time I
heard the word my grief would burst out afresh; but what
won't time do? I have come to like it now."

"And is she good, and gentle, and affectionate?" asked I.

"She is far too good and true-hearted to be in such company as ours. Would that some rich person—it should be a
lady—kind, and gentle, and compassionate, could see her and
take her away from such associates, and this life of shame,
ere it be too late. If I have a sorrow left me now, it is for
her."

I was silent, for though the wish only seemed fair and
natural enough on his part, I could not help thinking how
improbable such an incident would prove.

" She would repay it all," said he. " If ever there was a
nature rich in great gifts, it is hers. She can learn whatever
she will, and for a word of kindness she would hold her
hand in the fire for you. Hush!" whispered he, "she is
stirring. What is it, darling?" said he, creeping close to
her, as she lay, throwing her arms wildly open, but not
removing the handkerchief from her face.

She muttered something hurriedly, and then burst into a
laugh so joyous and so catching, it was impossible to refrain
from joining in it.

She threw back the kerchief at once and started to her
knees, gazing stedfastly, almost sternly, at me. I saw that
the old man comprehended the inquiry of her glance, and as
quickly whispered a few words in her ear. She listened till
he had done, and then springing towards me, she caught my
hand and kissed it.

I suspect he must have rebuked the ardour of her movement, for she hung her head despondingly, and turned away
from us both.

" Now for the road once more," said Vaterchen, " for if we
stay much longer here, we shall have the forest flies, which
are always worse towards evening."

It was not without great difficulty I could prevent his
carrying my knapsack for me, and even the girl herself
would gladly have borne some of my load. At last, however, we set forth, Tintefleck lightening the way with a
merry canzonette, that had the time of a quick step.

<hr />

CHAPTER XXXI.

WHAT a pleasant little dinner we had that day. It was
laid out in a little summer-house of the inn-garden. All
overgrown with a fine old fig-tree, through whose leaves the
summer wind played deliciously, while a tiny rivulet rippled
close by, and served to cool our " Achten-thaler "—an

amount of luxury that made Tintefleck quite wild with laughter.

"Is it cold enough?" she asked, archly, in her peasant dialect, each time the old man laid down his glass.

As I came gradually to pick up the occasional meaning of her words—a process which her expressive pantomime greatly aided—I was struck by the marvellous acuteness of a mind so totally without culture, and I could not help asking Vaterchen why he had never attempted to instruct her.

"What can I do?" said he, despondently; "there are no books in the only language she knows, and the only language she will condescend to speak. She can understand Italian, and I have read stories for her, and sonnets, too, out of Leopardi, but though she will listen in all eagerness till they are finished, no sooner over than she breaks out into some wild Calabrian song, and asks me is it not worth all the fine things I have been giving her, thrice told."

"Could you not teach her to write?"

"I tried that. I bought a slate, and I made a bargain with her that she should have a scarlet knot for her hair when she could ask me for it in written words. Well, all seemed to go on prosperously for a time; we had got through half the alphabet very successfully, till we came to the letter H. This made her laugh immediately, it was so like a scaffold we had in the circus for certain exercises; and no sooner had I marked down the letter, than she snatched the pencil from me, and drew the figure of a man on each bar of the letter. From that hour forth, as though her wayward humour had been only imprisoned, she burst forth into every imaginable absurdity at our lessons. Every ridiculous event of our daily life she drew, and with a rapidity almost incredible. I was not very apt, as you may imagine, in acquiring the few accomplishments they thought to give me, and she caricatured me under all my difficulties."

"Si, si," broke she in at this; for, with a wonderful acuteness, she could trace something of a speaker's meaning where every word was unknown to her. As she spoke she arose, and fled down the garden at top speed.

"Why has she gone? Is she displeased at your telling me all these things about her?" asked I.

16

"Scarcely that; she loves to be noticed. Nothing really seems to pain her so much as when she is passed over unremarked. When such an event would occur in the circus, I have seen her sob through her sleep all the night after. I half suspect now she is piqued at the little notice you have bestowed upon her. All the better if it be so."

"But here she comes again."

With the same speed she now came back to us, holding her slate over her head, and showing that she rightly interpreted what the old man had said of her.

"Now for my turn!" said Vaterchen, with a smile. "She is never weary of drawing me in every absurd and impossible posture."

"What is it to be, Tintefleck?" asked he. "How am I to figure this time?"

She shook her head without replying, and, making a sign that she was not to be questioned or interrupted, she nestled down at the foot of the fig-tree, and began to draw.

The old man now drew near me, and proceeded to give me further details of her strange temper and ways. I could mark that throughout all he said, a tone of intense anxiety and care prevailed, and that he felt her disposition was exactly that which exposed her to the greatest perils for her future. There was a young artist who used to follow her through all the South Tyrol, affecting to be madly in love with her, but of whose sincerity and honour Vaterchen professed to have great misgivings. He gave her lessons in drawing, and, what was less to be liked, he made several studies of herself. "The artless way," said the old man, "she would come and repeat to me all his raptures about her, was at first a sort of comfort to me. I felt reassured by her confidence, and also by the little impression his praises seemed to make, but I saw later on that I was mistaken. She grew each day more covetous of these flatteries, and it was no longer laughingly, but in earnest seriousness she would tell me that the 'Fornarina' in some gallery had not such eyes as hers, and that some great statue that all the world admired was far inferior to her in shape. If I had dared to rebuke her vanity, or to ridicule her pretensions, all my influence would have been gone for ever. She would have left us, gone who knows whither, and been lost, so that

I had nothing for it but to seem to credit all she said and yet hold the matter lightly, and I said beauty had no value except when associated with rank and station. If queens and princesses be handsome, they are more fitted to adorn this high estate, but for humble folk it is as great a mockery as these tinsel gems we wear in the circus.

" 'Max says not,' said she to me one evening, after one of my usual lectures. 'Max says, there are queens would give their coronets to have my hair, ay, or even one of the dimples in my cheek.'

" 'Max is a villain,' said I, before I could control my words.

" 'Max is a vero signor!' said she, haughtily, 'and not like one of us; and more, too, I'll go and tell him what you have called him.' She bounded away from me at this, and I saw her no more till nightfall.

" 'What has happened to you, poor child,' said I, as I saw her lying on the floor of her room, her forehead bleeding, and her dress all draggled and torn. She would not speak to me for a long while, but by much entreating and caressing I won upon her to tell me what had befallen her. She had gone to the top of the 'Glucksberg' and thrown herself down. It was a fearful height, and only was she saved by being caught by the brambles and tangled foliage of the cliff; and all this for 'one harsh word of mine,' she said. But I knew better; the struggle was deeper in her heart than she was aware of, and Max had gone suddenly away, and we saw no more of him."

"Did she grieve after him?"

"I scarcely can say she did. She fretted, but I think it was for her own loneliness and the want of that daily flattery she had grown so fond of. She became overbearing, and even insolent, too, with all her equals, and though for many a day she had been the spoiled child of the troop, many began to weary of her waywardness. I don't know how all this might have turned out, when, just as suddenly, she changed and became everything that she used to be."

When the old man had got thus far, the girl arose, and, without saying a word, laid the slate before us. Vaterchen, not very quick-sighted, could not at once understand the picture, but I caught it at once, and laughed immoderately. She

had taken the scene where I had presented Vaterchen and
herself to the ladies at the tea-table, and with an intense
humour, sketched all the varying emotions of the incident.
The offended dignity of the old lady, the surprise and mortification of Miss Herbert, and my own unconscious pretension
as I pointed to the "friends" who accompanied me, were
drawn with the spirit of high caricature. Nor did she spare
Vaterchen or herself; they were drawn, perhaps, with a
more exaggerated satire than all the rest.

The old man no sooner comprehended the subject than he
drew his hand across it, and turned to her with words of
anger and reproach. I meant, of course, to interfere in her
behalf, but it was needless; she fled, laughing, into the
garden, and before many minutes were over we heard her
merry voice, with the tinkle of a guitar to assist it.

"There it is," said Vaterchen, moodily. "What are you
to do with a temperament like that ? "

That was a question I was in no wise prepared to answer.
Tintefleck's temperament seemed to be the the very converse
of my own. I was over eager to plan out everything in life.
She appeared to be just as impulsively bent on risking all.
My head was always calculating eventualities; *hers*, it struck
me, never worried itself about difficulties till in the midst of
them. Now, Jean Paul tells us that when a man detects
any exaggerated bias in his character, instead of endeavouring, by daily watching, to correct it, he will be far more successful if he ally himself with some one of a diametrically
opposite humour. If he be rash, for instance, let him seek
companionship with the sluggish. If his tendency bear to
over-imagination, let him frequent the society of realists.
Why, therefore, should not I and Tintefleck be mutually
beneficial? Take the two different kinds of wood in a bow :
one will supply resistance, the other inflexibility. It was a
pleasant notion, and I resolved to test it.

"Vaterchen," said I, "call me to-morrow, when you get
ready for the road. I will keep you company as far as
Constance."

"Ah, Sir," said he, with a sigh, "you will be well weary
of us before half the journey is over ; but you shall be obeyed."

CHAPTER XXXII.

NEXT morning, just as day was breaking, we set out on foot on our road to Constance. There was a pinkish-grey streak of light on the horizon, sure sign of a fine day, and the bright stars twinkled still in the clear half-sombre sky, and all was calm and noiseless—nothing to be heard but the tramp of our own feet on the hard causeway.

With the cowardly caution of one who feels the water with his foot before he springs in to swim, I was glad that I made my first experiences of companionship with these humble friends while it was yet dark and none could see us. The old leaven of snobbery was unsubdued in my heart, and, as I turned to look at poor Vaterchen and then at the tinsel finery of Catinka, I bethought me of the little consideration the world extends to such as these and their belongings. "Vagabonds all!" would say some rich banker, as he rolled by in his massive travelling-carriage, creaking with imperials and jingling with bells; "Vagabonds all!" would mutter the Jew pedlar, as he looked down from the *banquette* of the diligence. How slight is the sympathy of the realist for the poor creature whose life-labour is to please. How prone to regard him as useless, or, even worse, forgetting, the while, how a wiser than he has made many things in this beautiful world of ours that they should merely minister to enjoyment, gladden the eye and ear, and make our pilgrimage less weary. Where would be the crimson jay? where the scarlet bustard? where the gorgeous peacock, with the nosegay on his tail? where the rose, and the honeysuckle, and the purple foxglove, mingling with the wild thorn in our hedgerows, if the universe were of *their* creation, and this great globe but one big workshop? You never insist that the daisy and the daffodil should be pot-herbs; and why are there not to be wild flowers in humanity as well as in the fields? Is it not a great pride to you who live under a bell-glass, nurtured and cared for, and with your name attached to a cleft-stick at

your side,—is not a great pride to know that you are not
like one of us poor dog-roses ? Be satisfied, then, with that
glory; we only ask to live! Shame on me for that " only!"
As if there could be anything more delightful than life.
Life, with all its capacities for love, and friendship, and
heroism, and self-devotion, for generous actions and noble
aspirations! Life to feel life, to know that we are in a
sphere specially constructed for the exercise of our senses
and the play of our faculties, free to choose the road we
would take, and with a glorious reward if our choice be the
right one !

" ' Vagabonds !' Yes," thought I, " there was once on a
time such a vagabond, and he strolled along from village to
village, making of his flute a livelihood; a poor performer,
too, he tells us he was, but he could touch the hearts of these
simple villagers with his tones as he could move the hearts
of thousands more learned than they with his marvellous
pathos, and this vagabond was called Oliver Goldsmith." I
have no words to say the ecstasy this thought gave me.
Many a proud traveller doubtless swept past the poor wayfarer as he went, dusty and footsore, and who was, neverthe-
less, journeying onward to a great immortality; to be a
name remembered with blessings by generations when the
haughty man that scorned him was forgotten for ever.
" And so now," thought I, " some splendid Russian or some
Saxon Crœsus will crash by and not be conscious that the
thin and weary-looking youth, with the girl's bundle on his
stick and the red umbrella under his arm, that this is Potts!
Ay, Sir, you fancy that to be threadbare and footsore is to
be vulgar-minded and ignoble, and you never so much as
suspect that the heart inside that poor plaid waistcoat is
throbbing with ambitions high as a Kaiser's, and that the
brain within that battered Jim Crow is the realm of thoughts
profound as Bacon's, and high-soaring as Milton's."

If I make my reader a sharer in these musings of mine,
it is because they occupied me for some miles of the way.
Vaterchen was not talkative, and loved to smoke on uninter-
ruptedly. I fancy that, in his way, he was as great a
dreamer as myself. Catinka would have talked incessantly
if anyone had listened, or could understand her. As it was,
she recited legends and sang songs for herself, as happy as

ever a blackbird was to listen to his own melody; and
though I paid no especial attention to her music, still the
sounds float through all my thoughts, bathing them with a
soothing flood; just as the air we breathe is often loaded
with a sweet and perfumed breath ere we know it. On the
whole, we journeyed along very pleasantly, and what between
the fresh morning air, the brisk exercise, and the novelty of
the situation, I felt in a train of spirits that made me delighted with everything. "This, after all," thought I, "is
more like the original plan I sketched out for myself. This
is the true mode to see life and the world. The student of
Nature never begins his studies with the more complicated
organisations; he sets out with what is simplest in structure,
and least intricate in function; he begins with the extreme
link of the chain; so, too, I start with the investigation of
those whose lives of petty cares and small ambitions must
render them easy of appreciation. This poor Mollusca
Vaterchen, for instance—to see is to know him; and the
girl, how absurd to connect such a guileless child of nature
as that, with those stereotyped notions of feminine craft and
subtlety!" I then went on to imagine some future biographer of mine engaged on this portion of my life, puzzled for
materials, puzzled, still more, to catch the clue to my meaning in it. "At this time," will he say, "Potts, by one of
those strange caprices which often were the mainspring of
his actions, resolved to lead a gipsy life. His ardent love of
nature, his heartfelt enjoyment of scenery, and, more than
even these, a certain breadth and generosity of character,
disposed him to sympathise with those who have few to pity
and fewer to succour them. With these wild children of the
roadside he lived for months, joyfully sharing the burdens
they carried, and taking his part in their privations. It was
here he first met Catinka." It stopped at this sentence, and
slowly repeated to myself, "'It was here he first met
Catinka!' What will he have next to record?" thought I.
"Is Potts now to claim sympathy as the victim of a passion
that regarded not station, nor class, nor fortune; that despised the cold conventionalities of a selfish world, and asked
only a heart for a heart? Is he to be remembered as the
faithful believer in his own theory—Love, above all? Are
we to hear of him clasping rapturously to his bosom the poor

forlorn girl ? " So intensely were my feelings engaged in
my speculations, that, at this critical pass, I threw my arms
around Catinka's neck, and kissed her. A rebuke, not very
cruel, not in the least angry or peevish, brought me quickly
to myself, and as Vaterchen was fortunately in front and saw
nothing of what passed, I speedily made my peace. I do
not know how it happened, but in that same peace-making,
I had passed my arm round her waist and there it remained
—an army of occupation after the treaty was signed—and
we went along, side by side, very amicably—very happily.

We are often told that a small competence—the just
enough to live on—is the bane of all enterprise ; that men
thus placed are removed from the stimulus of necessity, and
yet not lifted into the higher atmosphere of ambitions.
Exactly in the same way do I believe that equality is the
grave of love. The passion thrives on difficulty, and requires sacrifice. You must bid defiance to mankind in your
choice, or you are a mere fortune-hunter. Show the world
the blushing peasant girl you have made your wife, and say,
" Yes, I have had courage to do this." Or else strive for a
princess— a Russian princess. Better, far better, however,
the humble-hearted child of nature and the fields, the simple,
trusting, confiding girl, who regarding her lover as a sort of
demi-god, would, while she clung to him —— "

" You press me so hard !" murmured Catinka, half rebukingly, but with a sort of pouting expression that became
her marvellously.

" I was thinking of something that interested me, dearest,"
said I ; but I'm not sure that I made my meaning very clear
to her, and yet there was a roguish look in her black eye
that puzzled me greatly. I began to like her, or, if you
prefer the phrase, to fall in love with her. I knew it—I
felt it just the way that a man who has once had the ague
never mistakes when he is going to have a return of the
fever. In the same way, exactly did I recognise all the pre-
monitory symptoms ; the giddiness, the shivering, increased
action of the heart ——. Halt, Potts ! and reflect a bit ;
are you describing love, or a tertian ?

How will the biographer conduct himself here ? Whether
will he have to say, " Potts resisted manfully this fatal
attachment ; had he yielded to the seductions of this early

passion, it is more than probable we would never have seen him this, that, and t'other, nor would the world have been enriched with—Heaven knows what;" or shall he record, "Potts loved her, loved her as only such a nature as his ever loves? He felt keenly that, in a mere worldly point of view, he must sacrifice; but it was exactly in that love and that sacrifice was born the poet, the wondrous child of song, who has given us the most glorious lyrics of our language. He had the manliness to share his fortune with this poor girl. 'It was,' he tells us himself, in one of those little touching passages in his diary, which place him immeasurably above the mock sentimentality of Jean Jacques—'it was on the road to Constance, of a bright and breezy summer morning, that I told her of my love. We were walking along, our arms around each other, as might two happy, guileless children. I was very young in what is called the world, but I had a boundless confidence in myself; my theory was, "If I be strengthened by the deep devotion of one loving heart, I have no fears of failure." Beautiful words, and worthy of all memory! And then he goes on : 'I drew her gently over to a grassy bench on the roadside, and taking my purse from my pocket, poured out before her its humble contents, in all something less than twenty sovereigns, but to her eyes a very Pactolus of wealth.'"

"What if I were to try this experiment?" thought I; "what if I were, so to say, to anticipate my own biography?" The notion pleased me much. There was something novel in it, too. It was making the experiment in the *corpore vile* of accident, to see what might come of it.

"Come here, Catinka," said I, pointing to a moss-covered rock at the roadside, with a little well at its base—"come here, and let me have a drink of this nice clear water."

She assented with a smile and a nod, detaching at the same time a little cup from the flask she wore at her side, in *vivandière* fashion. "And we'll fill my flask, too," said she, showing that it was empty. With a sort of childish glee she now knelt beside the stream, and washed the cup. What is it, I wonder, that gives the charm to running water, and imparts a sort of glad feeling to its contemplation? Is it that its ceaseless flow suggests that "for ever" which contrasts so powerfully with all short-lived pleasures? I cannot tell, but I was still musing over the difficulty, when, having twice offered me the cup without my noticing it, she at last raised it to my lips. And I drank—oh, what a draught it was! so clear, so cold, so pure; and all the time my eyes were resting on hers, looking, as it were, into another well, the deepest and most unfathomable of all.

"Sit down here beside me on this stone, Catinka, and help me to count these pieces of money; they have got so mingled together that I scarcely know what is left me." She seemed delighted with the project, and sat down at once, and I, throwing myself at her feet, poured the contents of my purse into her lap.

"Madonna mia!" was all she could utter as she beheld the gold. Aladdin in the cave never felt a more overwhelming rapture than did she at sight of these immense riches. "But where did it come from?" cried she, wildly. "Have you got mines of gold and silver? Have you got gems, too —rubies and pearls? Oh, say if there be pearls; I love them so? And are you really a great prince, the son of a king; and are you wandering the world this way to seek adventures, or in search, mayhap, of that lovely princess you are in love with?" With wildest impetuosity she asked these and a hundred other questions, for it was only now and then that I could trace her meaning, which expressive pantomime did much to explain.

I tried to convince her that what she deemed a treasure was a mere pittance, which a week or two would exhaust; that I was no prince, nor had I a kingly father; "and last of all," said I, "I am not in pursuit of a princess. But I'll tell you what I am in search of, Catinka: one trusting, faithful, loving, heart; one that will so unite itself to mine, as to have no joys, or sorrows, or cares, but mine; one content to go wherever I go, live however I live, and no matter what my faults may be, or how meanly others think of me, will ever regard me with eyes of love and devotion."

I had held her hand while I uttered this, gazing up into her eyes with ecstasy, for I saw how their liquid depth appeared to move as though about to overflow, when at last she spoke, and said,

"And there are no pearls!"

"Poor child!" thought I, "she cannot understand one word I have been saying. Listen to me, Catinka," said I, with a slow utterance. "Would you give me your heart for all this treasure?"

"Si, si!" cried she, eagerly.

"And love me always—for ever?"

"Si," said she, again; but I fancied with less of energy than before.

"And when it was spent and gone, and nothing remaining of it, what would you do?"

"Send you to gather more, mio caro," said she, pressing my hand to her lips, as though in earnest of the blandishments she would bestow upon me.

Now, I cannot affect to say that all this was very reassuring. This poor simple child of the mountains showed a spirit as sordid and as calculating as though she were baptised in May Fair. It was a terrible shock to me to see this; a dire overthrow to a very fine edifice that I was just putting the roof on! "Would Kate Herbert have made me such a speech?" thought I. "Would she have declared herself so venal and so worldly?—and why not? May it not be, perhaps, simply that a mere question of good breeding, the usages of a polite world, might have made all the difference, and that she would have felt what poor Catinka felt and owned to. If this were true, the advantages were all on the side of sincerity. With honesty as the basis, what may not one build up of character? Where there is candour there are at least no disappointments. This poor simple child, untutored in the wiles of a scheming world, where all is false, unreal, and deceptive, has the courage to say that her heart can be bought. She is ready in her innocence, too, to sell it, just as the Indians sell a great territory for a few glass beads or bright buttons. And why should not I make the acquisition in the very spirit of a new settler? It was I discovered this lone island of the sea; it was I first landed on this unknown shore; why not claim a sovereignty so cheaply established." I put the question arithmetically before me: Given, a young girl, totally new to life and its seductions, deeply impressed with the value of wealth, to find the measure of venality in a well brought-up young lady, educated at Clapham, and finished at Boulogne-sur-Mer. I expressed it thus : $D - y = T - x$, or an unknown quantity.

"What strange marks are you drawing there?" cried she, as I made these figures on the slate.

"A caprice," said I, in some confusion.

"No," said she; "I know better. It was a charm. Tell truth—it was a charm."

"A charm, dearest; but for what?"

"*I* know," said she, shaking her head and laughing, with a sort of wicked drollery.

"*You* know! Impossible, child."

"Yes," she said with great gravity, while she swept her hand across the slate and erased all the figures. "Yes *I* know, and I'll not permit it."

"But what, in Heaven's name, is trotting through your head, Catinka? You have not the vaguest idea of what those signs meant."

"Yes," she said even more solemnly than before. "I know it all. You mean to steal away my heart in spite of me, and you are going to do it with a charm."

"And what success shall I have, Catinka?"

"Oh, do not ask me," said she, in a tone of touching misery. "I feel it very sore here." And she pressed her hand to her side. "Ah me," sighed sh , "if there were only pearls!"

The ecstasy her first few words gave me was terribly routed by this vile conclusion, and I started abruptly, and in an angry voice, said, "Let us go on; Vaterchen will fear we are lost."

"And all this gold; what shall I do with it?" cried she.

"What you will. Throw it into the well if you like," said I, angrily; for in good sooth I was out of temper with her, and myself, and all mankind.

"Nay," said she mildly, "it is yours; but I will carry it for you if it weary you."

I might have felt rebuked by the submissive gentleness of her words; indeed, I know not how it was that they did not so move me, and I walked on in front of her, heedless of her entreaties that I should wait till she came up beside me.

When she did join me, she wanted to talk immensely. She had all manner of questions to ask about where my treasure came from; how often I went back there to replenish it; was I quite sure that it could never, never be exhausted, and such-like. But I was in no gracious mood for such inquiries, and telling her that I wished to follow my own thoughts without interruption, I walked along in silence.

I cannot tell the weight I felt at my heart. I am not speaking figuratively. No; it was exactly as though a great mass of heavy metal filled my chest, forced out my ribs, and pressed down my diaphragm; and though I held my hands to my sides with all my force, the pressure still remained.

"What a bitter mockery it is," thought I, "if the only false thing in all the world should be the human heart! There are diamonds that will resist fire, gold that will stand the crucible; but the moment you come to man and his affections, all is hollow and illusory!"

Why do we give the name worldliness to traits of selfish advancement and sordid gain, when a young creature like this, estranged from all the commerce of mankind, who knows nothing of that bargain-and-barter system which we call civilisation, reared and nurtured like a young fawn in her native woods, should, as though by a very instinct of corruption, have a heart as venal as any hackneyed beauty of three London seasons.

Let no man tell me now, that it is our vicious system of female training, our false social organisation, our spurious morality, laxity of family ties, and the rest of it. I am firmly persuaded that a young squaw of the Choctaws has as many anxieties about her "*parti*" as any belle of Belgravia, even though the settlements be only paid in sharks' teeth and human toupees.

And what an absurdity is our whole code on this subject! A man is actually expected to court, solicit, and even worship the object that he is after all called upon to pay for. You do not smirk at the salmon in your fishmonger's window, or ogle the lamb at your butcher's; you go in boldly and say, "How much the pound?" If you sighed outside for a week, you'd get it never the cheaper. Why not then make an

honest market of what is so saleable. What a saving of
time to know that the splendid creature yonder, with the
queenly air, can only be had at ten thousand a-year, but that
the spicy article with the black ringlets will go for two!
Instead of all the heart-burnings and blank disappointments
we see now, we should have a practical, contented genera-
tion; and in the same spirit that a man of moderate fortune
turns away from the seductions of turtle and whitebait,
while he orders home his mutton chop, he would avert his
gaze from beauty, and fix his affections on the dumpy woman
that can be "got a bargain."

Why did not the poet say, Venality, thy name is Woman?
It would suit the prosody about as well, and the purpose
better. The Turks are our masters in all this; they are
centuries—whole centuries in advance of us. How I wish
some Babbage would make a calculation of the hours, weeks,
years, centuries of time, are lost in what is called love-making.
Time, we are told, is money, and here, at once, is the fund to
pay off our national debt. Take the "time that's lost in
wooing" by a nation, say of twenty-eight or thirty millions,
and at the cheapest rate of labour—take the prison rate if
you like—and see if I be not right. Let the population
who now heave sighs, pound oyster-shells, let those who
pick quarrels, pick oakum, and we need no income-tax!

"I'll not sing any more," broke in Catinka. "I don't think
you have been listening to me."

"Listening to you!" said I, contemptuously, "certainly
not. When I want a siren, I take a pit ticket and go to
the Opera; seven-and-sixpence is the price of Circe, and dear
at the money." With this rude rebuff I waved her off, and
walked along once more alone.

At a sudden bend in the road we found Vaterchen seated
under a tree waiting for us, and evidently not a little uneasy
at our long absence.

"What is this?" said he, angrily, to Catinka. "Why
have you remained so long behind?"

"We sat down to rest at a well," said she, "and then
he took out a great bag of money to count, and there was
so much in it, so many pieces of bright gold, that one
could not help turning them over and over, and gazing at
them."

"And worshipping them too, girl!" cried he, indignantly, while he turned on me a look of sorrow and reproach. I returned his stare haughtily, and he arose and drew me to one side.

"Am I, then, once more mistaken in my judgment of men? Have *you*, too, duped me?" said he, in a voice that shook with agitation. Was it for this you offered us the solace of your companionship? Was it for this you condescended to journey with us, and deigned to be our host and entertainer?"

The appeal came at an evil moment: a vile, contemptible scepticism was at work within me. The rasp and file of Doubt were eating away at my heart, and I deemed "all men liars."

"And is it to me—Potts—you address such words as these, you consummate old humbug? What is there about me that denotes dupe or fool?"

The old man shook his head, and made a gesture to imply he had not understood me; and now I remembered that I had uttered this rude speech in English and not in German. With the memory of this fact came also the consciousness of its cruel meaning. What if I should have wronged him? What if the poor old fellow be honest and upright? What if he be really striving to keep this girl in the path of virtue? I came close to him, and fixed my eyes stedfastly on his face. He looked at me fearlessly, as an honest man might look. He never tried to turn away, nor did he make the slightest effort to evade me. He seemed to understand all the import of my scrutiny, for he said at last:

"Well, are you satisfied?"

"I am, Vaterchen," said I, "fully satisfied. Let us be friends." And I took his hand and shook it heartily.

"You think me honest?" asked he.

"I do think so."

"And I am not more honest than she is. No," said he, resolutely, "Tintefleck is true-hearted."

"What of *me?*" cried she, coming up and leaning her arm on the old man's shoulder—"what of *me?*"

"I have said that you are honest, and would not deceive!"

"Not *you*, Vaterchen—not *you*," said she, kissing him. And then, as she turned away she gave me a look so full of meaning, and so strange withal, that if I were to speak for an hour I could not explain it. It seemed to mean sorrow and reproach and wounded pride, with a dash of pity, and, above all and everything, defiance; ay, that was its chief character, and I believe I winced under it.

"Let us step out briskly," said Vaterchen. "Constance is a good eleven miles off yet."

"He looks tired already," said she, with a glance at me.

"I? I'm as fresh as when I started," said I. And I made an effort to appear brisk and lively, which only ended in making them laugh heartily.

CHAPTER XXXIII.

RESPECTABLE reader, there is no use in asking you if you have ever been in the Hotel of the " Balance," at Constance. Of course you have not. It is neither recorded in the book of John, nor otherwise known to fame. It is an obscure hostel, only visited by the very humblest wayfarers, and such poor offshoots of wretchedness as are fain to sleep on a truckle-bed and sup meanly. Vaterchen, however, spoke of it in generous terms. There was a certain oniony soup he had tasted there years ago whose flavour had not yet left his memory. He had seen, besides, the most delicious schweine fleisch hanging down from the kitchen rafters, and it had been revealed to him in a dream that a solvent traveller might have rashers on demand.

Poor fellow! I had not the vaguest idea of the eloquence he possessed till he came to talk on these matters. From modest and distrustful, he grew assured and confident; his hesitation of speech was replaced by a fluent utterance and a rich vocabulary; and he repeatedly declared that though the exterior was unprepossessing, and the service generally homely, there were substantial comforts obtainable which far surpassed the resources of more pretentious houses. "You are served on pewter, it is true," said he; "but pewter is a rare material to impart relish to a savoury mess." Though we should dine in the kitchen, he gave me to understand that even in this there were advantages, and that the polite guest of the *salon* never knew what it was to taste that rich odour of the "roast," or that fragrant incense that steamed up from the luscious stew, and which were to cookery what bouquet was to wine.

"I will not say that, honoured Sir," continued he, "to you, in the mixed company which frequent such humble hearths there would be matter of interest and amusement; but, to a man like myself, these chance companionships are delightful. Here all are stragglers, all adventurers. Not a man that deposits his pack in the corner and draws in his chair to the circle but is a wanderer and a pilgrim of one sort or other." He drew me an amusing picture of one of these groups, wherein, even without telling his story, each gave such insight into his life and travels as to present a sort of drama.

Whether it was that my companion had drawn too freely on his imagination, or that we had fallen on an unfortunate moment, I cannot say, but, though we found the company at the "Balance" numerous and varied, there was none of the sociality I looked for, still less of that generous warmth and good greeting which he assured me was the courtesy of such places. The men were chiefly carriers, with their mule-teams and heavy wagons, bound for the Bavarian Tyrol. There was a sprinkling of Jew pedlars, on their way to the Vorarlberg; a deserter from the Austrian army, trying to get back to Hesse Cassel; and an Italian image carrier, with a green parrot and a well-filled purse, going back to finish his days at Lucca.

Now none of these were elements of a very exalted or exclusive rank; they were each and all of them taken from the very base of the social pyramid; and yet, would it be believed that they regarded our entrance amongst them as an act of rare impudence!

17

A more polished company might have been satisfied with
averted heads or cold looks; these were less equivocal. One
called out to the landlord to know if he expected any gipsies;
another, affecting to treat us as solicitors for their patronage,
said he had no "batzen" to bestow on buffoonery; a third
suggested we should get up our theatricals under the cart-
shed outside, and beat the drum when we were ready; and
the deserter, a poor weak-looking, mangy wretch, with a
ragged fatigue-jacket and broken boots, put his arm round
Catinka's waist, to draw her on his knee, for the which she
dealt him such a slap on the face as fairly sent him on the
floor, in which ignoble position Vaterchen kicked him again
and again. In an instant all were upon us. Carters, pedlars,
and image man assailed us furiously. I suppose I beat somebody; I know that several beat *me*. The impression left
upon me when all was over was of a sort of human kaleiod-
scope, where the people turned every way without ceasing.
Now we seemed all on our feet, now on our heads, now on the
floor, now in the air, Vaterchen flying about like a demon,
while Tintefleck stood in a corner, with a gleaming stiletto
in hand, saying something in Calabrian, which sounded like
an invitation to come and be killed.

The police came at last; and, after a noisy scene of
accusation and denial, the weight of evidence went against
us, and we were marched off to prison, poor old Vaterchen
crying like a child for all the disgrace and misery he had
brought on his benefactor : and while he kissed my hand,
swearing that a whole life's devotion would not be enough to
recompense me for what he had been the means of inflicting on me, Catinka took it more easily, her chief regret
apparently being, that nobody came near enough to give her
a chance with her knife, which she assured us she wielded
with a notable skill, and could, with a jerk, send flying
through a door, like a javelin, at full six paces' distance;
nor, indeed, was it without considerable persuasion she could
be induced to restore it to its sheath, which truth obliges me
to own was inside her garter. Our prison, an old tower
adjoining the lake, had been once the dungeon of John Huss,
and the torture chamber, as it was still called, continued to
be used for mild transgressors, such as we were. A small
bribe induced the gaoler's wife to take poor Tintefleck for the

night into her own quarters, and Vaterchen and I were sole possessors of the gloomy old hall, which opened by a balcony, railed like a sort of cage, over the lake.

If the torture chamber had been denuded of its flesh pincers and thumb-screws, and the other ingenious devices of human cruelty, I am bound to own that its traditions as a place of suffering had not died out, as the fleas left nothing to be desired on the score of misery. Whether it was that they had been pinched by a long fast, or that we were more tender, cutaneously, than the aborigines, I know not, but I can safely aver that I never passed such a night, and sincerely trust that I may never pass such another. Though the air from the lake was cold and chilly, we preferred to crouch on the balcony to remaining within the walls, but even here our persecutors followed us.

Vaterchen slept through it all; an occasional convulsive jerk would show, at times, when one of the enemy had chanced upon some nervous fibre; but on the whole, he bore up like one used to such martyrdom, and able to brave it. As for me, when morning broke, I looked like a strong case of confluent small-pox, with the addition that my heavy eyelids nearly closed over my eyes, and my lips swelled out like a Kaffir's. How that young minx, Catinka, laughed at me. All the old man's signs, warnings, menaces, were in vain; she screamed aloud with laughter, and never ceased, even as we were led into the tribunal and before the dread presence of the judge.

The judgment-seat was not imposing. It was a long, low, ill-lighted chamber, with a sort of raised counter at one end, behind which sat three elderly men, dressed like master sweeps—that is, of the old days of climbing-boys. The prisoners were confined in a thing like a fold, and there leaned against one end of the same pen as ourselves a square-built, thick-set man of about eight-and-forty, or fifty, dressed in a suit of coarse drab, and who, notwithstanding an immense red beard and moustache, a clear blue eye and broad brow proclaimed to be English. He was being interrogated as we entered, but from his total ignorance of German the examination was not proceeding very glibly.

"You're an Englishman, ain't you?" cried he, as I came in. "You can speak High Dutch, perhaps?"

17—2

"I can speak German well enough to to be intelligible, Sir."

"All right," said he, in the same free-and-easy tone. "Will you explain to those old beggars there that they're making fools of themselves. Here's how it is. My passport was made out for two; for Thomas Harper, that's me, and Sam Rigges. Now, because Sam Rigges ain't here, they tell me I can't be suffered to proceed. Ain't that stupid? Did you ever hear the like of that for downright absurdity before?"

"But where is he?"

"Well, I don't mind telling you, because you're a countryman, but I don't like blackening an Englishman to one of those confounded foreigners. Rigges has run."

"What do you mean by 'run'?"

"I mean, cut his stick; gone clean away; and what's worse, too, carried off a stout bag of dollars with him that we had for our journey?"

"Whither were you going?"

"That's neither here nor there, and don't concern you in any respect. What you're to do is, explain to the old cove yonder—the fellow in the middle is the worst of them—tell him it's all right, that I'm Harpar, and that the other ain't here; or, look here, I'll tell you what's better, do you be Rigges, and it's all right."

I demurred flatly to this suggestion, but undertook to plead his cause on its true merits.

"And who are you, Sir, that presume to play the advocate here?" said the judge, haughtily. "I fancied that you stood there to answer a charge against yourself."

"That matter may be very easily disposed of, Sir," said I, as proudly; "and you will be very fortunate if you succeed as readily in explaining your own illegal arrest of me to the higher court of your country."

With the eloquence which we are told essentially belongs to truth, I narrated how I had witnessed, as a mere passing traveller, the outrageous insult offered to these poor wanderers as they entered the inn. With the warm enthusiasm of one inspired by a good cause, I painted the whole incident with really scarcely a touch of embellishment, reserving the only decorative portion to a description of myself, whom I

mentioned as an agent of the British government, especially
employed on a peculiar service, the confirmation of which I
proudly established by my passport setting forth that I was
a certain " Ponto, Chargé des Dépêches."

Now if there be one feature of continental life fixed and
immutable, it is this, that wherever the German language
be spoken, the reverence for a government functionary is
supreme. If you can only show on documentary evidence
that you are grandson of the man who made the broom
that swept out a government office, it is enough. You are
from that hour regarded as one of the younger children of
Bureaucracy. You are under the protection of the state,
and though you be but the smallest rivet in the machinery,
there is no saying what mischief might not ensue if you
were either lost or mislaid.

I saw in an instant the dread impression I had created,
and I said, in a voice of careless insolence, " Go on, I beg of
you ; send me back to prison ; chain me ; perhaps you would
like to torture me ? The government I represent is especially
slow in vindicating the rights of its injured officials. It has
a European reputation for long-suffering, patience, and for-
bearance. Yes, Englishmen can be impaled, burned, flayed
alive, disembowelled. By all means, avail yourselves of your
bland privileges ; have me led out instantly to the scaffold,
unless you prefer to have me broken on the wheel ! "

" Will nobody stop him ! " cried the president, almost
choking with wrath.

" Stop me ; I suspect not, Sir. It is upon these declarations of mine, made thus openly, that my country will found
that demand for reparation which will one day cost you so
dearly. Lead on, I am ready for the block." And as I said
this, I untied my cravat, and appeared to prepare for the
headsman.

" If he will not cease, the court shall be dissolved," called
out the judge.

" Never, Sir. Never, so long as I live, shall I surrender
the glorious privileges of that freedom by which I assert my
birthright as a Briton."

" Well, you are as impudent a chap as ever I listened to,"
muttered my countryman at my side.

" The prisoners are dismissed, the court is adjourned,"

said the president, rising; and amidst a very disorderly
crowd, not certainly enthusiastic in our favour, we were all
hurried into the street.

"Come along down here," said Mr. Harpar. "I'm in a
very tidy sort of place they call the 'Golden Pig.' Come
along, and bring the vagabonds, and let's have breakfast
together."

I was hurt at the speech, but as my companions could not
understand its coarseness, I accepted the invitation, and we
followed him.

"Well, I ain't seen *your* like for many a day," said
Harpar, as we went along. "If you'd have said the half of
that to one of our 'Beaks,' I think I know where you'd be.
But you seem to understand the fellows well. Mayhap you
have lived much abroad ? "

"A great deal. I am a sort of citizen of the world," said
I, with a jaunty easiness.

"For a citizen of the world you appear to have strange
tastes in your companionship. How did you come to fore-
gather with these creatures ? "

I tried the timeworn cant about seeing life in all its gradations—exploring the cabin as well as visiting the palace,
and so on ; but there was a rugged sort of incredulity in his
manner that checked me, and I could not muster the glib
rudeness which usually stood by me on such occasions.

"You're not a man of fortune," said he, drily, as I finished ;
" one sees that plainly enough. You're a fellow that should
be earning his bread somehow; and the question is—Is this
the kind of life that you ought to be leading ? What humbug it is to talk about knowing the world and such like.
The thing is, to know a trade, to understand some art, to be
able to produce something, to manufacture something, to
convert something to a useful purpose. When you've done
that, the knowledge of men will come later on, never be
afraid of that. It's a school that we never miss one single
day of our lives. But here we are ; this is the ' Pig.' Now,
what will you have for breakfast? Ask the vagabonds, too,
and tell them there's a wide choice here ; they have everything you can mention in this little inn."

An excellent breakfast was soon spread out before us, and
though my humble companions did it the most ample justice,

I sat there, thoughtful and almost sad. The words of that
stranger rang in my ears like a reproach and a warning. I
knew how truly he had said that I was not a man of fortune,
and it grieved me sorely to think how easily he saw it. In
my heart of hearts, I knew it was the delusion I loved best.
To appear to the world at large an eccentric man of good
means, free to do what he liked and go where he would, was
the highest enjoyment I had ever prepared for myself: and
yet here was a coarse, common-place sort of man—at least
his manners were unpolished and his tone underbred—and
he saw through it all at once.

I took the first opportunity to slip away unobserved from
the company, and retired to the little garden of the inn, to
commune with myself and be alone. But ere I had been
many minutes there, Harpar joined me. He came up smoking
his cigar, with the lounging, lazy air of a man at perfect
leisure, and, consequently, quite free to be as disagreeable as
he pleased.

"You went off without eating your breakfast," said he,
bluntly. "I saw how it was. You didn't like *my* freedom
with you. You fancied that I ought to have taken all that
nonsense of yours about your rank and your way of life for
gospel; or, at least, that I ought to have pretended to do so.
That ain't my way. I hate humbug."

It was not very easy to reply good humouredly to such a
speech as this. Indeed, I saw no particular reason to treat
this man's freedom with an indulgence, and drawing myself
haughtily up, I prepared a very dry but caustic rejoinder.

"When I have learned two points," said I, "on which you
can inform me, I may be better able to answer what you
have said. The first is: By what possible right do you take
to task a person that you never met in your life till now?
and, secondly, What benefit on earth could it be to me to
impose upon a man from whom I neither want nor expect
anything?"

"Easily met, both," said he, quickly. "I'm a practical
sort of fellow, who never wastes time on useless materials;
that's for your first proposition. Number two: you're a
dreamer, and you hate being awakened."

"Well, Sir," said I, stiffly, "to a gentleman so remarkable
for perspicuity, and who reads character at sight, ordinary

intercourse must be wearisome. Will you excuse me if I take my leave of you here ? "

"Of course, make no ceremony about it; go or stay, just as you like. I never cross any man's humour."

I muttered something that sounded like a dissent to that doctrine, and he quickly added, " I mean, further than speaking my mind, that's all ; nothing more. If you had been a man of fair means, and for a frolic thought it might be good fun to consort for a few days with rapscallions of a travelling circus, all one could say was, it wasn't very good taste ; but being evidently a fellow of another stamp, a young man who ought to be in his father's shop or his uncle's counting-house, following some honest craft or calling—for you, I say, it was downright ruin."

" Indeed ! " said I, with an accent of intense scorn.

" Yes," continued he, seriously, "downright ruin. There's a poison in the lazy, good-for-nothing life of these devils, that never leaves a man's blood. I've a notion that it wouldn't hurt a man's nature so much were he to consort with housebreakers ; there's at least something real about these fellows."

" You talk, doubtless, with knowledge, Sir," said I, glad to say something that might offend him.

" I do," said he, seriously, and not taking the smallest account of the impertinent allusion. " I know that if a man hasn't a fixed calling, but is always turning his hand to this, that, and t'other, he will very soon cease to have any character whatsoever ; he'll just become as shifty in his nature as in his business. I've seen scores of fellows wrecked on that rock, and I hadn't looked at you twice till I saw you were one of them."

" I must say, Sir," said I, summoning to my aid what I felt to be a most cutting sarcasm of manner—" I must say, Sir, that, considering how short has been the acquaintance which has subsisted between us, it would be extremely difficult for me to show how gratefully I feel the interest you have taken in me."

" Well, I'm not so sure of that," said he, thoughtfully.

" May I ask, then, how ? "

" Are you sure, first of all, that you wish to show this gratitude you speak of ? "

"Oh, Sir, can you possibly doubt it?"

"I don't want to doubt it, I want to profit by it."

I made a bland bow that might mean anything, but did not speak.

"Here's the way of it," said he, boldly. "Rigges has run off with all my loose cash, and though there's money waiting for me at certain places, I shall find it very difficult to reach them. I have come down here on foot from Wildbad, and I can make my way, in the same fashion, to Marseilles or Genoa; but then comes the difficulty, and I shall need about ten pounds to get to Malta. Could you lend me ten pounds?"

"Really, Sir," said I, coolly, "I am amazed at the innocence with which you can make such a demand on the man whom you have, only a few minutes back, so acutely depicted as an adventurer."

"It was for that very reason I thought of applying to you. Had you been a young fellow of a certain fortune, you'd have naturally been a stranger to the accidents which now and then leave men penniless in out-of-the-way places, and it is just as likely that the first thought in your head would be, 'Oh, he's a swindler. Why hasn't he his letters of credit or his circular notes?' But, being exactly what I take you for, the chances are you'll say: 'What has befallen *him* to-day may chance to *me* to-morrow. Who can tell the day and the hour some mishap may not overtake him? and so I'll just help him through it.'"

"And that was your calculation?"

"That was my calculation."

"How sorry I feel to wound the marvellous gift you seem to possess of interpreting character. I am really shocked to think that for this time, at least, your acuteness is at fault."

"Which means that you'll not do it."

I smiled a benign assent.

He looked at me for a minute or more with a sort of blank incredulity, and then, crossing his arms on his breast, moved slowly down the walk without speaking.

I cannot say how I detested this man; he had offended me in the very sorest part of all my nature; he had wounded the nicest susceptibility I possessed; of the pleasant fancies

wherewith I loved to clothe myself he would not leave me
enough to cover my nakedness; and yet, now that I had
resented his cool impertinence, I hated myself far more than
I hated him.   Dignity and sarcasm, forsooth!   What a fine
opportunity to display them, truly!   The man might be
rude and underbred; he *was* rude and underbred; and was
that any justification for *my* conduct towards him?   Why
had I not had the candour to say, "Here's all I possess in the
world; you see yourself that I cannot lend you ten pounds."
How I wished I had said that, and how I wished, even more
ardently still, that I had never met him, never interchanged
speech with him!

"And why is it that I am offended with him—simply
because he has discovered that I am Potts?"   Now, these
reflections were all the more bitter, since it was only twenty-
four hours before that I had resolved to throw off delusion
either of myself or others; that I would take my place in
the ranks, and fight out my battle of life, a mere soldier.
For this it was that I made companionship with Vaterchen,
walking the high road with that poor old man of motley,
and actually speculating—in a sort of artistic way—whether
I should not make love to Tintefleck!   And if I were sincere
in all this, how should I feel wounded by the honest candour
of that plain-spoken fellow?   He wanted a favour at my
hands, he owned this; and yet, instead of approaching me
with flattery, he at once assails the very stronghold of my
self-esteem, and says, "No humbug, Potts; at least, none
with *me!*"   He opens acquaintance with me on that masonic
principle by which the brotherhood of Poverty is maintained
throughout all lands and all peoples, and whose great maxim
is, "He who lends to the poor man, borrows from the ragged
man."

"I'll go after him at once," said I, aloud.   "I'll have
more talk with him.   I'm much mistaken if there's not good
stuff in that rugged nature."

When I entered the little inn, I found Vaterchen fast
asleep; he had finished off every flask on the table, and lay
breathing stentoriously, and giving a long-drawn whistle in
his snore, that smacked almost of apoplexy.   Tintefleck was
singing to her guitar before a select audience of the inn
servants, and Harpar was gone!

I gave the girl a glance of rebuke and displeasure. I aroused the old man with a kick, and imperiously demanded my bill.

"The bill has been paid by the other stranger," said the landlord; "he has settled everything, and left a 'trenkgeld' for the servants, so that you have nothing to pay."

I could have almost cried with spite as I heard these words. It would have been a rare solace to my feelings if I could have put that man down for a rogue, and then been able to say to myself how cleverly I had escaped the snares of a swindler. But to know now that he was not only honest but liberal, and to think, besides, that I had been his guest—eaten of his salt—it was more than I well could endure.

"Which way did he take?" asked I.

Round the head of the lake for Lindau. I told him that the steamer would take him there to-morrow for a trifle, but he would not wait.'

"Ah me!" sighed Vaterchen, but half awake, and with one eye still closed, "and we are going to St. Gallen."

"Who said so?" cried I, imperiously. "We are going to Lindau; at least if I be the person who gives orders here. Follow!" And as I spoke, I marched proudly on, while a slipshod, shuffling noise of feet, and a low, half-smothered sob, told me that they were coming after me.

CHAPTER XXXIV.

MY poor companions had but a sorry time of it on that morning. I was in a fearful temper, and made no effort to control it. The little romance of my meeting with these creatures was beginning to scale off, and, there beneath, lay the vulgar metal of the natures exposed to view. As for old Vaterchen, shuffling along in his tattered shoes, half-stupid

with wine and shame together, I couldn't bear to look at
him; while Tintefleck, although at the outset abashed by
my rebukeful tone and cold manner, had now rallied, and
seemed well disposed to assert her own against all comers.
Yes, there was a palpable air of defiance about her, even to
the way that she sang as she went along; every thrill and
cadence seemed to say, " I'm doing this to amuse myself;
never imagine that I care whether you are pleased or not."
Indeed, she left me no means of avoiding this conclusion,
since at every time that I turned on her a look of anger or
displeasure, her reply was to sing the louder.

"And it was only yesterday," thought I, "and I dreamed
that I could be in love with this creature—dreamed that I
could replace Kate Herbert's image in my heart with that
coarse travestie of woman's gentleness. Why, I might as
well hope to make a gentleman of old Vaterchen, and present him to the world as a man of station and eminence."

What an insane hope was this ! As well might I shiver
a fragment from a stone on the road-side, and think to give
it value by having it set as a ring. The caprice of keeping
them company for a day might be pardonable. It was the
whim of one who is, above all, a student of mankind. But
why continue the companionship ? A little more of such
intimacy, and who is to say what I may not imbibe of their
habits and their natures; and Potts, the man of sentiment,
the child of impulse, romance, and poetry, become a slave of
the "Ring"—a saltimbanque ! Now, though I could implicitly rely upon the rigidity of my joints to prevent the
possibility of my ever displaying any feats of agility, I could
yet picture myself in a long-tailed blue coat and jack-boots
walking round and round in the sawdust circle, with four or
five other creatures of the same sort, and who have no consciousness of any function till they are made the butt of some
extempore drollery by the clown.

The creative temperament has this great disadvantage,
that one cannot always build castles, but must occasionally
construct hovels, and sometimes even dungeons and gaols;
and here was I now, with a large contract order for this
species of edifice, and certainly I set to work with a will.
The impatience of my mind communicated itself to my gait,
and I walked along at a tremendous rate.

"I can scarcely keep up with you at this pace," said Tintefleck; "and see, we have left poor Vaterchen a long way behind."

I made some rude answer—I know not what—and told her to come on.

"I will not leave him," said she, coming to a halt, and standing in a composed and firm attitude before me.

"Then I will," said I, angrily. "Farewell!" And waving my hand in a careless adieu, I walked briskly onward, not even turning a look on her as I went. I think I'm almost certain I heard a heavy sob close behind me, but I would not look round for worlds. I was in one of those moods—all weak men know them well—when a harsh or an ungracious act appears something very daring and courageous. The very pain my conduct gave myself, persuaded me that it must be heroic, just as a devotee is satisfied after a severe self-castigation.

"Yes, Potts," said I, "you are doing the right thing here. A little more of such association as this, and you would be little better than themselves. Besides, and above all, you ought to be 'real.' Now, these are not real any more than the tinsel gems and tinfoil splendours they wear on their tunics." It broke on me, too, like a sudden light, that to be the fictitious Potts, the many-sided, many-tinted—what a German would call "der mitviele-farben bedeckte Potts"—I ought to be immensely rich, all my changes of character requiring great resources and unlimited "properties," as stage folk call them; whereas, "der echte wahrhaftige maun Potts" might be as poor as Lazarus. Indeed, the poorer the more real, since more natural.

While I thus speculated, I caught sight of a man scaling one of the precipitous paths by which the winding road was shortened for foot-travellers; a second glance showed me that this was Harpar, who, with a heavy knapsack, was toiling along. I made a great effort to come up with him, but when I reached the high road, he was still a long distance in front of me. I could not, if there had been anyone to question me, say why I wished to overtake him. It was a sort of chase suggested simply by the object in front; a rare type, if we but knew it, of one half the pursuits we follow throughout life.

As I mounted the last of these by-paths which led to the crest of the mountain, I felt certain that, with a lighter equipment, I should come up with him; but scarcely had I gained the top, than I saw him striding away vigorously on the road fully a mile away beneath me. "He shall not beat me," said I; and I increased my speed. It was all in vain. I could not do it; and when I drew nigh Lindau at last, very weary and foot-sore, the sun was just sinking on the western shore of the lake.

"Which is the best inn here?" asked I of a shopkeeper who was lounging carelessly at his door.

"Yonder," said he, "where you see that post-carriage turning into."

"To-night," said I, "I will be guilty of an extravagance. I will treat myself to a good supper, and an honest glass of wine." And on these hospitable thoughts intent I unslung my knapsack, and, throwing as much of distinction as I could into my manner, strolled into the public room.

So busied was the household in attending to the travellers who arrived "extra post," that none condescended to notice me, till at last, as the tumult subsided, a venerable old waiter approached me, and said, in a half friendly, half rebukeful tone, "It is at the 'Swan' you ought to be, my friend; the next turning but two to the left hand, and you'll see the blue lantern over the gateway."

"I mean to remain where I am," said I, imperiously, "and to remember your impertinence when I am about to pay my bill. Bring me the *carte*."

I was overjoyed to see the confusion and shame of the old fellow. He saw at once the grievous error he had committed, and was so overwhelmed, that he could not reply. Meanwhile, with all the painstaking accuracy of a practised *gourmand*, I was making a careful note of what I wished for supper.

"Are you not ashamed," said I, rebukefully, "to have *ortolans* here, when you know in your heart they are swallows?"

He was so abject that he could only give a melancholy smile, as though to say, "Be merciful, and spare us!"

"Bohemian pheasant, too—come, come, this is too bad!

Be frank and confess; how often has that one speckled tail done duty on a capon of your own raising?"

"Gracious Herr!" muttered he, "do not crush us altogether."

I don't think that he said this in actual words, but his terrified eyes and his shaking cheeks declared it.

"Never mind," said I, encouragingly, "it will not hurt us to make a sparing meal occasionally; with the venison and steak, the fried salmon, the duck with olives, and the apricot tart, we will satisfy appetite, and persuade ourselves, if we can, that we have fared luxuriously."

"And the wine, Sir?" asked he.

"Ah, there we *are* difficult. No little Baden vintage, no small wine of the Bergstrasse, can impose upon us! Liebfrauen-milch, or, if you can guarantee it, Marcobrunner will do; but, mind, no substitutes!"

He laid his hand over his heart and bowed low; and, as he moved away, I said to myself, "What a mesmerism there must be in real money, since, even with the mockery of it, I have made that creature a bond slave." Brief as was the interval in preparing my meal, it was enough to allow me a very considerable share of reflection, and I found that, do what I would, a certain voice within would whisper, "Where are your fine resolutions now, Potts? Is this the life of reality that you had promised yourself? Are you not at the old work again? Are you not masquerading it once more? Don't you know well enough that all this pretension of yours as bad money, and that at the first ring of it on the counter you will be found out?"

"This you may rely on, gracious Sir," said the waiter, as he laid a bottle on the table beside me with a careful hand. "It is the orange seal;" and he then added, in a whisper, "taken from the Margrave's cellar in the revolution of '93, and every flask of it worth a province."

"We shall see—we shall see," said I, haughtily; "serve the soup!"

If I had been Belshazzar, I believe I should have eaten very heartily, and drunk my wine with a great relish, notwithstanding that drawn sword. I don't know how it is, but if I can only see the smallest bit of *terra firma* between myself and the edge of a precipice, I feel as though I had a whole

vast prairie to range over. For the life of me I cannot
realise anything that may, or may not, befal me remotely.
"Blue are the hills far off," says the adage; and on the converse of the maxim do I aver, that faint are all dangers that
are distant. An immediate peril overwhelms me; but I
could look forward to a shipwreck this day fortnight with a
fortitude truly heroic.

"This is a nice old half-forgotten sort of place," thought
I, "a kind of vulgar Venice, water-washed, and muddy, and
dreary, and do-nothing. I'll stay here for a week or so; I'll
give myself up to the drowsy 'genius loci;' I'll Germanise
to the top of my bent; who is to say what metaphysical
melancholy, dashed with a strange diabolic humour, may
not come of constantly feeding on this heavy cookery, and
eternally listening to their gurgling gutturals? I may come
out a Wieland or a Herder, with a sprinkling of Henri
Heine! Yes," said I, "this is the true way to approach
life; first of all, develop your own faculties, and then mark
how in their exercise you influence your fellow-men. Above
all, however, cultivate your individuality, respect this the
greatest of all the unities."

"Ja, gnädiger Herr," said the old waiter, as he tried to
step away from my grasp, for, without knowing it, I had
laid hold of him by the wrist while I addressed to him this
speech. Desirous to re-establish my character for sanity,
somewhat compromised by this incident, I said:

"Have you a money-changer in these parts? If so, let
me have some silver for this English gold." I put my hand
in my pocket for my purse; not finding it, I tried another
and another. I ransacked them all over again, patted myself, shook my coat, looked into my hat, and then, with a
sudden flash of memory, I bethought me that I had left it
with Catinka, and was actually without one sou in the world!
I sat down, pale and almost fainting, and my arms fell power-
less at my sides.

"I have lost my purse!" gasped I out, at length.

"Indeed!" said the old man, but with a tone of such palpable scorn that it actually sickened me.

"Yes," said I, with all that force which is the peculiar
prerogative of truth; "and in it all the money I possessed."

"I have no doubt of it," rejoined he, in the same dry tone as before.

"You have no doubt of what, old man? Or what do you mean by the supercilious quietness with which you assent to my misfortune? Send the landlord to me."

"I will do more; I will send the police," said he, as he shuffled out of the room.

I have met scores of men on my way through life who would not have felt the slightest embarrassment in such a situation as mine, fellows so accustomed to shipwreck, that the cry of "Breakers ahead!" or "Man the boats!" would have occasioned neither excitement nor trepidation. What stuff they are made of instead of nerves, muscles, and arteries, I cannot imagine, since, when the question is self-preservation, how can it possibly be more imminent than when not alone your animal existence is jeopardised, but the dearer and more precious life of fame and character is in peril?

For a moment I thought that though this besotted old fool of a waiter might suspect my probity, the more clear-sighted intelligence of the landlord would at once recognise my honest nature, and with the confidence of a noble conviction say, "Don't tell me that the man yonder is a knave. I read him very differently. Tell me your story, Sir." And then I would tell it. It is not improbable that my speculation might have been verified had it not been that it was a land-lady and not a landlord who swayed the destinies of the inn. Oh, what a wise invention of our ancestors was the Salique law! How justly they appreciated the unbridled rashness of the female nature in command! How well they understood the one-idea'd impetuosity with which they rush to wrong conclusions!

Until I listened to the Frau von Wintner, I imagined the German language somewhat weak in the matter of epithets. She undeceived me on this head, showing resources of abusive import that would have done credit to a Homeric hero. Having given me full ten minutes of a strong vocabulary, she then turned on the waiter, scornfully asking him if, at his time of life, he ought to have let himself be imposed upon by so palpable and undeniable a swindler as myself? She clearly showed that there was no extenuation of his fault, that rogue and vagabond had been written on my face, and

10

inscribed in my manner; not to mention that I had followed the well-beaten track of all my fraternity in fraud, and ordered everything the most costly the house could command. In fact, so strenuously did she urge this point, and so eager did she seem about enforcing a belief in her statement, that I almost began to suspect she might suggest an anatomical examination of me to sustain her case. Had she been even less eloquent, the audience would still have been with her, for it is a curious but unquestionable fact that in all little visited localities the stranger is ungraciously regarded and ill looked on.

Whenever I attempted to interpose a word in my defence, I was overborne at once. Indeed, public opinion was so decidedly against me, that I felt very happy in thinking Lynch law was not a Teutonic institution. The room was now filled with retainers of the inn, strangers, town-folk, and police, and, to judge by the violence of their gestures and the loud tones of their voices, one would have pronounced me a criminal of the worst sort.

"But what is it that he has done? What's his offence?" I heard a voice say from the crowd, and I fancied his accent was that of a foreigner. A perfect inundation of vituperative accusation, however, now poured in, and I could gather no more. The turmoil and uproar rose and fell, and fell and rose again, till at last, my patience utterly exhausted, I burst out into a very violent attack on the uncivilised habits of a people who could thus conduct themselves to a man totally unconvicted of any offence.

"Well, well, don't give way to passion; don't let temper get the better of you," said a fat, citizen-like man beside me. "The stranger there has just paid for what you have had, and all is settled."

I thought I should have fainted as I heard these words. Indeed, until that instant, I had never brought home to my own mind the utter destitution of my state; but now, there I stood, realizing to myself the condition of one of those we read of in our newspapers as having received five shillings from the poor-box, while D 490 is deputed to "make inquiries after him at his lodgings," and learn particulars of his life and habits. I could have borne being sent to prison. I could have endured any amount of severity, so long as I revolted against its injustice; but the sense of being an object of actual charity crushed me utterly, and I could nearly have cried with vexation.

By degrees the crowd thinned off, and I found myself sitting alone beside the table where I had dined, with the hateful old waiter, as though standing sentinel over me.

"Who is this person," asked I, haughtily, "who, with an indelicate generosity, has presumed to interfere with the concerns of a stranger?"

"The gracious nobleman who paid for your dinner is now eating his own at No. 8," said the old monster with a grin.

"I will call upon him when he has dined," said I, transfixing the wretch with a look so stern, as to make rejoinder impossible; and then, throwing my plaid wrapper and my knapsack on a table near, I strolled out into the street.

Lindau is a picturesque old place, as it stands rising, as it were, out of the very waters of the Lake of Constance, and the great mountain of the Sentis, with its peak of six thousand feet high, is a fine object in the distance; while the gorge of the Upper Rhine offers many a grand effect of Alpine scenery, not the less striking when looked at with a setting sun, which made the foreground more massive and the hill-tops golden; and yet I carried that in my heart which made the whole picture as dark and dreary as Poussin's Deluge. It was all very beautiful. There, was the snow-white summit, reflected in the still water of the lake; there, the rich wood, browned with autumn, and now tinted with a golden glory, richer again; there, were the white-sailed boats, asleep on the calm surface, streaked with the variegated light of the clouds above, and it was peaceful as it was picturesque. But do what I could, I could not enjoy it, and all because I had lost my purse, just as if certain fragments of a yellow metal the more or the less, ought to obscure eyesight, lull the sense of hearing, and make a man's whole existence miserable. "And after all," thought I, "Catinka will be here this evening, or to-morrow at furthest. Vaterchen was tired, and could not come on. It was *I* who left *them*; I, in my impatience and ill-humour.

The old man doubtless knew nothing of the purse confided to
the girl, nor is it at all needful that he should. They will
certainly follow me, and why, for the mere inconvenience of
an hour or two, should I persist in seeing the whole world
so crape-covered and sad-looking? Surely this is not the
philosophy my knowledge of life has taught me. I ought to
know and feel that these daily accidents are but stones on
the road one travels. They may, perchance, wound the foot
or damage the shoe, but they rarely delay the journey, if the
traveller be not faint-hearted and craven. I will treat the
whole incident in a higher spirit. I will wait for their
coming in that tranquil and assured condition of mind which
is the ripe fruit of a real insight into mankind. Pitt said,
after long years of experience, that there was more of good
than of bad in human nature. Let it be the remark of some
future biographer that Potts agreed with him."

When I got back to the inn, I was somewhat puzzled what
to do. It would have been impossible with any success to
have resumed my former tone of command, and for the life of
me I could not bring myself down to anything like entreaty.
While I thus stood, uncertain how to act, the old waiter
approached me, almost courteously, and said my room was
ready for me when I wished it.

" I will first of all wait upon the traveller in No. 8,"
said I.

" He has retired for the night," was the answer. " He
seems in very delicate health, and the fatigue of the journey
has overcome him."

" To-morrow will do, then," said I, easily; and not
venturing upon an inquiry as to the means by which my
room was at my disposal, I took my candle and mounted
the stairs.

As I lay down in my bed, I resolved I would take a calm
survey of my past life: what I had done, what I had failed
to do, what were the guiding principles which directed me,
and whither they were likely to bear me. But scarcely had
I administered to myself the preliminary oath to tell
nothing but the truth, than I fell off sound asleep.

My first waking thought the next morning was to inquire
if two persons had arrived in search of me—an elderly man
and a young woman. I described them. None such had

been seen. "They will have sought shelter in some of the humbler inns," thought I; "I'll up and look after them." I searched the town from end to end; I visited the meanest halting-places of the wayfarer; I inquired at the police bureaus—at the gate—but none had arrived who bore any resemblance to those I asked after. I was vexed—only vexed at first—but gradually I found myself. growing distrustful. The suspicion that the ice is not strong enough for your weight, and then, close upon that, the shock of fear that strikes you when the loud crash of a fracture breaks on the ear, are mere symbols of what one suffers at the first glimmering of a betrayal. I repelled the thought with indignation; but certain thoughts there are which, when turned out, stand like sturdy duns at the gate, and will not be sent away. This was one of them. It followed me wherever I went, importunely begging for a hearing, and menacing me with sad consequences if I were obdurate enough to listen. "You are a simpleton, Potts, a weak, foolish, erring creature! and you select as the objects of your confidence those whose lives of accident present exactly as the most irresistible of all temptations to them—the Dupe! How they must have laughed—how they must yet be laughing at you! How that old drunken fox will chuckle over your simplicity, and the minx Tintefleck indulge herself in caricatures of your figure and face! I wonder how much of truth there was in that old fellow's story? Was he ever the syndic of his village, or was the whole narrative a mere fiction like—like ——" I covered my face with my hands in shame as I muttered out, "like one of your own, Potts?"

I was very miserable, for I could no longer stand proudly forward as the prosecutor, but was obliged to steal ignominiously into the dock and take my place beside the other prisoners. What became of all my honest indignation as I bethought me, that I of all men could never arraign the counterfeit and the sham?

"Let them go, then," cried I, "and prosper if they can; I will never pursue them. I will even try and remember what pleased and interested me in their fortunes, and, if it may be, forget that they have carried away my little all of wealth."

A loud tramping of post-horses, and the cracking of whips, drew me to the window, and I saw beneath in the court-

yard, a handsome travelling britschka getting ready for the
road. Oh how suggestive is a well-cushioned calèche, with
its many appliances of ease and luxury, its trim imperials, its
scattered litter of wrappers and guide-books—all little
episodes of those who are to journey in it!

"Who are the happy souls about to travel thus enjoy-
ably?" thought I, as I saw the waiter and the courier discussing the most convenient spot to deposit a small hamper
with eatables for the road; and then I heard the landlady's
voice call out:

"Take up the bill to No. 8."

So, then, this was No. 8 who was fast getting ready to
depart—No. 8 who had interposed in my favour the evening
before, and towards whom a night's rest and some reflection
had modified my feelings and changed my sentiments very
remarkably.

"Will you ask the gentleman at No. 8 if I may be permitted to speak with him?" said I to the man who took in
the bill.

"He'll scarcely see you now—he's just going off."

"Give the message as I speak it," said I; and he disappeared.

There was a long interval before he issued forth again,
and when he did so he was flurried and excited. Some
overcharges had been taken off and some bad money in
change to be replaced by honest coin, and it was evident that
various little well-intended rogueries had not achieved their
usual success.

"Go in, you'll find him there," said the waiter, insolently,
as he went down to have the bill rectified.

I knocked, a full round voice cried "Come in!" and I
entered.

CHAPTER XXXV.

"Well, what next? have you bethought you of anything more to charge me with?" cried a large full man, whose angry look and manner showed how he resented these cheatings.

I staggered back sick and faint, for the individual before me was Crofton, my kind host of long ago in Ireland, and from whose hospitable roof I had taken such an unceremonious departure.

"Who are you?" cried he, again. "I had hoped to have paid everything and everybody. Who are you?"

Wishing to retire unrecognised, I stammered out something very unintelligibly indeed about my gratitude, and my hope for a pleasant journey to him, retreating all the while towards the door.

"It's all very well to wish the traveller a pleasant journey," said he, "but you innkeepers ought to bear in mind that no man's journey is rendered more agreeable by roguery. This house is somewhat dearer than the 'Clarendon' in London, or the 'Hôtel du Rhin' at Paris. Now, there might be perhaps some pretext to make a man pay smartly who travels post, and has two or three servants with him, but what excuse can you make for charging some poor devil of a foot-traveller, taking his humble meal in the common room, and, naturally enough, of the commonest fare, for making him pay eight florins—eight florins and some kreutzers—for his dinner? Why, our dinner here for two people was handsomely paid at six florins a head, and yet you bring in a bill of eight florins against that poor wretch."

I saw now, that, what between the blinding effects of his indignation, and certain changes which time and the road had worked in my appearance, it was more than probable I should escape undetected, and so I affected to busy myself

with some articles of his luggage that lay scattered about
the room until I could manage to slip away.

"Touch nothing, my good fellow!" cried he, angrily;
"send my own people here for these things. Let my courier
come here—or my valet!"

This was too good an opportunity to be thrown away, and
I made at once for the door, but at the same instant it was
opened, and Mary Crofton stood before me. One glance
showed me that I was discovered, and there I stood, speechless with shame and confusion. Rallying, however, after a
moment, I whispered, "Don't betray me," and tried to pass
out. Instead of minding my entreaty, she set her back to
the door, and laughingly cried out to her brother:

"Don't you know whom we have got here?"

"What do you mean?" exclaimed he.

"Cannot you recognise an old friend, notwithstanding all
his efforts to cut us?"

"Why—what—surely it can't be—it's not possible—eh?"
And by this time he had wheeled me round to the strong
light of the window. and then, with a loud burst, he cried
out, "Potts. by all that's ragged! Potts himself! Why,
old fellow, what could you mean by wanting to escape us?"
and he wrung my hand with a cordial shake that at once
brought the blood back to my heart, while his sister completed my happiness by saying:

"If you only knew all the schemes we have planned to
catch you, you would certainly not have tried to avoid us."

I made an effort to say something—anything, in short—
but not a word would come. If I was overjoyed at the
warmth of their greeting, I was no less overwhelmed with
shame; and there I stood, looking very pitiably from one to
the other, and almost wishing that I might faint outright,
and so finish my misery.

With a woman's fine tact, Mary Crofton seemed to read
the meaning of my suffering. and, whispering one word in
her brother's ear, she slipped away and left us alone together.

"Come," said he good-naturedly, as he drew his arm
inside of mine, and led me up and down the room, "tell me
all about it. How have you come here? What are you
doing?"

I have not the faintest recollection of what I said. I know that I endeavoured to take up my story from the day I had last seen him, but it must have proved a very strange and bungling narrative, from the questions which he was forced occasionally to put, in order to follow me out.

"Well," said he, at last, "I will own to you that, after your abrupt departure, I was sorely puzzled what to make of you, and I might have remained longer in the same state of doubt, when a chance visit that I made to Dublin led me to Dycer's, and there, by a mere accident, I heard of you—heard who you were, and where your father lived. I went at once and called upon him, my object being to learn if he had any tidings of you, and where you then were. I found him no better informed than myself. He showed me a few lines you had written on the morning you had left home, stating that you would probably be absent some days, and might be even weeks, but that since that date nothing had been heard of you. He seemed vexed and displeased, but not uneasy or apprehensive about your absence, and the same tone I observed in your college tutor, Doctor Tobin. He said : 'Potts will come back, Sir, one of these days, and not a whit wiser than he went. His self-esteem is to his capacity, in the reduplicate ratio of the inverse proportion of his ability, and he will be always a fool.' I wrote to various friends of ours travelling about the world, but none had met with you ; and at last, when about to come abroad myself, I called again on your father, and found him just re-married."

"Re-married!"

"Yes! he was lonely, he said, and wanted companionship, and so on; and all I could obtain from him was a note for a hundred pounds, and a promise that, if you came back within the year, you should share the business of his shop with him."

"Never! never!" said I. "Potts may be the fool they deem him, but there are instincts and promptings in his secret heart that they know nothing of. I will never go back. Go on."

"I now come to my own story. I left Ireland a day or two after and came to England, where business detained me some weeks. My uncle had died and left me his heir—not, indeed, so rich as I had expected, but very well off for a man

who had passed his life on very moderate means. There
were a few legacies to be paid, and one which he especially
entrusted to me by a secret paper, in the hope that, by
delicate and judicious management, I might be able to persuade the person in whose interest it was bequeathed to
accept. It was, indeed, a task of no common difficulty, the
legatee being the widow of a man who had, by my uncle's
cruelty, been driven to destroy himself. It is a long story,
which I cannot now enter upon; enough that I say it had
been a trial of strength between two very vindictive unyield-
ing men which should crush the other, and my uncle being
the richer—and not from any other reason—conquered.

"The victory was a very barren one. It embittered every
hour of his life after, and the only reparation in his power,
he attempted on his death-bed, which was to settle an annuity
on the family of the man he had ruined. I found out at once
where they lived, and set about effecting this delicate charge.
I will not linger over my failure—but it was complete. The
family was in actual distress, but nothing would induce them
to listen to the project of assistance; and, in fact, their indignation compelled me to retire from the attempt in despair.
My sister did her utmost in the cause, but equally in vain,
and we prepared to leave the place, much depressed and cast
down by our failure. It was on the last evening of our stay
at the inn of the little village, a townsman of the place,
whom I had employed to aid my attempt by his personal
influence with the family, asked to see me and speak with
me in private.

"He appeared to labour under considerable agitation, and
opened our interview by bespeaking my secresy as to what
he was about to communicate. It was to this purport: A
friend of his own, engaged in the Baltic trade, had just declared to him that he had seen W., the person I allude to,
alive and well, walking on the quay at Riga, that he traced
him to his lodging, but, on inquiring for him the next day,
he was not to be found, and it was then ascertained that he
had left the city. W was, it would seem, a man easily recognised, and the other declared that there could not be the
slightest doubt of his identity. The question was a grave one
how to act, since the assurance company with which his life
was insured were actually engaged in discussing the pro-

priety of some compromise by paying to the family a moiety of the policy, and a variety of points arose out of this contingency; for while it would have been a great cruelty to have conveyed hopes to the family that might, by possibility, not be realised, yet, on the other band, to have induced them to adopt a course on the hypothesis of his death when they believed him still living, was almost as bad.

"I thought for a long while over the matter, and with my sister's counsel to aid me, I determined that we should come abroad and seek out this man, trusting that, if we found him, we could induce him to accept of the legacy which his family rejected. We obtained every clue we could think of to his detection. A perfect description of him, in voice, look, and manner; a copy of his portrait, and a specimen of his handwriting; and then we bethought ourselves of interesting you in the search. You were rambling about the world in that idle and desultory way in which any sort of a pursuit might be a boon—as often in the by-paths as on the high roads— you might chance to hit off this discovery in some remote spot, or, at all events, find some clue to it. In a word, we grew to believe, that, with you to aid us, we should get to the bottom of this mystery; and now that by a lucky chance we have met you, our hopes are all the stronger."

"You'll think it strange," said I, "but I already know something of this story; the man you allude to was Sir Samuel Whalley."

"How on earth have you guessed that?"

"I came by the knowledge on a railroad journey, where my fellow-passengers talked over the event, and I subsequently travelled with Sir Samuel's daughter, who came abroad to fill the station of a companion to an elderly lady. She called herself Miss Herbert."

"Exactly! The widow resumed her family name after W.'s suicide—if it were a suicide."

"How singular to think that you should have chanced upon this link of the chain. And do you know her?"

"Intimately; we were fellow-travellers for some days."

"And where is she now?"

"She is, at this moment, at a villa on the Lake of Como, living with a Mrs. Keats, the sister of her Majesty's Envoy at Kalbbratonstadt."

"You are marvellously accurate in this narrative, Potts," said he, laughing; "the impression made on you by this young lady can scarcely have been a transcient one."

I suppose I grew very red—I felt that I was much confused by this remark—and I turned away to conceal my emotion. Crofton was too delicate to take any advantage of my distress, and merely added:

"From having known her, you will naturally devote yourself with more ardour to serve her. May we then count upon your assistance in our project?"

"That you may," said I. "From this hour, I devote myself to it."

Crofton at once proposed that I should order my luggage to be placed on his carriage, and start off with them; but I firmly opposed this plan. First of all, I had no luggage, and had no fancy to confess as much; secondly, I resolved to give at least one day for Vaterchen's arrival—I'd have given a month rather than come down to the dreary thought of his being a knave, and Tintefleck a cheat! In fact, I felt that if I were to begin any new project in life with so slack an experience, that every step I took would be marked with distrust, and tarnished with suspicion. I therefore pretended to Crofton that I had given rendezvous to a friend at Lindau, and could not leave without waiting for him. I am not very sure that he believed me, but he was most careful in not dropping a word that might show incredulity; and once more we addressed ourselves to the grand project before us.

"Come in, Mary!" cried he, suddenly rising from his chair, and going to meet her. "Come in, and help us by your good counsel."

It was not possible to receive me with more kindness than she showed. Had I been some old friend who came to meet them there by appointment, her manner could not have been more courteous nor more easy; and when she learnt from her brother how warmly I had associated myself in this plan, she gave me one of her pleasantest smiles, and said:—

"I was not mistaken in you."

With a great map of Europe before us on the table, we proceeded to plan a future line of operations. We agreed to take certain places, each of us, and to meet at certain others, to compare notes and report progress. We scarcely permitted ourselves to feel any great confidence of success, but we all concurred in the notion that some lucky hazard might do for us more than all our best-devised schemes could accomplish ; and, at last, it was settled that, while *they* took Southern Germany and the Tyrol, *I* should ramble about through Savoy and Upper Italy, and our meeting-place be in Italy. The great railway centres, where Englishmen of every class and gradation were much employed, offered the best prospect of meeting with the object of our search, and these were precisely the sort of places such a man would be certain to resort to.

Our discussion lasted so long, that the Croftons put off their journey till the following day, and we dined all together very happily, never wearied of talking over the plan before us, and each speculating as to what share of acuteness he could contribute to the common stock of investigation. It was when Crofton left the room to search for the portrait of Whalley, that Mary sat down at my side, and said :—

"I have been thinking for some time over a project in which you can aid me greatly. My brother tells me that you are known to Miss Herbert. Now I want to write to her; I want to tell her that there is one who, belonging to a family from which hers has suffered heavily, desires to expiate so far, maybe, the great wrong, and, if she will permit it, to be her friend. While I can in a letter explain what I feel on this score, I am well aware how much aid it would afford me to have the personal corroboration of one who could say, " She who writes this is not altogether unworthy of your affection ; do not reject the offer she makes you, or, at least, reflect and think over it before you refuse it.' Will you help me so far ?"

My heart bounded with delight as I first listened to her plan ; it was only a moment before, that I remembered how difficult, if not impossible, it would be for me to approach Miss Herbert once more. How or in what character could I seek her ? To appear before her in any feigned part would be, under the circumstances, ignoble and unworthy, and yet was I, out of any merely personal consideration, any regard for the poor creature Potts, to forego the interests, mayhap the whole happinesss, of one so immeasurably better and worthier ? Would not any amount of shame and exposure to myself be a cheap price for even a small quantity of benefit bestowed on *her?* What signified it that I was poor and ragged—unknown, unrecognised—if *she* were to be the gainer? Would not, in fact, the very sacrifice of self in the affair be ennobling and elevating to me, and would I not stand better in my own esteem for this one honest act, than I had ever done after any mock success or imaginary victory ?

"I think I can guess why you hesitate," cried she; "you fear that I will say something indiscreet—something that would compromise you with Miss Herbert—but you need not dread that; and, at all events, you shall read my letter."

"Far from it," said I; "my hesitation had a very different source. I was solely thinking whether, if you were aware of how I stood in my relations to Miss Herbert, you would have selected me as your advocate; and though it may pain me to make a full confession, you shall hear everything."

With this I told her all—all, from my first hour of meeting her at the railway station, to my last parting with her at Schaffhausen. I tried to make my narrative as grave and common-place as might be, but, do what I would, the figure in which I was forced to present myself overcame all her attempts at seriousness, and she laughed immoderately. If it had not been for this burst of merriment on her part, it is more than probable I might have brought down my history to the very moment of telling, and narrated every detail of my journey with Vaterchen and Tintefleck. I was, however, warned by these circumstances, and concluded in time to save myself from this new ridicule.

"From all that you have told me here," said she, "I only see one thing—which is, that you are deeply in love with this young lady."

"No," said I; "I was so once—I am not so any longer. My passion has fallen into the chronic stage, and I feel myself her friend—only her friend."

"Well, for the purpose I have in mind, this is all the better. I want you, as I said, to place my letter in her hands, and, so far as possible, enforce its arguments—that is, try and persuade her that to reject our offers on her behalf, is to throw upon us a share of the great wrong our uncle worked, and make us, as it were, participators in the evil he did them. As for myself," said she, boldly, "all the happiness that I might have derived from ample means is dashed with remembering what misery it has been attended with to that poor family. If you urge that one theme forcibly, you can scarcely fail with her.'

"And what are your intentions with regard to her?" asked I.

"They will take any shape she pleases. My brother would either enable her to return home, and, by persuading her mother to accept an annuity, live happily under her own roof; or she might—if the spirit of independence fires her—she might yet use her influence over her mother and sister to regard our proposals more favourably; or she might come and live with us, and this I would prefer to all; but you must read my letter, and more than once, too. You must possess yourself of all its details, and, if there be anything to which you object, there will be time enough still to change it.'

"Here he is—here is the portrait of our lost sheep," said Crofton, now entering with a miniature in his hand. It represented a bluff, bold, almost insolently bold man in full civic robes, the face not improbably catching an additional expression of vulgar pride from the fact that the likeness was taken in that culminating hour of greatness when he first took the chair as chief magistrate of his town.

"Not an over-pleasant sort of fellow to deal with, I should say," remarked Crofton. "There are some stern lines here about the corners of the eyes, and certain very suspicious-looking indentations next the mouth."

"His eye has no forgiveness in it," said his sister.

"Well, one thing is clear enough, he ought to be easily recognised; that broad forehead, and those wide-spread nostrils and deeply divided chin, are very striking marks to guide one. I cannot give you this," said Crofton to me, "but I'll take care to send you an accurate copy of it at the first favourable moment; meanwhile, make yourself master of its details, and try if you cannot carry the resemblance in your memory."

" Disabuse yourself, too," said she, laughing, " of all this accessorial grandeur, and bear in mind that you'll not find him dressed in ermine, or surrounded with a collar and badge. Not very like his daughter, I'm sure," whispered she in my ear, as I continued to gaze stedfastly at the portrait. "Can you trace any likeness?"

" Not the very faintest; she is beautiful," said I, " and her whole expression is gentleness and delicacy."

" Well, certainly," said Crofton, shutting up the miniature, " these are not the distinguishing traits of our friend here, whom I should call a hard-natured, stern, obstinate fellow, with great self-reliance, and no great trust of others."

" I was just thinking," said I, " that were I to come up with such a man as this, what chance would my poor, frail, yielding temperament have, in influencing the rugged granite of his nature? He'd terrify me at once."

"Not when your object was a good and generous one," said Miss Crofton. "You might well enough be afraid to confront such a man as this if your aim was to over-reach and deceive him ; but bear in mind the fable of the man who had the courage to take the thorn out of the lion's paw. The operation, we are told, was a painful one, and there might have been an instant in which the patient felt disposed to eat his doctor ; but, with all these perils, strong in a good purpose, the surgeon persevered, and by his skill and his courage made the king of the beasts his fast friend for life. The lesson is worth remembering."

I was still pondering over this apophthegm, when Crofton aroused me by pushing across the table a great heap of gold. " This is all yours, Potts," said he ; " and remember, that as you are now my agent, travelling for the house of Crofton and Co., that you journey at my cost."

Of course I would not listen to this proposal, and, although urged by Miss Crofton with all a woman's tact and delicacy, I persisted so firmly in my refusal, that they were obliged to yield. I now had a hundred pounds all my own, and though the sum be not a very splendid one, I remember some French writer—I'm not sure it is not Jules Janin—saying, " Any man who can put his hand into his pocket and find five Napoleons there, is rich ;" and he certainly supports his theory with considerable sophistry and cleverness, mainly depending on the assumption, that any of the reasonable daily necessities of life, even in a luxurious point of view, are attainable with such means. Now, although a hundred pounds would not very long supply resources for such a life, yet, as I am not a Frenchman, nor living in Paris, still less had I habits or tastes of a costly kind, I might very well eke out three months pleasantly on this sum, and in these three months what might not happen? In a "hundred days" the great Napoleon crushed the whole might of the Austrian empire, and secured an emperor's daughter for his bride; and in another "hundred days" he made the tour of France, from Cannes to Rochefort, and lost an empire by the way! Wonderful things might then be compassed within three months.

"What are you saying about three months, Potts?" asked Crofton, for unwittingly I had uttered these words aloud.

"I was observing," said I, "that in three months from this day, we should arrange to meet somewhere. Where shall we say?"

"Geneva is very central; shall we name Geneva?"

"Oh, on no account. Let our rendezvous be in Italy. Let us say Rome."

"Rome be it then," cried Crofton. "Now for another point: let us have a wager as to who first discovers the object of our search. I'll bet you twenty Napoleons, Potts, to ten—for as we are two to one, so should the wager be."

"I take you," cried I, entering into his humour, "and I feel as certain of success as if I had your money in my hands."

"Will you have another wager with *me?*" whispered Mary Crofton, as she came behind my chair. "It is, that you'll not persuade Miss Herbert to wear this ring for *my* sake."

"I'll bet my life on it," said I, taking the opal ring she drew from her finger, as she spoke; "I'm in that mood of confidence now, I feel there is nothing I could not promise."

"If so then, Potts, let me have the benefit of this fortunate interval, and ask you to promise me one thing, which is, not to change your mind more than twice a day; don't be angry

with me, but hear me out. You are a good-hearted fellow,
and have excellent intentions; I don't think I know one less
really selfish, but at the same time you are so fickle of purpose, so undecided in action, that I'd not be the least
astonished to hear, when we asked for you to-morrow at
breakfast-time, that you had started for a tour in Norway, or
on a voyage to the Southern Pacific."

"And is this your judgment of me also, Miss Crofton ? "
said I, rising from my seat.

"Oh, no, Mr. Potts. I would only suspect you of going
off into the Tyrol, or the Styrian Alps, and forgetting all
about us, amidst the glaciers and the cataracts."

"I wish you a good night, and a better opinion of your
humble servant," said I, bowing.

"Don't go, Potts—wait a minute—come back. I have
something to tell you."

I closed the door behind me, and hastened off, not, however, perfectly clear whether I was the injured man, or one
who had just achieved a great outrage.

<hr />

CHAPTER XXXVI.

I am obliged to acknowledge that I was vain-glorious
enough to accept a seat in the Crofton carriage on the morning of their departure, and accompany them for a mile or so
of the way—even at the price of returning on foot—just that
I might show myself to the landlady and that odious old
waiter in a position of eminence, and make them do a bitter
penance for the insults they had heaped on an illustrious
stranger. It was a poor and paltry triumph, and over very
contemptible adversaries, but I could not refuse it to myself.
Crofton, too, contributed largely to the success of my little
scheme, by insisting that I should take the place beside his
sister, while he sat with his back to the horses; and though
I refused at first, I acceded at last, with the bland com-

pliance of a man who feels himself once more in his accustomed station.

As throughout this true history I have candidly revealed the inmost traits of my nature—well knowing the while how deteriorating such innate analogy must prove—I have ever felt that he who has small claims to interest by the events of his life, can make some compensation to the world by an honest exposure of his motives, his weaknesses, and his struggles. Now, my present confession is made in thi¹ spirit, and is not absolutely without its moral, for, as the adage tells us, " Look after the pence, and the pounds will take care of themselves;" so would I say, Guard yourself carefully against petty vices. You and I, most esteemed reader, are—I trust fervently—little likely to be arraigned on a capital charge. I hope sincerely that transportable felonies, and even misdemeanours, may not picture among the accidents of our life; such-like are the pounds that take care of themselves, but the "small pence," which require looking after, are little envies, and jealousies, and rancours, petty snobberies of display, small exhibitions of our being better than this man or greater than that; these, I repeat to you, accumulate on a man's nature just the way barnacles fasten on a ship's bottom—from mere time, and it is wonderful what damage can come of such paltry obstacles.

I very much doubt if a Roman conquerer regarded the chained captive who followed his chariot with a more supreme pride than I bestowed upon that miserable old waiter who now bowed himself to the ground before me, and when I ordered my dinner for four o'clock, and said, that probably I might have a friend to dine with me, his humiliation was complete.

"I wish I knew the secret of your staying here," said Mary Crofton, as we drove along ; "why will you not tell it?"

"Perhaps it might prove indiscreet, Mary, our friend Potts may have become a *mauvais sujet* since we have seen him last?"

I wrapped myself in a mysterious silence, and only smiled.

"Lindau, of all places, to stop at!" resumed she, pettishly. "There is nothing remarkable in the scenery,

19—⌐

no art treasures, nothing socially agreeable; what can it possibly be that detains you in such a place?"

"My dear Mary," said Crofton, "you are, without knowing it, violating a hallowed principle; you are no less than leading into temptation. Look at poor Potts there, and you will see that, while he knows in his inmost heart the secret which detains him here is some passing and insignificant circumstance unworthy of mention, you have, by imparting to it a certain importance, suggested to his mind the necessity of a story; give him now but five minutes to collect himself, and I'll engage that he will 'come out' with a romantic incident that would never have seen the light but for a woman's curiosity."

"Good Heavens!" thought I, "can this be a true interpretation of my character? Am I the weak and impressionable creature this would bespeak me?" I must have blushed deeply at my own reflection, for Crofton quickly added:—

"Don't get angry with me, Potts, any more than you would with a friend who'd say, 'Take care how you pass over that bridge, I know it is rotten and must give way.'"

"Let me answer you," said I, courageously, for I was acutely hurt to be thus arraigned before another. "It is more than likely that you, with your active habits and stirring notions of life, would lean very heavily on him who, neither wanting riches nor honours, would adopt some simple sort of dreamy existence, and think that the green alleys of the beech wood, or the little path beside the river, pleasanter sauntering than the gilded antechamber of a palace; and just as likely is it that you would take him roundly to task about wasted opportunities, misapplied talents, and stigmatise as inglorious indolence what might as possibly be called a contented humility. Now, I would ask you, why should one man be the measure of another? The load you could carry with ease might serve to crush me, and yet there may be some light burdens that would suit *my* strength, and in bearing which I might taste a sense of duty grateful as your own."

"I have no patience with you," began Crofton, warmly; but his sister stopped him with an imploring look, and then, turning to me, said:—

"Edward fancies that everyone can be as energetic and active as himself, and occasionally forgets what you have just so well remarked as to the relative capacities of different people."

"I want him to do something, to be something besides a dreamer!" burst he in, almost angrily.

"Well, then," said I, "you shall see me begin this moment, for I will get down here and walk briskly back to the town." I called to the postillions to pull up at the same time, and in spite of remonstrances, entreaties—almost beseeching from Mary Crofton—I persisted in my resolve, and bade them farewell.

Crofton was so much hurt that he could scarcely speak, and when he gave me his hand it was in the coldest of manners.

"But you'll keep our rendezvous, won't you?" said Mary; "we shall meet at Rome?"

"I really wonder, Mary, how you can force our acquaintanceship where it is so palpably declined. Good-bye—farewell," said he to me.

"Good-bye," said I, with a gulp that almost choked me; and away drove the carriage, leaving me standing in the train of dust it had raised. Every crack of the postboys' whips gave me a shock as though I had felt the thong on my own shoulders; and, at last, as sweeping round a turn of the road the carriage disappeared from view, such was the sense of utter desolation that came over me, that I sat down on a stone by the wayside, overwhelmed. I do not know if I ever felt such an utter sense of destitution as at that moment. "What a wealth of friends must a man possess," thought I, "who can afford to squander them in this fashion! How could I have repelled the counsels that kindness alone could have prompted? Surely Crofton must know far more of life than I did?" From this I went on to inquire why it was that the world showed itself so unforgiving to idleness in men of small fortune, since, if no burden to the community, they ought to be as free as their richer brethren. It was a puzzling theme, and though I revolved it long, I made but little of it, the only solution that occurred to me was, that the idleness of the humble man is not relieved by the splendours and luxuries which surround a rich man's leisure, and that the world resents the pretensions of ease unassociated with riches. In what a profound philosophy was it, then, that Diogenes rolled his tub about the streets! there was a mock purpose about it, that must have flattered his fellow-citizens. I feel assured that a great deal of the butterfly-hunting and beetle-gathering that we see around us is done in this spirit. They are a set of idle folk anxious to indulge their indolence without reproach.

Thus pondering and musing, I strolled back to the town. So still and silent was it, so free from all movement of traffic or business, that I was actually in the very centre of it without knowing it. There were streets without passengers, and shops without customers, and even *cafés* without guests, and I wondered within myself why people should thus congregate to do nothing, and I rambled on from street to alley, and from alley to lane, never chancing upon one who had anything in hand. At last I gained the side of the lake, along which a little quay ran for some distance, ending in a sort of terraced walk, now grass-grown and neglected. There were at least the charms of fresh air and scenery here, though the worthy citizen seemed to hold them cheaply, and I rambled along to the end, where, by a broad flight of steps, the terrace communicated with the lake ; a spot, doubtless, where, once on a time, the burghers took the water and went out a pleasuring with fat fraus and fräuleins. I had reached the end, and was about to turn back again, when I caught sight of a man, seated on one of the lower steps, employed in watching two little toy ships which he had just launched. Now this seemed to me the very climax of indolence, and I sat myself down on the parapet to observe him. His proceedings were indeed of the strangest, for as there was no wind to fill the sails and his vessels lay still and becalmed, he appeared to have bethought him of another mode to impart interest to him. He weighted one of them with little stones till he brought her gunwale level with the water, and then pressing her gently with his hand he made her sink slowly down to the bottom. I'm not quite certain whether I laughed outright, or that some exclamation escaped me as I looked, but some noise I must unquestionably have made, for he started and turned up his head, and

I saw Harpar, the Englishman whom I had met the day before at Constance.

"Well, you're not much the wiser after all," said he, gruffly, and without even saluting me.

There was in the words, and fierce expression of his face, something that made me suspect him of insanity, and I would willingly have retired without reply had he not risen and approached me.

"Eh," repeated he with a sneer, " ain't I right? You can make nothing of it?"

"I really don't understand you!" said I. "I came down here by the merest accident, and never was more astonished than to see you."

"Oh, of course; I am well used to that sort of thing," went he on in the same tone of scoff. "I've had some experience of these kinds of accidents before; but, as I said, it's no use, you're not within one thousand miles of it, no, nor any man in Europe."

It was quite clear to me now that he *was* mad, and my only care was to get speedily rid of him.

"I'm not surprised," said I, with an assumed ease—"I'm not surprised at your having taken to so simple an amusement, for really in a place so dull as this any mode of passing the time would be welcome."

"Simple enough when you know it," said he, with a peculiar look.

"You arrived last night, I suppose?" said I, eager to get conversation into some pleasanter channel.

"Yes, I got here very late. I had the misfortune to sprain my ankle, and this detained me a long time on the way, and may keep me for a couple of days more."

"I learned where he was stopping in the town, and seeing with what pain and difficulty he moved, I offered him my aid to assist him on his way.

"Well, I'll not refuse your help," said he, dryly; "but just go along yonder, about five-and-twenty or thirty yards, and I'll join you. You understand me, I suppose?"

Now, I really did not understand him, except to believe him perfectly insane, and suggest to me the notion of profiting by his lameness to make my escape with all speed. I conclude some generous promptings opposed this course, for

I obeyed his injunctions to the very letter, and waited till he
came up to me. He did so very slowly, and evidently in
much suffering, assisted by a stick in one haud, while he
carried his two little boats in the other.

"Shall I take charge of these for you ? " said I, offering
to carry them.

"No don't trouble yourself," said he, in the same rude
tone. "Nobody touches these but myself."

I now gave him my arm, aud we moved slowly along.

"What has become of the vagabonds ? Are they here
with you ? " asked he, abruptly.

" I parted with them yesterday," said I, shortly, and not
wishing to enter into further explanations.

"And you did wisely," rejoined he, with a serious air.
"Even when these sort of creatures have nothing very bad
about them, they are bad company, out of the hap-hazard
chance way they gain a livelihood. If you reduce life to a
game, you must yourself become a gambler. Now, there's
one feature of that sort of existence intolerable to an honest
man : it is, that to win himself, some one else must lose.
Do you understand me ? "

" I do, and am much struck by what you say."

"In that case," said be, with a nudge of his elbow against
my side—"in that case you might as well have not come
down to watch *me ?*—eh ? "

I protested stoutly against this mistake, but I could plainly
perceive with very little success.

"Let it be, let it be," said he, with a shake of the head.
"As I said before, if you saw the thing done before your eyes
you'd make nothing of it. I'm not afraid of you, or all the
men in Europe! There now, there's a challenge to the
whole of ye! Sit down every man of ye, with the problem
before ye, and see what you'll make of it."

"Ah," thought I, "this is madness. Here is a poor
monomaniac led away into the land of wild thoughts and
fancies by one dominating caprice; who knows whether out
of the realm of this delusion he may not be a man acute and
sensible."

"No, no," muttered he, half aloud; "there are, maybe, half
a million of men this moment manufacturing steam-engines ;
but it took one head, just one head, to set them all working,

and if it wasn't for old Watt, the world at this day wouldn't
be five miles in advance of what it was a century back. I
see," added he, after a moment, "you don't take much interest
in these sort of things. Your line of parts, is the walking
gentleman, eh ? Well, bear in mind it don't pay; no, Sir, it
don't pay! Here, this is my way ; my lodging is down this
lane. I'll not ask you to come further; thank you for your
help, and good-bye."

"Let us not part here; come up to the inn and dine
with me," said I, affecting his own blunt and abrupt
manner.

"Why should I dine with you?" asked he, roughly.

"I can't exactly say," stammered I, "except out of good-
fellowship, just as, for instance, I accepted your invitation
t'other morning to breakfast."

"Ah, yes, to be sure, so you did. Well, I'll come. We
shall be all alone, I suppose? "

"Quite alone."

"All right, for I have no coat but this one," and he looked
down at the coarse sleeve as he spoke, with a strange and
sad smile, and then waving his hand in token of farewell, he
said, " I'll join you in half an hour," and disappeared up the
lane.

I have already owned that I did not like this man; he had
a certain short abrupt way that repelled me at every moment.
When he differed in opinion with me, he was not satisfied to
record his dissent, but he must set about demolishing my
conviction, and this sort of intolerance pervaded all he
said. There was, too, that business-like practical tone about
him that jars fearfully on the sensitive fibre of the idler's
nature.

It was exactly in proportion as his society was distasteful
to me, that I felt a species of pride in associating with him,
as though to say "I am not one of those who must be fawned
on and flattered. I am of a healthier and manlier stamp; I
can afford to hear my judgments arraigned, and my opinions
opposed." And in this humour I ascended the stairs of the
hotel, and entered the room where our table was already laid
out.

To compensate, so far as they could, for the rude reception
of the day before, they had given me now the " grand apart-

ment" of the inn, which, by a long balcony, looked over the lake, and that fine mountain range that leads to the Splugen pass. A beautiful bouquet of fresh flowers ornamented the centre of the small dinner-table, tastily decked with Bohemian glass, and napkins with lace borders. I rather liked this little display of elegance. It was a sort of ally on my side against the utilitarian plainness of my guest.

As I walked up and down the room, awaiting his arrival, I could not help a sigh, and a very deep one too, over the thought of what had been my enjoyment that moment if my guest had been one of a different temperament—a man willing to take me on my own showing, and ready to accept any version I should like to give of myself. How gracefully, how charmingly I could have played the host to such a man! What vigour would it have imparted to my imagination—what brilliancy to my fancy! With what a princely grace might I have dispensed my hospitalities, as though such occasions were the daily habit of my life : whereas a dinner with Harpar would be nothing more or less than an airing with a " slave in the chariot "—a perpetual reminder like the face of a poor relation, that my lot was cast in an humble sphere, and it was no use trying to disguise it.

" What's all this for ? " said Harpar's harsh voice, as he entered the room. " Why didn't you order our mutton-chop below stairs in the common room, and not a banquet in this fashion ? You must be well aware I couldn't do this sort of thing by *you*. Why, then, have you attempted it with *me !* "

" I have always thought it was a host's prerogative," said I, meekly, " to be the arbiter of his own entertainment."

" So it might where he is the arbiter of his purse, but you know well enough neither you nor I have any pretension to these costly ways, and they have this disadvantage, that they make all intercourse stilted and unnatural. If you and I had to sit down to table, dressed in court suits, with wigs and bags, ain't it likely we'd be easy and cordial together? Well, this is precisely the same."

" I am really sorry," said I, with a forced appearance of courtesy, " to have incurred so severe a lesson, but you must allow me this one transgression before I begin to profit by it." And so saying, I rang the bell and ordered dinner.

Harpar made no reply, but walked the room, with his hands deep in his pockets, humming a tune to himself as he went.

At last we sat down to table; everything was excellent and admirably served, but we ate on in silence, not a syllable exchanged between us. As the dessert appeared I tried to open conversation. I affected to seem easy and unconcerned, but the cold half stern look of my companion repelled all attempts, and I sat very sad and much discouraged sipping my wine.

"May I order some brandy-and-water? I like it better than these French wines," asked he, abruptly; and, as I arose to ring for it, he added, "and you'll not object to me having a pipe of strong Cavendish?" And therewith he produced a leather bag and a very much smoked meerschaum, short and ungainly as his own figure. As he thrust his hand into the pouch, a small boat, about the size of a lady's thimble, rolled out from amidst the tobacco, he quickly took it and placed it in his waistcoat pocket—the act being done with a sort of hurry that with a man of less self-possession might have perhaps evinced confusion.

"You fancy you've seen something, don't you?" said he, with a defiant laugh. "I'd wager a five-pound note, if I had one, that you think at this moment you have made a great discovery. Well, there it is, make much of it!" As he spoke, he produced the little boat and laid it down before me. I own that this speech and the act convinced me that he was insane; I was aware that intense suspectfulness is the great characteristic of madness, and everything tended to show that he was deranged.

Rather to conceal what was passing in my own mind than out of curiosity, I took up the little toy to examine it. It was beautifully made, and finished with a most perfect neatness: the only thing I could not understand being four small holes on each side of the keel, fastened by four little plugs.

"What are these for?" asked I.

"Can't you guess?" said he, laughingly.

" No; I have never seen such before."

" Well," said he, musingly, " perhaps they *are* puzzling—
I suppose they are. But mayhap, too, if I thought you'd
guess the meaning, I'd not have been so ready to show it to
you." And with this he replaced the boat in his pocket and
smoked away. " You ain't a genius, my worthy friend,
that's a fact," said he, sententiously.

" I opine that the same judgment might be passed upon a
great many ? " said I, testily.

" No," continued he, following on his own thoughts
without heeding my remark, " *you'll* not set the Thames
a-fire."

" Is that the best test of a man's ability ? " asked I,
sneeringly.

" You're the sort of fellow that ought to be—let us see
now what you ought to be—yes, you're just the stamp of man
for an apothecary."

" You are so charming in your frankness," said I, " that
you almost tempt me to imitate you."

" And why not? sure we oughtn't to talk to each other
like two devils in waiting. Out with what you have to
say."

" I was just thinking," said I—" led to it by that specu-
lative turn of yours—I was just thinking in what station
your abilities would have pre-eminently distinguished you."

" Well, have you hit it ? "

" I'm not quite certain," said I, trying to screw up my
courage for an impertinence, " but I half suspect that in our
great national works—our lines of railroad, for instance—
there must be a strong infusion of men with tastes and
habits resembling yours."

" You mean the navvies? " broke he in. " You're right,
I was a navvy once; I turned the first spadeful of earth on
the Coppleston Junction, and seeing what a good thing
might be made of it, I suggested task-work to my comrades, and we netted from four-and-six to five shillings a day
each. In eight months after, I was made an inspector: so
that you see strong sinews can be good allies to a strong
head and a stout will."

I do not believe that the most angry rebuke, the most
sarcastic rejoinder, could have covered me with a tenth part

of the shame and confusion than did these few words. I'd
have given worlds, if I had them, to make a due reparation
for my rudeness, but I knew not how to accomplish it. I
looked into his face to read if I might hit upon some trait
by which his nature could be approached ; but I might as
well have gazed at a line of of railroad to guess the sort of
town that it led to. The stern, rugged, bold countenance
seemed to imply little else than daring and determination,
and I could not but wonder how I had ever dared to take a
liberty with one of his stamp.

"Well," said I, at last, and wishing to lead him back to
his story, " and after being made inspector ——"

" You can speak German well," said he, totally inattentive
to my question; "just ask one of these people when there
will be any conveyance from this to Ragatz."

" Ragatz of all places ! " exclaimed I.

"Yes; they tell me it's good for the rheumatics, and I
have got some old shoulder pains I'd like to shake off before
winter. And then this sprain too : I foresee I shall not be
able to walk much for some days to come."

" Ragatz is on my road ; I am about to cross the Splugen
into Italy; I'll bear you company so far, if you have no
objection."

"Well, it may not seem civil to say it, but I have an
objection," said he, rising from the table. "When I've got
weighty things on my mind I've a bad habit of talking of
them to myself aloud. I can't help it, and so I keep strictly
alone till my plans are all fixed and settled; after that,
there's no danger of my revealing them to anyone. There
now, you have my reason, and you'll not dispute that it's a
good one."

"You may not be too distrustful of yourself," said I,
laughing, "but assuredly you are far too flattering in your
estimate of *my* acuteness."

" I'll not risk it," said he, bluntly, as he sought for his
hat.

"Wait a moment," said I. " You told me at Constance
that you were in want of money : at the time I was not
exactly in funds myself. Yesterday, however, I received a
remittance, and if ten or twenty pounds be of any service,
they are heartily at your disposal."

He looked at me fixedly, almost sternly, for a minute or two, and then said,

"Is this true, or is it that you have changed your mind about me?"

"True," said I—"strictly true."

"Will this loan—I mean it to be a loan—inconvenience you much?"

"No, no; I make you the offer freely."

"I take it, then. Let me have ten pounds; and write down there an address where I am to remit it some day or other, though I can't say when."

"There may be some difficulty about that," said I. "Stay! I mean to be at Rome some time in the winter; send it to me there."

"To what banker?"

"I have no banker, I never had a banker. There's my name, and let the post-office be the address."

"Whichever way you're bent on going, you're not on the road to be a rich man," said Harpar, as he deposited my gold in his leather purse; "but I hope you'll not lose by me. Good-bye." He gave me his hand, not very warmly or cordially either, and was gone ere I well knew it.

CHAPTER XXXVII.

I WENT the next morning to take leave of Harpar before starting, but found to my astonishment that he was already off! He had, I learned, hired a small carriage to convey him to Bregenz, and had set out before daybreak. I do not know why this should have annoyed me, but it did so, and set me a thinking over the people whom Echstein, in his "Erfährungen," says, are born to be dupes. "There is," says he, "a race of men who are 'eingeborne Narern'—'native numbskulls,' one might say—who muddy the

streams of true benevolence by indiscriminating acts of kindness, and who, by always aiding the wrong-doer, make themselves accomplices of vice." Could it be that I was in this
barren category? Harpar had told me, the evening before,
that he would not leave Lindau till his sprain was better,
and now he was off, just as if, having no further occasion for
me, he was glad to be rid of my companionship—just as if
—— I was beginning again to start another conjecture, when
I bethought me that there is not a more deceptive formula in
the whole cyclopædia of delusion than that which opens with
these same words, "just as if." Rely upon it, amiable
reader, that whenever you find yourself driven to explain a
motive, trace a cause, or reconcile a discrepancy, by "just as
if," the chances are about seven to three you are wrong. If
I was not in the bustle of paying my bill and strapping on
my knapsack, I'd convince you on this head, but as the
morning is a bright, but mellow one of early autumn, and
my path lies along the placid lake, waveless and still, with
many a tinted tree reflected in its fair mirror, let us not
think of knaves and rogues, but rather dwell on the
pleasanter thought of all the good and grateful things which
daily befal us in this same life of ours. I am full certain
that almost all of us enter upon what is called the world in
too combative a spirit. We are too fond of dragon slaying,
and rather than be disappointed of our sport, we'd fall foul
of a pet lamb, for want of a tiger. Call it self-delusion,
credulity, what you will, it is a faith that makes life very
livable, and, without it,

> We feel a light has left the world,
>   A nameless sort of treasure,
> As though one pluck'd the crimson heart
>   From out the rose of pleasure.
> I could forgive the fate that made
>   Me poor and young to-morrow,
> To have again the soul that played
>   So tenderly in sorrow,
> So buoyantly in happiness.
>   Ay, I would brook deceiving,
> And even the deceiver bless,
>   Just to go on believing!

"Still," thought I, "one ought to maintain self-respect;
one should not willingly make himself a dupe." And then

I began to wish that Väterchen had come up, and that Tintefleck was rushing towards me with tears in her eyes, and
my money-bag in her hands.   I wanted to forget them.   I
tried in a hundred ways to prevent them crossing my
memory; but though there is a most artful system of artificial "mnemonics" invented by some one, the Lethan art
has met no explorer, and no man has ever yet found out the
way to shut the door against by-gones.   I believe it is
scarcely more than five miles to Bregenz from Lindau, and
yet I was almost as many hours on the road.   I sat down,
perhaps, twenty times, lost in reverie; indeed, I'm not very
sure that I didn't take a sound sleep under a spreading
willow, so that, when I reached the inn, the company was
just going in to dinner. at the *table d'hôte.*   Simple and un-
pretentious as that board was, the company that graced it
was certainly distinguished, being no less than the Austrian
field-marshal in command of the district, and the officers of
his staff.   To English notions, it seemed very strange to see
a nobleman of the highest rank, in the proudest state of
Europe, seated at a dinner-table open to all comers, at a
fraction less than one shilling a head, and where some of the
government officials of the place daily came.

It was not without a certain sense of shame that I found
myself in the long low chamber, in which about twenty officers
were assembled, whose uniforms were all glittering with stars,
medals, and crosses; in fact, to a weak-minded civilian like
myself, they gave the impression of a group of heroes fresh
come from all the triumphant glories of a campaign.   Between the staff which occupied one end of the long table and
the few townsfolk who sat at the other, there intervened a
sort of frontier territory uninhabited, and it was here that
the waiter located me—an object of observation and remark
to each.   Resolving to learn how I was treated by my critics,
I addressed the waiter in the very worst French, and protested my utter ignorance of German.   I had promised myself
much amusement from this expedient, but was doomed to a
severe disappointment—the officers coolly setting me down
for a servant, while the townspeople pronounced me a pedlar;
and when these judgments had been recorded, instead of
entering upon a psychological examination of my nature,
temperament, and individuality, they never noticed me any

more. I felt hurt at this, more indeed for their sakes than my own, since I bethought me of the false impression that is current of this people throughout Europe, where they have the reputation of philosophers deeply engaged in researches into character, minute anatomists of human thought and man's affections; "and yet," muttered I, "they can sit at table with one of the most remarkable of men, and be as ignorant of all about him, as the husbandman who toils at his daily labour is of the mineral treasures that lie buried down beneath him.

"I will read them a lesson," thought I. "They shall see that in the humble guise of foot-traveller it may be the pleasure of men of rank and station to journey." The towns-folk when the dessert made its appearance, rose to take their departure, each before he left the room making a profound obeisance to the general, and then another but less lowly act of homage to the staff, showing by this that strangers were expected to withdraw, while the military guests sat over their wine. Indeed, a very significant look from the last person who left the room conveyed to me the etiquette of the place. I was delighted at this—it was the very opportunity I longed for—and so, with a clink of my knife against my wine-glass, the substitute for a bell in use amongst humble hostels, I summoned the waiter, and asked for his list of wines. I saw that my act had created some astonishment amongst the others, but it excited nothing more, and now they had all lighted their pipes, and sat smoking away quite regardless of my presence. I had ordered a flask of Steinberger at four florins, and given most special directions that my glass should have a "roped rim," and be of a tender green tint, but not too deep to spoil the colour of the wine.

My admonitions were given aloud, and in a tone of command, but I perceived that they failed to create any impression upon my moustached neighbours. I might have ordered nectar or hypocras for all that they seemed to care about me. I raked up in memory all the impertinent and insolent things Henri Heine had ever said of Austria; I bethought me how they tyrannised in the various provinces of their scattered empire, and how they were hated by Hun, Slavac, and Italian; I revelled in those slashing leading articles that used to show up the great but bankrupt bully,

20

and I only wished I was "own correspondent" to something
at home to give my impressions of "Austria and her military
system."

Little as you think of that pale sad-looking stranger, who
sits sipping his wine in solitude at the foot of the table, that
he is about to transmit yourselves and your country to a remote posterity. "Ay!" muttered I, "to be remembered
when the Danube will be a choked-up rivulet, and the park
of Schönbrunn a prairie for the buffalo." I am not exactly
aware how or why these changes were to have occurred, but
Lord Macaulay's New Zealander might have originated
them.

While I thus mused and brooded, the tramp of four horses
came clattering down the street, and soon after swept into
the arched door-way of the inn with a rolling and thunderous
sound.

"Here he comes—here he is at last!" said a young officer,
who had rushed in haste to the window, and at the announcement a very palpable sentiment of satisfaction seemed to
spread itself through the company, even to the grim old
field-marshal, who took his pipe from his mouth to say :

"He is in time—he saves 'arrest!'"

As he spoke, a tall man in uniform entered the room, and
walking with military step till he came in front of the
general, said, in a loud but respectful voice :

"I have the honour to report myself as returned to duty.'

The general replied something I could not catch, and then
shook him warmly by the hand, making room for him to sit
down next him.

"How far did your royal highness go? Not to Coire?'
said the general.

"Far beyond it, Sir," said the other. "I went the whole
way to the Splugen, and if it were not for the terror of your
displeasure, I'd have crossed the mountain and gone on to
Chiavenna."

The fact that I was listening to the narrative of a royal
personage was not only the bond of fascination to me, for
somehow the tone of the speaker's voice sounded familiarly
to my ears, and I could have sworn I had heard it before
As he was at the same side of the table with myself, I could
not see him, but while he continued to talk, the impression

grew each moment more strong that I must have met him previously.

I could gather—it was easy enough to do so—from the animated looks of the party, and the repeated bursts of laughter that followed his sallies, that the newly-arrived officer was a wit and authority amongst his comrades. His elevated rank, too, may have contributed to this popularity. Must I own that he appeared in the character that to me is particularly offensive? He was a " narrator." That vulgar adage of " two of a trade " has a far wider acceptance when applied to the operations of intellect than when addressed to the work of men's hands. To see this jealousy at its height, you must look for it amongst men of letters, artists, actors, or, better still, those social performers who are the bright spirits of dinner-parties—the charming men of society. All the animosities of political or religious hate are mild compared to the detestation this rivalry engenders; and now, though the audience was a foreign one, which I could have no pretension to amuse, I conceived the most bitter dislike for the man who had engaged their attention.

I do not know how it may be with others, but to myself there has always been this difficulty in a foreign language, that until I have accustomed myself to the tone of voice and the manner of a speaker, I can rarely follow him without occasional lapses. Now, on the present occasion, the narrator, though speaking distinctly, and with a good accent, had a very rapid utterance, and it was not till I had familiarised my ear with his manner that I could gather his words correctly. Nor was my difficulty lessened by the fact that, as he pretended to be witty and epigrammatic, frequent bursts of laughter broke from his audience and obscured his speech. He was, as it appeared, giving an account of a fishing excursion he had just taken to one of the small mountain lakes near Poppenheim, and it was clear enough he was one who always could eke an adventure out of even the most ordinary incident of daily life.

This fishing story had really nothing in it, though he strove to make out fifty points of interest or striking situations out of the veriest common-place. At last, however, I saw that, like a practised story-teller, he was hoarding up his great incident for the finish.

"As I have told you," said he, "I engaged the entire of the little inn for myself; there were but five rooms in it altogether, and though I did not need more than two, I took the rest, that I might be alone and unmolested. Well, it was on my second evening there, as I sat smoking my pipe at the door, and looking over my tackle for the morrow there came up the glen the strange sound of wheels, and, to my astonishment, a travelling carriage soon appeared, with four horses driven in hand, and I saw in a moment it was a lohnkutscher, who had taken the wrong turning after leaving Ragatz, and mistaken the road, for the highway ceases about two miles above Poppenheim, and dwindles down to a mere mule-path. Leaving my host to explain the mistake to the travellers, I hastily re-entered the house, just as the carriage drove up. The explanation seemed a very prolix one, for when I looked out of the window, half an hour afterwards, there were the horses still standing at the door, and the driver, with a large branch of alder, whipping away the flies from them, while the host continued to hold his place at the carriage door. At last he entered my room, and said that the travellers, two foreign ladies—he thought them Russians—had taken the wrong road, but that the elder, what between fatigue and fear, was so overcome, that she could not proceed further, and entreated that they might be afforded any accommodation—mere shelter for the night—rather than retrace their road to Ragatz.

"'Well,' said I, carelessly, 'let them have the rooms on the other side of the hall; so that they only stop for one night, the intrusion will not signify.' Not a very gracious reply, perhaps, but I did not want to be gracious. The fact was, as the old lady got out, I saw something like an elephant's leg, in a fur boot, that quite decided me on not making acquaintance with the travellers, and I was rash enough to imagine they must be both alike. Indeed, I was so resolute in maintaing my solitude undisturbed, that I told my host on no account whatever to make me any communication from the strangers, nor, on any pretext, to let me feel that they were lodged under the same roof with myself. Perhaps, if the next day had been one to follow my usual sport, I should have forgotten all about them, but it was one of such rain as made it perfectly impossible to leave the house. I doubt if I ever saw rain like it. It came down in sheets, like water splashed out of buckets, flattening the small trees to the earth, and beating down all the light foliage into the muddy soil beneath ; meanwhile the air shook with the noise of the swollen torrents, and all the mountain-streams crashed and thundered away, like great cataracts. Rain can really become grand at such moments, and no more resembling a mere shower than the cry of a single brawler in the streets is like the roar of a mighty multitude. It was so fine, that I determined I would go down to a little wooden bridge over the river, whence I could see the stream as it came down, tumbling and splashing, from a cleft in the mountain. I soon dressed myself in all my best waterproofs —hat, cape, boots, and all—and set out. Until I was ·fully embarked on my expedition, I had no notion of the severity of the storm, and it was with considerable difficulty I could make head against the wind and rain together, while the slippery ground made walking an actual labour.

"At last I reached the river, but of the bridge, the only trace was a single beam, which, deeply buried in the bank at one extremity, rose and fell in the surging flood, like the arm of a drowning swimmer. The stream had completely filled the channel, and swept along, with fragments of timber, and even furniture, in its muddy tide ; farm produce, and implements too, came floating by, showing what de-struction had been effected higher up the river. As I stood gazing on the current, I saw, at a little distance from me, a man, standing motionless beside the river, and apparently lost in thought—so at least he seemed—for though not at all clad in a way to resist the storm, he remained there, wet and soaked through, totally regardless of the weather. On in-quiring at the inn, I learned that this was the lohnkutscher —the ' vetturino '—of the travellers, and who, in attempting to ascertain if the stream were fordable, had lost one of his best horses, and barely escaped being carried away himself. Until that, I had forgotten all about the strangers, whom, it now appeared, were close prisoners like myself. While the host was yet speaking, the lohnkutscher came up, and in a tone of equality, that showed me he thought I was in his own line of business, asked if I would sell him one of my nags then in the stable.

"Not caring to disabuse him of his error regarding my
rank, I did not refuse him so flatly as I might, and he
pressed the negotiation very warmly in consequence. At
last, to get rid of him, I declared that I would not break up
my team, and retired into the house. I was not many
minutes in my room, when a courier came, with a polite
message from his mistress, to beg I would speak with her.
I went at once, and found an old lady—she was English, as
her French bespoke—very well mannered and well bred,
who apologized for troubling me, but having heard from her
vetturino that my horses were disengaged, and that I might,
if not disposed to sell one of them, hire out the entire team,
to take their carriage as far as Andeer—— By the time
she got thus far, I perceived that she, too, mistook me for a
lohnkutscher. It just struck me what good fun it would be
to carry on the joke. To be sure, the lady herself presented
no inducement to the enterprise, and as I thus balanced the
case, there came into the room one of the prettiest girls I
ever saw. She never turned a look towards where I was
standing, nor deigned to notice me at all, but passed out of
the room as rapidly as she entered; still, I remembered that
I had already seen her before, and passed a delightful evening in her company at a little inn in the Black Forest."

When the narrator had got thus far in his story, I
leaned forward to catch a full view of him, and saw, to my
surprise, and I own to my misery, that he was the German
count we had met at the Titi-See. So overwhelming was
this discovery to me, that I heard nothing for many minutes
after. All of that wretched scene between us on the last
evening at the inn came full to my memory, and I bethought
me of lying the whole night on the hard table, fevered with
rage and terror alternately. If it were not that his narrative
regarded Miss Herbert now, I would have skulked out of the
room, and out of the inn, and out of the town itself, never
again to come under the insolent stare of those wicked grey
eyes, but in that name there was a fascination—not to say
that a sense of jealousy burned at my heart like a furnace.

The turmoil of my thoughts lost me a great deal of his
story, and might have lost me more, had not the hearty
laughter of his comrades recalled me once again to attention.

He was describing how, as a " vetturino," he drove their

carriage with his own spanking grey horses to Coire, and thence to Andeer. He had bargained, it seemed, that Miss Herbert should travel outside in the cabriolet, but she failed to keep her pledge, so that they only met at stray moments during the journey. It was in one of these she said, laughingly, to him,—

"'Nothing would surprise me less than to learn, some fine morning, that you were a prince in disguise, or a great count of the empire, at least. It was only the other day we were honoured with the incognito presence of a royal personage; I do not exactly know who, but Mrs. Keats could tell you. He left us abruptly at Schaffhausen.'

"'You can't mean the creature,' said I, 'that I saw in your company at the Titi-See?'

"'The same,' said she, rather angrily.

"'Why, he is a saltimbanque; I saw him the morning I came through Constance with some others of his troop dragged before the maire for causing a disturbance in a cabaret; one of the most consummate impostors, they told me, in Europe.'"

"An infamous falsehood, and a base liar the man who says it," cried I, springing to my legs, and standing revealed before the company in an attitude of haughty defiance. "I am the person you have dared to defame. I have never assumed to be a prince, and as little am I a rope-dancer. I am an English gentleman, travelling for his pleasure, and I hurl back every word you have said of me with contempt and defiance."

Before I had finished this insolent speech, some half-dozen swords were drawn and brandished in the air, very eager, as it seemed, to cut me to pieces, and the count himself required all the united strength of the party to save me from his hands. At last, I was pushed, hustled, and dragged out of the room to another smaller one on the same floor, and, the key being turned on me, left to my very happy reflections.

CHAPTER XXXVIII.

I HAD no writing materials, but I had just composed a long letter to the *Times* on "the outrageous treatment and false imprisonment of a British subject in Austria," when my door was opened by a thin, lank-jawed, fierce-eyed man in uniform, who announced himself as the Rittmeister von Mahony, of the Keyser Hussars.

"A countryman—an Irishman," said I, eagerly, clasping his hand with warmth.

"That is to say, two generations back," replied he; "my grandfather Terence was a lieutenant in Trenck's Horse, but since that none of us have ever been out of Austria."

If these tidings fell coldly on my heart just beginning to glow with the ardour of home and country, I soon saw that it takes more than two generations to wash out the Irishman from a man's nature. The honest Rittmeister, with scarcely a word of English in his vocabulary, was as hearty a country-man as if he had never journeyed out of the land of Bog.

"He had heard 'all about it,'" he said, by way of arrest-ing the eloquent indignation that filled me; and he added, "And the more fool myself to notice the matter;" asking me, quaintly, if I had never heard of our native maxim that says, "One man ought never to fall upon forty"? "Well," said he, with a sigh, "what's done can't be undone; and let us see what's to come next? I see you are a gentleman, and the worse luck yours."

"What do you mean by that?" asked I.

"Just this: you'll have to fight; and if you were a 'Gemeiner'—a plebeian—you'd get off."

I turned away to the window to wipe a tear out of my eye; it had come there without my knowing it, and, as I did so, I devoted myself to the death of a hero.

"Yes," said I, "*she* is in this incident—she has her part in this scene of my life's drama, and I will not disgrace her presence. I will die like a man of honour rather than that her name should be disparaged."

He went on to tell me of my opponent, who was brother to

a reigning sovereign, and himself a royal highness—Prince
Max of Swabia. "He was not," he added, "by any means
a bad fellow, though not reputed to be perfectly sane on
certain topics." However, as his eccentricities were very
harmless ones, merely offshoots of an exaggerated personal
vanity, it was supposed that some active service, and a little
more intercourse with the world, would cure him. "Not,"
added he, "that one can say he has shown many signs of
amendment up to this, for he never makes an excursion of
half-a-dozen days from home, without coming back filled
with the resistless passion of some young queen or arch-
duchess for him. As he forgets these as fast as he imagines
them, there is usually nothing to lament on the subject.
Now you are in possession of all that you need know about
him. Tell me something of yourself; and first, have you
served ? "

"Never."

"Was your father a soldier, or your grandfather ? "

"Neither."

"Have you any connections on the mother's side in the
army ? "

"I am not aware of one."

He gave a short, hasty cough, and walked the room twice
with his hands clasped at his back, and then, coming
straight in front of me, said, "And your name ? What's
your name ? "

"Potts ! Potts !" said I, with a firm energy.

"Potztausend !" cried he, with a grim laugh; "what a
strange name !"

"I said Potts, Herr Rittmeister, and not Potztausend,"
rejoined I, haughtily.

"And I heard you," said he; "it was involuntary on my
part to add the termination. And who are the Pottses?
Are they noble ? "

"Nothing of the kind—respectable middle-class folk ;
some in trade, some clerks in mercantile houses, some holding small government employments, one, perhaps the chief of
the family, an eminent apothecary !"

As if I had uttered the most irresistible joke, at this
word, he held his hands over his face and shook with
laughter.

"Heilege Joseph!" cried he, at last, "this is too good! The Prince Max going out with an apothecary's nephew, or, maybe, his son!"

"His son upon this occasion," said I, gravely.

He did not reply for some minutes, and then, leaning over the back of a chair, and regarding me very fixedly he said :—

"You have only to say who you are, and what your belongings, and nothing will come of this affair. In fact, what with your little knowledge of German, your imperfect comprehension of what the Prince said, and your own station in life, I'll engage to arrange everything and get you off clear!"

"In a word," said I, "I am to plead in *formâ inferioris*— isn't that it?"

"Just so," said he, puffing out a long cloud from his pipe.

"I'd rather die first!" cried I, with an energy that actually startled him.

"Well," said he, after a pause, "I think it is very probable that will come of it; but, if it be your choice, I have nothing to say."

"Go back, Herr Rittmeister," cried I, "and arrange the meeting for the very earliest moment."

I said this with a strong purpose, for I felt if the event were to come off at once I could behave well.

"As you are resolved on this course," said he, "do not make any such confidences to others as you have made to me; nothing about those Pottses in haberdashery and dry goods, but just simply you are the high and well-born Potts of Pottsheim. Not a word more."

I bowed an assent, but so anxious was he to impress this upon me that he went over it all once more.

"As it will be for me to receive the prince's message, the choice of weapons will be yours. What are you most expert with? I mean, after the pistol?" said he, grinning.

"I am about equally skilled in all. Rapier, pistol, or sabre are all alike to me."

"Der Teufel!" cried he: "I was not counting upon this; and as the sabre is the prince's weakest arm, we'll select it."

I bowed again, and more blandly.

"There is but one thing more," said he, turning about just as he was leaving the room. "Don't forget that in this case the gross provocation came from *you*, and, therefore, be satisfied with self-defence, or at most a mere flesh wound. Remember that the prince is a near connection of the royal family of England, and it would be irreparable ruin to you were he to fall by your hand." And with this he went out.

Now, had he gravely bound me over not to strangle the lions in the Tower it could not have appeared more ridiculous to me than this injunction, and if there had been in my heart the smallest fund of humour, I could have laughed at it; but, Heaven knows, none of my impulses took a mirthful turn at that moment, and there never was invented the drollery that could wring a smile from me.

I was sitting in a sort of stupor—I know not how long—when the door opened, and the Rittmeister's head peered in.

"To-morrow morning at five!" cried he. "I will fetch you half an hour before." The door closed, and he was off.

It was now a few minutes past eight o'clock, and there were, therefore, something short of nine hours of life left to me. I have heard that Victor Hugo is an amiable and kindly disposed man, and I feel assured, if he ever could have known the tortures he would have inflicted, he would never have designed the terrible record entitled *Le Dernier Jour d'un Condamné*. I conclude it was designed as a sort of appeal against death punishments. I doubt much of its efficacy in altering legislation, while I feel assured, that if ever it fall in the way of one whose hours are numbered, it must add indescribably to his misery.

When, how, or by whom my supper was served, I never knew. I can only remember that a very sleepy waiter roused me out of a half drowsy reverie about midnight, by asking if he were to remove the dishes, or let them remain till morning. I bade him leave them, and me also, and when the door was closed I sat down to my meal. It was cold and unappetising. I would have deemed it unwholesome, too, but I remembered that the poor stomach it was destined for would never be called on to digest it, and that for once I might transgress without the fear of dyspepsia. My case was precisely that of the purseless traveller, who, we are told, can sing before the robber, just as if want ever suggested melody, or that being poor was a reason for song. So with me any excess was open to me just because it was impossible!

"Still," thought I, " great criminals—and surely I am not as bad as they—eat very heartily." And so I cut the tough fowl vigorously in two, and placed half of it on my plate. I filled myself out a whole goblet of wine, and drank it off. I repeated this, and felt better. I fell to now with a will, and really made an excellent supper. There were some potted sardines that I secretly resolved to have for my breakfast, when the sudden thought flashed across me that I was never to breakfast any more. I verily believe that I tasted in that one instant a whole lifelong of agony and bitterness.

There was in my friendless, lone condition, my youth, the mild and gentle traits of my nature, and my guileless simplicity, just that combination of circumstances which would make my fate peculiarly pathetic, and I imagined my countrymen standing beside the gravestone and muttering "Poor Potts!" till I felt my heart almost bursting with sorrow over myself.

"Cut off at three-and-twenty!" sobbed I; "in the very opening bud of his promise!"

"Misfortune is a pebble with many facets," says the Chinese adage, " and wise is he who turns it around till he find the smooth one."

"Is there such here?" thought I. "And where can it be?" With all my ingenuity I could not discover it, when at last there crossed my mind, how the event would figure in the daily papers, and be handed down to remote posterity. I imagined the combat itself described in the language almost of a lion-hunt. "Potts, who had never till that moment had a sword in his had—Potts, though at this time severely wounded, and bleeding profusely, nothing dismayed by the ferocious attack of his opponent—Potts maintained his guard with all the coolness of a consummate swordsman." How I wished my life might be spared just to let me write the narrative of the combat. I would like, besides, to show the world how generously I could treat an adversary, with what delicacy I could respect his motives, and how nobly deal even with his injustice.

"Was that two o'clock?" said I, starting up, while the humming sound of the gone bell filled the room. "Is it possible that but three hours now stand between me and —— " I gave a shudder that made me feel as if I was standing in a fearful thorough draught, and actually looked up to see if the window were not open ; but no, it was closed, the night calm, and the sky full of stars. "Oh!" exclaimed I, "if there are Pottses up amongst you yonder, I hope destiny may deal more kindly by them than down here. I trust that in those glorious regions a higher and purer intelligence prevails, and, above all things, that duelling is proclaimed the greatest of crimes." Remnant of barbarism ! it is worse ten thousand times; it is the whole suit, costume, and investure of an uncivilised age. "Poor Potts!" said I; "you went out upon your life-voyage with very generous intentions towards posterity. I wonder how it will treat *you?* Will it vindicate your memory, uphold your fame, and dignify your motives? Will it be said in history, 'Amongst the memorable events of the period was the duel between the Prince Max of Swabia and an Irish gentleman named Potts? To understand fully the circumstance of this remarkable conflict, it is necessary to premise that Potts was not what is vulgarly called constitutionally brave ; but he was more. He was ——' Ah! there was the puzzle. How was that miserable biographer ever to arrive at the secret of an organization fine and subtle as mine? If I could but leave it on record—if I could but transmit to the ages that will come after me the invaluable key to the mystery of my being—a few days would suffice—a week certainly would do it—and why should I not have time given me for this? I will certainly propose this to the Rittmeister when he comes. There can be little doubt but he will see the matter with my own eyes."

As if I had summoned him by enchantment, there he stood at the door, wrapped in his great white cavalry cloak, and looking gigantic and ominous together.

"There is no carriage-road," said he, "to the place we are going, and I have come thus early that we may stroll along leisurely, and enjoy the fresh air of the morning."

Until that moment I had never believed how heartless human nature could be! To talk of enjoyment, to recal the world and its pleasures, in any way, to one situated like I, was a bold and scarcely credible cruelty ; but the words did me good service—they armed me with a sardonic contempt for life and mankind—and so I protested that I was charmed with the project, and out we set.

My companion was not talkative; he was a quiet, almost depressed man, who had led a very monotonous existence, with little society among his comrades ; so that he did not offer me the occasion I sought for, of saying saucy and sneering things of the world at large. Indeed, the first observation he made was, that we were in a locality that ought to be interesting to Irishmen, since an ancient shrine of St. Patrick marked the spot of the convent to which we were approaching. No remark could have been more ill-timed; to look back into the past, one ought to have some vista of the future. Who can sympathise with bygones when he is counting the minutes that are to make him one of them ?

What a bore that old Rittmeister was with his antiquities, and how I hated him as he said, "If your time was not so limited, I'd have taken you over to St. Gallen to inspect the manuscripts." I felt choking as he uttered these words. How was my time so limited ? I did not dare to ask. Was he barbarous enough to mean that if I had another day to live, I might have passed it pleasantly in turning over musty missals in a monastery ?

At last we came to a halt in a little grove of pines, and he said, "Have you any address to give me of friends or relatives, or have you any peculiar directions on any subject."

"You made a remark last night, Herr Rittmeister," said I, "which did not at the moment produce the profound impression upon me that subsequent reflection has enforced. You said that if his royal highness were fully aware that his antagonist was the son of a practising chemist and apothecary —— "

"That I could have put off this event; true enough, but when you refused that alternative, and insisted on satisfaction, I myself, as your countryman, gave the guarantee for your

rank, which nothing now will make me retract. Understand
me well—nothing will make me retract."

"You are pleased to be precipitate," said I, with an
attempt to sneer; "my remark had but one object, and that
was my personal disinclination to obtain a meeting under a
false pretext."

"Make your mind easy on that score. It will be all precisely the same in about an hour hence."

I nearly fainted as I heard this, it seemed as though a cold
stream of water ran through my spine and paralysed the
very marrow inside.

"You have your choice of weapons," said he, curtly;
"which are you best at ?"

I was going to say the "javelin," but I was ashamed, and
yet should a man sacrifice life for a false modesty; while I
reasoned thus, he pointed to a group of officers close to the
garden wall of the convent, and said :

"They are all waiting yonder, let us hasten on."

If I had been mortally wounded, and was dragging my
feeble limbs along to rest them for ever on some particular
spot, I might have, probably, effected my progress as easily
as I now did. The slightest inequality of ground tripped
me, and I stumbled at every step.

"You are cold," said my companion, "and probably
unused to early rising, taste this."

He gave me his brandy-flask, and I finished it off at a
draught. Blessings be on the man who invented alcohol !
all the ethics that ever were written cannot work the same
miracle in a man's nature as a glass of whiskey. Talk of all
the wonders of chemistry, and what are they to the simple
fact that two-pennyworth of cognac can convert a coward
into a hero?

I was not quite sure that my antagonist had not
resorted to a similar sort of aid, for he seemed as light-
hearted and as jolly as though he was out for a pic-nic.
There was a jauntiness, too, in the way he took out his
cigar, and scraped his lucifer match on a beech-tree, that
quite struck me, and I should like to have imitated it if I
could.

"If it's the same to you, take the sabre, it's his weakest
weapon," whispered the Rittmeister in my ear, and I agreed.

And now there was a sort of commotion about the choice of
the ground and the places, in which my friend seemed to
stand by me most manfully. Then there followed a general
measurement of swords, and a fierce comparison of weapons.
I don't know how many were not thrust into my hand, one
saying, " Take this, it is well balanced in the wrist, or if you
like a heavy guard, here's your arm ! "

" To *me*, it is a matter of perfect indifference, said I,
jauntily. " All weapons are alike."

" He will attack fiercely, and the moment the sword is
given," whispered the Rittmeister, " so be on your guard;
keep your hilt full before you, or he'll slice off your nose
before you are aware of it."

" Be not so sure of that till you have seen my sword play,"
said I, fiercely ; and my heart swelled with a fierce sentiment
that must have been courage, for I never remember to have
felt the like before. I know I was brave at that moment,
for if, by one word, I could have averted the combat, I would
not have uttered it.

" To your places," cried the umpire, " and on your guard!
Are you ready ? "

" Ready," re-echoed I, wildly, while I gave a mad flourish
of my weapon round my head that threw the whole company into a roar of laughter ; and, at the same instant, two
figures, screaming fearfully, rushed from the beech copse,
and, bursting their way through the crowd, fell upon me
with the most frantic embraces, amidst the louder laughter
of the others. O shame and ineffable disgrace ! O misery
never to be forgotten! It was Vaterchen who now grasped
my knees, and Tinteflect who clung round my neck and
kissed me repeatedly. From the time of the Laocoon,
no one ever struggled to free himself as I did, but all in
vain—my efforts, impeded by the sword, lest I might
unwillingly wound them, were all fruitless, and we rolled
upon the ground inextricably commingled and struggling.

" Was I right? " cried the prince. " Was I right in
calling this fellow a saltimbanque? See him now with his
comrades around him, and say if I was mistaken."

" How is this ? " whispered the Rittmeister. " Have you
dared to deceive *me ?* "

" I have deceived no one," said I, trying to rise, and I

poured forth a torrent of not very coherent eloquence, as the mirth of my audience seemed to imply; but, fortunately, Vaterchen had now obtained a hearing, and was detailing in very fluent language, the nature of the relations between us. Poor old fellow, in his boundless gratitude I seemed more than human; and his praises actually shamed me to hear them. How I had first met them, he recounted in the strain of one assisted by the gods in classic times; his description made me a sort of Jove coming down on a rosy cloud to succour suffering humanity; and then came in Tintefleck with her broken words, marvellously aided by "action," as she poured forth the heap of gold upon the grass and said it was all mine!

Wonderful metal, to be sure, for enforcing conviction on the mind of man: there is a sincerity about it far more impressive than any vocal persuasion. The very clink of it implies that the real and the positive are in question, not the imaginary and the delusive. "This is all his!" cried she, pointing to the treasure with the air of one showing Aladdin's cave; and though her speech was not very intelligible, Vaterchen's "vulgate" ran underneath and explained the text.

"I hope you will forgive me. I trust you will be satisfied with my appologies, made thus openly," said the prince, in the most courteous of manners. "One who can behave with such magnanimity can scarcely be wanting in another species of generosity." And ere I could well reply, I found myself shaking hands with everyone, and everyone with me; nor was the least pleasurable part of this recognition the satisfaction displayed by the Rittmeister at the good issue of this event. I had great difficulty in resisting their resolution to carry me back with them to Bregenz. Innumerable were the plans and projects devised for my entertainment. Field sports, sham fights, rifle-shooting, all were displayed attractively before me; and it was clear, that if I accepted their invitations, I should be treated like the most favoured guest. But I was firm in my refusal; and, pleading a pretended necessity to be at a particular place by a particular day, I started once more, taking the road with the "vagabonds," who now seemed bound to me by an indissoluble bond; at least, so Vaterchen assured me by the most emphatic of

21

declarations, and that, do with him what I might, he was my slave till death.

"Who is ever completely happy?" says the sage; and with too good reason is the doubt expressed. Here, one might suppose, was a situation abounding with the most pleasurable incidents. To have escaped a duel, and come out with honour and credit from the issue; to have refound not only my missing money, but to have my suspicions relieved as to those whose honest name was dear to me, and whose discredit would have darkened many a bright hope of life,— these were no small successes; and yet—I shame to own it— my delight in them was dashed by an incident so small and insignificant, that I have scarce courage to recal it. Here it is, however: While I was taking a kindly farewell of my military friends, hand-shaking and protesting interminable friendships, I saw, or thought I saw, the prince, with even a more affectionate warmth, making his adieus to Tintefleck! If he had not his arm actually round her waist, there was certainly a white leather cavalry glove curiously attached to her side, and one of her cheeks was deeper coloured than the other, and her bearing and manner seemed confused so that she answered, when spoken to, at cross purposes.

"How did you come by this brooch, Tintefleck? I never saw it before."

"Oh, is it not pretty? It is a violet; and these leaves, though green, are all gold."

"Answer me, girl! who gave it thee?" said I, in the voice of Othello.

"Must I tell?" murmured she, sorrowfully.

"On the spot—confess it!"

"It was one who bade me keep it till he should bring me a prettier one."

"I do not care for what he said, or what you promised, I want his name."

"And that I was never to forget him till then— never."

"Do you say this to irritate and offend me, or do you prevaricate out of shame?" said I, angrily.

"Shame!" repeated she, haughtily.

"Ay, shame or fear."

"Or fear! Fear of what, or of whom?"

"You are very daring to ask me. And now, for the last time, Tintefleck—for the last time, I say, who gave you this?"

As I said these words we had just reached the borders of a little rivulet, over which we were to cross by stepping-stones. Vaterchen was, as usual, some distance behind, and now calling to us to wait for him. She turned at his cry, and answered him, but made no reply to me.

This continued defiance of me overcame my temper altogether, sorely pushed as it was by a stupid jealousy, and seizing her wrist with a strong grasp, I said, in a slow, measured tone, "I insist upon your answer to my question, or ——"

"Or what?"

"That we part here, and for ever."

"With all my heart. Only remember one thing," said she, in a low, whispering voice : "you left me once before—you quitted me, in a moment of temper, just as you threaten it now. Go, if you will, or if you must; but let this be our last meeting and last parting."

"It is as such I mean it—good-bye!" I sprang on the stepping-stone as I spoke, and at the same instant a glittering object splashed into the stream close to me. I saw it, just as one might see the lustre of a trout's back as it rose to a fly. I don't know what demon sat where my heart ought to have been, but I pressed my hat over my eyes, and went on without turning my head.

CHAPTER XXXIX.

VERY conflicting and very mixed were my feelings, as I set forth alone. I had come well, very well, out of a trying emergency. I was neither driven to pretend I was some-

21—2

thing other than myself, with grand surroundings, and
illustrious belongings, nor had I masqueraded under a feigned
name and a false history; but as Potts, son of Potts the
apothecary, I had carried my head high and borne myself
creditably.

"*Magna est veritas*," indeed!   I am not so sure of the
"*prævalebit semper*," but assuredly where it does succeed, the
success is wonderful.

Heaven knows into what tortuous entanglements might
my passion for the "imaginative"—I liked this name for it
—have led me, had I given way to one of my usual temptations.   In more than one of my flights have I found myself
carried up into a region, and have had to sustain an atmosphere very unsuited to my respiration, and now, with the
mere prudence of walking on the *terra firma*, and treading
the common highway of life, I found I had reached my goal
safely and speedily.   Flowers do not assume to be shrubs,
nor shrubs affect to be forest trees ; the limestone and granite
never pretend that they are porphyry and onyx.   Nature is
real, and why should man alone be untruthful and unreal ?
If I liked these reflections, and tried to lose myself in them
it was in the hope of shutting out others less gratifying ; but,
do what I would, there before me arose the image of Catinka,
as she stood at the edge of the rivulet, that stream which
seemed to cut me off from one portion of my life, and make
the past irrevocably gone for ever.

I am certain I was quite right in parting with that girl.
Any respectable man, a father of a family, would have
applauded me for severing this dangerous connection.
What could come of such association except unhappiness?
"Potts," would the biographer say—"Potts saw, with the
unerring instinct of his quick perception, that this young
creature would one day or other have laid at his feet the
burnt-offering of her heart, and then, what could he have
done?   If Potts had been less endowed with genius, or less
armed in honesty, he had not anticipated this peril, or, fore-
seeing, had undervalued it.   But he both saw and feared it.
How very differently had a libertine reasoned out this situation!"   And then I thought how wicked I might have been ;
a monster of crime and atrocity.   Every one knows the
sensation of lying snugly a-bed on a stormy night, and, as

the rain plashes and the wind howls, drawing more closely around him the coverlet, and the selfish satisfaction of his own comfort, heightened by all the possible hardships of others outside. In the same benevolent spirit, but not by any means so reprehensible, is it pleasant to imagine oneself a great criminal, standing in the dock, to be stared at by a horror-struck public, photographed, shaved, prison costumed, exhorted, sentenced, and then, just as the last hammer has driven the last nail into the scaffold, and the great bell has tolled out, to find that you are sitting by your wood fire, with your curtain drawn, your uncut volume beside you, and your peculiar weakness, be it tea, or sherry-cobbler, at your elbow. I constantly take a "rise" out of myself in this fashion, and rarely a week goes over that I have not either poisoned a sister or had a shot at the Queen. It is a sort of intellectual Russian bath, in which the luxury consists in the exaggerated alternative between being scalded first and rolled in the snow afterwards. It was in this figurative snow I was now disporting myself, pleasantly and refreshingly, and yet remorse, like a sturdy dun, stood at my gate, and refused to go away.

Had I, indeed, treated her harshly? had I rejected the offer of her young and innocent heart? Very puzzling and embarrassing question this, and especially to a man who had nothing of the coxcomb in his nature, none of that prompting of self-love that would suggest a vain reply. I felt that it was very natural *she* should have been struck by the attractive features of my character, but I felt this without a particle of conceit. I even experienced a sense of sorrow as I thought over it, just as a conscientious syren might have regretted that nature had endowed her with such a charming voice; and this duty—for it was a duty—discharged, I bethought me of my own future. I had a mission, which was to see Kate Herbert and give her Miss Crofton's letter. In doing so, I must needs throw off all disguises and mockeries, and be Potts, the very creature she sneered at, the man whose mere name was enough to suggest a vulgar life and a snob's nature! No matter what misery it may give, I will do it manfully. *She* may never appreciate—the world at large may never appreciate—what noble motives were hidden beneath these assumed natures, mere costumes as

they were, to impart more vigour and persuasiveness to
sentiments which, uttered in the undress of Potts, would
have carried no convictions with them. Play Macbeth in a
paletot, perform Othello in "pegtops," and see what effect
you will produce! Well, my pretended station and rank
were the mere gaudes and properties that gave force to my
opinions. And now to relinquish these, and be the actor, in
the garish light of the noonday, and a shabby-genteel coat
and hat! "I will do it," muttered I, "I will do it, but the
suffering will be intense!" When the prisoner sentenced to
a long captivity is no more addressed by his name, but
simply called No. 18, or 43, it is said that the shock seems
to kill the sense of identity with him, and that nothing more
tends to that stolid air of indifference, that hopeless inactivity
of feature, so characteristic of a prison life; in the very same
way am I affected when limited to my Potts nature, and condemned to confine myself within the narrow bounds of that
one small identity. From what Prince Max had said at the
table d'hôte at Bregenz, it was clear that Mrs. Keats had
already learned I was not the young prince of the House of
Orleans; but, in being disabused of one error, she seemed to
have fallen into another, and it behoved me to explain that I
was not a rope-dancer or a mountebank. "She, too, shall
know me in my Potts nature," said I; "she also shall
recognise me in the 'majesty of myself.'" I was not very
sure of what that was, but found it in Hegel.

And when I have completed this task, I will throw myself
like a waif upon the waters of life. I will be that which the
moment or the event shall make me—neither trammelled by
the past nor awed by the future. I will take the world as
the drama of a day. Were men to do this, what breadth
and generosity would it impart to them! It is in self-
seeking and advancement that we narrow our faculties and
imprison our natures. A man fancies he owns a palace and
a demesne, but it is the palace that owns *him*, obliges him to
maintain a certain state, live in a certain style, surrounded
with certain observances, not one of which may be perhaps
native to him. It is the poor man, who comes to visit and
gaze on his splendours, who really enjoys them; *he* sees
them without one detracting influence—not to say that in
his heart are no corroding jealousies of some other rich man,

who has a finer Claude, or a grander Rubens. Instead, besides, of owning one palace and one garden, it is the universe he owns : the vast Savannah is his race-ground; Niagara his own private cascade.

My heart bounded with these buoyant fancies, and I stepped out briskly on my road. Now that I had made this vow of poverty to myself, I felt very light-hearted and gay. So long as a man is struggling for place and pre-eminence in life, how can he be generous, how even gracious? "Thou shalt not covet thy neighbour ox," says the commandment, but surely it must have been your neighbour's before it was yours, and if you have striven for it, it is likely that you have coveted it. Now, I will covet nothing—positively nothing—and I will see if in this noble spirit there will not be a reward proportionately ample and splendid.

My road led through that wild and somewhat dreary valley by which the Upper Rhine descends, fed by many an Alpine stream and torrent, to reach the fertile plains of Germany. It was a desolate expanse or shingle, with here and there little patches of oak scrub, or, at rare intervals, small enclosures of tillage, though how tilled, or for whom, it was hard to say, since not a trace of inhabitant could be seen, far or wide. Deep fissures, the course of many a mountain stream, cut the road at places, and through these the foot traveller had to pass on stepping-stones; while wheel carriages, descending into the chaos of rocks and stones, fared even worse, and incurred serious peril to spring and axle in the passage. On the mountain-sides, indeed, some châlets were to be seen, very high up, and scarcely accessible, but ever surrounded with little tracts of greener verdure and more varied foliage. From these heights, too, I could hear the melodious ring of the bells worn by the cattle—sure signs of peasant comfort. "Might not a man find a life of simple cares and few sorrows, up yonder?" asked I, as I gazed upward. While I continued to look, the great floating clouds that soared on the mountain-tops began to mass and to mingle together, thickening and darkening at every moment, and then, as though overweighted, slowly to descend, shutting out châlet and shady copse and crag, as they fell, on their way to the plain beneath. It was a grievous change from the bright picture a few moments back, and not the less disheartening, that the heavily charged mist now melted into rain, that soon fell in torrents. With not a rock nor a shrub to shelter under, I had nothing for it but to trudge onward to the nearest village, wherever that might be. How speedily the slightest touch of the real will chase away the fictitious and imaginary! No more dreams nor fancies now, as wet and soaked I plodded on, my knapsack seeming double its true weight, and my stick appearing to take root each time it struck the ground. The fog, too, was so dense that I was forced to feel my way as I went. The dull roar of the Rhine was the only sound for a long time; but this at length became broken by the crashing noise of timber carried down by the torrents, and the louder din of the torrents themselves as they came tumbling down the mountain. I would have retraced my steps to Bregenz, but that I knew the places I had passed dryshod in the morning would by this time have become impassable rivers. My situation was a dreary one, and not without peril, since there was no saying when or where a mountain cataract might not burst its way down the cliffs and sweep clean across the road towards the Rhine.

Had there been one spot to offer shelter, even the poorest and meanest, I would gladly have taken it, and made up my mind to await better weather; but there was not a bank, nor even a bush, to cower under, and I was forced to trudge on. It seemed to me at last that I must have been walking many hours; but having no watch, and being surrounded with impenetrable fog, I could make no guess of the time, when at length a louder and deeper sound appeared to fill the air, and make the very mist vibrate with its din. The surging sound of a great volume of water, sweeping along through rocks and fallen trees, apprised me that I was nearing a torrent; while the road itself, covered with some inches of water, showed that the stream had already risen above its embankments. There was real danger in this; light carriages—the great lumbering diligence itself—had been known to be carried away by these suddenly swollen streams, and I began seriously to fear disaster. Wading cautiously onward, I reached what I judged to be the edge of the torrent, and felt with my stick that the water was here borne madly onward, and at considerable depth. Though through the fog I could make out the opposite bank, and see that the stream was not a wide one, I plainly perceived that the current was far too powerful for me to breast without assistance, and that no single passenger could attempt it with safety. I may have stood half-an-hour thus, with the muddy stream surging over my ankles, for I was stunned and stupified by the danger, when I thought I saw through the mist two gigantic figures looming through the fog, on the opposite bank. When and how they had come there, I knew not, if they were indeed there, and if these figures were not mere spectres of my imagination. It was not till having closed my eyes, and opening them again, beheld the same objects, that I could fully assure myself of their reality.

CHAPTER XL.

THE two great figures I had seen looming through the fog while standing in the stream, I at last made out to be two horsemen, who seemed in search of some safe and fordable part of the stream to cross over. Their apparent caution was a lesson by which I determined to profit, and I stood a patient observer of their proceedings. At times I could catch their voices, but without distinguishing what they said, and suddenly I heard a plunge, and saw that one had dashed boldly into the flood, and was quickly followed by the other. If the stream did not reach to their knees, as they sat, it was yet so powerful that it tested all the strength of the horses and all the skill of the riders to stem it; and as the water splashed and surged, and as the animals plunged and struggled, I scarcely knew whether they were fated to reach the bank, or be carried down in the current. As they gained about the middle of the stream, I saw that they were mounted gendarmes, heavy men, with heavy equipments,

favourable enough to stem the tide, but hopelessly incapable
to save themselves if over-turned. "Go back—hold in—go
back! the water is far deeper here!" I cried out at the top
of my voice; but either not hearing, or not heeding my
warning, on they came, and, as I spoke, one plunged forward
and went headlong down under the water, but, rising immediately, his horse struck boldly out, and, after a few
struggles, gained the bank.   The other, more fortunate,
had headed up the stream, and reached the shore without
difficulty.

With the natural prompting of a man towards those who
had just overcome a great peril, I hastened to say how glad
I felt at their safety, and from what intense fear their landing had rescued me; when one, a corporal, as his cuff
bespoke, muttered a coarse exclamation of impatience, and
something like a malediction on the service that exposed
men to such hazards, and at the same instant the other
dashed boldly up the bank, and with a bound placed his
horse at my side, as though to cut off my retreat.

"Who are you?" cried the corporal to me, in a stern
voice.

"A traveller," said I, trying to look majestic and
indignant.

"So I see; and of what nation?"

"Of that nation which no man insults with impunity."

"Russia?"

"No; certainly not—England."

"Whence from last?"

"From Bregenz."

"And from Constance by Lindau?" asked he quickly,
as he read from a slip of paper he had just drawn from his
belt.

I assented, but not without certain misgivings, as I saw so
much was known as to my movements.

"Now for your passport. Let me see it," said the corporal
again. "Just so," said he, folding it up. "Travelling on
foot, and marked 'suspected.'"

Though he muttered these words to his companion, I
perceived that he cared very little for my having overheard
them.

"Suspected of what, or by whom?" asked I, angrily.

Instead of paying any attention to my question, the two men now conversed together in a low tone and confidentially.

"Come," said I, with an assumed boldness, "if you have quite done with that passport of mine, give it to me, and let me pursue my journey."

So eager were they in their own converse, that this speech, too, was unheeded; and now, grown rasher by impunity and impatience, I stepped stoutly forward, and attempted to take the passport from the soldier's hand.

"Sturm und Gewitter!" swore out the fellow, while he struck me sharply on the wrist, "do you mean to try force with us?" And the other drew his sabre, and flourishing it over his head, held the point of it within a few inches of my chest.

I cannot imagine whence came the courage that now filled my heart, for I know I am not naturally brave, but I felt for an instant that I could have stormed a breach; and, with an insulting laugh, I said, "Oh, of course, cut me down. I am unarmed and defenceless. It is an admirable opportunity for the display of Austrian chivalry."

"Bey'm Henker! It's very hard not to slice off his ear," said the soldier, seeming to ask leave for this act of valour.

"Get out your cords," said the corporal; "we're losing too much time here."

"Am I a prisoner, then?" asked I, in some trepidation.

"I suspect you are, and likely to be for some time to come," was the gruff answer.

"On what charge—what is alleged against me?" cried I, passionately.

"What has sent many a better-looking fellow to Spielberg," was the haughty rejoinder.

"If I *am* your prisoner," said I, haughtily—"and I warn you at once of your peril in daring to arrest a British subject travelling peacefully—You are not going to tie my hands! You are not going to treat me as a felon?" I screamed out these words in a voice of wildest passion, as the soldier, who had dismounted for the purpose, was now proceeding to tie my wrists together with a stout cord, and in a manner that displayed very little concern for the pain he occasioned me.

As escape was totally out of the question, I threw myself upon the last resource of the injured. I fell back upon eloquence. I really wish I could remember even faintly the outline of my discourse; for though not by any means a fluent German, the indignation that makes men poets converted me into a great master of prose, and I told them a vast number of curious, but not complimentary, traits of the land they belonged to. I gave, too, a rapid historical sketch of their campaigns against the French, showing how they were always beaten, the only novelty being whether they ran away or capitulated. I reminded them that the victory over *me* would resound through Europe, being the only successful achievement of their arms for the last half-century. I expressed a fervent hope that the corporal would be decorated with the "Maria Theresa," and his companion obtain the "valour medal," for what they had done. Pensions, I hinted, were difficult in the present state of their finances, but rank and honour certainly ought to await them. I don't know at what exact period of my peroration it was that I was literally "pulled up," each of the horsemen holding a line fastened to my wrists, and giving me a drag forward that nearly carried me off my feet, and flat on my face. I stumbled, but recovered myself; and now saw that, bound as I was, with a gendarme on each side of me, it required all the activity I could muster, to keep my legs.

Another whispered conversation here took place across me, and I thought I heard the words Bregenz and Feldkirch interchanged, giving me to surmise that they were discussing to which place they should repair. My faint hope of returning to the former town was, however, soon extinguished, as the corporal, turning to me, said, "Our orders are to bring you alive to head-quarters. We'll do our best; but if, in crossing these torrents, you prefer to be drowned, it's no fault of ours."

"Do you mean by that," cried I, "that I am to be dragged through the water in this fashion?"

"I mean that you are to come along as best you may."

"It is all worthy of you, quite worthy!" screamed I, in a voice of wildest rage. "You reserve all your bravery for those who cannot resist you—and you are right, for they are your only successes. The Turks beat you"—here they chucked me close up, and dashed into the stream. "The Prussians beat you!" I was now up to my waist in water. "The Swiss beat you!" Down I went over head and ears. "The French always—thrashed you"—down again—"at Ulm—Auster—litz—Aspern"—nearly suffocated, I yelled out, "Wagram!"—and down I went, never to know any further consciousness till I felt myself lying on the soaked and muddy road, and heard a gruff voice saying, "Come along—we don't intend to pass the night here!"

CHAPTER XLI.

BENUMBED, bedraggled, and bewildered, I entered Feldkirch late at night, my wrists cut with the cords, my clothes torn by frequent falls, my limbs aching with bruises, and my wet rags chafing my skin. No wonder was it that I was at once consigned from the charge of a gaoler to the care of a doctor, and ere the day broke I was in a raging fever.

I would not if I could, preserve any memory of that grievous interval. Happily for me, no clear traces remain on my mind—pangs of suffering are so mingled with little details of the locality, faces, words, ludicrous images of a wandering intellect, long hours of silent brooding, sound of church bells and such other tokens as cross the lives of busy men in the daily walk of life, all came and went within my brain, and still I lay there in fever.

In my first return of consciousness I perceived I was the sole occupant of a long arched gallery, with a number of beds arranged along each side of it. In their uniform simplicity, and the severe air of the few articles of furniture, my old experiences at once recalled the hospital; not that I arrived at this conclusion without much labour and a considerable mental effort. It was a short journey, to be sure, but I was walking with sprained ankles. It was, however, a great joy and a great triumph to me to accomplish even this much. It was the recognition to myself that I was once more on the road to health, and again to feel the sympathies that make a brotherhood of this life of ours; and so happy was I with the prospect, that when I went to sleep at night my last thought was of the pleasure that morning would bring me. And I was not disappointed; the next day, and the next, and several more that followed, were all passed in a calm and tranquil enjoyment. Looking back upon this period, I have often been disposed to imagine that when we lie in the convalescence that follows some severe illness, with no demands upon our bodily strength, no call made upon our muscular energies, the very activity of digestion not evoked, as our nourishment is of the simplest and lightest, our brain must of necessity exercise its functions more freely, untrammelled by passing cares or the worries incident to daily life, and that at such times our intellect has probably a more uncontested action than at any other period of our existence. I do not want to pursue my theory, or endeavour to sustain it, my reader has here enough to induce him to join his experience to my own, or reject the notion altogether.

I lay thus, not impatiently, for above a fortnight. I regained strength very slowly; the least effort or exertion was sure to overcome me. But I wished for none; and as I lay there, gazing for whole days long at a great coat of arms over the end of the gallery, where a hugh double-headed eagle seemed to me screaming in the agony of strangulation, but yet never to be choked outright, I revelled in many a strange rambling as to the fate of the land of which it was the emblem and the shield. Doubtless some remnant of my passionate assault on Austria lingered in my brain, and gave this turn to its operations.

My nurse was one of that sisterhood whose charities call down many a blessing on the Church that organises their benevolences. She was what is called a " graue Schwester; " and of a truth she seemed the incarnation of greyness. It was not her dress alone, but her face and hands, her noiseless gait, her undemonstrative stare, her half-husky whisper, and her monotonous ways, had all a sort of pervading greyness that enveloped her, just as a cloud mist wraps a landscape.

There was besides a kind of fog-like indistinctness in her few and muttered words that made a fitting atmosphere of drowsy uniformity for the sick room.

Her first care, on my recovery, was to supply me with a number of little religious books—lives of saints and martyrs, accounts of miracles, and narratives of holy pilgrimages—and I devoured them with all the zest of a devotee. They seemed to supply the very excitement my mind craved for, and the good soul little suspected how much more she was ministering to a love for the marvellous than to a spirit of piety. In the " Flowers of St. Francis," for instance, I found an adventure seeker after my own heart. To be sure, his search was after sinners in need of a helping hand to rescue them, but as his contests with Satan were described as stand-up encounters, with very hard knocks on each side, they were just as exciting combats to read of, as any I had ever perused in stories of chivalry.

Mistaking my zest for these readings for something far more praiseworthy, " the grey sister " enjoined me very seriously to turn from the evil advisers I had formerly consorted with, and frequent the society of better-minded and wiser men. Out of these counsels, dark and dim at first, but gradually growing clearer, I learned that I was regarded as a member of some terrible secret society, banded together for the direst and blackest of objects; the subversion of thrones, overthrow of dynasties, and assassination of sovereigns being all labours of love to us. She had a full catologue of my colleagues from Saud, who killed Kotzebue, to Orsini, and seemed thoroughly persuaded that I was a very advanced member of the order. It was only after a long time, and with great address on my part, that I obtained these revelations from her, and she owned that nothing but witnessing how the holy studies had influenced me would ever have induced her to make these avowals. As my convalescence progressed, and I was able to sit up for an hour or so in the day, she told me that I might very soon expect a visit from the Staats Procurator, a kind of district attorney-general, to examine me. So little able was I to carry my mind back to the bygone events of my life, that I heard this as a sort of vague hope that the inquiry would strike out some clue by which I could connect myself with the past, for I was sorely

puzzled to learn what and who I had been before I came
there. Was I a prosecutor or was I a prisoner? Never
was a knotty point more patiently investigated, but, alas!
most hopelessly. The intense interest of the inquiry, however, served totally to withdraw me from my previous readings, and "the grey sister" was shocked to see the mark in
my book remain for days long unchanged. She took
courage at length to address me on the subject, and even
went so far as to ask if Satan himself had not taken occasional opportunity of her absence to come and sit beside my
bed? I eagerly caught at the suggestion, and said it was as
she suspected: that he never gave me a moment's peace,
now torturing me with menaces, now asking for explanations, how this could be reconciled with that, and why such
a thing should not have prevented such another?

Instead of expressing any astonishment at my confession,
she appeared to regard it as one of the most ordinary incidents, and referred me to my books, and especially to St.
Francis, to see that these were usual and every-day snares in
use. She went further, and in her zeal actually showed a
sort of contempt for the Evil One in his intellectual capacity
that startled me; showing how St. Jude always got the
better of him, and that he was a mere child when opposed
by the craft of St. Anthony of Pavia.

"It is the truth," said she, "always conquers him.
Whenever, by any chance, he can catch you concealing or
evading, trying to make out reasons that are inconsistent, or
affecting intentions that you had not, then he is your
master."

There was such an air of matter of fact about all she
said, that when—our first conversation on this theme over
—she left the room, a cold sweat broke over me at the
thought that my next visitor would be the "Lebendige
Satan" himself.

It had come to this, that I had furnished my own mind
with such a subject of terror that I could not endure to be
alone, and lay there trembling at every noise, and shrinking at every shadow that crossed the floor. Many and
many times, as the dupe of my own deceivings, did I find
myself talking aloud in self-defence, averring that I
wanted to be good, and honest, and faithful, and that

whenever I lapsed from the right path, it was in moments of erring reason, sure to be followed after by sincere repentance.

It was after an access of this kind, "the grey sister" found me one morning, bathed in cold perspiration, my eyes fixed, my lips livid, and my fingers fast knotted together.

"I see," said she, "he has given you a severe turn of it to-day. What was the temptation?"

For a long while I refused to answer; I was weak as well as irritable, and I desired peace, but she persisted, and pressed hard to know what subject we had been discussing together.

"I'll tell you, then," said I, fiercely, for a sudden thought prompted perhaps by a sense of anger, flashed across me: "he has just told me that you are his sister."

She screamed out wildly, and rushing to the end of the gallery, threw herself at the foot of a little altar.

Satisfied with my vengeance, I lay back and said no more. I may have dropped into a half-slumber afterwards, for I remember nothing till, just as evening began to fall, one of the servants came up and placed a table and two chairs beside my bed, with writing materials and a large book, and shortly after two men dressed in black, and with square black caps on their heads, took their places at the table, and conversed together in low whispers.

Resolving to treat them with a show of complete indifference, I turned away and pretended to go asleep.

"The Herr Staats Procurator Schlässel has come to read the act of accusation," said the shorter man, who seemed a subordinate; "take care that you pay proper respect to the law and the authorities."

"Let him read away," said I, with a wave of my hand, "I will listen."

In a low, sing-song, dreary tone, he began to recite the titles and dignities of the Emperor. I listened for a while, but as he got down to the Banat and Herzegovine, sleep overcame me, and I dozed away, waking up to hear him detailing what seemed his own greatness, how he was "Ober" this, and "Unter" that, till I fairly lost myself in the maze of his description. Judging from the monotonous, business-

like persistence of his manner, that he had a long road before
him, I wrapped myself comfortably in the bed-clothes, closed
my eyes, and soon slept.

There were two candles burning on the table when I next
opened my eyes, and my friend the procurator was reading
away as before. I tried to interest myself for a second or
two; I rubbed my eyes, and endeavoured to be wakeful ; but
I could not, and was fast settling down into my former
state, when certain words struck on my ear and aroused
me :

" ' The well-born Herr von Rigges further denounces the
prisoner Harpar —— ' "

" Read that again," cried I, aloud, "for I cannot clearly
follow what you say."

" ' The well-born Herr von Rigges ' " repeated he,
" ' further denounces the prisoner Harpar as one of a
sect banded together for the darkest purposes of revolution ! ' "

" Forgive my importunity, Herr Procurator," said I, in
my most insinuating tone, " but in compassion for the weakness of faculties sorely tried by fever, will you tell me who is
Rigges ? "

" Who is Rigges?   Is that your question ? " said he,
slowly.

" Yes, Sir ; that was my question."

He turned over several pages of his voluminous report,
and proceeded to search for the passage he wanted.

" Here it is," said he, at last: and he read out : " ' The
so-called Rigges, being a well-born and not-the-less-from-a-
mercantile-object-engaging pursuit highly-placed and much-
honoured subject of her Majesty the Queen of England,
of the age of forty-two years and eight months, unmarried, and professing the Protestant religion.' Is that
sufficient ? "

" Quite so ; and now, will you, with equal urbanity, inform
me who is Harpar ? "

" Who is Harpar ? Who is Harpar ? You surely do not
ask me that ? "

" I do ; such is my question."

" I must confess that you surprise me. You ask me for
information about yourself ! "

"Oh, indeed! So that I am Harpar?"

"You can, of course, deny it. We are in a measure prepared for that. The proofs of your identity will be, however, forthcoming; not to add, that it will be difficult to disprove the offence."

"Ha, the offence! I'm really curious about that. What is the offence with which I am charged?"

"What I have been reading these two hours. What I have recited with all the clearness, brevity, and perspicuity that characterize our imperial and royal legislation, making our code at once the envy and admiration of all Europe."

"I'm sure of that. But what have I done?"

"With what for a dulness-charged and much-beclouded intellect are you afflicted," cried he, "not to have followed the greatly-by-circumstances-corroborated, and in-various-ways-by-proofs-brought-home narrative that I have already read out?"

"I have not heard one word of it!"

"What a deplorable, and all-the-more-therefore-hopeless intelligence is yours! I will begin it once more." And with a heavy sigh he turned over the first pages of his manuscript.

"Nay, Herr Procurator," interposed I, hastily. "I have the less claim to exact this sacrifice on your part, that even when you have rendered it, it will be all fruitless and unprofitable. I am just recovering from a severe illness. I am, as you have very acutely remarked, a man of very narrow and limited faculties in my best of moments, and I am now still lower in the scale of intelligence. Were you to read that lucid document till we were both grey-headed, it would leave me just as uninformed as to imputed crime as I now am."

"I perceive," said he, gravely. Then, turning to his clerk, he bade him write down, "'And the so-called Harpar, having duly heard and with decorously-lent attention listened to the foregoing act, did thereupon enter his plea of mental incapacity and derangement.'"

"Nay, Herr Procurator, I would simply record that, however open to follow some plain narrative, the forms and subtleties of a legal document only bewilder me."

"What for an ingeniously-worded and with-artifice-cunningly-conceived excuse have we here?" exclaimed he, indignantly. "Is it from England, with her seventeen hundred and odd volumes of an incomplete code, that the imperial and royal government is to learn legislation? You are charged with offences that are known to every state of civilization : highway assault and molestation—attack with arms and deadly implements, stimulated by base and long-heretofore and with-bitterness-imagined plans of vengeance on your countryman and former associate, the so-named Rigges. From him, too, proceeds the information as to your political character, and the ever-to-be-deplored, and only-with-blood-expiated, error of republicanism by which you are actuated. This brief, but not-the-less-on-that-account lucid exposition, it is my duty first to read out, and then leave with you. With all your from-a-wrong-impulse-pro-ceeding and a-spirit-of-opposition-suggested objections, I have no wish nor duty to meddle. The benign and ever-paternal rule under which we live, gives even to the most-with-accusation-surrounded, and with-strong-presumption-implicated prisoner, every facility of defence. Having read and matured this indictment, you will, after a week, make choice of an advocate."

"Am I to be confronted with my accuser?"

"I sincerely hope that the indecent spectacle of insulting attack and offensive rejoinder thus suggested, is unknown to the administration of our law."

"How, then, can you be certain that I am the man he accuses of having molested him?"

"You are not here to assail, nor I to defend, the with-ages-consolidated and by-much-tact-accumulated wisdom of our imperial and royal code."

"Might he not say, when he saw me, 'I never set eyes on this man before?'"

He turned again to his clerk, and dictated something of which I could but catch the concluding words—"And thereby imputing perjury to the so-called Rigges."

It was all I could do to repress an outburst of anger at this unjustifiable system of inference, but I did restrain myself, and merely said, "I impute nothing Herr Procurator; I simply suggest a possible case, that everything suffered by Rigges was inflicted by some other than I."

" If you had accomplices, name them," said he, solemnly.

This overcame all my prudent resolves. I was nowise prepared for such a perversity of misconception, and, losing all patience, and all respect for his authority, I burst out into a most intemperate attack on Austria, her code, her system, her ignorant indifference to all European enlightenment, her bigoted adherence to forms either unmeaning or pernicious, winding up all with a pleasant prediction that in a few short years the world would have seen the last of this stolid and unteachable empire.

Instead of deigning a reply, he merely bent down to the table, and I saw by the movement of his lips, and the rapid course of the clerk's pen, that my statement was being reduced to writing.

" When you have completed that," said I, gravely, " I have some further observations to record."

"In a moment—in a moment," patiently responded the procurator ; " we have only got to ' the besotted stupidity of her pretentious officials. ' "

The calm quietude of his manner as he said this threw me into a fit of laughter, which lasted several minutes.

"There, there," said I, " that will do; I will keep the remainder of my remarks for another time and place."

" ' Reserving to himself,' " dictated he, " ' the right of uttering still more bitter and untruthful comments on a future occasion.' " And the clerk wrote the words as he spoke them.

" You will sign this here," said he, presenting me with the pen.

" Nothing of the kind, Herr Procurator. I will not lend myself to any, even the most ordinary, form of your stupid system."

" ' And refuses to sign the foregoing,' " dictated he, in the same unmoved voice. This done, he arose, and proceeded to draw on his gloves. " The act of allegation I now commit to your hands," said he, calmly, "and you will have a week to reflect upon the course you desire to adopt."

" One question before you go : Is the person called Rigges here at this moment, and can I see him ? "

He consulted for a few seconds with his subordinate, and

then replied : "These questions we are of opinion are irrele-
vant to the defence, and need not be answered."

"I only ask you, as a favour, Herr Procurator," said I.

"The law recognises no favours, nor accepts courte-
sies."

"Does it also reject common sense?—is it deaf to all
intelligence?—is it indifferent to every appeal to reason?—
is it dead to —— "

But he would not wait for more, and having saluted me
thrice profoundly, retired from the gallery and left me alone
with my indignation.

The great pile of paper still lay on the table next me, and
in my anger I hurled it from me to the middle of the room,
venting I know not what passionate wrath at the same time
on everything German : "This the land of primitive simplicity and patriarchal virtues, forsooth ! This the country
of elevated tastes and generous instincts ! Why, it is all
Bureau and Barrack !" I went on for a long time in this
strain, and I felt the better for it. The operative surgeons
tell us that no men recover so certainly or so speedily after
great operations as the fellows who scream out and make a
terrible uproar. It is your patient, self-controlling creature
who sinks under the suffering he will not con'ess; and I am
confident that it is a wise practice to blow off the steam of
one's indignation, and say all the most bitter things one can
think of in moments of disappointment, and, so to say, prepare the chambers of your mind for the reception of better
company.

After a while I got up, gathered the papers together, and
prepared to read them. Legal amplifications and circumlo-
cutions are of all lands and peoples ; but for the triumph of
this diffusiveness commend me to the Germans. To such an
extent was this the case, that I reached the eighth page of
the precious paper before I got finally out of the titular
description of the vice-governor in whose district the event
was laid. Armed, however, with heroic resolution, I persevered, and read on through the entire night—I will not say
without occasional refreshers in the shape of short snaps—
but the day was already breaking when I turned over the
last page, and read the concluding little blessing on the
Emperor under whose benign reign all the good was

encouraged, all evil punished, and the Hoch-gelehrter—
Hoch wohl-geborner Herr der Hofrath, Ober Procurators-
fiscal-Secretär, charged with the due execution of the present
decree.

In the language of *précis* writing the event might be stated
thus: "A certain Englishman named Rigges, travelling by
post, arrived at the torrent of Dornbirn a short time before
noon, and while waiting there for the arrival of some
peasants to accompany his carriage through the stream, was
joined by a foot-traveller, by whom he was speedily recognised. Whatever the nature of the relations previously sub-
sisting between them—and it may be presumed they were
not of the most amiable—no sooner had they exchanged
glances than they engaged in deadly conflict. Rigges was
well armed; the stranger had no weapon whatever, but was
a man of surpassing strength, for he tore the door of the
carriage from its hinges, and dragged Rigges out upon the
road before the other could offer any resistance. The
postillion, who had gone to summon the peasants, was
speedily recalled by the report of fire-arms; three shots were
fired in rapid succession, and when he reached the spot it
was to see two men struggling violently in the torrent, the
stranger dragging Rigges with all his might towards the
middle of the stream, and the other screaming wildly for
succour. The conflict was a terrible one, for the foot-
traveller seemed determined on self-destruction, if he
could only involve the other in his own fate. At last
Rigges' strength gave way, and the other threw himself upon him, and they both went down beneath the
water.

"The stranger emerged in an instant, but one of the
peasants on the bank struck him a violent blow with his ash
pole, and he fell back into the stream. Meanwhile, the
others had rescued Rigges, who lay panting, but unconscious,
on the ground. They were yet ministering to his recovery
when they heard a wild shout of derisive triumph, and now
saw that the other, though carried away by the torrent, had
gained a small shingly bank in the middle of the Rhine, and
was waving his hat in mockery of them. They were too
much occupied with the care of the wounded man, however,
to bestow more attention on him. One of Rigges' arms was

badly fractured, and his jaw also broken, while he complained
still more of the pain of some internal injuries : so severe,
indeed, were his sufferings, that he had to be carried on a
litter to Feldkirch.   His first care on arriving was to denounce the assailant, whose name he gave as Harpar,
declaring him to be a most notorious member of a
" Rouge " society, and one whose capture was an object of
European interest.   In fact, Rigges went so far as to pretend that he had himself perilled life in the attempt to secure
him.

   " Detachments of mounted gendarmes were immediately
sent off in pursuit, the order being to arrest any foot-
traveller whose suspicious appearance might challenge
scrutiny."

   It is needless to say how much I appeared to fulfil the
signs they sought for, not to add that the intemperance of
my language, when captured, was in itself sufficient to
establish a grave charge against me.   It is true, there was
in the act of allegation a lengthened description of me, with
which my own appearance but ill corresponded.   I was described as of middle age, of a strong frame and muscular
habit, and with an expression that denoted energy and
fierceness.   How much of that vigour must they imagine
had been washed away by the torrent, to leave me the poor
helpless-looking thing I now appeared!

   I know it is a very weak confession, I feel as I make it
how damaging to my character is the acknowledgment, and
how seriously I compromise myself in my reader's estimation;
but I cannot help owning that I felt very proud to be thought
so wicked, to be classed with those Brutuses of modern history, who were scattering explosive shells like bonbons, and
throwing grenades broadcast like "confetti" in a carnival.
I fancied how that miserable Staats Procurator must have
trembled in his inmost heart as he sat there in close proximity
with such an infuriate desperado as I was.   I hoped that
every look, every gesture, every word of mine, struck terror
into his abject soul.   It must also unquestionably do them
good, these besotted, self-satisfied, narrow-minded Germans,
to learn how an Englishman, a born Briton, regards their
miserable system of government, and that poor and meagre
phantasm they call their " civilisation."   Well, they have

had their opportunity now, and I hope they will make much of it.

As I pondered over the late incident as recorded in the allegation, I remembered the name of Rigges as that of the man Harpar mentioned as having "run" or escaped with their joint finances, and had very little difficulty in filling up the probable circumstances of their rencontre. It was easy to see how Rigges, travelling "extra-post," with all the appearance of wealth and station, could impute to the poor wayfarer any criminality he pleased. Cunningly enough, too, he had hit upon the precise imputation which was sure to enlist Austrian sympathies in the pursuit, and calling him a "Socialist and a Rogue" was almost sealing his fate at once. How glad I felt that the poor fellow had escaped, even though it cost me all the penalty of personating him; yes, I really was generous enough for that sentiment, though I perceive that my reader smiles incredulously as I declare it. "No, no," mutters he, "the arrant snob must not try to impose upon us in that fashion. He was trembling to the very marrow of his bones, and nothing was further from his thoughts than self-sacrifice or devotion." I know your opinion of me takes this lively shape, I feel it, and I shrink under it; but I know, besides, that I owe all this depreciating estimate of me to nothing so much as my own frankness and candour. If my reader, therefore, scruples to accord me the merit of the generosity that I lay claim to, let him revel in the depreciating confession that I am about to make. I knew that when it was discovered I was not Harpar, I must instantly be set at liberty. I felt this, and could therefore be at any moment the arbiter of my own freedom. To do this, of course, would set in motion a search after the real delinquent, and I determined I would keep my secret till he had ample time to get away. When I had satisfied myself that all pursuit of him must be hopeless, I would declare myself to be Potts, and proudly demand my liberation.

My convalescence made now such progress that I was able to walk about the gallery, and indeed occasionally to stroll out upon a long terrace which flanked the entire building, and gaze upon a garden, beyond which again I could see the town of Feldkirch and the open Platz in which

the weekly market was held. By the recurrence of these
—they always fell upon a Saturday—was I enabled to mark
time, and I now reckoned that three weeks had gone over
since the day of the Herr Procurator's visit, and yet I had
heard nothing more of him, nor of the accusation against
me. I was seriously thinking whether my wisest plan
might not be to take French leave and walk off, when my
gaoler came one morning to announce that I was to be trans-
ferred to Innspruck, where, in due course, my trial would
take place.

"What if I refuse to go?" said I; "what if I demand
my liberation here on the spot?"

"I don't imagine that you'd delay your journey much by
that, my good friend," said he; "the Imperial and Royal
Government takes little heed of foolish remonstrances."

"What if the Imperial and Royal Government, in the
plenitude of its sagacity, should be in the wrong? What
if I be not the person who is accused of this crime? What
if the real man be now at liberty? What if the accuser
himself will declare, when he sees me, that he never met me
before, nor so much as heard of me?"

"Well, all that may happen; I won't say it is impossible, but it cannot occur here, for the Herr von Rigges has
already set off for Innspruck, and you are to follow him
to-morrow."

CHAPTER XLII

If there be anything in our English habits upon which no
difference of opinion can exist, it is our proneness to extend
to a foreigner a degree of sympathy and an amount of
interest that we obstinately deny to our own people. The
English artist struggling all but hopelessly against the
town's indifference has but to displace the consonants or

multiply the vowels of his name to be a fashion and a success. Strange and incomprehensible tendency in a nation so overwhelmingly impressed with a sense of its own vast superiority! But so it is. Mr. Brady may sing to empty benches, while il Signor Bradini would "bring down the house." What set me thinking over this was, that, though Silvio Pellico was a stock theme for English pity and compassion, I very much doubted if a single tear would fall for the misfortunes of a Potts. And yet there was a marvellous similarity in our sufferings. In each case was the Austrian the gaoler; in each case was the victim a creature of tender mould and gentle nature.

I travelled in a sort of covered cart, with a mounted gendarme at either side of me. Indeed the one faintly alleviating circumstance of my captivity was the sight of those two heavily equipped giants, armed to the teeth, who were supposed to be essential to my safe conduct. It was such an acknowledgment of what they had to apprehend from my well-known prowess and daring, so palpable a confession that every precaution was necessary against the bold intrepidity of a man of my stamp! At times, I almost wished they had put chains upon me. I thought how well it would read in my Memoirs; how I was heavily "manacled"—a great word that—"orders being given to the escort to shoot me if I showed the slightest intention to escape." It was an intense pleasure to me to imagine myself a sort of Nana Sahib, and whenever we halted at some way-side public, and the idle loungers would draw aside the canvass covering and stare in at me, I did my utmost to call up an expression of ogre-like ferocity and wildness, and it was with a thrill of ecstasy I saw a little child clasp its mother by the neck, and scream out to come away as it beheld me.

On the second night of our journey we halted at a little village at the foot of the Arlberg, called Steuben, where, in default of a regular prison, they lodged me in an old tower, the lower part of which was used for a stable. It stood in the very centre of the town, and from its narrow and barred windows I could catch glimpses of the little world that moved about in happy freedom beneath me. I could see the Marktplatz, from which the booths were now being taken down, and could mark that preparations for some approaching ceremony were going on, but of what nature I could not guess. A large place was neatly swept out, and at last strewn with sawdust—signs unerring of some exibition of legerdemain or conjuring, of which the Tyrolese are warm admirers. The arrangements were somewhat more portentous than are usually observed in open air representations, for I saw seats prepared for the dignitaries of the village, and an evident design to mark the entertainment as under the most distinguished protection. The crowd—now considerable—observed all the decorous bearing of citizens in presence of their authorities.

I nestled myself snugly in the deep recess of the window to watch the proceedings, nor had I long to wait; some half-dozen gaily-dressed individuals having now pierced their way through the throng, and commenced those peculiar gambols which bespeak backbones of gristle and legs of pasteboard. It is a class of performance I enjoy vastly. The two fellows who lap over each other like the links of a chain, and the creature who rolls himself about like a ball, and the licensed freedoms of that man of the world—the clown—never weary me, and I believe I laugh at them with all the more zest that I have so often laughed at them before. It was plain, after a while, that a more brilliant part of the spectacle was yet to come, for a large bluff-looking man, in cocked-hat and jack-boots, now entered the ring and indignantly ejected the clowns by sundry admonitions with a lash-whip, which I perceived were not merely make-believes.

"Ah, here he comes! here he is!" was now uttered in accents of eager interest, and an avenue was quickly made through the crowd for the new performer. There was delay after this, and though doubtless the crowd below could satisfy their curiosity, I was so highly perched and so straightened in my embrasure that I had to wait, with what patience I might, the new arrival. I was deep in my guesses what sort of "artist" he might prove, when I saw the head of a horse peering over the shoulders of the audience, and then the entire figure of the quadruped as he emerged into the circle, all sheeted and shrouded from gaze. With one dexterous sweep the groom removed all the clothing, and there stood before me my own lost treasure—Blondel himself! I would have known him among ten thousand. He was thinner, perhaps, certainly thinner, but in all other respects the same; his silky mane and his long tassel of a tail hung just as gracefully as of yore, and, as he ambled round, he moved his head with a courteous inclination, as though to acknowledge the plaudits he met with.

There was in his air the dignity that said, "I am one who has seen better days. It was not always thus with me. Applaud if you must, and if you will; but remember that I accept your plaudits with reserve, perhaps even with reluctance." Poor fellow, my heart bled for him! I felt as though I saw a cathedral canon cutting somersaults, and all this while, by some strange inconsistency, I had not a sympathy to bestow on the human actors in the scene. "As for them," thought I, "they have accepted this degradation of their own free will. If they had not shirked honest labour they need never have been clowns or pantaloons; but Blondel —Blondel, whom fate had stamped as the palfrey of some high-born maiden, or, at least, the favourite steed of one who would know how to lavish care on an object of such perfection—Blondel, who had borne himself so proudly in high places, and who, even in his declining fortunes, had been the friend and fellow traveller of —— Yes, why should I shame to say it? Posterity will speak of Potts without the detracting malice and envious rancour of contemporaries; and when, in some future age, a great philanthropist or statesman should claim the credit of some marvellous discovery, some wondrous secret by which humanity may be bettered, a learned critic will tell the world how this great invention was evidently known to Potts, how at such a line, or such a page, we shall find that Potts knew it all."

The wild cheering of the crowd beneath cut short these speculations, and now I saw Blondel cantering gaily round the circle, with a handkerchief in his mouth. If in sportive levity it chanced to fall, he would instantly wheel about and seize it, and then, whisking his tail and shaking his long forelock, resume his course again. It was fine, too, to mark the haughty indifference he manifested towards that whip-cracking monster who stood in the centre, and affected to direct his motions. Not alone did he reject his suggestions, but in a spirit of round defiance did he canter up behind him, and alight with his fore-legs on the fellow's shoulders. I am not sure whether the spectators regarded the tableau as I did, but to *me* it seemed an allegorical representation of man and his master.

The hard breathing of a person close behind me now made me turn my head, and I saw the gaoler, who had come with my supper. A thought flashed suddenly across me. "Go down to those mountebanks, and ask if they will sell that cream-coloured pony," said I. "Bargain as though you wanted him for yourself—he is old and of little value, and you may perhaps secure him for eighty or ninety florins, and if so, you shall have ten more for your pains. It is a caprice of mine, nothing more, but help me to gratify it."

He heard me with evident astonishment, and then gravely asked if I had forgotten the circumstance that I was a prisoner, and likely to remain so for some time.

"Do as I bade you," said I, "and leave the result to me. There, lose no more time about it, for I see the performance is drawing to a close."

"Nay, nay," said he; "the best of all is yet to come. The pretty Moorish girl has not yet appeared. Ha! here she is."

As he spoke he crept up into the window beside me, not less eager for the spectacle than myself. A vigorous cheer, and a loud clapping of hands below, announced that the favourite was in sight long before she was visible to our eyes.

What can she do?" asked I, peevishly, perhaps, for I was provoked how completely she had eclipsed poor Blondel in public favour. "What can she do? Is she a rope-dancer, or does she ride in the games of the ring?"

"There, there! Look at her—yonder she goes! and there's the young prince—they call him a prince, at least—who follows her everywhere."

I could not but smile at the poor gaoler's simplicity, and would willingly have explained to him that we have outlived the age of Cinderellas. Indeed, I had half turned towards him with this object, when a perfect roar of the crowd beneath me drew off my attention from him to what was going on below. I soon saw what it was that entranced the public: it was the young girl, who now, standing on Blondel's back, was careering round the circle at full speed. It is an exercise in which neither the horse nor the rider are seen to advantage; the heavy monotonous tramp of the beast, cramped by the narrow limits, becomes a stilty, wooden gallop. The rider, too, more careful of her balance than intent upon graceful action, restricts herself to a few, and by no means picturesque, attitudes. With all this, the girl now before me seemed herself so intensely to enter into the enjoyment of the scene, that all her gestures sprang out of a sort of irrepressible delight. Far from unsteadying her foot, or limiting her action, the speed of the horse appeared to assist the changeful bendings of her graceful figure, as now, dropping on one knee, she would lean over to caress him, or now, standing erect, with folded arms and leg advanced, appear to dare him to displace her. Faultlessly graceful as she was, there was that in her own evident enjoyment that imparted a strange delight to the beholder, and gave to the spectacle the sort of magnetism by which pleasure finds its way from heart to heart throughout a multitude. At least, I suppose this must have been so, for in the joyous cheering of that crowd there was a ring of wild delight far different from mere applause.

At last, poor Blondel, blown and wearied, turned abruptly into the middle of the ring, and with panting sides and shaking tail came to a dead halt. The girl, with a graceful slide seated herself on his back and patted him playfully. And to me this was by far the most graceful movement of the whole.

It was really a picture! and so natural and so easy withal, that one forgot all about her spangles and tinsel, the golden fillet of her hair, and the tawdry fringe of her sandals; and, what was even harder still, heard not the hoarse-mouthed enthusiasm that greeted her. At length, a tall man, well-dressed and of striking appearance, pushed his way into the ring, and politely presented her with a bouquet, at which piece of courtesy the audience, noways jealous, again redoubled their applause. She now looked round her with an air of triumphant pleasure, and while, with a playful gesture, she flung back the ringlets on her neck, she lifted

her face full to my view and it was Tintefleck ! With all my
might I cried out, "Catinka ! Catinka !" I know not why,
but the impulse never waited to argue the question. Though
I screamed my loudest, the great height at which I was
placed, and the humming din of the crowd, totally drowned
my words. Again and again I tried it, but to no purpose.
There she sat, slowly making the round of the circus, while
the stranger walked at her side, to all seeming conversing as
though no busy and prying multitude stood watching and
observing them. Wearied with my failure to attract notice,
I turned to address the gaoler, but he had already gone, and
I was alone. I next endeavoured by a signal to call attention to me, and, at last, saw how two or three of the crowd
had observed my waving a handkerchief, aud were pointing
it out to others. Doubtless they wondered how a poor
captive could care for the pleasant follies of a life of whose
commonest joys he was to be no sharer, and still greater was
their astonishment as I flung forth a piece of money—a
gold Napoleon it was—which they speedily caught up and
gave to Catinka. How I watched her as she took it and
showed it to the stranger. He, by his gesture, seemed
angry, and made a motion as though asking her to throw it.
away ; and then there seemed some discussion between them,
and his petulance increased ; and she, too, grew passionate,
and, leaping from the horse, strode haughtily across the
circus and disappeared. And then arose a tumult and confusion, the mob shouting madly for the Moorish girl to come
back, and many much disposed to avenge her absence on the
stranger. As for him, he pushed the mob haughtily aside
and went his way, and though for a while the crowd continued to vent its expressions of displeasure and disappointment, the performance soon concluded, and all went their
several roads homeward ; and when I looked out upon the
empty Platz, over which the dusky shadows of the old
houses were now stealing to mingle together, and instead of
the scene of bustle and excitement saw a few lingering
townsfolk moody and purposeless, I asked myself if the
whole incidents were not a vision mind-drawn and invented.
There was not one single clue by which I could trace it to
reality.

More than once in my life had my dreamy temperament

played me such pranks, and, strangely too, even when I had assured myself of the deception, there would yet linger in my mind thoughts and impressions strong enough to influence my actions, just as we often see that our disbelief in a scandalous story is not sufficient to disabuse us of a certain power it wields over us.

Oh, what a long and dreary night was that, harassed with doubts, and worn out with speculations. My mind had been much weakened by my fever, and whenever I followed a train of thought too long, confusion was sure to ensue. The terror of this chaotic condition, where all people, and lands, and ideas, and incidents, jostle against each other in mad turmoil, can only be estimated by one who has felt it. Like the awful rush of sensations of him who is sliding down some steep descent to a tremendous precipice, one feels the gradual approach of that dreamy condition where reason is lost, and the mind a mere waif upon the waters.

" Here's your breakfast," said the gaoler, as he stopped the course of my reverie. " And the brigadier-hopes you'll be speedy with it, for you must reach Maltz by nightfall."

" Tell me," said I, eagerly, " was there a circus company here yesterday evening? Did they exhibit on the Platz there ? "

" You are a deep one, you are!" muttered he, sulkily to himself, and left the cell.

CHAPTER XLIII.

I BORE up admirably on my journey. I felt I was doing a very heroic thing. By my personation of Harpar, I was securing that poor fellow's escape, and giving him ample time to get over the Austrian frontier, and many a mile away from the beaks of the Double Eagle. I had read of such

23

things in history, and I resolved I would not derogate from
the proudest records of such self-devotion. Had I but
remembered how long my illness had lasted, I might have
easily seen that Harpar could by this time have arrived at
Calcutta ; but, unfortunately for me, I had no gange of time
whatever, and completely forgot the long interval of my
fever.

On reaching Innspruck, I was sent on to an old
château some ten miles away, called the Ambras Schloss,
and being consigned to the charge of a retired artillery
officer there, they seemed to have totally forgotten all
about me. I lived with my old gaoler just as if I were
his friend : we worked together in the garden, pruned and
raked, and hoed, and weeded ; we smoked and fished, and
mended our nets on wet days, and read, living exactly
as might any two people in a remote out-of-the-world
spot.

There is a sort of armoury at the Ambras, chiefly of old
Tyrolese weapons of an early period—maces and halberds,
and double-handed swords, and such like—and one of our
pastimes was arranging, and settling, and cataloguing them,
for which, in the ancient records of the Schloss, there was
ample material. This was an occupation that amused me
vastly, and I took to it with great zeal, and with such
success that old Hirsch, the gaoler, at last consigned the
whole to my charge, along with the task of exhibiting
the collection to strangers—a source from which the
honest veteran derived the better part of his means of
life.

At first, I scarcely liked my function as showman, but
like all my other experiences in life, habit sufficed to reconcile
me, and I took to the occupation as though I had been born
to it. If now and then some rude or vulgar traveller would
ruffle my temper by some illiterate remark or stupid question, I was well repaid by intercourse with a different stamp.
They were to me such peeps at the world as a monk might
have from the windows of his cloister, tempting, perhaps,
but always blended with the sense of the security that
encompassed him, and defended him from the cares of
existence.

Perhaps the consciousness that I could assert my innocence

and procure my freedom at any moment, for the first few months reconciled me to this strange life; but certainly after a while I ceased to care for any other existence, and never troubled my head either about past or future. I had, in fact, arrived at the great monastic elevation, in which a man, ceasing to be human, reaches the dignity of a vegetable.

I had begun, as I have said, by an act of heroism, in accepting all the penalties of another, and, long after I ceased to revert to this sacrifice, the impulse it had once given still continued to move me. If Hirsch never alluded to my imputed crime to me, I was equally reserved towards him.

CHAPTER XLIV.

FROM time to time, a couple of grave, judicial-looking men would arrive and pass the forenoon at the Ambras Schloss, in reading out certain documents to me. I never paid much attention to them, but my ear at moments would catch the strangest possible allegations as to my exalted political opinions, the dangerous associates I was bound up with, and the secret societies I belonged to. I heard once, too, and by mere accident, how, at Steuben, I had asked the gaoler to procure me a horse, and thrown gold in handfuls from the windows of my prison to bribe the townsfolk to my rescue, and I laughed to myself to think what a deal of pleading and proof it would take to rebut all these allegations, and how little likely it was I would ever engage in such a conflict.

By long dwelling on the thought of my noble devotion, and how it would read when I was dead and gone, I had

23—ɪ

extinguished within my heart all desire for other distinction,
speculating only on what strange and ingenious theories men
would spin for the secret clue to my motives. "True," they
would say, "Potts never cared for Harpar. He was not a
man to whom Potts would have attached himself under any
circumstances; they were, as individuals, totally unlike and
unsympathetic. How, then, explain this extraordinary act
of self-sacrifice? Was he prompted by the hope that the
iniquities of the Austrian police system would receive their
death-blow from his story, and that the mound that covered
him in the churchyard would be the altar of Liberty to
thousands? or was Potts one of those enthusiastic creatures
only too eager to carry the load of some other pilgrim in
life?"

While I used thus to reason and speculate, I little knew
that I had become a sort of European notoriety. Some
English woman, however, some vagrant tourist, had put me
in her book as the half-witted creature who showed the coins
and curiosities at Ambras, and mentioned how for I know
not how many years I was never heard to utter a syllable
except on questions of old armour and antiquities. In consequence I was always asked for by my travelling countrymen, and my peculiarities treated with all that playful good
taste for which tourists are famous. I remember one day
having refused to perform the showman to a British family.
I had a headache, or was sulky, or a fit of rebellion had got
hold of me, but I sauntered out into the grounds and would
not see them. In my walk through a close alley of laurels,
I chanced to overhear the stranger conversing with Hirsch,
and making myself the subject of his inquiries; and as I
listened, I heard Hirsch say that one entire room of the
château was devoted to the papers and documents in my
case, and that probably it would occupy a quick reader about
twelve months to peruse them. He added, that as I made
no application for a trial myself, nor any of my friends
showed an inclination to bestir themselves about me, the
government would very probably leave me to live and die
where I was. Thereupon, the Briton broke out into a worthy
fit of indignant eloquence. He denounced the Hapsburgs
and praised the Habeas Corpus; he raved of the power of
England, our press, our public opinion, our new frigates.

He said he would make Europe ring with the case. It was as bad, it was worse than Caspar Hauser's, for he was an idiot outright, and *I* appeared to have the enjoyment of certain faculties. He said it should appear in the *Times* and be mentioned in the House; and as I listened, the strangest glow ran through me, a mild and pleasurable enthusiasm, to think that all the right, majesty, and power of Great Britain was about to interest itself in behalf of Potts!

The Briton kept his word; the time, too, favoured him. It was a moment when wandering Englishmen were ex-huming grievances throughout every land of Europe; and while one had discovered some case of religious intolerance in Norway, another beat him out of the field with the cold-blooded atrocities of Naples. My Englishman chanced to be an M.P., and therefore he asked, "in his place," if the Foreign Secretary had any information to afford the House with respect to the case of the man called Harper, or Harpar, he was not certain which, and who had been confined for upwards of ten months in a dungeon in Austria, on allegations of which the accused knew nothing whatever, and attested by witnesses with whom he had never been confronted.

In the absence of his chief, the under-secretary rose to assure the right honourable gentleman that the case was one which had for a considerable time engaged the attention of the department he belonged to, and that the most unremit-ting exertions of her Majesty's envoy at Vienna were now being devoted to obtain the fullest information as to the charges imputed to Harpar, and he hoped in a few days to be able to lay the result of his inquiry on the table of the House.

It was in about a week after this that Hirsch came to tell me that a member of her Majesty's legation at Vienna had arrived to investigate my case, and interrogate me in person. I am half-ashamed to say how vaingloriously I thought of the importance thus lent me. I felt somehow as though the nation missed me. Waiting patiently, as it might be, for my return, and yet no tidings coming, they said, "What has become of Potts?" It was clearly a case upon which they would not admit of any mystification or deceit. "No secret tribunals, no hole-and-corner commitments with us! Where is he? Produce him. Say, with what is he charged?" I

was going to be the man of the day. I knew it, I felt it; I
saw a great tableau of my life unrolling itself before me.
Potts, the young enthusiast after virtue—hopeful, affectionate,
confiding, giving his young heart to that fair-haired girl as
freely as he would have bestowed a moss-rose; and she,
making light of the gift, and with a woman's coquetry, torturing him by a jealous levity till he resented the wrong,
and tore himself away. And then Catinka—how I tried the
gold of my nature in that crucible, and would not fall in love
with her before I had made her worthy of my love; and
when I had failed in that, how I had turned from love to
friendship, and offered myself the victim for a man I never
cared about. No matter; the world will know me at last.
Men will recognise the grand stuff that I am made of. If
commentators spend years in exploring the recondite passages
of great writers, and making out beauties where there were
only obscurities, why should not all the dark parts of my
nature come out as favourably, and some flattering interpreter
say, " Potts was for a long time misconceived; few men
were more wrongfully judged by their contemporaries. It
was to a mere accident, after all, we owe it that we are now
enabled to render him the justice so long denied him. His
was one of those remarkable natures in which it is difficult
to say whether humility or self-confidence predominated? "
    Then I thought of the national excitement to discover the
missing Potts ; just as if I had been a lost Arctic voyager.
Expeditions sent out to track me—all the thousand speculations as to whether I had gone this way or that—where
and from whom the latest tidings of me could be traced—the
heroic offers of new discoverers to seek me living, or, sad
alternative, restore to the country that mourned me the
reliqui Pottsi. I always grew tender in my moods of self-
compassion, and I felt my eyes swimming now in pity for
my fate; and let me add in this place my protest against the
vulgar error which stigmatises as selfishness the mere fact
of a man's susceptibility. How, I would simply ask, can he
feel for others who has no sense of sympathy with his own
suffering nature ? If the well of human kindness be dried
up within him, how can he give to the parched throats the
refreshing waters of compassion ?
    Deal with the fact how you may, I was very sorry for

myself, and seriously doubted if as sincere a mourner would bewail me when I was gone.

If a little time had been given me, I would have endeavoured to get up my snug little chamber somewhat more like a prison cell : I would have substituted some straw for my comfortable bed, and gracefully draped a few chains upon the walls and some stray torture implements out of the Armoury ; but the envoy came like a " thief in the night," and was already on the stairs when he was announced.

" Oh ! this is his den, is it ? " cried he from without, as he slowly ascended the stairs. " Egad ! he hasn't much to complain of in the matter of a lodging. I only wish our fellows were as well off at Vienna." And with these words there entered into my room a tall young fellow, with a light brown moustache, dressed in a loose travelling suit, and with the lounging air of a man sauntering into a *café*. He did not remove his hat as he came in, or take the cigar from his mouth ; the latter circumstance imparting a certain confusion to his speech that made him occasionally scarce intelligible. Only deigning to bestow a passing look on me, he moved towards the window, and looked out on the grand panorama of the Tyrol Alps, as they enclose the valley of Innspruck.

" Well," said he to himself, " all this ain't so bad for a dungeon."

The tone startled me. I looked again at him, I rallied myself to an effort of memory, and at once recalled the young fellow I had met on the South-Western line and from whom I had accidently carried away the dispatch-bag. To my beard, and my long imprisonment, I trusted for not being recognised, and I sat patiently awaiting my examination.

" An Englishman, I suppose ? " asked he, turning hastily round. " And of English parents ? "

" Yes," was my reply, for I determined on brevity whereever possible.

" What brought you into this scrape ?—I mean, why did you come here at all ? "

" I was travelling."

" Travelling ? Stuff and nonsense ! Why should fellows like you travel ? What's your rank in life ? "

" A gentleman."

" Ah! but whose gentleman, my worthy friend? Ain't you a flunkey? There, it's out! I say, have you got a match to light my cigar? Thanks—all right. Look here, now—don't let us be beating about the bush all the day—I believe this goverument is just as sick of you as you are of them. You've been here two months, ain't it so?"

" Ten months and upwards."

" Well, ten mouths. And you want to get away?"

I made no answer; indeed, his free-and-easy manner so disconcerted me that I could not speak, and he went on :

" I suspect they haven't got much against you, or that they don't care about it; and, besides, they are civil to us just now. At all events, it can be done—you understand? —it can be done."

" Indeed," said I, half superciliously.

" Yes," resumed he, " I think so; not but you'd have managed better in leaving the thing to *us.* That stupid notion you all have of writing letters to newspapers and getting some troublesome fellow to ask questions in the House, that's what spoils everything! How can *we* nego- tiate when the whole story is in the *Times* or the *Daily News ?*"

" I opine, Sir, that you arc ascribing to me an activity ard energy I have no claim to."

" Well, if you didn't write those lctters, somebody else did. I don't care a rush for the difference. You see, here's how the matter stands. This Mr. Brigges, or Rigges, has gone off, and doesn't care to prosecute, and all his allegations against you fall to the ground. Well, these peoplc fancy they could carry on the thing themselves, you understand; we think not. They say they have got a strong case; perhaps they have; but we ask, 'What's the use of it? Sending the poor beggar to Spielberg won't save you, will it?' Aud so we put it to them this way : 'Draw stakes, let him off, and both can cry quits.' There, give me another light. Isn't that the common-sense view of it?"

" I scarcely dare to say that I understand you aright."

" Oh, I can guess why. I havo had dealings with fellows of your sort before. You don't fancy my not alluding to compensation, eh ? You want to hear about the money part of the matter ? "

And he laughed aloud, but whether at *my* mercenary spirit or *his own* shrewdness in detecting it, I do not really know.

"Well, I'm afraid," continued he, "you'll be disappointed there. These Austrians are hard up; besides, they never do pay. It's against their system, and so we never ask them."

"Would it be too much, Sir, to ask why I have been imprisoned?"

"Perhaps not; but a great deal too much for me to tell you. The confounded papers would fill a cart, and that's the reason I say, cut your stick, my man, and get away." Again he turned to the window, and, looking out, asked, "Any shooting about here ? There ought to be cocks in that wood yonder ?" and without caring for reply, went on : "After all, you know what Bosh it is to talk about chains and dungeons, and bread-and-water, and the rest of it. You've been living in clover here. That old fellow below tells me that you dine with him every day; that you might have gone into Innspruck, to the theatre if you liked it.—I'll swear there are snipes in that low land next the river.— Think it over, Rigges, think it over."

"I am not Rigges."

"Oh, I forgot! you're the other fellow. Well, think it over, Harpar."

"My name is not Harpar, Sir."

"What do I care for a stray vowel or two? Maybe you call yourself Harpar or Harpér? It's all the same to *us*."

"It is not the question of a vowel or two, Sir; and I desire you to remark it is the graver one of a mistaken identity!" I said this with a high-sounding importance that I thought must astound him, but his light and frivolous nature was impervious to rebuke.

"*We* have nothing to say to that," replied he, carelessly. "You may be Noakes or Styles. I believe they are the names of any fellows who are supposed by courtesy to have no name at all, and it's all alike to *us*. What I have to observe to you is this : nobody cares very much whether you are detained here or not ; nobody wants to detain you. Just reflect, therefore, if it's not the best thing you can do to slope off, and make no more fuss about it?"

"Once for all, Sir," said I, still more impressively, "I am not the person against whom this charge is made. The authorities have all along mistaken me for another."

"Well, what if they have? Docs it signify one kreutzer? We have had trouble enough about the matter already, and do not embroil us any further."

"May I ask, Sir, just for information, who are the ' we' you have so frequently alluded to?"

Had I asked him in what division of the globe he under-stood us then to be conversing, he would not have regarded me with a look of more blank astonishment.

"Who are we?" repeated he. "Did you ask who are we?"

"Yes, Sir, that was what I made bold to ask."

"Cool, certainly; what might be called uncomman cool. To what line of life were you brought up to, my worthy gent? I have rather a curiosity about your antecedents."

"That same curiosity cost you a trifle once before," said I, no longer able to control myself, and dying to repay his impertinence. "I remember, once upon a time, meeting you on a railroad, and you were so eager to exhibit the skill with which you could read a man's calling, that you bet me a sovereign you would guess mine. You did so, and lost."

"You can't be—no, it's impossible. Are you really the goggle-eyed fellow that walked off with the bag for Kalbbratonstadt?"

"I did, by mistake, carry away a bag on that occasion, and so punctiliously did I repay my error, that I travelled the whole journey to convey those dispatches to their destination."

"I know all about it," said he, in a frank, gay manner. "Doubleton told me the whole story. You dined with him and pretended you were I don't remember whom, and then you took old Mamma Keats off to Como and made her believe you were Louis Philippe, and you made fierce love to your pretty companion, who was fool enough to like you. By Jove! what a rig you must have run. We have all laughed over it a score of times."

"If I knew who ' we' were, I am certain I should feel

flattered by any amusement I afforded them, notwithstanding
how much more they are indebted to fiction than fact regarding me. I never assumed to be Louis Philippe, nor affected
to be any person of distinction. A flighty old lady was
foolish enough to imagine me a prince of the Orleans
family——"

"You—a prince! Oh, this is too absurd!"

"I confess, Sir, I cannot see the matter in this light.
I presume the mistake to be one by no means difficult to
have occurred. Mrs. Keats has seen a deal of life and the
world——"

"Not so much as you fancy," broke he in. "She was a
long time in that private asylum up at Brompton, and then
down in Staffordshire; altogether she must have passed
five-and-twenty or thirty years in a rather restricted
circle."

"Mad! Was she mad?"

"Not what one would call mad, but queer. They were all
queer. Hargrave, the second brother, was the fellow that
made that shindy in the Mauritius, and our friend Shalley
isn't a conjuror. And we thought you were larking the old
lady, I assure you we did."

"'We' were once more mistaken, then," said I,
sneeringly.

"We all said, too, at the time, that Doubleton had been
'let in.' He gave you a good round sum for expenses on
the road, didn't he, and you sent it all back to him?"

"Every shilling of it."

"So he told us, and that was what puzzled us more than
all the rest. Why did you give up the money?"

"Simply, Sir, because it was not mine."

"Yes, yes, to be sure, I know that; but I mean, what
suggested the restitution?"

"Really, Sir, your question leads me to suppose that the
'we' so often referred to are not eminently remarkable for
integrity."

"Like their neighbours, I take it—neither better nor
worse. But won't you tell why you gave up the tin?"

"I should be hopeless of any attempt to explain my
motives, Sir; so pray excuse me."

"You were right, at all events," said he, not heeding the

sarcasm of my manner. "There's no chance for the knaves now, with the telegraph system. As it was, there were orders flying through Europe to arrest Pottinger—I can't forget the name. We used to have it every day in the Chancellerie: Pottinger, five feet nine, weak-looking and vulgar, low forehead, light hair and eyes, slight lisp, talks German fluently, but ill. I have copied that portrait of you twenty, ay, thirty times."

"And yet, Sir, neither the name nor the description apply. I am no more Pottinger than I am ignoble-looking and vulgar."

"What's the name, then?—not Harpar, nor Pottinger? But who cares a rush for the name of fellows like you? You change them just as you do the colour of your coat."

"May I take the liberty of asking, Sir, just for infor- mation, as you said a while ago, how you would take it were I to make as free with you as you have been pleased to do with *me?* To give a mock inventory of your external characteristics, and a false name to yourself?"

"Laugh, probably, if I were amused—throw you out of the window, if you offended me."

"The very thing I'd do with you this moment if I was strong enough," said I, resolutely. And he flung himself into a chair, and laughed as I did not believe he could laugh.

"Well," cried he, at last, "as this room is about fifty feet or so from the ground, it's as well as it is. But now let us wind up this affair. You want to get away from this, I suppose; and as nobody wants to detain you, the thing is easy enough. You needn't make a fuss about compensation, for they'll not give a kreutzer, and you'd better not write a book about it, because 'we' don't stand fellows who write books; so just take a friend's advice, and go off without military honours of any kind."

"I neither acknowledge the friendship nor accept the advice, Sir. The motives which induced me to suffer im- prisonment for another are quite sufficient to raise me above any desire to make a profit of it."

"I think I understand *you*," said he, with a cunning ex- pression in his half-closed eyes. "You go in for being a 'character.' Haven't I hit it? You want to be thought a strange, eccentric sort of fellow. Now, there was a time the world had a taste for that kind of thing. Romeo Coates, and Brummel, and that Irish fellow that walked to Jerusalem, and half a dozen others, used to amuse the town in those days, but it's all as much bygone now as starched neckcloths and Hessian boots. Ours is an age of paletots and easy manners, and you are trying to revive what our grand-fathers discarded and got rid of. It won't do, Pottinger; it will not."

"I am not Pottinger; my name is Algernon Sydney Potts."

"Ah! there's the mischief all out at last. What could come of such a collocation of names but a life of incongruity and absurdity! You owe all your griefs to your godfathers, Potts. If they'd have called you Peter, you'd have been a well-conducted poor creature. Well, I'm to give you a pass-port. Where do you wish to go?"

"I wish, first of all, to go to Como."

"I think I know why. But you're on a wrong cast there. They have left that long since."

"Indeed, and for what place?"

"They've gone to pass the winter at Malta. Mamma Keats required a dry, warm climate, and you'll find them at a little country-house about a mile from Valetta: the Jasmines, I think it's called. I have a brother quartered in the island, and he tells me he has seen them, but they won't receive visits, nor go out anywhere. But, of course, a royal highness is always sure of a welcome. Prince Potts is an Open, sesame! wherever he goes."

"What atrocious tobacco this is of yours, Buller," said I, taking a cigar from his case as it lay on the table. "I suppose that you small fry of diplomacy cannot get things in duty free, eh?"

"Try this cheroot; you'll find it better," said he, opening a secret pocket in the case.

"Nothing to boast of," said I, puffing away, while he con-tinued to fill up the blanks in my passport.

"Would you like an introduction to my brother? He's on the government staff there, and knows everyone. He's a jolly sort of fellow, besides, and you'll get on well together."

"I don't care if I do," said I, carelessly, " though, as a
rule, your red-coat is very bad style—flippant without smartness, and familiar without ease."

"Severe, Potts, but not altogether unjust; but you'll find
George above the average of his class, and I think you'll like
him."

"Don't let him ask me to his mess," said I, with an
insolent drawl. "That's an amount of boredom I could
not submit to. Caution him to make no blunder of that
kind."

He looked up at me with a strange twinkle in his eyes,
which I could not interpret. He was either in intense
enjoyment of my smartness, or Heaven knows what other
sentiment then moved him. At all events, I was in ecstasy
at the success of my newly discovered vein, and walked the
room, humming a tune, as he wrote the letter that was to
present me to his brother.

"Why had I never hit upon this plan before?" thought
I. "How was it that it had not occurred that the maxim of
homœopathy is equally true in morals as in medicine, and
that ' *similia similibus curantur !*' So long as I was meek,
humble, and submissive, Buller's impertinent presumption
only increased at every moment. With every fresh con-
cession of mine he continued to encroach, and now that I
had adopted his own strategy, and attacked, he fell back at
once. I was proud, very proud of my discovery. It is a
new contribution to that knowledge of life which, notwithstanding all my disasters, I believed to be essentially my
gift.

At last he finished his note, folded, sealed, and directed it—
" The Hon. George Buller, A.D.C., Government House, Malta,
favoured by Algernon Sydney Potts, Esq."

"Isn't that all right?" asked he, pointing to my name.
"I was within an ace of writing Hampden-Russell, too."
And he laughed at his own very meagre jest.

"I hope you have merely made this an introduction?"
said I.

"Nothing more; but why so?"

"Because it's just as likely that I never present it! I am
the slave of the humour I find myself in, and I rarely do
anything that costs me the slightest effort." I said this with

a close and, indeed, a servile imitation of Charles Matthews in "Used Up"; but it was a grand success, and Buller was palpably vanquished.

"Well, for George's sake, I hope your mood may be the favourable one. Is there anything more I can do for you? Can you think of nothing wherein I may be serviceable?"

"Nothing. Stay, I rather think our people at home might with propriety show my old friend Hirsch here some mark of attention for his conduct towards me. I don't know whether they give a C.B. for that sort of thing, but a sum— a handsome sum—something to mark the service, and the man to whom it was rendered. Don't you think 'we' could manage that?"

"I'll see what can be done. I don't despair of success."

"As for your share in the affair, Buller, I'll take care that it shall be mentioned in the proper quarter. If I *have* a characteristic—my friends say I have many—but if I have one, it is that I never forget the most trifling service of the humblest of those who have aided me. You are young, and have your way to make in life. Go back, therefore, and carry with you the reflection that Potts is your friend."

I saw he was affected at this, for he covered his face with his handkerchief and turned away, and for some seconds his shoulders moved convulsively.

"Yes," said I, with a struggle to become humble, "there are richer men, there are men more influential by family ties and connections, there are men who occupy a more conspicuous position before the public eye, there are men who exercise a wider sway in the world of politics and party; but this I will say, that there is not one—no, not one—individual in the British dominions who, when you come to consider either the difficulties he has overcome, the strength of the prejudices he has conquered, the totally unassisted and unaided struggle he has had to maintain against not alone the errors, for errors are human, but still worse, the ungenerous misconceptions, the—I will go further, and call them the wilful misrepresentations of those who, from education and rank and condition, might be naturally supposed—indeed confidently affirmed to be—to be——"

"I am certain of it!" cried he, grasping my hand, and

rescuing me from a situation very like smothering—" I am certain of it!" And with a hurried salutation, for his feelings were evidently overcoming him, he burst away, and descended the stairs five steps at a time, and although I was sorry he had not waited till I finished my peroration, I was really glad that the act had ended and the curtain fallen.

" What a deal of bad money passes current in this world," said I, as I was alone; " and what a damper it is upon honest industry to think how easy it is to eke out life with a forgery."

" What do you say to a dinner with me at the ' Swan' in Innspruck, Potts ? " cried out Buller, from the court-yard.

" Excuse me, I mean to eat my last cutlet here, with my old gaoler. It will be an event for the poor fellow as long as he lives. Good-bye, and a safe journey to you."

CHAPTER XLV.

I WAS now bound for the first port in the Mediterranean from which I could take ship for Malta, and the better to carry out my purpose, I resolved never to make acquaintance with anyone, or be seduced by any companionship, till I had seen Miss Herbert, and given her the message I was charged with. This time, at least, I would be a faithful envoy, at least as faithful as a man might be who had gone to sleep over his credentials for a twelvemonth. And so I reached Maltz, and took my place by diligence over the Stelvio down to Lecco, never trusting myself with even the very briefest intercourse with my fellow-travellers, and suffering them to indulge in the humblest estimate of me, morally and intellectually—all that I might be true to my object and firm to my fixed purpose. For the first time in my life I tried to present myself in an unfavourable aspect, and I was astonished to find the experiment by no means unpleasing, the reason being, probably, that it was an eminent success. I began to see how the surly people are such acute philosophers in life, and what a deal of selfish gratification they must derive from their uncurbed ill humour. I reached Genoa in time to catch a steamer for Malta. It was crowded, and with what, in another mood, I might have called pleasant people; but I held myself estranged and aloof from all. I could mark many an impertinent allusion to my cold and distant manner, and could see that a young sub on his way to join was even witty at the expense of my retiring disposition. The creature, Groves he was called, used to try to "trot me out," as he phrased it; but I maintained both my resolve and my temper, and gave him no triumph.

I was almost sorry on the morning we dropped anchor in the harbour. The sense of doing something, anything, with a firm persistence had given me cheerfulness and courage. However, I had now a task of some nicety before me, and addressed myself at once to its discharge. At the hotel I learned that the cottage inhabited by Mrs. Keats was in a small nook of one of the bays, and only an easy walk from the town; and so I dispatched a messenger at once with Miss Crofton's note to Miss Herbert, enclosed in a short one from myself, to know if she would permit me to wait upon her, with reference to the matter in the letter. I spoke of myself in the third person and as the bearer of the letter.

While I was turning over the letters and papers in my writing-desk, awaiting her reply, I came upon Buller's note to his brother, and, without any precise idea why, I sent it by a servant to the Government House, with my card. It was completely without a purpose that I did so, and if my reader has not experienced moments of the like "inconsequence," I should totally break down in attempting to account for their meaning.

Miss Herbert's reply came back promptly. She requested that the writer of the note she had just read would favour her with a visit at his earliest convenience.

I set forth immediately. What a strange and thrilling sensation it is when we take up some long-dropped link in life, go back to some broken thread of our existence, and try to attach it to the present! We feel young again in the

24

bygone, and yet far older even than our real age in the thought of the changes time has wrought upon us in the meanwhile. A week or so before I had looked with impatience for this meeting, and now I grew very faint-hearted as the moment drew nigh. The only way I could summon courage for the occasion was by thinking that in the mission entrusted to me *I* was actually nothing. There were incidents and events not one of which touched me, and I should pass away off the scene when our interview was over, and be no more remembered by her.

It was evident that the communication had engaged her attention to some extent by the promptitude of her message to me ; and with this thought I crossed the little lawn, and rang the bell at the door.

"The gentleman expected by Miss Herbert, Sir," asked a smart English maid. "Come this way, Sir. She will see you in a few minutes."

I had fully ten minutes to inspect the details of a pretty little drawing-room, one of those little female temples where scattered drawings and books and music, and, above all, the delicious odour of fresh flowers, all harmonise together, and set you a thinking how easily life could glide by with such appliances were they only set in motion by the touch of the enchantress herself. The door opened at last, but it was the maid, she came to say that Mrs. Keats was very poorly that day, and Miss Herbert could not leave her at that moment ; and if it were not perfectly convenient to the gentleman to wait, she begged to know when it would suit him to call again?

"As for me," said I, "I have come to Malta solely on this matter; pray say that I will wait as long as she wishes. I am completely at her orders."

I strolled out after this through one of the windows that opened on the lawn, and gaining the sea-side, I sat down upon a rock to bide her coming. I might have sat about half-an-hour thus, when I heard a rapid step approaching, and I had just time to arise when Miss Herbert stood before me. She started back, and grew pale, very pale, as she recognised me, and for fully a minute there we both stood, unable to speak a word.

"Am I to understand, Sir," said she, at last, "that you

are the bearer of this letter?" And she held it open towards me.

"Yes," said I, with a great effort at collectedness. " I have much to ask your forgiveness for. It is fully a year since I was charged to place that in your hands, but one mischance after another has befallen me; not to own that in my own purposeless mode of life I have had no enemy worse than my fate."

"I have heard something of your fondness for adventure," said she, with a strange smile that blended a sort of pity with a gentle irony. "After we parted company at Schaff-hausen, I believe you travelled for some time on foot? We heard, at least, that you took a fancy to explore a mode of life few persons have penetrated, or, at least, few of your rank and condition."

"May I ask, what do you believe that rank and condition to be, Miss Herbert?" asked I, firmly.

She blushed deeply at this; perhaps I was too abrupt in the way I spoke, and I hastened to add,—

"When I offered to be the bearer of the letter you have just read, I was moved by another wish than merely to render you some service. I wanted to tell you, once for all, that if I lived for a while in a fiction land of my own in-vention, with day-dreams and fancies, and hopes and ambitions all unreal, I have come to pay the due penalty of my deceit, and confess that nothing can be more humble than I am in birth, station, or fortune—my father an apothecary, my name Potts, my means a very few pounds in the world; and yet, with all that avowal, I feel prouder now that I have made it, than ever I did in the false assumption of some condition I had no claim to."

She held out her hand to me with such a significant air of approval, and smiled so good-naturedly, that I could not help pressing it to my lips, and kissing it rapturously.

Taking a seat at my side, and with a voice meant to recal me to a quiet and business-like demeanour, she asked me to read over Miss Crofton's letter. I told her that I knew every line of it by heart, and, more still, I knew the whole story to which it related. It was a topic that required the nicest delicacy to touch on, but with a frankness that charmed me, she said,—

24—2

"You have had the candour to tell me freely your story; let me imitate you, and reveal mine.

"You know who we are, and whence we have sprung; that my father was a simple labourer on a line of railroad, and by dint of zeal and intelligence, and an energy that would not be baulked or impeded, that he raised himself to station and affluence. You have heard of his connection with Sir Elkanah Crofton, and how unfortunately it was broken off; but you cannot know the rest—that is, you cannot know what we alone know, and what is not so much as suspected by others; and of this I can scarcely dare to speak, since it is essentially the secret of my family."

I guessed at once to what she alluded; her troubled manner, her swimming eyes, and her quivering voice, all betraying that she referred to the mystery of her father's fate; while I doubted within myself whether it were right and fitting for me to acknowledge that I knew the secret source of her anxiety. She relieved me from my embarrassment by continuing thus :—

"Your kind and generous friends have not suffered themselves to be discouraged by defeat. They have again and again renewed their proposals to my mother, only varying the mode, in the hope that by some stratagem they might overcome her reasons for refusal. Now, though this rejection, so persistent as it is, may seem ungracious, it is not without a fitting and substantial cause."

Again she faltered, and grew confused, and now I saw how she struggled between a natural reserve and an impulse to confide the sorrow that oppressed her to one who might befriend her.

"You may speak freely to me," said I, at last. "I am not ignorant of the mystery you hint at. Crofton has told me what many surmise and some freely believe in."

"But we know it, know it for a certainty," cried she, clasping my hand in her eagerness. "It is no longer a surmise or a suspicion. It is a certainty—a fact! Two letters in his handwriting have reached my mother; one from St. Louis, in America, where he had gone first; the second from an Alpine village, where he was laid up in sickness. He had had a terrible encounter with a man who had done him some gross wrong, and he was wounded in the shoulder.

After which he had to cross the Rhine, wading or swimming, and travel many miles ere he could find shelter. When he wrote, however, he was rapidly recovering, and as quickly regaining all his old courage and daring."

" And from that time forward have you had no tidings of him ? "

"Nothing but a cheque on a Russian banker in London to pay to my mother's order a sum of money, a considerable one, too ; and although she hoped to gain some clue to him through this, she could not succeed, nor have we now any trace of him whatever. I ought to mention," said she, as if catching up a forgotten thread in her narrative, " that in his last letter he enjoined my mother not to receive any payment from the assurance company, nor enter into any compromise with them ; and, above all, to live in the hope that we should meet again and be happy."

" And are you still ignorant of where he now is ? "

" We only know that a cousin of mine, an officer of engineers at Aden, heard of an Englishman being engaged by the Shah of Persia to report on certain silver mines at Kashan, and from all he could learn, the description would apply to him. My cousin had obtained leave of absence expressly to trace him, and promised in his last letter to bring me himself any tidings he might procure here to Malta. Indeed, when I learned that a stranger had asked to see me, I was full sure it was my Cousin Harry."

Was it that her eyes grew darker in colour as this name escaped her—was it that a certain tremor shook her voice —or was it the anxiety of my own jealous humour, that made me wretched as I heard of that cousin Harry, now mentioned for the first time?

" What reparation can I make you for so blank a disappointment? " said I, with a sad, half-bitter tone.

" Be the same kind friend that he would have proved himself if it had been his fortune to have come first," said she ; and though she spoke calmly, she blushed deeply! " Here," said she, hurriedly, taking a small printed paragraph from a letter, and eagerly, as it seemed, trying to recover her former manner—" here is a slip I have cut out of the *Levant Herald*. I found it about two months since. It ran thus : 'The person who had contracted for the works at Pera, and

who now turns out to be an Englishman, is reported to have
had a violent altercation yesterday with Musted Pasha, in
consequence of which he has thrown up his contract, and
demanded his passport for Russia. It is rumoured here that
the Russian ambassador is no stranger to this rupture.'
Vague as this is, I feel persuaded that he is the person
alluded to, and that it is from Constantinople we must trace
him."

"Well," cried I, "I am ready. I will set out at once."

"Oh! can I believe you will do us this great service?"
cried she, with swimming eyes and clasped hands.

"This time you will find me faithful," said I, gravely.
"He who has said and done so many foolish things as I
have, must, by one good action, give bail for his future
character."

"You are a true friend, and you have all my confidence."

"Mrs. Keats's compliments, miss," said the maid at this
moment, "and hopes the gentleman will stay to dinner with
you, though she cannot come down herself."

"She imagines you are my cousin, whom she is aware I
have been expecting," said Miss Herbert, in a whisper, and
evidently appearing uncertain how to act.

"Oh!" said I, with an anguish I could not repress,
"would that I could change my lot with his."

"Very well, Mary," said Miss Herbert; "thank your
mistress from me, and say the gentleman accepts her invitation with pleasure. Is it too much presumption on my
part, Sir, to say so?" said she, with a low whisper, while
a half malicious twinkle lit up her eyes, and I could not
speak with happiness.

Determined, however, to give an earnest of my zeal in her
cause, I declared I would at once return to the town, and
learn when the first packet sailed for Constantinople. The
dinner hour was seven, so that I had fully five hours yet to
make my inquiries ere we met at table. I wondered at
myself how business-like and practical I had become; but a
strong impulse now impelled me, and seemed to add a sort
of strength to my whole nature.

"As Cousin Harry is the mirror of punctuality, and you
now represent him, Mr. Potts," said she, shaking my hand,
"pray remember not to be later than seven."

CHAPTER XLVI.

"CONSTANTINOPLE, ODESSA, and the LEVANT.—The *Cyclops*, five hundred horse-power, to sail on Wednesday morning, at eight o'clock. For freight or passage apply to Captain Robert B. Rogers."

This announcement, which I found amidst a great many others in a frame over the fire-place in the coffee-room, struck me forcibly, first of all, because, not belonging to the regular mail packets, it suggested a cheap passage; and, secondly, it promised an early departure, and the vessel was to sail on the very next morning, an amount of promptitude that I felt would gratify Miss Herbert.

Now, although I had been living for a considerable time back at the cost of the Imperial House of Hapsburg, my resources for such an expedition as was opening before me were of the most slender kind. I made a careful examination of all my worldly wealth, and it amounted to the sum of forty-three pounds some odd shillings. On *terra firma* I could, of course, economise to any extent. With self-denial and resolution I could live on very little. Life in the East, I had often heard, was singularly cheap and inexpensive. All I had read of Oriental habits in the "Arabian Nights" and "Tales of the Genii" assured me that with a few dates and a water-melon a man dined fully as well as need be; and the delicious warmth of the climate rendered shelter a complete superfluity. Before forming anything like a correct budget, I must ascertain what would be the cost of my passage to Constantinople, and so I rang for the waiter to direct me to the address of the advertiser.

"That's the captain yonder, Sir," whispered the waiter, and he pointed to a stout, weather-beaten man, who, with his hands in the pockets of his pilot-coat, was standing in front of the fire, smoking a cigar.

Although I had never seen him before, the features reminded me of some one I had met with, and suddenly I bethought me of the skipper with whom I had sailed from Ireland for Milford, and who had given me a letter for

his brother "Bob"—the very Robert Rogers now before
me.

"Do you know this handwriting, captain?" said I, drawing the letter from my pocket-book.

"That's my brother Joe's," said he, not offering to take
the letter from my hand, or removing the cigar from his
mouth, but talking with all the unconcern in life. "That's
Joe's own scrawl, and there ain't a worse from this to himself."

"The letter is for you," said I, rather offended at his
coolness.

"So I see. Stick it up there, over the chimney; Joe has
never anything to say that won't keep."

"It is a letter of introduction, Sir," said I, still more
haughtily.

"And what if it be? Won't that keep? Who is it to
introduce?"

"The humble individual before you, Captain Rogers."

"So, that's it!" said he, slowly. "Well, read it out for
me, for, to tell you the truth, there's no harder navigation to
me than one of Joe's scrawls."

"I believe I can master it," said I, opening and reading
what originally had been composed and drawn up by
myself. When I came to "Algernon Sydney Potts, a
man so completely after your own heart," he drew his
cigar from his mouth, and laying his hand on my
shoulder, turned me slowly around till the light fell full
upon me.

"No, Joseph," said he, deliberately, "not a bit of it, my
boy. This ain't my sort of chap at all!"

I almost choked with anger, but somehow there was such
an apparent earnestness in the man, and such a total absence
of all wish to offend, that I read on to the end.

"Well," said he, as I concluded, "he usedn't to be so
wordy as that. I wonder what came over him. Mayhap
he wasn't well."

What a comment on a style that might have adorned the
Correct Letter Writer!

"He was, on the contrary, in the enjoyment of perfect
health, Sir," said I, tartly.

"All I can pick out of it is, I ain't to offer you any money;

and as there isn't any direction easier to follow, nor pleasanter to obey, here's my hand!" And he wrung mine with a grip that would have flattened a chain cable.

"What's your line, here? You ain't sodgering, are you?"

"No; I'm travelling, for pleasure, for information, for pastime, as one might say."

"In the general do-nothing and careless line of business? That ain't mine. No, by jingo! I don't eat my fish without catching, ay, and salting them, too, I ain't ashamed to say. I'm captain, supercargo, and pilot of my own craft; take every lunar that is taken aboard; I've writ every line that ever is writ in the log-book, and I vaccinated every man and boy aboard for the natural small-pox with these fingers and this tool that you see here!" And he produced an old and very rusty instrument of veterinary surgery from his vest-pocket, where it lay with copper money, tobacco quids, and lucifer matches.

I quickly remembered the character for inordinate boastfulness his brother had given me, and of which he thus, without any provocation on my part, afforded me a slight specimen. Now, perhaps at this stage of my narrative, I might never have alluded to him at all, if it were not for the opportunity it gives me of recording how nobly and how resolutely I resisted what may be called the most trying temptation of human nature. An inveterate dram-drinker has been known to turn away from the proffered glass; an incurable gambler has been seen to decline the invitation to "cut in;" dignitaries of the church have begged off being made bishops; but is there any mention in history of an anecdote-monger suffering himself to be patiently vanquished, and retiring from the field without firing off at least an "incident that occurred to himself?" If ever a man was sorely tried, I was. Here was this coarsely-minded vulgar dog, with nothing pictorial or imaginative in his nature, heaping story upon story of his own feats and achievements, in which not one solitary situation ever suggested an interest or awakened an anxiety; and I, who could have shot my tigers, crippled my leopards, hamstrung my lionesses, rescued men from drowning, and women from fire—with little life touches to thrill the heart and force tears from the eyes of a stockbroker—I, I say, had to stand there and listen in silence! Watching a creature banging away at a target that he never hit, with an old flint musket, while you held in your hand a short Enfield that would have driven the ball through the bull's eye is nothing to this; and to tell the truth, it nearly choked me. Twice I had to cough down the words, "Now let me mention a personal fact." But I did succeed, and I am proud to say I only grew very red in the face, and felt that singing noise in the ears and general state of muddle that forbodes a fit. But I rallied, and said in a voice, slow from the dignity of a self-conquest,—

"Can you take me as a passenger to Constantinople?"

"To Constantinople? Ay, to the Persian Gulf, to Point de Galle, to Cochin China, to Ross River; don't think to puzzle me with navigation, my lad."

"Are there many other passengers?"

"I could have five hundred, if I'd take 'em! Put Bob Rogers on a placard, and see what'll happen. If I said, 'I'm agoing to sea on a plank, to-morrow,' there's men would rather come along with me than go in the *Queen*, or the *Hannibal*. I don't say they're right, mind ye; but I won't say they's wrong, neither."

"Oh, why did'nt I meet this wretch when I was a child? Why didn't my father find a Helot like this, to tell lies before me, and frighten me with their horrid ugliness?" This was the thought that flashed through me as I listened. I felt, besides, that such stupid, purposeless inventions, corrupted and blunted the taste for graceful narrative, just in the same way that an undeserving recipient of charity offends the pleasure of real benevolence.

"May I ask, Captain Rogers, what is the fare?" said I, with a bland courtesy.

"That depends upon the man, Sir. If you was Ramsam Can-tankcr-abad, I'd say five hundred gold pagodas. If you was a Cockney stripling, with a fresh-water face, and a spunyarn whisker, I'd call it a matter of seven or eight pound."

"And you sail at eight?"

"To the minute. When Bob Rogers says eight o'clock, the first turn of the paddles will be the first stroke of the hour."

"Then book me, pray, for a berth; and, for surety's sake, I'll go aboard to-night."

"Meet me, then, here at ten o'clock, and I'll take you off in my gig, an honour to be proud on, my lad; but as Joe's friend, I'll do it."

I bowed my acknowledgments and went off, neither delighted with my new acquaintance, nor myself for the patience I had shown him. After all, I had secured an early passage, and was thus able to show Kate Herbert that I was not going to let the grass grow under my feet this time, and that she might reckon on my zeal to serve her in future. As I retraced my road to the cottage, I forgot all about Captain Rogers, and only thought of Kate, and the interests that were hers. It was next to a certainty that her father was yet alive; but how to find him in a strange land, with a feigned name, and most probably with every aid and appliance to complete his disguisement! It was, doubtless, a noble enterprise to devote oneself for such as she was, but not very hopeful withal; and then I went over various plans for my future guidance: what I should do if I fell sick? what if my money failed me? what if I were waylaid by Arabs, or carried away to some fearful region in the mountains, and made to feed a pet alligator, or a domestic boa-constrictor? I hoped sincerely that I was over-estimating my possible perils, but it was wise to give a large margin to the unknown; and so I did not curb myself in the least.

As I entered the grounds, the night was falling, and I could see that the lamps were already lighted in the drawing-room. What surprised me, however, was to see a very smart groom, well mounted, and leading another horse up and down before the door. There was evidently a vi 'tor within, and I felt indisposed to enter till he had gone away. My curiosity, however, prompted me to ask the groom the name of his master, and he replied, "The Honourable Captain Buller."

The very essence of all jealousy is, that it is unreasoning. It is well known that husbands—that much-believing and much-belied class—always suspect everyone but the right man; and now, without the faintest clue to a suspicion, I grew actually sick with jealousy!

Nor was it altogether blamable in me, for as I looked through the uncurtained window, I could see the captain, a fine-looking, rather tigerish sort of fellow, standing with his back to the fireplace, while he talked to Miss Herbert, who sat some distance off at a work-table. There was in his air that amount of jaunty ease and self-possession that said, " I'm at home here; in this fortress I hold the chief command." There was about him, too, the tone of an assumed superiority, which when displayed by a man towards a woman, takes the most offensive of all possible aspects.

As he talked, he moved at last towards a window, and, opening it, held out his hand to feel if it were raining.

" I hope," cried he, " you'll not send me back with a refusal ; her ladyship counts upon you as the chief ornament of her ball."

" We never do go to balls, Sir," was the dry response.

" But make this occasion the exception. If you only knew how lamentably we are off for pretty people, you'd pity us. Such garrison wives and daughters are unknown to the oldest inhabitant of the island. Surely Mrs. Keats will be quite well by Wednesday, and she'll not be so cruel as to deny you to us for this once."

" I can but repeat my excuses—I never go out."

" If you say so, I think I'll abandon all share in the enterprise. It was a point of honour with me to persuade you; in fact, I pledged myself to succeed, and if you really persist in a refusal, I'll just pitch all these notes in the fire, and go off yachting till the whole thing is over." And with this he drew forth a mass of notes from his sabretasche, and proceeded to con over the addresses : " ' Mrs. Hilyard,' ' Mr. Barnes,' ' Mr. Clintosh,' ' Lady Blagden.' Oh, Lady Blagden ! Why it would be worth while coming only to see her and Sir John; and here are the Crosbys, too; and what have we here? Oh! this is a note from Grey. You don't know my brother Grey—he'd amuse you immensely. Just listen to this, by way of a letter of introduction:

" ' DEAR GEORGE,—Cherish the cove that will hand you this note as the most sublime Snob I have ever met in all my home and foreign experiences. In a large garrison like yours, you can have no difficulty in finding fellows to give him a field-day. I commit him, therefore, to your worthy keeping, to dine him, draw him forth, and pitch him out of the window when you've done with him. No harm if it is from the topmost story of the highest barrack in Malta. His name is Potts—seriously and truthfully, Potts. Birth, parentage, and belongings all unknown to   " 'Yours ever,

" ' Grey Buller.' "

"You are unfortunate, Sir, in confiding your correspondence to me," said Kate, rising from her seat, "for that gentleman is a friend, a sincere and valued friend, of my own, and you could scarcely have found a more certain way to offend me than to speak of him slightingly."

"You can't mean that you know him—ever met him?"

"I know him and respect him, and I will not listen to one word to his disparagement. Nay, more, Sir, I will feel myself at liberty, if I think it fitting, to tell Mr. Potts the honourable mode in which your brother has discharged the task of an introduction, its good faith, and gentlemanlike feeling."

"Pray let us have him at the mess first. Don't spoil our sport till we have at least one evening out of him."

But she did not wait for him to finish his speech, and left the room.

It is but fair to own he took his reverses with great coolness : he tightened his sword-belt, set his cap on his head before the glass, stroked down his moustache, and then lighting a cigar, swaggered off to the door with the lounging swing of his order.

As for myself, I hastened back to the town, and with such speed that I traversed the mile in something like thirteen minutes. I had no very clear or collected plan of action but I resolved to ask Captain Rogers to be my friend, and see me through this conjuncture. He had just dined as I entered the coffee-room, and consented to have his brandy-and-water removed to my bedroom while I opened my business with him.

I will not at this eleventh hour of revelations, inflict upon

my reader the details, but simply be satisfied to state that I
found the skipper far more practical than I looked for. He
evidently, besides, had a taste for these sort of adventures,
and prided himself on his conduct of them. "Go back now,
and eat your dinner comfortably with your friends; leave
everything to me, and I promise you one thing—the *Cyclops*
shall not get full steam up till we have settled this small
transaction."

CHAPTER XLVII.

THOUGH I was a few minutes late for dinner, Miss Herbert
did not chide me for delay. She was charming in her reception of me; nor was the fascination diminished to me
by feeling with what generous warmth she had defended
and upheld me.

There is a marvellous charm in the being defended by one
you love, and of whose kind feeling towards you, you had never
dared to assure yourself till the very moment that confirmed
it. I don't know if I ever felt in such spirits in my life.
Not that I was gay or light-hearted so much as happy—
happy in the sense of a self-esteem I had not known till
then. And what a spirit of cordial familiarity was there
now between us! She spoke to me of her daily life, its
habits and even of its trials; not complainingly nor fretfully,
far from it, but in a way to imply that these were the
burdens meted out to all, and that none should arrogantly
imagine he was to escape the lot of his fellows. And then
we talked of the Croftons, of whom she was curious to hear
details—their ages, appearance, manner, and so on—lastly,
how I came to know them, and thus imperceptibly led me to
tell of myself and of my story. I am sure that we each of
us had enough of care upon our hearts, and yet none would
have ever guessed it to have seen how joyously and

merrily we laughed over some of the incidents of my
chequered career. She bantered me, too, on the feeble
and wayward impulses by which I had suffered myself to
be moved, and gravely asked me, had I accomplished
any single one of all objects I had set before my mind in
starting.

Far more earnestly, however, did we discuss the future.
She heard with joy that I had already secured a passage for
Constantinople, and declared that she could not dismiss from
her mind the impression that I was destined to aid their return to happiness and prosperity. I liked the notion, too, of
there being a fate in our first meeting; a fate in that
acquaintanceship with the Croftons, which gave the occasion
to seek her out again; and last of all, if it might be so, a
fate in the influence I was to exercise over their fortunes. I
was so absorbed in these pleasant themes, that I, with as
little of the lion in my heart as any man breathing, never
once thought of the quarrel and its impending consequences.
How my heart beat as her soft breath fanned me while she
spoke! As she was telling when and from whence I was to
write to her, the servant came to say that a gentleman outside begged to see Mr. Potts. I hurried to the hall.

"Not come to disturb you, Potts," said the skipper, in a
brisk tone; "only thought it best to made your mind easy.
It's all right."

"A thousand thanks, captain," said I, warmly. "I
knew when the negotiation was in your hands, it would
be so."

"Yes; his friend, a Major Colesby, boggled a bit at first.
Couldn't see the thing in the light I put it. Asked very
often 'who were you?' asked, too, 'who I was?' Good
that! it made me laugh. Rather late in the day, I take it,
to ask who Bob Rogers is! But in the end, as I said, it all
comes right, quite right."

"And his apology was full, ample, and explicit? Was it
in writing, Rogers? I'd like it in writing."

"Like what in writing?"

"His apology, or explanation, or whatever you like to
call it."

"Who ever spoke of such a thing? Who so much as
dreamed of it? Haven't I told you the affair is all

right? and what does all right mean, eh?—what does it
mean?"

"I know what it ought to mean," said I, angrily.

"So do I, and so do most men in this island, Sir. It
means twelve paces under the Battery wall, fire together,
and as many shots as the aggrieved asks for. That's all
right, isn't it?"

"In one sense it is so," said I, with a mock composure.

"Well, that's the only sense I ever meant to consider it
by. Go back now to your tea, or your sugar-and-water, or
whatever it is, and when you come home to-night, step into
my room, and we'll have a cozy chat and a cigar. There's
one or two trifling things that I don't understand in this
affair, and I put my own explanation on them, and maybe it
ain't the right one. Not that it signifies *now*, you perceive,
because you are here to the fore, and can set them right.
But as by this time to-morrow you might be where—
I won't mention—we may as well put them straight this
evening."

"I'll beat you up, depend upon it," said I, affecting
a slap-dash style. "I can't tell you how glad I am
to have fallen into your hands, Rogers. You suit me
exactly."

"Well it's more than I expected when I saw you first,
and I kept saying to myself, 'Whatever could have
persuaded Joe to send me a creature like that?' To tell
you the truth, I thought you were in the cheap funeral
line."

"Droll dog!" said I, while my fingers were writhing and
twisting with passion.

"Not that it's fair to take a fellow by his looks. I'm
aware of that, Potts. But go back to the parlour—that's
the second time the maid has come out to see what keeps
you. Go back, and enjoy yourself; maybe you won't have
so pleasant an opportunity soon again."

This was the parting speech of the wretch as he buttoned
the collar of his coat, and with a short nod bade me good-
bye, and left me.

"Why did you not ask your friend to take a cup of tea
with us?" said Kate, as I re-entered the drawing-room.

"Oh! it was the skipper, a rough sort of creature, not

exactly made for drawing-room life; besides, he only came to ask me a question."

"I hope it was not a very unpleasant one, for you look pale and anxious."

"Nothing of the kind—a mere formal matter about my baggage."

It was no use; from that moment, I was the most miserable of mankind. What availed it to speculate any longer on the future? How could I interest myself in what years might bring forth? Hours, and a very few of them, were all that were left to me. Poor girl! how tenderly she tried to divert my sorrow; she, most probably, ascribed it to the prospect of our speedy separation; and with delicacy and tact, she tried to trace out some faint outlines of what painters call "extreme distance"—a sort of future, where all the skies would be rose-coloured and all the mountains blue. I am sure, if a choice had been given me at that instant, I would rather have been a courageous man than the greatest genius in the universe. *I* knew better what was before me. At last it came to ten o'clock, and I arose to say good-bye. I found it very hard not to fall upon her neck, and say, "Don't be angry with poor Potts; this is his last as it is his first embrace."

"Wear that ring for me and for my sake," said she. giving me one from her finger; "don't refuse me—it has no value save what you may attach to it from having been mine."

Oh dear! what a gulp it cost me not to say, "I'll never take it off while I live, and then add, "which will be about eight hours and a half more."

When I got into the open air, I ran as if a pack of wolves were in pursuit of me. I cannot say why, but the rapid motion served to warm my blood, so that when I reached the hotel, I felt more assured and more resolute.

Rogers was asleep, and so soundly, that I had to pull the pillow from beneath his head before I could awaken him; and when I had accomplished the feat, either the remote effect of his brandy-and-water, or his drowsiness, had so obscured his faculties, that all he could mumble out was, "Hit him where he can't be spliced—hit him where they can't splice him!" I tried for a long time to recal him to sense and intelligence, but I got nothing from him save the one inestimable precept; and so I went to my room, and throwing myself on my bed in my cloak, prepared for a night of gloomy retrospect and gloomier anticipation; but, odd enough, I was asleep the moment I lay down.

"Get up, old fellow," cried Rogers, shaking me violently, just as the dawn was breaking; "we're lucky if we can get aboard before they catch us."

"What do you mean?" said I. "What's happened?"

"The governor has got wind of our shindy, and put all the red-coats in arrest, and ordered the police to nab us too."

"Bless him! bless him!" muttered I.

"Ay, so say I. He be blessed!" cried he, catching up my words: "but let us make off through the garden; my gig is down in the offing, and they'll pull in when they hear my whistle. Ain't it provoking—ain't it enough to make a man swear?"

"I have no words for what I feel, Rogers," said I, bustling about to collect my stray articles through the room. "If I ever chance upon that governor—he has only five years of it—I believe ——"

"Come along! I see the boat coming round the point yonder." And with this we slipped noiselessly down the stairs, down the street, and gained the jetty.

"Steam up?" asked the skipper, as he jumped into the gig.

"Ay, ay, Sir; and we're short on the anchor, too."

In less than half an hour we were under weigh, and I don't think I ever admired a land prospect receding from view with more intense delight than I did that, my last glimpse of Malta.

CHAPTER XLVIII.

Our voyage had nothing remarkable to record: we reached Constantinople in due course, and during the few days the *Cyclops* remained I had abundant time to discover that there was no trace of anyone resembling him I sought for. By the advice of Rogers, I accompanied him to Odessa There, too, I was not more fortunate; and though I instituted the most persevering inquiries, all I could learn was that some Americans were employed by the Russian Government in raising the frigates sunk at Sebastopool, and that it was not impossible an Englishman, such as I described, might have met an engagement amongst them. At all events, one of the coasting craft was already at Odessa, and I went on board of her to make my inquiry. I learned from the mate, who was a German, that they had come over on rather a strange errand, which was to convey a corps of circus people to Balaclava. The American contractor at that place being in want of some amusement, had arranged with these people to give some weeks' performances there, but that, from an incident that had just occurred, the project had failed. This was no less than the elopement of the chief dancer, a young girl of great beauty, with a young Prince of Bavaria. It was rumoured that he had married her, but my informant gave little credence to this version, and averred that he had bought, not only herself, but a favourite old Arab horse she rode, for thirty thousand piastres. I asked eagerly where the others of the corps were to be found, and heard they had crossed over to Simoom, all broken up and disjointed, the chief clown having died of grief after the girl's flight.

If I heard this tale rudely narrated, and not always with the sort of comment that went with my sympathies, I sorrowed sincerely over it, for I guessed upon whom these events had fallen, and recognised poor old Vaterchen and the dark-eyed Tintefleck.

25—2

"You've fallen into the black melancholies these some days back," said Rogers to me. "Rouse up, and take a cruise with me. I'm going over to Balaclava with these steam-boilers, and then to Sinope, and so back to the Bosphorus. Come aboard to-night, it will do you good."

I took his counsel, and at noon next day we dropped anchor at Balaclava. We had scarcely passed our "health papers," when a boat came out with a message to inquire if we had a doctor on board who could speak English, for the American contractor had fallen from one of the scaffolds that morning, and was lying dreadfully injured up at Sebastopol, but unable to explain himself to the Russian surgeons. I was not without some small skill in medicine; and, besides, out of common humanity, I felt it my duty to set out, and at about sunset I reached Sebastopol.

Being supposed to be a physician of great skill and eminence, I was treated by all the persons about with much deference, and, after very few minutes' delay, introduced into the room where the sick man lay. He had ordered that when an English doctor could be found, they were to leave them perfectly alone together; so that as I entered, the door was closed immediately, and I found myself alone by the bedside of the sufferer. The curtain was closely drawn across the windows, and it was already dusk, so that all I could discover was the figure of a man, who lay breathing very heavily, and with the irregular action that implies great pain.

"Are you English?" said he, in a strong, full voice. "Well, feel that pulse, and tell me if it means sinking—I suspect it does."

I took his hand and laid my finger on the artery. It was beating furiously—far too fast to count, but not weakly nor faintly.

"No," said I; "this is fever, but not debility."

"I don't want subtleties," rejoined he, roughly. "I want to know am I dying. Draw the curtain there, open the window full, and have a look at me."

I did as he bade me, and returned to the bedside. It was all I could do not to cry out with astonishment; for, though terribly disfigured by his wounds, his eyes actually covered by the torn scalp that hung over them, I saw that it was

Harpar lay before me, his large reddish beard now matted and clotted with blood.

"Well, what's the verdict?" cried he, sternly; "don't keep me in suspense."

"I do not perceive any grave symptoms so far——"

"No cant, my good friend, no cant! It's out of place just now. Be honest, and say what is it to be—live or die?"

"So far as I can judge, I say, live."

"Well, then, set about the repairs at once. Ask for what you want—they'll bring it."

Deeming it better not to occasion any shock whatever to a man in his state, I forbore declaring who I was, and set about my office with what skill I could.

With the aid of a Russian surgeon, who spoke German well, I managed to dress the wounds and bandage the fractured arm, during which the patient never spoke once, nor, indeed, seemed to be at all concerned in what was going on.

"You can stay here, I hope," said he to me, when all was finished. "At least, you'll see me through the worst of it. I can afford to pay, and pay well."

"I'll stay," said I, imitating his own laconic way; and no more was said.

Now, though it was not my intention to pass myself off for a physician, or derive any, even the smallest advantage from the assumption of such a character, I saw that, remote as the poor sufferer was from his friends and country, and totally destitute of even companionship, it would have been cruel to desert him until he was sufficiently recovered to be left with servants.

From his calm composure, and the self-control he was able to exercise, I had formed a far too favourable opinion of his case. When I saw him first, the inflammatory symptoms had not yet set in; so that, at my next visit, I found him in a high fever, raving wildly. In his wanderings he imagined himself ever directing some gigantic enterprise, with hundreds of men at his command, whose efforts he was cheering or chiding alternately. The indomitable will of a most resolute nature was displayed in all he said; and though his bodily sufferings must have been intense, he only alluded to them to show how little power they had to arrest his activity. His ever-recurring cry was, "It can be done, men! It can be done! See that we do it!"

I own that, even though stretched on a sick-bed, and raving madly, this man's unquenchable energy impressed me greatly; and I often fancied to myself what must have been the resources of such a bold spirit in sad contrast to a nature pliant and yielding like mine. To the violence of the first access, there soon succeeded the far more dangerous state of low fever, through which I never left him. Care and incessant watching could alone save him, and I devoted myself to the last with the resolve to make this effort the first of a new and changed existence.

Day and night in the sick room, I lost appetite and strength, while an unceasing care preyed upon me and deprived me even of rest. The very vacillations of the sick man's malady had affected my nerves, rendering me over-anxious, so that just as he had passed the great crisis of the malady, I was stricken down with it myself.

My first day of convalescence, after seven weeks of fever, found me sitting at a little window that looked upon the sea, or rather the harbour of Sebastopol, where two frigates and some smaller vessels were at anchor. A group of lighters and such unpicturesque craft occupied another part of the scene, engaged as it seemed in operations for raising other vessels. It was in gazing for a long while at these, and guessing their occupation, that I learned to trace out the past, and why and how I had come to be sitting there. Every morning the German servant who tended me through my illness, used to bring me the "Herr Baron's" compliments to know how I was, and now he came to say, that as the "Herr Baron" was able to walk so far, he begged that he might be permitted to come and pay me a visit. I was aware of the Russian custom of giving titles to all who served the government in positions of high trust, and was, therefore, not astonished when the announcement of the "Herr Baron" was followed by the entrance of Harpar, who, sadly reduced, and leaning on a crutch, made his way slowly to where I sat. I attempted to rise to receive him, but he cried out, half sternly:—

"Sit still! we are neither of us in good trim for ceremony."

He motioned to the servants to leave us alone; then laying his wasted hand in mine, for we were each too weak to
grasp the other, he said :—

"I know all about it. It was you saved my life, and
risked your own to do it."

I muttered out some unmeaning words—I know not well
what—about duty and the like.

" I don't care a brass button for the motive. You stood to
me like a man." As he said this, he looked hard at me, and
shading the light with his hand, peered into my face.
" Haven't we met before this ? Is not your name Potts ? "

" Yes, and you're Harpar."

He reddened, but so slightly, that but for the previous
paleness of his sickly cheek it would not have been
noticeable.

"I have often thought about *you*," said he, musingly.
"This is not the only service you have done me; the first
was at Lindau; mayhap you have forgotten it. You lent me
two hundred florins, and, if I'm not much mistaken, when
you were far from being rich yourself."

He leaned his head on his hand, and seemed to have fallen
into a musing fit.

"And after all," said I, "of the best turn I ever did you,
you have never heard in your life, and what is more, might
never hear, if not from myself. Do you remember an
altercation on the road to Feldkirch, with a man called
Rigges ? "

" To be sure I do ; he smashed the small-bone of this arm
for me; but I gave worse than I got. They never could find
that bullet I sent into his side, and he died of it at Palermo.
But what share in this did you bear? "

" Not the worst nor the best; but I was imprisoned for a
twelvemonth in your place."

" Imprisoned for *me ?* "

" Yes; they assumed that I was Harpar, and as I took no
steps to undeceive them, there I remained till they seemed to
have forgotten all about me."

Harpar questioned me closely and keenly as to the reasons
that prompted this act of mine—an act all the more remarkable, as, to use his own words, " We were men who had no
friendship for each other, actually strangers;" and, added

he, significantly, "the sort of fellows who, somehow, do not usually 'hit it off' together. You a man of leisure, with your own dreamy mode of life; I, a hard worker, who could not enjoy idleness; and in this sense, far more likely to hold each other cheaply than otherwise."

I attempted to account for this piece of devotion as best I might, but not very successfully, since I was only endeavouring to explain what I really did not well understand myself. Nor could a vague desire to do something generous, merely because it *was* generous, satisfy the practical intelligence of him who heard me.

"Well," said he, at last, "all that machinery you have described is so new and strange to me, I can tell nothing as to how it ought to work; but I'm as grateful to you as a man can be for a service which he could not have rendered *himself*, nor has the slightest notion of what could have prompted *you* to do. Now, let me hear by what chance you came here?"

"You must listen to a long story to learn that," said I; and as he declared that he had nothing more pressing to do with his time, I began, almost as I have begun with my reader. On my first mention of Crofton, he asked me to repeat the name; and when I spoke of meeting Miss Herbert at the Milford station, he slightly moved his chair, as if to avoid the strong light from the window; but from that moment till I finished, he never interrupted me by a word, nor interposed a question.

"And it was she gave you that old seal-ring I see on your finger?" said he, at last.

"Yes," said I. "How came you to guess that?"

"Because *I* gave it to her the day she was sixteen! I am her father."

I drew a long breath, and could only clutch his arm with astonishment, without being able to speak.

"It's all well known in England, now. Everybody has been paid in full, my creditors have met in a body, and signed a request to me to come back and recommence business. They have done more; they have bought up the lease of the Foundry, and sent it out to me. Ay, and old Elkanah's mortgage, too, is redeemed, and I don't owe a shilling."

" You must have worked hard to accomplish all this ? "

" Pretty hard, no doubt. You remember those little boats with the holes in 'em at Lindau. *They* did the business for me. I was fool enough at that time to imagine that you had got a clue to my discovery, and were after me to pick up all the details. I ought to have known better! It was easy enough to see that *you* could have no head for anything with a ' tough bone ' in it! Light, thoughtless creatures of *your* kind are never dangerous anywhere ! "

I was not quite sure whether I was expected to return thanks for this speech in my favour, and, therefore, only made some very unintelligible mutterings.

" There's only one liner now to be raised, and all the guns are already out of her, but I can return to-morrow. I am free ; my contract is completed ; and the *Ignatief* sloop-of-war is at my orders at Balaclava to convey me to any port I please in Europe."

He said this so boastfully and so vaingloriously, that I really felt Potts in his humility was not the smaller man of the two. Nor, perhaps, was my irritation the less, at seeing how little surprise our singular meeting had caused him, and how much he regarded all I had done in his behalf as being ordinary and commonplace services. But, perhaps, the *coup de grace* of my misery came as he said :—

" Though I forwarded that ten-pound note you lent me to Rome, perhaps you'll like to have it now. If you need any more, say so."

My heart was in my mouth, and I felt that I'd have died of starvation rather than accept the humblest benefit at his hands.

" Very well," said he to my refusal; " all the better that you've no need of cash, for, to tell the truth, Potts, you're not much of a doctor, nor are you very remarkable as a man of genius; and it is a kind thing of Providence when such fellows as you are born with even a ' pewter spoon ' in their mouths."

I nearly choked, but I said nothing.

" If you'd like me to land you anywhere in the Levant, or down towards the Spanish coast, only tell me."

" No, nothing of the kind. I'm going north ; I'm going

to Moscow, to Tobolsk: I'm going to Persia and Astracan,"
said I, in wildest confusion.

"Well, I can give you a capital travelling cloak—it's one
of those buntas they make in the Banat, and you'll need it,
for they have fearfully severe cold in those countries."

With this, and not waiting my resolute refusal, he rose,
hobbled out of the room, and I—ay, there's no concealing it—
burst out a crying!

Weak and sick as I was, I procured an "araba" that
night, and, without one word of adieu, set out for Krim.

*   *   *   *   *   *

*   *   *   *   *   *

It was about two years after this—my father had died in
the interval, leaving me a small but sufficient fortune to live
on, and I had just arrived in Paris, after a long desultory
ramble through the east of Europe—I was standing one
morning early in one of the small alleys of the Champs
Elysées, watching with half listless curiosity the various
grooms as they passed to exercise their horses in the Bois de
Boulogne. Group after group passed me of those magnificent animals in which Paris is now more than the rival of
London, and at length I was struck by the appearance of a
very smartly-dressed groom, who led along beside him a
small-sized horse, completely sheeted and shrouded from
view. Believing that this must prove some creature of rare
beauty, an Arab of purest descent, I followed them as they
went, and at last overtook them.

The groom was English, and by my offer of a cigar, somewhat better than the one he was smoking, he was very
willing to satisfy my curiosity.

"I suppose he has Arab blood in him," said he, half contemptuously; "but he's forty years old now if he's a day.
What they keep him for I don't know, but they make as
much work about him as if he was a Christian: and, as for
myself, I have nothing else to do than walk him twice a day
to his exercise, and take care that his oats are well bruised
and mixed with linseed, for he hasn't a tooth left."

"I suppose his master is some very rich man, who can
afford himself a caprice like this."

"For the matter of money, he has enough of it. He is the

Prince Ernest Maximilian of Würtemberg, and, except the Emperor, has the best stable in all Paris. But I don't think that *he* cares much for the old horse; it's the *Princess* likes him, and she constantly drives out to the wood here, and when we come to a quiet spot, where there are no strangers, she makes me take off all the body-clothes and the hood, and she'll get out of the carriage and pat him. And he knows her, that he does! and lifts up that old leg of his when she comes towards him, and tries to whinny, too. But here she comes now, and it won't do if I'm seen talking to you, so just drop behind, Sir, and never notice me."

I crossed the road, and had but reached the opposite pathway, when a carriage stopped, and the old horse drew up beside it. After a word or two, the groom took off the hood, and there was Blondel! But my amazement was lost in the greater shock, that the Princess, whose jewelled hand held out the sugar to him, was no other than Catinka!

I cannot say with what motive I was impelled—perhaps the action was too quick for either—but I drew nigh to the carriage, and raising my hat respectfully, asked if her highness would deign to remember an old acquaintance.

" I am unfortunate enough, Sir, not to be able to recal you," said she, in the most perfect Parisian French.

" My name you may have forgotten, madame, but scarcely so either our first meeting at Schaffhausen, or our last at Bregenz."

" These are all riddles to me, Sir; and I am sure you are too well bred to persist in an error after you have recognised it to be such." With a cold smile and a haughty bow, she motioned the coachman to drive on, and I saw her no more.

Stung to the very quick, but yet not without a misgiving that I might be possibly mistaken, I hurried to the police department, where the list of strangers was preserved. By sending in my card I was admitted to see one of the chiefs of the department, who politely informed me that the princess was totally unknown as to family, and not included in the Gotha Almanack.

" May I ask," said he, as I prepared to retire, "if this letter here—it has been with us for more than a year—is for your address? It came with an enclosure covering any possible expense in reaching your address, and has lain nere ever since."

"Yes," said I, "my name is Algernon Sydney Potts."

Strange are the changes and vicissitudes of life! Just as I stood there, shocked and overwhelmed with one trait of cold ingratitude, I found a letter from Kate (she who was once Kate Herbert), telling me how they had sent messenger afters me through Europe, and begging, if these lines should ever reach me, to come to them in Wales. "My father loves you, my mother longs to know you, and none can be more eager to thank you than your friend Kate Whalley."

I set off for England that night—I left for Wales the next morning—and I have never quitted it since that day.

THE END.

Printed by W. H. Smith & Son, 186, Strand, London.